A HANDFUL OF SEEDS

The England of 1666 sits fragilely in a peace between two wars. Sir Rollo Fitzmedwin returns to his homeland to find Anna Ruyter, the woman he loves. When he arrives in London, Anna is not there and in his efforts to trace her he encounters her foster sister, Alice. As Rollo's quest takes him to Africa, Alice faces brutal consequences as her husband also sets sail leaving her alone and vulnerable. In a terrible twist of fate, two lives begin as two others end, and Alice decides to take destiny into her own hands as the uneasy peace with Holland falters and fails...

A HANDFUL OF SEEDS

A HANDFUL OF SEEDS

by

Elizabeth Daish

Magna Large Print Books
Long Preston, North Yorkshire,
BD23 4ND, England.

British Library Cataloguing in Publication Data.

Daish, Elizabeth
    A handful of seeds.

    A catalogue record of this book is
    available from the British Library

    ISBN   0-7505-1820-0

First published in Great Britain 2000 by Robert Hale Ltd.

Published in Large Print 2002 by arrangement with
Robert Hale Limited

Magna Large Print is an imprint of Library Magna Books Ltd.

Printed and bound in Great Britain by
T.J. (International) Ltd., Cornwall, PL28 8RW

Chapter 1

Light from a high window made the loft bright and showed the dust on the canvases stacked against the wooden walls. Pieter Van Steen glanced at the man by his side and smiled, then turned to see the expression on the face of the young man more clearly, his own smile wavering. 'You do like it?'

'Of course. It looks very expensive.' Sir Rollo Fitzmedwin gathered his thoughts and nodded, laughing. 'It's very impressive.'

The older man seemed reassured. 'It cost me a few guilders,' he admitted, 'But it was well worth it. Every member of my family in one picture, and so like them.' He frowned. 'I would like you to have been with them but the artist said there was no room and your colouring was different and didn't match the others.' His note of regret made Rollo smile more naturally. It mattered so much to Pieter that his daughter had married into an aristocratic family and when the trouble with England was settled once and for all, the marriage would add much to the status of the Van Steens.

It was one thing to be a respected burgomaster with a fine house in one of the best parts of Amsterdam and enough wealth to see his daughters married to men of rank and influence, but for Helena his eldest girl to marry a noble-

7

man was beyond his dreams.

'It is like them,' said Rollo. He stared in a kind of fascinated horror at the dozen faces, pale against the flat dark background. The women all stared as if in a trance and the men looked vaguely uneasy as if the lace on the dull fabric of their tunics was over-starched and rubbed their necks raw. The dark wide hats of the men, some worn and some held low over the knee britches were elegant but rather like those worn in a play by actors unused to finery.

'Your wife looks well,' said Pieter, mistaking Rollo's absorption for real interest.

Rollo almost said, which is she? but bit back the words. He could pick out Helena's mother for her bulk and heavy features, and the aunt who lived with the family stared pale and thin and sanctimonious from the oils as if she didn't trust the world, but the three daughters were alike in life and here, caught and imprisoned by paint, they were all the same. Rollo saw the silk kerchief that had been one of his first gifts to the girl he had wooed and won with no difficulty when travelling through Belgium, and with relief was able to remark on the dress she was wearing and to praise the way her hair was portrayed.

'God's Death,' he whispered in English. 'They are just so many bladders of lard or some of their round Dutch cheeses.'

'The artist has done well, but he has not brought out Helena's vivacity and the light in her eyes,' he said in good Dutch.

'There speaks a man in love,' Pieter laughed. He hoped that the other men in the party were listening. Sometimes, he wondered if the bride-groom of only six months was really as attentive as he should be to his new bride, but Helena spoke little of any tongue but her own and this must be a strain even though Rollo spoke French with ease and Dutch with careful fluency. Rollo shook out a pure white handkerchief and pretended to use it. Pieter watched, admiring the effortless panache of the man who had erupted into their lives on the day when their carriage broke down and he came to their aid in his huge yellow and black vehicle with the rich velvet cushions that quite silenced his wife and two daughters travelling with Pieter from France, through Belgium to their home in The Nether-lands. For his own safety and to please the family who had helped him far more than they would ever suspect in his flight from England in 1666, he had put aside his silk and velvets and the fine silk stockings and elegant shoes and now wore the dark fustian and worsted and lace collars of the soberly clad Netherlanders. The knitted woollen stockings had irritated his delicate skin at first but now he could put them on without even thinking it odd that he, of all people, should dress like a puritan or an English peasant.

'Who is the artist?' Pieter shrugged and looked embarrassed. 'Not Rembrandt or Hals,' Rollo went on with a slight sneer. 'That background was painted by pupils and the hands aren't good.' He was becoming tired of the complacency of the rich man who could have given the commission to the very best artist that the country with so many skilled craftsmen and painters could produce.

'It wasn't Rembrandt but it is from his school. It cost enough,' added Pieter as if that made the painting better. Rollo looked for some relief in the dark and light of the background and could find none. The flat portraits could have been cut out and stuck on to the darkness, and he thought of the pictures in his own gallery at home in England, the faces of lovely women, handsome men and beasts, country scenes where he felt he could almost pick the ripe and glistening fruit from the painted trees. He sighed and walked away to look at other paintings. He thought of his farms and elegant town houses, of soft English countryside with rolling downland and good horses to gallop along the bird-loud valleys. His own sudden anguish frightened him. Such scenes had never moved him until now when he had to be exiled until such a time when it was safe to return: flatness and canals and women who went about their daily tasks as if the future of the world depended on scrubbed floors and clean linen and the everlasting lace-making.

Even his desires had lessened and he had no stomach for the whores who thronged the market-places and the docks, even if he felt free to go to them. He looked back to the group he had left. All were sipping fine French wine but one man was watching him, quietly and never intruding, but there, a kind of guide and servant, a personal factotum put to his service by his father-in-law as befitted a man of rank and who was only absent when Sir Rollo was safe in the family circle or being entertained by friends and business contacts.

'Do you paint portraits?' Rollo asked idly of a man who was cleaning brushes in a large earthenware bowl.

'No, Menhir.' The man laughed. 'I paint but in my own time. I work to buy brushes and oils and canvas and I paint the sea and the polders.' He saw that the men at the other end of the studio were still talking, their laughter rising as they drank more to celebrate the finished picture. 'You didn't care for that one?' He gave an expressive shudder. 'Every house of quality has one now and others to hang in the banks and places of business. Students paint the background and most of the clothes and sometimes the painter does no more than put his name to it and to paint a few skin tones. I can show you better work.' He led Sir Rollo Fitzmedwin to an alcove where the light was poor. Quickly, he pulled aside a thick curtain to let the light fall on a shrouded easel. 'There!'

'It's beautiful.' The deep vibrant colours and the almost living flesh glowed with warmth and the scene beyond the figures was real. Rollo looked up and asked the name of the artist.

'The Master,' the man said simply. 'Menhir Rembrandt in trouble again and having to give this to pay his debts. The students copy it and learn but it isn't for the eyes of rich merchants who can pay for trash. If they saw this against that one even they would see the difference.' He eyed the neatly dressed but elegant man with a quizzical look. 'You are English and yet you dress as we do and move safely with some of the most influential in the land. Have you not heard of our

11

victory in the Medway, Englander?' He laughed. 'I saw the ROYAL CHARLES brought in like a lame swan and I painted her as she lay at the moorings by the Amstel. A beautiful ship and truly great craftsmen built her,' he conceded. He grinned. 'But our sailors are better fed and our Admiral De Ruyter a better tactician.'

Sir Rollo shrugged and gave a wry smile. 'Politics? War? I know nothing of such matters. I came here to live in peace and to escape my creditors in England.' It was the easy excuse he gave to any curious enough to enquire too closely about his private affairs, and it came naturally now as more and more people came to wonder how the handsome and obviously well-bred Englishman came to live in Amsterdam while war still grumbled fitfully between the British and the Netherlanders.

'They say you fled the country for other reasons.' The young man scraped paint from the wooden handle of a large sable brush and swished the hairs briskly in the dark liquid. He glanced up and Rollo saw that his gaze was sharp and guarded. 'They say that you took the fair Helena for a bride almost before you had time to change your hose.' He nodded. 'A very shrewd move, my friend, if you wanted to be accepted into our society quickly and without too much fuss.'

'A man has the right to fall in love and want his nuptials.' Rollo laughed. 'I think that English blood is warmer and English faces have more charm for the ladies than you cheese-eaters.'

'You have a lot to learn about us, but you speak

our language well if slowly. Hoe lang bent u hier al?'

'Six months.' Rollo sighed. 'Six months without English faces, English trees and hills. Tell me, have you ever seen a hill?' His tone was derisive. 'What can you know of life outside this watery city?'

'I know the Court of the French and I have been to Whitehall. I made the Grand Tour when there was better feeling between our countries and I heard of you in London, Sir Rollo Fitz-medwin.' He now spoke in good English with a hint of a Scottish accent.

'Then why are you here?' Rollo eyed the stained smock and frayed fustian, the heavy hose and thick ungainly shoes of an artisan and the hands now dyed brown in the cleaning fluid.

'I am an artist and that is not to the liking of my family. I am not entirely disinherited, but have only enough for my modest needs, but there is a trust that I cannot touch for another year. My grandfather was one of the leading men in the city, a burgomaster in the Regent Class that came into being in 1660.' He grinned. 'It isn't easy. They were against the House of Orange and loyalties flow as deviously as the floods by the Amrack. My father lost all ambition for political power and now tends his lands outside the city where the new polders are being built. He hopes that one of his sons will bring him glory but as yet neither my brother nor I are willing to join the entourage of the mighty. I say it rests with Johann as he will inherit, being the elder son. I want nothing more than to paint and eat well and to

13

whore a little.'

'You know my name, sir, and you have the advantage,' said Rollo.

'I am Willem de Graeff.'

Rollo put out his hand and took the damp and stained fingers of the other man in a warm grip. He didn't even glance at his own dirtied palm or wipe it clean. Willem grinned with delight. He handed Rollo a piece of old cotton cloth. 'Only a man of breeding would have been so courteous. I think we can be friends. Too many men never look below the dirt and see nothing.'

The servant walked past them with the tray of empty glasses and Willem let fall the heavy curtain to hide the Rembrandt picture. The silent man who seemed to Rollo to be his shadow came slowly towards them with the message that Menhir Van Steen and his party were ready to leave.

'My compliments and tell him that I am interested in commissioning another painting, of my wife alone.' It came as an inspiration and would serve to have more freedom. 'There is no need for you to stay with me. I can find my way from here to the house alone. I am not a child.'

The man looked discomforted but inclined his head slightly and followed the rest of the party to the carriages where the painting was already secured to the box of the heavy family carriage.

'Be careful,' said Willem, softly. 'Even if your guard has gone, Amsterdam is full of eyes and tongues ready to spy on you. If you were short and less pleasing to the eye, you might have a better chance of freedom, but that family will keep you for Helena as a good and faithful husband. You are the jewel in the family bosom and must shine for them alone.'

His words held an undercurrent of real warning, but Rollo felt that they were kindly meant. 'And you?' said Rollo. 'Do you spy for the Van Steens?'

'I am my own man and let others live as they wish, but when my trust is mine, I may offer for Helena's sister. I have lain with women from every country in Europe but for marriage I want a virgin who will be there when I need her.' He held up his hands and laughed. 'I shall wash and be finely dressed and borrow some of your manners, but until then, I can show you Holland and make you aware of its beauty.'

'When you were in London, did you see work by artists such as Lely? He has painted portraits of most of the ladies of the Court of St James's and is held in as high a regard as your Vermeer or Hals or even Rembrandt,' said Rollo.

Willem walked across the room and looked down towards the group of apprentices who were listening to their tutor and engrossed in his treatment of draped velvet as he smoothed on highlights and shadow. 'I am not supposed to touch these, but I look at them whenever I have the chance. They are the most beautiful copies that have come to this studio and could be mistaken for the originals.' He pushed Rollo towards a small door and opened it. 'If I am discovered, I shall tell them that the Englander married to the daughter of Menhir Van Steen demanded to be shown the other pictures.'

'Are you such a low vassal here?' Rollo sounded amused.

'I am tolerated as I work hard but they don't really trust me, as the master here is an Orangeman, and they know my name.'

'Then show me the paintings and I will promise not to let them flog you,' Rollo laughed.

'That they would never dare to do,' said Willem, grimly. 'I am stronger than many think. They also have an inborn respect for the Regents and so leave me alone, but I need to work here so that I can observe and use their brains.'

He pushed back the wooden shutters at the wide windows and turned a large canvas to face them. Rollo gasped and once again a poignant stab of nostalgia took him back to London. The portrait of Lady Castlemaine, the mistress of King Charles II of England seemed to spill out on to the dusty floor the extravagance of lace, the softness of velvet and the sheer voluptuousness of the woman who stared out of the picture with all the arrogance and beauty of the mother of seven of the King's bastards.

'You knew her?' asked Willem. 'You spoke with her, touched her, saw her at dinner and in the theatre? I saw her once in her carriage with the King, but not to kiss her hand or speak with her.'

'I have kissed her hand and sat with her in the Royal Box and eaten with them at Court,' Rollo admitted. 'She is as lovely as a rose overblown, drenching the King with fragrant petals and fascinating many men who dare not touch her if they value their lives.' He laughed. 'If you intend bedding a Dutch girl you must never look at such paintings or it will take away your manhood.'

'You manage to do that,' said Willem.

'Helena has freshness and charm and an amazing willing heart and her youth makes a man of me. I have given up the Court and the joys of sophisticated women.'

'What of this? Surely this can inflame you?'

The next picture was a nude reclining on cushions, with a small cherub watching her at her toilette. 'Pretty but not for me.' Rollo walked towards a canvas that still bore the hessian cover as if it had not been fully unpacked.

Willem took out a sharp knife from under the soiled smock and cut the bindings. 'This should have been done in case of damage. My master would be angry to see it wrapped two days after its arrival. Is something wrong?' Hastily, he flung the hessian into a corner and propped the canvas against the wall where the best light fell on it. 'It's perfect,' Willem said with relief. 'I thought from your face that it was damaged. It's a very good copy of a recent one by Lely and we had to bring it through France and Belgium in a sealed carriage. You look quite pale, my friend. What is wrong? It is a beautiful picture of an amazingly lovely lady.'

'I think I know the subject.' said Rollo with difficulty. He turned away to take snuff in an effort to compose his features. It was impossible!

'On the back will be the name and history of the painting.' Willem squinted along the back of the frame. 'Yes, it was painted by Lely originally and this is the first copy in a series of three. Commissioned by Colonel Daniel Bennet as a gift to Lady Marian Verney and Mr Edward Verney on the occasion of his marriage with their ward, Miss Anna Maria Ruyter.'

'A pretty gesture,' Rollo admitted. He gazed at the face he knew so well, the delicate but healthy colouring and the sweet tilt to her chin.

'She is proud,' said Willem. 'Too proud for you?' he asked, slyly.

'She is proud and virtuous and intelligent as any man; fond of stargazing and other sciences best left to the professors, and skilled in the art of healing.'

'She bore a proud name,' said Willem. 'Do you have such a love for the Dutch that you choose their women to bed and marry?'

'I was never so fortunate.' He lapsed into silence for a minute and Willem eyed him with a mixture of curiosity and disbelief. 'She is half Dutch and not a De Ruyter, just a sprig of the admiral's family and plain Ruyter, brought up in England by distant relatives and now wasted on that, that solemn and unworthy soldier.' Rollo spoke with a terrible restraint as if he could curse and rant about the marriage but dared not show his feelings.

'And yet you love her,' stated Willem. 'All the virtues a man avoids for his own comfort and yet you love her. Better have a warm soft and pliant wife who sets a fine table and knows so little that she can never answer back.

'You are right. I have such a wife and in time she will bear me sons.' Rollo set his mouth in a hard line. 'Is there a price on the picture? I must have it.'

'And what would the Van Steens say if you took that to your rooms? You live with them until your house is finished?'

'You know everything about me, so tell me how I can buy this painting and not offend.'

'It isn't wise but if you are serious, let me act as your agent and keep it in my rooms until you can safely claim it.'

'Buy it even if it is almost beyond my purse. I have land in France and Switzerland as well as England and revenues will come soon.'

'And now, go home to your wife and praise her dinner. I will send messages when I have secured it.'

'How can I thank you? I had no idea the painting could move me as much.'

'We can be friends,' said Willem. He hesitated. 'Never ask me to do something outside the law.'

'Why say that? Look at me!' Rollo laughed. 'I dress soberly and lead a quiet life, married to a woman of whom I am very fond. I am watched far too well even to visit the stews and I cannot go back to England to indulge in the sports I took so much for granted, so how could I be guilty of anything?'

'Why did you leave England and all your estates?'

'Surely you know that I offended the Church? I have no strong beliefs and I am content to worship with the Van Steens or any others who ask me, but after the fire when most of London was burned, my enemies pointed a finger and shouted papist and spy, so I fled the country.' It had served as an excuse well enough until now, but under the level gaze of the young Dutchman, Rollo sensed that it was a thin excuse.

'Go home, Rollo. Go to your innocent wife,' said Willem, quietly. Rollo turned away and strode from the small room without another glance at the painting. Willem called him back and Rollo paused, his heavy cloak swinging from one shoulder, and his sword loosely touched. What now? he thought.

'Is it true you fled because you killed a man?'

'Is that what they say?'

'I have heard it whispered,' said Willem. 'Any foreigner is open to conjecture.'

'They lie!' Willem watched him leave and saw him striding angrily over the cobbled square towards the canal where the Van Steens had their home, overlooking the calm water. He turned to the painting again and wondered how any man could leave everything he loved and valued, perhaps to lose everything, as Rollo had lost this woman, to live in near obscurity in a strange and fairly dull landscape...

Chapter 2

'You really must not encourage her, Vincent,' said Lady Marian Verney with a hint of affectionate reproach. 'Alice is a married lady and your wife and yet you allow her to act like a hoyden, riding to hounds and taking part in all the sports that her brother Peter enjoys so much.'

Vincent Clavell laughed and leaned out of the window to watch his young bride playing with the latest litter of kittens in the stable yard. 'She's a child yet, ma'am, and I would have her no different. My sister Sarah is so like my dearest Alice that I find it difficult to deny them anything.'

Marian sighed. 'She is your wife and your care now, Vincent, but while you are away at sea it is my task to make sure that nothing bad can happen to them.' Her laugh was tinged with irritation. 'If Anna was here it would be well enough, but she has left me and Kate is too far away to be of use.'

Vincent Clavell sat where he could see his wife, as if he couldn't bear the thought of her being out of sight for five minutes, but now became serious. 'I had considered the possibility of Alice and Sarah staying in Surrey with your daughter Kate but it seems that they are not in favour of the idea.' He frowned. 'I thought that now Kate is to be a mother it would be good for Alice to see

21

how a nursery should be managed.'

'My dear boy, Alice is as you say, yet a child herself. If she has not taken, it is the will of God and you have not been married for more than a few months. Kate is far too busy with her Parish duties and her own marriage to have the care of two heedless young beauties, and John and Mattie at the Manor are frail and not inclined for the kind of boisterous amusements that the young seem to think are essential for happiness.' He gave her a sweet smile that melted her planned opposition. 'Of course Alice must stay with us if she has no suitable lady to attend her. I do see that we must do what we can while you are at sea, but I doubt if this household will amuse her for very long.'

'It is my dearest wish that we should have a child soon, partly to ensure the inheritance of the Clavell lands and partly to settle my wife into more gentle pursuits. I love the child I married and bless the day that I met her, but I shall feel safer when she grows into a more sober matron.'

Marian watched the pleasant face as he frowned. Not really handsome, but wholesome and good, with humour of a sort and far too much trust in his wife and sister. The girls of fourteen and fifteen who had run wild together in the Surrey copses and who rode across the Downs like fair wood nymphs were now two years older and had not lost their kittenish ways.

'You spoil them both,' Marian said. The heavy silk of the well-made suit that Alice now ignored as she sat on a log and let the kittens scratch her skirt, had cost more than an artisan could earn in

22

a year, and yet Alice would pout and cry if she was accused of waste.

'I leave tomorrow for the Indies, ma'am, and know that Alice will be in good hands and your excellent husband will oversee my business.' He unbuttoned the deep pocket in his plain jacket and handed a bundle of papers to his mother-in-law. 'Mr Verney will know what to do with these but I shall not see him again before I leave, if as you say he is in Greenwich today.'

'Is there a message?' The package was thick and heavy and Lady Marian handled it as if it might sting her. 'I know very little about business, Vincent.'

'Keep them safe, ma'am. They are the proof that I have lent a considerable sum to the King and State, badly needed in these hard times for the rebuilding of the City of London after the terrible fire.' His expression became more calculating. 'There are many who refused the request for funds and I feel they are listed as hostile to the throne but even a King cannot ignore his debts for ever, so this loan gives me power. I have the command I wanted in the Navy and a place at Court if I ever wanted to join that profligate crew.' His tone indicated how much he despised the life in St James's and Whitehall and the people who toadied and flattered to gain preferment.

He uncrossed legs clad in fine silk and adjusted the huge silver buttons on his dull green jacket, the only visible signs of his immense wealth. The sound of harness and the voice of the groom below made him glance at the face of the marble clock and to gather up his hat and stick and to take his leave of Lady Marian.

'I'll see that she leaves the kittens, and to-morrow, after I've gone, Alice will come to you for a few days until her new companion-duenna arrives and Sarah will be with you shortly. God bless you, ma'am. I am easy in my mind if you take a care for my wife and if by some mischance I should not return, she is safe from want and care for ever.'

'My dear boy!' said Marian, alarmed and suddenly conscious that men did die at sea. 'If only you were like our son, Christopher. Surely a life farming and breeding fine horses is enough to fill a man's time?'

He laughed. 'Pastimes, ma'am. I hunt and shoot for pleasure, but after Alice, the sea is the love of my life.' His eyes sparkled and he looked almost handsome. 'Give me timbers under foot and a good crew with volunteers and few pressed men, a fair wind and sweet water and I'd change with no man alive.'

'God speed you and bring you back safe, my son,' she said, and the tears flowed freely.

'I'll bring you a monkey and exotic feathers,' he replied, holding her close and almost afraid that he too would show signs of emotion. This family into which he had married had given him more warmth and more affection than any of his own blood.

Vincent Clavell walked slowly down to the yard. Below him, far away, he could see the black stumps of trees and the ruins of once good houses, the heaps of broken and charred hurdles and the dusty spent fields. Even now, a year after the great fire that had consumed most of the two cities of London and Westminster the signs remained and the devastation that he saw from the freshly tended grounds of the house above the city was only a hint of the ruins beyond Holborn and Lincoln's Inn Fields, as far as the river and the Tower of London.

'The horses are ready?' It was an unnecessary question. Vincent looked on with approval as Sam, the Vernes's coachman, slapped the flank of the near horse and grinned.

'I saw to them myself, sir. That one needs more exercise with a heavy load, or send her to the country while you are away. The ladies need only a curricle and the small carriage, and without a good coachman and you to see that all is well, your stable will suffer.' He spoke with the ease of one who liked his work and knew his own worth.

'Come to sea with me, Sam,' said Clavell, then shook his head as if he knew he had said the wrong words.

'Never again, sir. I am a free man with a family who have looked after me and mine for too long for me to desert them now.'

'So Lord Chalwood has given up hope of you running his stud?'

'I never wanted to work for him and his kind and Debbie is expecting. We stay here for as long as Mr Verney wants us, and bless the good Lord for this family.'

'May I ask you to give an eye to my horses from time to time, Sam?' Clavell smiled. 'I ask too many favours of the Verneys as it is but they make me feel that I leave a solid, honest wall against anything that could go amiss.'

'I can look in at the house on the Strand, sir, and you have men enough in the estates, and the new coachman will settle well enough. He's clean and willing and doesn't drink enough to make a monkey drunk.'

'Vincent, I must take these two!' Alice held up two black and white kittens and laughed. Her hair was fast escaping from the snood in which it was meant to be restrained and her skirts were spotted with mud and what looked suspiciously like urine from the kittens.

'You will not! Put them down madam, and wash your face and hands. I shall make you walk home if you can't present yourself like a lady.'

'Please don't scold me, Vincent. They would be company and amusement while you are away.' Her lip trembled and she glanced up at him to see his reaction to the pathos that seldom failed, but saw only his displeasure. She remembered his promise to take her to the theatre on the last night before he sailed and she knew that there were limits to his patience. She put the kittens on to the mounting block and laughed when they fell to the ground and ran back into the stable yard. Alice went into the house where Debbie waited anxiously with a bowl of warm water and a soft towel. While Alice washed, she fetched a stiff brush to rid the skirt of mud and made almost the same sounds as an ostler brushing a horse.

'Miss Alice! You are no better than my Lucy,' Deborah said. 'She's but a babe and you a

26

married lady, and I swear she does not dirty her clothes like this.' She brushed the skirt harder, marvelling at the slender waist and curving hips, aware of her own thickening waistline and puffy ankles. 'You need a baby to slow you down, my love.'

'I don't want a baby, Debbie. I want to have a few years of enjoyment first. All the ladies I know who have children are so serious or they leave their children to servants and wonder why they get the croup and die. When I have babies, I shall look after them and teach them how to ride and play and look for nuts when we go in to the country.'

'You might let them learn to walk first, Miss Alice.'

Alice giggled. 'Vincent wants me safely with child before he goes to his ship, but as yet he's been disappointed. Perhaps I shall be like Abigail, the girl who my brother Christopher married. She has no baby and they say that her family start very late in bearing or never have children. I shall grow into a beautiful lady with a place at Court and many admirers and even the King will look on me with favour.'

'Not too much favour, I hope, Miss Alice. He has no difficulty when it comes to siring bastards.'

Alice pulled away and stamped her foot. 'I didn't mean that. Men *do* admire me but they know I am married and they do no more than kiss my hand. My husband would never allow any further liberty and would kill whoever tried to seduce me.'

27

Vincent called, impatiently, and Alice ran out to the carriage with a surprising show of obedience. Debbie watched them leave in the gleaming coach and wondered if the rumours were true, but it had all happened last year while Sir Vincent Clavell was ashore in the East Indies. She shrugged. A swelling of the glands was common enough in any climate and even more so where the weather was hot and disease rampant, and sailors from the ship who knew Sam were ignorant fellows and wouldn't know mumps from a sore throat.

'Debbie?' Lady Marian opened the door and handed the keys of the linen press to the girl who had been in her employ since before the plague and had stayed to marry Sam when his wife died and left a baby girl. 'Take the keys and keep them for a while. If Alice and Sarah come here, there will be a run on clean linen and fresh collars and it is better that you now act as housekeeper.' She smiled. 'You are a good woman, Debbie and it's time you took over the linen and the kitchen staff.' She hesitated. 'Mr Verney thinks as I do, that now Sam is head coachman with full livery, you must have the rank of housekeeper and show some authority. I shall need you even after your baby is born, so choose a girl to look after Lucy and your baby when the time comes and she can have the room next to theirs, and free you for your duties.'

She turned away as Debbie cried out in delight. 'I am doing this because you and Sam are good servants and friends, but also so that when Alice has children, there will be a nursery here ready

28

with a nursery maid and I shall not have the worry and noise of small children except when I want them.' She smiled and her expression was gentle. 'Alice will have such handsome children, and I am sure that Sir Vincent will be able to hold his child in his arms when he returns from the Indies. You will of course have gowns made as will befit your new position, but for the present, loose gowns of good wool for this autumn and winter.

'And now,' she added, briskly. 'I shall need my blue silk and the gold wrap for the theatre tonight. I am sharing a box with Lady Chalwood as Mr Verney will be too busy to accompany us. Miss Alice will see the same play but her husband has a box with other friends and men from the diplomatic.'

When Debbie had gone to tell Sam her good news and to press the clothes that her mistress wanted ready for the theatre, Marian sat by the window and drew her shawl over her shoulders. The fine weather was becoming dull and a hint of autumn pressed through the still green leaves and shed the petals of the late summer flowers. She wandered down to the herb garden and picked a spray of sage. Its bitter smell made her think of the bunches of herbs she had worn to fend off the pestilence and she threw it down and picked a late moss rose that took away the memory.

This part of the garden is very neglected, she thought, then realized that the herb garden had been tended by dear Anna, and since she married Colonel Bennet and changed her name from

29

Anna Maria Ruyter, nobody had thought to take over her garden. Memories came back as Marian picked thyme and parsley and rosemary for the cook. Anna with a handful of sweet herbs making tisanes, and Anna with strange plants soothing bruised and torn muscles and deeper wounds with special poultices, as she had done when Daniel Bennet lay sorely wounded after an attack on his life.

And now, Anna was far away with her husband, welcoming the challenge of a life in Tangier or wherever the King saw fit to send one of his most trusted officers, and if Anna stayed true to herself, she would make use of whatever herbs and simples she could find however strange the land. I wonder if she misses us? I wonder when we shall see her again? A wave of depression flooded the eyes of the woman who had seen her daughter Kate and son Christopher married to people living in the deep countryside of Surrey and never willing to come to the huge house above the City, except for mothering Sunday or on business.

A distant church bell, one of the few to survive even if badly cracked after the Fire, warned her that she must see to her duties inside the house. The air was misty over the City and she could not get used to the lack of noise from the once busy and crowded streets below the house. She made sure that there was fresh water in the ewer in the dressing room and that Debbie had put out fine glasses and sack for the master. A savoury smell from the kitchens and the bustle of the new serving maid as she set out platters, left

30

Marian free to tidy her hair and to be ready to receive her husband when he came back from his offices in the City.

She heard the wheels drag on the gravel below the window and heard Sam call to the groom to take the horses, and a minute later, Edward Verney strode into the drawing-room and pulled off his periwig. His now sparse natural hair stood on end and Marian wished that he would wear a lighter wig and so avoid overheating. He left the wig on a chair and went to wash, coming back tidy, with hair brushed and neat and his face shining with cleanliness.

'It was a good day,' he replied to her question. 'Two more ships came into the river safely and are full of good booty.' He rubbed his hands together then poured out generous glasses of sack for both Marian and himself, keeping up the habit taught by his doctor brother who had insisted that sack was a specific guard against the plague. What had been taken in fear now had become a pleasant habit and one that Edward valued after a day working over his books and papers and clients.

'Are they ships in which you have an interest, Edward?'

'A good share but do not talk about it as there is rumour that the Dutch demand an end to privateering if the treaty of Breda is to be signed and we can be rid of them for ever.'

'But the Navy Secretary, Mr Pepys, owns a share in the *Greyhound* and no word is said against him,' Marian replied.

'Even Mr Pepys looks over his shoulder at times

and makes us all think that it may be time to sell off some of our shares in the traffic.' Edward frowned and refilled his glass. 'I dislike some of the trade and hate what I see on board at times. Trade in black slaves who die and spread disease in the holds may taint the other goods and I have a care for human life even if they have no souls.'

'We do not have slaves here, Edward!'

'There is no need for alarm. The ships take them from Africa to the Indies and if they call in at ports here, it is usually in the West in Bristol and Plymouth and when we see the wretches, they have been vetted and free of distemper. Some of the men are magnificent and make a fine showing as carriage footmen but I cannot imagine Sam taking one into the stables.'

'You recall our arrangement for the theatre, Edward?' said Marian hopefully.

'I recall the arrangement you made, my dear. Sam will drive you and collect you and you will be so busy talking about the fashions that you will never notice that I am missing. I enjoy a good tragedy but not the flimsy offerings of the kind acted at the King's theatre, to please the emptyheaded fops of the Court.'

Marian sighed. 'Vincent is taking Alice and I thought we might have supped with them after the play. It is their last night before he leaves for the Indies and Alice wanted to go on to Vauxhall gardens.'

'To look at burned ruins and felled trees? It's true that the ale-houses are open again and the entertainments restored in part,' he admitted, grudgingly. 'But it is now a place of assignation for every cut-purse left after the pestilence, and Vincent would do well to forbid his wife to go there when he is away.'

'Vincent was here today with Alice and has asked that we act as guardians while he is away. It is a heavy responsibility, Edward. Alice is a child in a woman's body but as a married lady is allowed to do much that was forbidden before she married Vincent. I hope when Sarah comes, they will settle down as loving friends and spend more time riding and visiting the estates. London and the Court could be far too full of adventure and intrigue for two young women alone.'

'She will have a duenna and you, my dear, to make sure she comes to no harm.'

'The woman does not arrive until next week and Sarah comes at the same time. I am getting too old to chase over London after the daughter I truly thought was safely off my hands,' said Marian with some heat. Edward shrugged and picked up the package that she now held out to him. 'Vincent asked me to give this to you, Edward. Has he loaned a great deal to the Crown?'

'More than most men and the King is grateful as Vincent hasn't demanded a high interest. It is a good position to occupy in the Royal favour,' Edward added, drily. 'It protects his sister and his wife as none would dare to insult or try to seduce them, and Vincent will leave with an easy mind. That young man has more steel in his fibre than you might imagine. He is older than Alice and so more jealous of her reputation and any man who violated his trust in any matter, wife, sister or

33

business should look beyond that mild face and see the man who can captain a ship and manage a raw crew.'

'I have noticed a change since he came into his inheritance and even Alice senses that she can ask for so much and no more, but how those two girls will fare after the ship leaves makes me very anxious.'

'Without cause now, Marian. I would be far more worried about Alice if she was unwedded. With the wealth and rank of her husband to protect her and the fact that the King has sent more than one seducer to The Tower when the murmurings grew too loud for even His Majesty to ignore, nobody would dare to step over the bounds of discretion. That young puppy, Routh, who attempted rape when Alice and Sarah were with us in the country has been banished to his estates in Scotland and dares not show his face south of the border.'

'There are others, sir.'

'Young, eager bloods without a penny between them until they inherit? Alice would scorn to have them near her and the older men have no fascination for her. Even Sir Rollo Fitzmedwin has disappeared and some say was killed as he tried to pass through France.' There was a note of regret in his voice as he continued. 'Bad and dangerous, they said, but there was much to like in the boy, and he could charm the birds from the bushes, as well you know, madam. Anna was in real danger before we knew his evil intentions, but I find it hard to believe that he killed that watchman and the only finger that pointed at

34

him in accusation has rotted long since in the ashes of the Strand.'

'So he may return, if he is alive?'

'I think he would be welcomed back for his humour and good manners and looks and the ladies would flutter behind their fans as if they had never heard anything wrong with his character.' Edward looked sad. 'Such waste if he is dead. I know that once he had finished with the brawls and women and the arrogant trials of skill and strength on the hunting field, he could have settled down to being a good man.'

'Anna is better off married to Colonel Bennet,' said Marian firmly.

'Well, she's out of harm's way where she is now but I miss her sweet smile and generous ways,' said Edward with a sigh. 'Has nothing come from the artist? I promised Daniel to leave the picture until two copies had been made, the one for Daniel and Anna to take with them to Tangier which was packed safely in the hold of the boat before they left, and the other copy which should be finished now and be on the way to an artist in Holland. Mr Lely is now so famous that this was the only way that Daniel could afford to pay for the original as a gift to us.'

'Deborah?' Marian called. 'Has any large picture arrived? It was promised for today and I had hoped that Vincent would see it before he left.'

'Sam is unloading it now, My Lady. He waited until the stable lad was clean as it is very big and takes two to carry it safely.'

'Tell them to hurry. Lady Marian is anxious to

see it,' said Edward, trying to hide his own excitement, and when five minutes later, the two servants came into the drawing-room, he could hide his impatience no longer. 'Over here, Sam. No, turned more to the light and rest it against that wall until we choose where it shall hang. A knife, Sam! But be careful and don't let the blade go deep into the hessian.'

With stolid patience, Sam carefully cut the bindings and dragged the rough covering from the face of the canvas. 'Take this and go back to your work and stop gawping,' he ordered the stable lad who seemed transfixed. 'Ha'nt you seen a painting before?'

'It's Miss Anna!' said the boy. 'She's a-looking at me and I swear she could walk out of that frame!' He grabbed the pile of hessian and coarse string and made for the door, pausing for a further glance filled with awe, then clattered down the wooden stairs and out into the yard.

Edward blew his nose, loudly. 'What do you think of it, me dear?' he asked and placed a chair so that Marian could sit facing it and not collapse with the vapours. 'What do you think, Sam?' Edward needed to hide his joy and the sudden tenderness he felt on seeing the calm and beautiful face in the portrait. 'Ale for you and Sam and fill our glasses, Debbie! This is a celebration and one you can think of forever as it came on the day you were made housekeeper.' As always in moments of family feeling and stress, the master and mistress of the house above the City felt close to the two servants who had been with them and given much to the family during the plague and since the fire.

The two couples stood and sipped their drinks, unable to voice their feelings. My Anna, thought Marian. My dear sweet Anna who I miss more than my own daughters. She couldn't decide if the sight of the picture gave her more pleasure than pain, but the wonder of the painting made Anna almost living flesh. The lights in the dark hair looked as if she walked under a sunbeam and the soft cool skin of her shoulders seemed to pulsate down to the creamy hidden breasts. One hand rested on a volume bound in rich dark leather and the other held a small bunch of fresh flowers. How did the artist know that learning and natural growing things were the passionate interest of the young woman?

'He's caught that look,' said Sam at last, and there were tears in his eyes. Debbie slipped her hand in his and pressed his fingers. Today, she had sorted out the baby clothes that Lucy had worn and showed Sam the gowns that Miss Anna had made with her own hands, soft and warm and cut from one of her own garments to fit a new-born baby, when Lottie, Lucy's mother, was alive.

'She's wearing the dress she wore when Christopher was married. I remember when she chose it from a bundle of silks we had sent from London and the bird's eye pattern in amber on that blue background suited her well,' said Marian. 'Many said that she looked as well as any at the Court in Westminster and Sir Rollo was quite overcome.'

'Humph! The less said about that the better,

37

madam. He'd have run off with her if he'd had the chance and what would have happened to our dear Anna then?'

'He was so handsome, My Lady.' Debbie sighed. 'He had a word for everyone and all the girls in the kitchen watched for his comings and goings.' She glanced at Sam's face, now stony and thought it best to forget the times when Sir Rollo had kissed her soundly and fumbled her behind the kitchen door. 'She has a sad look about her behind that gentle smile,' she added. 'It must be hard to leave those you love.'

'She loves her husband and her duty is at his side,' said Lady Marian, reprovingly. 'She will miss us all, but her happiness lies with Colonel Bennet, Deborah.'

'Yes, My Lady,' the girl said and took the tray out of the room.

Chapter 3

The heat from the pit rose with all the smells of dirty linen and sweat mingled with crushed apples under foot and torn orange peel. Lady Marian sat back in the box and hoped that her headache would leave her soon. Lady Chalwood was in one of her more boastful moods, and had been a little too inquisitive both about the business that Edward did regarding privateering and the state of health of Alice who sat with her husband in the opposite box, blooming like a delicate wind-flower but obviously not sickening for anything, least of all a pregnancy.

'My eldest daughter is lying in with her fifth and as healthy as with the first. Some families breed well and some must have something of inferior stock somewhere in their background that makes them almost barren,' said Lady Chalwood.

Marian pursed her lips. 'Is that so, madam? Then our stable hand must have very noble blood in his veins as I hear he has ten children and is yet not twenty five.' She sniffed as if she recalled the smell of the stables and disliked it. 'Edward allows only his coachman to have rooms within the house as the stink of dung follows the men everywhere. He often says that good manure breeds good fruit as our gardens have never looked better this year.' She smiled, suddenly feeling better, and Lady Chalwood turned her attention to the play, the vulgar redness of the paint and the badly made wigs of the actors.

Marian watched her daughter with a mixture of pride and misgivings. Many of the men in the better seats and boxes seemed to find Alice much more interesting than the women on stage, and the little minx was fully aware of the fact even when her husband was deep in conversation with another navy officer and paid no heed to what was under his nose. The rose-coloured damask gown hugged the girlish body and gave bloom to the exquisite line of her bosom, tantalizing through a froth of fine lace, and the golden hair gleamed and showed off the bands of pearls and fine turquoise that adorned it.

The wife of the other navy man sat close to Alice and looked bored. She talked loudly to one of the others in the party and tried to forget that Alice Clavell was beautiful enough to turn even the hard head of her unimaginative husband. Marian sent a note to Vincent inviting the party to supper after the play but saw him frown when he received it and shake his head although Alice turned pink and set her mouth in a mutinous line.

'I leave tomorrow and must have rest,' Vincent said. He smiled, tenderly. 'And what man would want to share his wife on this last evening together? I agreed to the play but nothing more. We leave as soon as is civil and sup alone at home.' Alice bit back a retort. There had been an interesting parcel in Vincent's study and she knew it must be a present for her that he would

40

give her before leaving. He had caught her trying to feel what it was through the wrappings and lifted her high in the air before kissing her and carrying her off to make love in their four-poster bed.

He was ardent enough to satisfy any woman and perhaps it might be better at home, but now, from the safety of the box, she could flirt with her eyes and make the handsome Frenchman blush. She glanced along to the next box where he sat forward, watching little of the play and taking a delight in smiling boldly as soon as he knew she was watching him.

'Who is he?' she asked, casually. His dark good looks were exciting and his manners exquisite. 'I thought that the French were not welcome here.'

'He is with the ambassador from France. As such, they have safe passage and come and go as any honest Englishman, but many will not give them hospitality as they are from an enemy country until such times when we can agree with the French and Dutch and the Danes as to the freedom of the seas.' Vincent glanced along to the next box and nodded in greeting. 'I know him from the Court and he might be useful if your brother makes the Grand Tour of Europe. It is still possible with the right letters of introduction and I have promised your father to pave the way for a good journey, using what connections I have.'

'You will ask him to call on us?' Alice looked engagingly innocent.

'Of course not! My dear girl I am leaving you tomorrow and you will live with your parents until the new woman arrives and Sarah is with you again. It would set tongues wagging if he so much as set foot in our house until you are well-chaperoned.'

'But if he is to help Peter, surely he must call on father?'

'He can meet your father in his chambers in the City. Many men meet foreigners in that way so that they keep business apart from their families. Now, thankfully, I think we may leave. Come my dear. The carriage will take us straight home and I have ordered a good fowl and venison from Lord Carnegie's own herd.' As if they had been waiting all the evening for such an order, the coachman and footman appeared at the back of the box and cleared a way for the couple and their party. Vincent firmly but courteously refused all offers of hospitality, and by the time that Lady Chalwood had levered her fat body from her seat and walked breathless down the narrow stairs, Alice and Vincent were nearly home in the new house by the Strand.

'I'm so hungry,' said Alice. She surveyed the well-ordered table and the fragile finger bowls that Vincent had brought back from Venice during earlier travels, and threw off her shawl. Vincent looked on as she picked a piece of fowl from the dressed bird with her fingers, and when she looked up he was laughing. 'I *am* hungry,' she repeated but sat more demurely and they ate in a hungry and companionable silence.

Vincent filled her glass with fine Rhenish wine and hoped that her unusual hunger was due to more than the needs of a youthful body. Alice was replete and hazy with good wine and he dismissed the servant and picked up the shawl and fan that Alice had dropped on the window seat. 'Who will run after you and pick up the things you drop after tomorrow?' he asked.

'Oh, Vincent! You must not go! I shall die if you leave me now.' She twined her arms round his neck and he picked her up as if she was a leaf and carried her to the room overlooking the river. 'You love your ship more than you love me,' she grumbled, and shivered with delight as he unbuttoned her bodice. 'Why is this wicked unless we are married?' she asked dreamily as he lay at her side caressing her breasts and bending to kiss her navel. She held him close as if he could never merge enough with her body and they made passionate love until dawn. Long after Alice lay asleep, her gentle breathing bubbling through moist lips, he sat watching her, quietly exulting that he knew that she would bear his child.

Vincent dressed and checked his papers and lighted a candle to examine the book that Edward had obtained from the Navy Office. His interest grew as he saw the excellent charts and illustrations of the coasts of Northern Europe and the lands along the coasts of the new colonies, Dutch and English and French. He had seen old copies of the *Mariner's Mirror* before today and as yet it was only in Dutch, but the charts on copperplate were clear and instructive in any language. Lucas Janszoon Wagenaer had compiled the best-known sailing manual in Europe, and Vincent was grateful to Edward for this gift of what in England was called the *Waggoner*.

Vincent went down to the library and consulted some of the heavy volumes published by the house of Blau, mercifully translated, and wished that someone would publish as good an atlas in English showing more of our colonies. The servants stirred and made up fires and laid the table with bread and ale and cheese. 'I'll take the first draught of the day with my wife,' he said and left his books to take his leave of Alice. She lay half asleep and held out her arms to him, and suddenly the puritanical streak in his nature made him wonder if Alice was not too fond of lust for a well-brought-up girl of good family. His own passion was spent and he had been asleep for only an hour, and now, the smell of the sea seemed to come up the river with the sound of oars and the slap of sails.

'Is it today?' asked Alice, sitting up and yawning.

'Today, my love,' he said, tenderly. 'I have brought you a present so that you can see it and not be lonely.' He gave her the package that she had seen in the study and she opened the small box, with excitement.

'Take good care of it. It has my heart as well as my likeness.' Alice lifted out the exquisite miniature set in diamonds and opened the back. Inside was a lock of hair; not fair and not dark but one cut from his own hair, and in the frame were tiny portraits of the young couple.

'It's pretty,' she said but wished it was surrounded by sapphires to match her eyes. She sensed that he was disappointed. 'I do love it, Vincent, but it makes me sad to think of you

44

being so far away.'

'Get dressed my love and you shall come with me to the ship and watch the men prepare for sailing.' He turned away wondering if he should prolong the parting, but unable to help his feelings. He sent for the maid and left them to select suitable clothes for the deck of a ship, but he laughed when Alice declared that she was ready, as the tall feathers in her hat would be enough to sail the ship down to Chatham. The leather-covered box and various pieces of luggage awaited collection in the hall and Vincent was dressed soberly in uniform with the gold epaulettes of his rank making the only bright touch in his sombre attire. His natural hair was neatly plaited and tied with a black ribbon in the nape of his neck and to Alice, he appeared as almost a stranger.

'Is that all you can take?' she asked, shocked at the paucity of his luggage. 'But you rule the ship. Surely you will have space for comfort? I could not exist for a week with such few things.'

'Which is as good a reason as any for not taking wives,' said Vincent and laughed. 'Besides, you would have all the officers and men looking at you and never doing a hand's turn on deck.'

Alice smiled and looked pleased. 'I promise to let them do their work today,' she said, but as the carriage drew up by the side of the ship and she gazed up at the vast wooden sides and the open gun ports, she hoped that there were many curious eyes watching her.

'Welcome aboard, sir.' It was obvious that Vincent was held in great respect by his officers and to her surprise and chagrin, Alice was almost ignored once she had been greeted and set down in a leather chair in the forward dining room with a glass of malmsey wine as if they had to give her a sweetmeat to keep her occupied.

Curiosity made her leave the shelter of the room and venture on deck, but there, the deck hands were coarse and dirty and eyed her with something like hate and she heard one mutter, 'Bad luck to bring a woman on board if she isn't of the company.'

'I want to go home,' she said, pulling at Vincent's sleeve as he looked up at the missen.

'And so you shall, my love.' There was a hint of relief in his voice as he said goodbye and vowed eternal love in the privacy of his small cabin. He kissed her and held her close, murmuring words of love but feeling the pull of the sea once more. 'There's a fair wind coming and the tide is right to take us clear of the river, so we shall be gone by midnight. I have given instructions to the coachman to take you straight to your mother and to fetch your clothes later. Your maid will see to all that and be with you to see you into bed.'

'If we could only be close as we were last night,' she whispered and clung to him.

'Not here,' he said in alarm. 'There isn't time and I must check the victualling tallies before the rogues leave the ship. There are a hundred and one things that must be done before we sail and I should have come earlier.'

'Please don't let me detain you, sir,' she said, with offended dignity. 'I hate your old ship. I want to be put ashore and I hope I never have to see it again.'

'Alice!' His face was pale. 'I am going away for perhaps a year and we cannot part with angry words. I love you dearly and once this voyage is over I may never go to sea again. When I come back, I promise that you shall be presented to the Queen and do what you have asked, apply for a place in her entourage.'

'My dearest love,' gasped Alice. 'Forget my temper and remember that I am your little Alice who loves you and wants you home again as soon as possible.' It surpassed her wildest dreams as Vincent had refused each time she had mentioned going to Court, even to watch the Royal Family at dinner as did many people of wealth and influence.

From the dock she kissed her hand towards him and climbed into the carriage, sinking back into the soft velvet cushions and smiling, and Vincent turned back to his men and work and the open sea. Alice forgot that she was returning to her parents' home until Sarah, Vincent's sister and the companion arrived, and she felt vaguely put out to be under their guardianship again. There was nobody to greet her in the hall until Debbie came from the back regions where Sam had told her the carriage had come.

'Where is my mother?' she asked. Did they not know that she must be heartbroken now that her husband had gone away for maybe a year or at least nine months? A tear forced its way down her cheek and she left it there hoping to look neglected.

'Your father has company and wants you to join

them in the drawing-room, Miss Alice,' said Debbie.

'I am Lady Clavell, not Miss anything! My husband has gone away and I am far too sad to see any of my father's business friends.'

'He asked particular, Miss Alice,' said Debbie firmly, too used to the tantrums of the girl to take any real notice of the latest outburst.

'They said you'd be back for dinner Miss and that Mr Vincent was making sure you'd be here as you wouldn't stay long on the boat.'

Alice glared at the girl. It was too bad! For all they knew she might have wanted to stay and to sail down the river to the mouth of the Thames and be brought back by Navy launch rowed by a crew of lusty sailors. She saw the warning in Debbie's eyes and snatched up her hat again. 'Please go to my mother and say that I shall be with them in half an hour when I have got the smell of that ship out of my nostrils.'

'Did it upset you, my lamb?' Debbie was contrite. 'Poor little Miss Alice. Your handsome husband gone away and you sick with the rolling of a boat.'

Alice managed a tremulous smile. She was hungry and the air on the river had stimulated her but the movement of the boat could be a good excuse for loitering and keeping her parents waiting. By then, the visitors might have gone and she wouldn't have to play the gracious lady but could go into the stable yard and play with the kittens.

'Your boxes have come, miss, and your maid is unpacking now. I put fresh warm water in the ewer and a few drops of scent in it for your hands.'

'Thank you Debbie,' Alice smiled, once more the bright and pleasant girl. 'I shall wear my new locket and show my mother what Vincent gave me before he left.' She ran to the stairs and forgot that she intended keeping the company waiting. Within ten minutes, she appeared at the door of the wide with-drawing room, her hair gleaming from brushing and her face glowing after being in the open air. The new locket hung on a gold chain over the front of her pale green dress which was forced into the cleft of her breasts by the heavy jewel. She stopped and looked confused.

'Come in, my dear,' her father said. 'Monsieur Le Comte, may I present my daughter, Lady Alice Clavell?'

'*Enchanté, madame!* Marc Lefèvre and your humble servant.' Alice found her hand taken gently and raised to the full and red lips of the man she had seen at the theatre. 'Exquisite,' he whispered. '*Madame* smells of summer and looks like spring.' He held her hand more firmly as she tried to take it away. 'How could any man leave such a treasure.'

'You Frenchmen!' said Edward, laughing. 'It's a wonder we have any territories left. You can get what you want by charm, and as for our women, it's as well we have the sea between us, or their heads would be turned by your flattery.' He gave Alice a keen glance. 'Come miss. You've kept the man from his dinner long enough and he has very little time to spare as he leaves for Guinea in a week.' Edward tired of his efforts to speak

49

French. 'Count Marc is very kind. He has agreed to give me letters of introduction for Peter when he starts out on the tour next year.'

The count spoke carefully in perfect English with an attractive accent. 'I am a diplomat, *madame*, and as such travel the world and have *entré* to all the royal courts and parliaments.'

'And have you been received by our King?' Alice asked, eagerly. 'Have you seen Mistress Stewart and Lady Castlemaine? And all the noble lords and ladies who follow the Royal Family?'

'*Madame* has not been presented?'

'Not yet. Vincent has promised that when he returns I shall go to Court and he will apply for me to join the ladies in waiting.'

'The devil he has!' said Edward. 'He swore that you would never go within a mile of the Court.'

'He promised today before he left and when he gave me this.' Alice slipped the locket from her neck and handed it to her father. The diamonds flashed as he held it and examined the pictures. The count held out his hand as soon as Lady Marian had seen the miniatures and exclaimed over the chased gold and the pattern of the diamonds.

Alice watched as the sensitive fingers turned the locket over and found the tiny clasp hiding the lock of hair. 'Not your hair, Madame! This is your husband's?' He smiled. 'You have more gold than this metal and your fortunate husband must carry a treasure with him indeed if he has a lock of your hair with him, against his heart.' Alice gave a bleak smile. Vincent had given her his

50

likeness but had asked for no lock of hair, no portrait to love and to muse over while he was away.

'He has the whole of me,' she said, proudly. 'This is a pretty thing but we need no tokens.'

The count smiled, showing good strong teeth and his eyes sparkled as if amused. 'Indeed, that is how it must be when you love.'

Edward carved the venison, proud that he had it as a gift from Lord Chalwood and his estates in Somerset and Surrey, and Alice forgot her ill-humour as she ate and drank and basked in the flattery of the good-looking Frenchman.

'I have not eaten as well since supping with the Duc at Fontainebleau,' asserted the count. 'You are indeed fortunate to eat deer flesh as I believe it is the prerogative of the King as it is in our country.' Edward waved a deprecatory hand but glowed under the implied compliment and even Lady Marian warmed to this well-mannered stranger.

'And now that you are alone, *madame*, how will you amuse yourself?' asked the man who now insisted that they ignore his rank and call him Marc.

They were walking in the garden and Alice was holding one of the kittens while Edward talked to Sam about a badly shod mare, and Lady Marian was giving orders for supper and ordering for the following day. They had admired the portrait of Anna, and Alice was pleased to see that her new friend looked at it with admiration for the painting rather than for the subject. 'We have many handsome women with dark hair such as your cousin, Lady Alice, but rarely do we see such blonde hair and skin,' he said as if Alice was a portrait about which he could comment. 'The diamonds are fine and very expensive, but for skin like a white rose, sapphires would match the eyes and be even more precious.' Alice frowned. He had said nothing against Vincent but each time he praised her looks it was as if he knew that Vincent fell far short of him in observation and flattery. Alice put the kitten down and smoothed her skirt free of dust and felt as if he knew that she was a grown woman and not a child to be petted and scolded in turns.

'With regret I must take my leave, Lady Alice,' he said at last. 'I have neglected my duties to come here today and I am expected at a soirée this evening at Whitehall.'

'We shall see you again?' Alice was surprised at her own despondency.

'If you wish it, Lady Alice.' His eyes seemed darker and had lost the careless humour. 'If you wish it,' he repeated.

Alice caught her breath. She recalled Sir Rollo Fitzmedwin who had courted and nearly seduced Anna and the expression in this man's eyes reminded her of him. He took her hand and kissed it, then turned the palm upwards and pressed his lips against the warm flesh, curling the fingers over the kiss before he released her hand.

'Lady Marian is in the house. I will find her before you go,' she said to hide her sudden disquiet, and hurried into the house. She shivered as if the air was suddenly cool and yet the Autumn was mild and still, and she touched her breasts through her gown as they felt heavy and tender as they did when she and Vincent made love.

'I will finish the letters tomorrow, sir, and send them to you by messenger.' The count didn't look at Alice and she felt discarded as if his need to see her was not real and he was only being polite in a gallant French way.

'My dear sir, you must dine with us again before you go. If you can say when you are available, I will make all the arrangements for a feast and invite more of our friends.' Edward frowned. 'You say you will send the letters by messenger tomorrow? If you could bring them with you and dine, we could combine business with our great pleasure.'

'*Helas, mon vieux*, I borrow everything. Today, I have the carriage of the ambassador's secretary, but tomorrow, I ride alone on a borrowed nag, and I pray for fine weather. All my goods are ready for transport to Guinea and my carriage is already on board ship. In five days, I leave for France and then to the tropics.'

'That is insupportable,' said Lady Marian. 'We have horses idle in the stables and a small closed carriage that would suit your needs well.' She glanced at her husband who wasn't in the habit of lending his valued horseflesh to anyone, but to her relief, he was smiling. 'Tomorrow, Alice must go to her own house with her maid to collect more boxes and to oversee the servants and tell them what to do while she lives here. I will tell the groom who will be driving the carriage to call for you from Whitehall at noon and you can fetch Alice home for dinner.'

'I shall await the carriage with thanks and pleasure, Lady Marian and I shall remember the kindness you have shown to a poor alien long after I am in the heat of Guinea.' Lady Marian blushed and her eyes were bright. The count brushed Alice's hand once more with a perfunctory salute and left for Whitehall.

A row of female faces hastily disappeared from an upstairs window before Mr Verney could see who was staring at the guest and when Alice went to her room, her maid babbled on about the looks and demeanour of the foreigner so much that Alice lost patience, and told her to be silent.

'But madam, he is so romantic. He had eyes only for you and seemed to follow you wherever you went.' She giggled. 'I saw him kiss your hand and it was as if he kissed me!' She brushed the long golden hair and Alice sat as if in a trance of self-indulgence, remembering his voice, his touch and what he had said about her hair, her looks and her dress.

'We must be ready when he calls for us tomorrow,' she said, at last. 'He will not be at the house until a quarter of an hour after noon and we have to buy many things from the stalls in the Strand and select more clothes. Be ready by nine by the clock and tell Sam that we need the small carriage first before it goes to collect the count. You shall shop while I choose what you must pack and I shall offer him some of my husband's best wine while we wait for you to have the boxes bound to the carriage.'

'You will be alone with him, Lady Alice.'

'Silly girl. How long does it take to tie a few boxes to a carriage? And you will not do it alone. The groom will see to all but the arrangement of the boxes so that my hats do not get crushed.'

Marian called to ask Alice to help unravel silks for a tapestry. 'Don't stay alone in your room, dear, even if you feel sad. Help me here, and tonight, your father has said we may go with him to Tothill gardens to walk in the dusk and have supper in the new ale-house by Wapping Stairs.' She kissed her youngest daughter with affection. 'You were brave to be gracious to our guest when you had just left your dear husband and can't say when you will meet again.'

Alice stared at her as if she didn't understand. 'Of course. I miss Vincent already but I doubt if I shall feel it fully until a few days have past and I know his ship has gone from the shore.' It was as if she was convincing herself that she was married and loved her husband enough to miss him sorely. 'I must fill my mind with other matters, Mother. Tomorrow, I shall ask Debbie to make one of the syllabubs that she makes so well, just as Anna made them.'

'You have no objection to travelling with the count? You will not be alone and we shall be here as soon as you arrive.'

'Mother, I think you should come too.' Alice felt cold and slightly apprehensive.

'No, my dear, this is good practice for when you really set up your own establishments. Many a time I've had to talk to people with whom I had

55

little in common before your father came home and it is a part of our duty as wives to offer hospitality to guests. The count has been more than kind and I shall let Peter go on his tour without any worries.'

So I am here with the blessing of my dear mother, thought Alice the following morning. She stood by the window of her boudoir and looked across at the river, wondering if Vincent was far away. She folded a gown and put it with the rest on the bed and took another that she had not worn for months and didn't think she wanted to keep. She stood in her shift and the warm breeze stirred the fine cambric and made it cling to her body. Her hair was unbound as it shook loose during the many fittings that she had done with the help of her maid and now she had one more to try on and then get dressed ready in an hour to greet the count. Margaret, the maid, had gone to buy lace and pale blue trimmings and some silks that Lady Marian had asked her to get, and the house was quiet.

Alice folded the gown and turned as she heard a sound by the door. She gasped and clutched her shift tightly across her bosom as Le Comte Marc Lefèvre advanced from the door. 'I did not expect you, Sir! You are not here until after noon!'

He raised his shoulders in mock humility. 'As you see, I am here now and I have to say good-bye.'

'You are going away today?' She forgot her state of undress and let him take her hands in his. She felt a wave of desolation pass over her as he kissed the small hands and then before she really knew what was happening, his lips traced a path from lips to chin, to throat and the gentle rise of her breast, while he murmured passionately in a language that she did not understand, yet understood too well.

The clothes on the bed flew in every direction as he lifted her up and placed her on the soft down cover. Alice tried to struggle but he was stronger than she and gradually, his mouth and questing hands aroused her as Vincent had never done and she moaned her submission.

It was over as violently as it started, leaving her sore and yet complete, as if she had found a new source of desire, and filled a gap in her education in lust.

'I hear your maid coming,' he said, calmly, adjusting his clothes with the expertise of long practise. 'I suggest that you dress and join me downstairs where I shall make my peace with the coachman for sending him on a fruitless journey to Whitehall. I came by hackney carriage and brought the papers for your father. Are you listening?' She nodded. 'I had to see you again *ma chère*, and one day, I will come back to you. I shall dream of you for the rest of my life.'

As if in a dream so terrible and so wonderful that she might die, Alice dressed and was putting the bed to rights when Margaret came in. 'My head ached and I lay on the bed for a while, but it is better now. I suppose the count will be here soon.'

Margaret eyed the crumpled bed with curiosity and saw that her mistress was flushed and wild-eyed. 'I think you have a fever, my lady. I will make a tisane and bring it here until the count arrives.' But she returned with the warm drink and a cool cloth for Alice to put on her brow, with the news that the count had come early and left a bundle of papers and his humble apologies as he could not dine with the Verneys but must take the next boat for France.

Chapter 4

The sound of gunfire made Anna Maria Bennet stir but not waken. She sighed in her sleep and turned over, pushing away the light covering and moving further to the edge of the wide bed where her husband lay beside her. The hot still night was full of muted sound, disturbed at intervals by the routine firing of guns just to show the Moors that the settlement and fort were defended and alert.

A sharper sound of heavy fire and shouting made her start and waken and her husband was already buckling on his bandolier over the uniform that he had pulled on in a matter of seconds. His sword clashed against the metal frame of the bed and he called for his servant.

'What now?' asked Anna, wearily. 'Be careful, Daniel.'

'I think it is nothing more than a guard half asleep and seeing the movement of the sand, but I must investigate.' He kissed her brow and left and she heard men's voices raised, and one, more frightened, shouting.

Anna stood by her bed and let the warm air find her body. Her hair felt damp and the thin sheet had clung to her in uncomfortable ridges. She followed the routine of dressing and making sure that her jewel case and other valuables were safe at hand and ventured as far as the arched doorway to find out if this was the third false

59

alarm during the night or an attack that might be serious.

Daniel Bennet strode back into the room, his face grim and angry. 'One guard killed and another asleep and now taking his medicine for the oversight.'

Anna tried to shut the sound of the flogged man from her ears but even after four months of trying to make a home for Daniel in the God-forsaken territory of Tangier, she could not reconcile her thoughts to the violence and brutality that seemed essential to the running of the fortifications. 'Is it morning?' The lack of light could change rapidly and make night day with a fiery swift dawn but as yet the sky was dark and starlit. She lit another tallow candle and watched her husband as he slipped out of his tunic and trousers and lay naked on the bed. Anna went slowly back to bed, wearing a long shift of fine cambric that she would wear under her clothes during the day. Outside the room, servants and soldiers walked and talked, close enough to threaten the privacy of her bedroom, and unused to a commander who had his wife with him. The rattan screen at the archway was barely enough to keep away any who wanted to speak to the colonel and Anna had no intention of inflaming the passions of men who were by way of their work deprived of women from home unless their rank and inclination allowed wives to accompany them abroad.

'Be easy, my love. I have posted Ali by the door with orders that I am not to be disturbed again tonight unless the whole of Gayland's horde come battering at the defences.' Daniel held her in his arms as the warmth of the night waned with the coming dawn. Hungrily, he kissed her lips and dragged away the shift, and Anna forgot the ever-encroaching sand, the heat, the dust and the flies and the coarseness of the soldiery as she wondered again at the depth and strength of the passion she shared with the man who was tender in moments of love but hard when giving orders, stern with miscreants and ever more conscious of the part he played in making Tangier secure for King Charles II of England.

At last, with the candle-light killed by morning, they called for fresh water and ale. Anna brushed her hair and twisted it high on her head to be as cool as possible during the day. Her simple cotton gown and supple leather slippers made her look cool and dignified with a hint of aloofness essential when dealing with the kind of servants she had to endure in North Africa. Without complaint, she began to mend a dress and a tunic of her husband's, tasks that, in London, she would have given to her maid.

The mending thread broke and Anna began to show impatience. Lady Marian Verney would now be washing in scented water and being served fresh bread and cool ale or better still, a sweet infusion of tea made from Indian leaves and fine white sugar. She would have to do nothing more taxing than order the menu for dinner and tell the maids which rooms to scour and which shops to patronise. Today, Anna silently vowed, I shall teach one of the Arab women how to sew on fine fabric and to clean the grease from uniforms; and when Daniel had gone to inspect the progress made on the building foundations of the Mole, she ventured out in the sun to see to the domestic arrangements.

Women squatted by fires made of camel dung and dried cactus leaves, making flat loaves of dark bread which they cooked on heated stones over the red embers. Others boiled water in iron pots and set it to cool for drinking in the shade of the white-walled garrison. Anna smiled encouragement and a few women smiled and offered her fresh bread, but others looked away with hatred in their eyes.

A young woman in a black robe that hid her body so effectively that she could have been small or gross under the swirling folds, looked tense and ill. Anna called for her interpreter, a girl who had been to school in Algiers and could speak some English and better French as well as Arabic. 'Find out what ails her,' Anna said, and listened for words that she had learned in an effort to understand the women under her care.

The women murmured and looked hostile and the girl dragged herself to her feet and ran into one of the huts by the wall of the compound. The interpreter shrugged and began to walk away.

'Ayesha! Come here and tell me what was said.'

Reluctantly, Ayesha returned. 'She is with child, My Lady.'

'Tell her that she is excused all heavy work and must rest. She looks ill. How far is it?'

'Not many moons, My Lady, and not for many more.'

'What do you mean? Four moons?' The girl had looked sick as if in very early pregnancy and Anna was thankful that so far, she had not become pregnant herself in this hot and inhospitable country.

'Two or less,' said Ayesha.

'And the father?' Anna remembered the sudden hostility of the women and knew that this was another case of rape or casual liaison with the local women. Daniel had told her, when she had burst into his office one day demanding that the men under his command should be forbidden to take advantage of the slaves and locally enrolled paid servants, that men must take their pleasure where they could find it and the heathen women were as hot for it as any Vauxhall whore.

'But what happens when they bear children?' she demanded.

Daniel frowned. 'The Crown has given leave for men to take honest women as concubines and live as man and wife until they leave for home. It gives rein to the natural lusts and often becomes a permanent arrangement.' He shrugged. 'The Netherlanders allow marriage with local women and they return to Holland with the men if they are not too black. Some of the women here are handsome and light skinned and I often wish that our laws were less rigid.'

'Do they often marry the Moroccan women? Some are very beautiful,' Anna said, and tried not to think that in the past when Daniel was unmarried, he might have slaked his lust with such women.

'But what of any children of such marriages

and liaisons?' she asked.

'It's strange but the women here never seem to bear them. They take well and then abort as if the seed and the women do not match and repel each other.' Daniel looked puzzled. 'The black slaves bear children well enough and some who have no religion, but the women we have taken from villages that have allegiance to Mohammed and Gayland never bring children to life.'

'It is a strange country.' Anna thought for a while. 'I try to master certain phrases but it is difficult. Even the names are hard to say and to remember. No wonder the men call the commander of the Moorish troops Gayland, instead of Abd Allah al-Ghailan.'

Again she thought of their conversation as she tried to find out more about the girl. 'She is Kezia, My Lady, and has been here for two months. She was taken from a village where all the men were killed and has been living in one of the huts with a soldier on the other side of the inner compound where she was safe from the guns.'

'Do you mean a woman gives her body so that she can be safe?'

'Yes, My Lady.' Ayesha sounded patient as if a child asked questions to which the answers were obvious.

'Have they no feelings for their babies?' Anna sounded wistful. A child would make this awful place possible to endure when Daniel was away inspecting forts and troops and arranging supplies.

For an instant, Ayesha let down her usual

placid guard and her eyes flashed with hate. She spat into the sand and walked away, her rounded hips fluid and sensual under the loose black robe.

Anna walked over to the hut where Kezia lay on a mound of sand covered with rugs. A pitcher of water stood by the rough bed and already flies and dust floated on the surface. It smelled stale and brackish and had not been boiled. Kezia glanced up but when she saw who had come into her hut, she covered her face with her robe and moaned, softly.

'Are you in pain?' Anna spoke slowly, using one of the phrases that had become very useful during the past few weeks. She had asked the same question of prisoners and slaves and men who had defected to the British commanders and now lay suffering wounds on their behalf after skirmishes with the Berbers and Moroccans.

Kezia shook her head vigorously and sat up, holding her belly but trying to appear normal. A sound from the doorway made Anna turn and she saw a woman retreating with an earthenware cup and a pad of soft rags. She hurried after her, knowing that Ayesha was the woman to whom many went to with minor aches and pains and who Anna suspected of using witchcraft, but nothing bad was known about her so she wandered freely among the servants and certainly had a wide knowledge of the herbs and plants growing in the barren region and in the oasis. She also had a working knowledge of French and English and was not as hostile as some of the other younger women.

'Wait!' Anna ordered. 'Tell me what is wrong

with the girl and what is that you are hiding?'

Ayesha seemed to recede into her robe and her eyes were hooded. '*Rien, madame,*' she said, firmly. 'Just a potion to ease the pain. It is from plants and soothes the women at certain times.'

'But Kezia is pregnant, and in pain. Is she about to miscarry?'

'It will not be long now.' Ayesha stated, calmly. 'It is the will of Allah.' Reluctantly when Anna persisted, she held out the cup to her and Anna sniffed at the warm dark fluid. With caution, she dipped a finger into the brew and tasted it, then shuddered at the bitterness. 'It is a good medicine,' Ayesha said, firmly. 'I help the women and give you time to rest, *madame.*' The inference was plain, firm and hidden under the smooth tones but Anna felt threatened – Go away and don't interfere in things that are no concern to you. You are our enemy, the woman of the colonel and so nothing to us – Anna's dark eyes looked into the even darker eyes of the Arab woman. Both recognized the pride and breeding in the other and Ayesha smiled, slightly. A cry from the hut made them both hurry back in time to see Kezia fall fainting to the floor. Anna soaked her handkerchief in water from the ewer and placed the wet coolness on the girl's brow while Ayesha lifted the heavy skirts and examined the tense but nearly flat abdomen. She held the cup to the girl's lips as soon as she stirred and looked up.

'No more! No more!' she said, but Ayesha spoke roughly and rapidly so that Anna could not understand, and the girl took one shuddering sip after another and finally drained the cup.

'What is it? That isn't the first draught you have given her,' Anna accused.

'It takes one or two or three but she will sleep now and be well soon. She will be able to work in a few days and it will be forgotten.' Ayesha called sharply to a woman waiting outside, and told her to sit by the girl and fetch her when there was a change. She pointed to the basket of soft rags and a large dish that lay empty on the floor, and Anna was now in no doubt as to the purpose of the noxious-tasting brew. No wonder none of the Muslim women bore live babies, if Ayesha went to each one as soon as they knew they were with child, dosing them with some potent abortifacient.

Curiosity overcame her repugnance and Anna asked to see the plant that Ayesha had used. 'I study plants and their uses,' she explained when the closed-in expression came back. 'I have books about herbs that we use in England. I use them for wounds and headaches and boils, and for purges.' She became animated. 'I miss having them to hand. I know good cures for loosening of the fluids and for gout and scurvy and the pox. Some of the soldiers have the King's Evil and yet I can do nothing for them. The surgeon has very little and knows less about herbs and I could do much to help if I had my herb garden here.'

'You grow many plants? Such as do not grow here and are good for healing?' Ayesha smiled. 'Your country is green and grows well but we have to travel far to find some that I need. I have books of ancient remedies and am called often to some of the mighty in the land.'

'Why do you not use them here?'

'It is not permitted. They think I might do harm.'

'They think that you might poison them?' Anna looked at the strong face and eyes that had seen the agony of her country under many rulers. 'And would you?' she asked, quietly.

'It might come to pass, My Lady.' She looked embarrassed but the urge to ask a favour was irresistible even though the lady was the wife of the colonel and her enemy. 'You say you have books? With you in Tangier?' Anna nodded. 'I could show you plants that I have collected and have sent to me when the camel trains come and leave them for me in a village over the hills.'

'Come to my house when the sun is high and my husband is away and I have only Azziza to attend me,' Anna suggested. 'Now I must go to the hospital and talk to the wounded. My heart bleeds for them when I know I could help if only I had the means.' She left Ayesha to return to the hut and walked slowly across the wide cleanly-swept compound where the houses of the officers stood dazzling white in the brilliant sunlight, through to the next where the buildings, although still Moorish in design with deep shadowy porches against the glare of the sun, were less big and more crowded, where the other ranks had their lodgings. The hospital was at the back of the last compound near the stables and victualling stores, as if the wounded were to be thrust away in the background and were already on the way to the grave, in a country where wounds festered quickly and men went mad with the heat and dust.

Daniel was already on the half-finished Mole, consulting the builders and giving judgement on two men who had tried to avoid working by hiding in a gulley until the workforce had gone, and Anna felt relieved that he would be gone for some time. She lifted the curtain over the arch and went into the ward where two men lay stinking in their own ordure and others looked at her with dull sick eyes. There was no one in charge and she called for the man who had the care of the sick men.

He hurried from a side room and looked flushed, his breath smelling of drink and there was no sign of the women who Anna had detailed to clean the hospital and to minister to the physical needs of the very ill. He made every excuse possible for the state of affairs in the hospital and hotly denied that he was drunk. 'Where are the women?' she asked.

Sullenly he said that they refused to come after the first day and he could find no others willing to take their places. 'And why was that? You had strict orders to treat them well and they seemed willing enough when I gave the order,' Anna said.

A man sitting on a chair in the corner, recovering from a fall from a horse laughed. 'He tried to take too many into the back room and they didn't fancy him,' he said.

Anna felt her temper rising. It was bad enough being far from every comfort she had taken for granted all her life and from all her friends and relatives but to have her orders flagrantly disobeyed when the men were in obvious discomfort and degradation was too much. 'You will hear more of this,' she exclaimed. 'You will clean up these beds yourself and I shall return in an hour to see that all is well.' She wondered where the surgeon was and when she asked one of the guards, was told that he was out on the Mole treating a man who had crushed a leg when trying to move a log into a pit to form a part of the foundations.

The sun took up its station in a relentless sky and the shade within the thick white walls was a relief as Anna returned to her quarters. The wife of one of the other officers was sitting languorously on a pile of cushions waiting for her and Anna felt only irritation when she saw her. She was offered some of her own precious tea which Mistress Dulcie Meredith had demanded as soon as she found that Anna was absent, and she was forced to listen fairly politely to the endless tale of woe about bad and dishonest servants, the heat and the lack of diversions.

'Come to the hospital with me,' suggested Anna. 'There is plenty of *divertisement* there.'

The woman's tinkling laugh was incredulous. 'What would I do there, except to hold my nose and wish I held a posy of sweet and bitter herbs to take away the smell of decay?'

'You are the wife of a serving officer and as such it is your duty to oversee the welfare of the wives of other ranks and to tend the sick, even if only by making sure that there are local women to clean and see to their needs,' Anna said at last, unable to keep silent.

'In this heat? At home, I follow my husband but can get to civilized company in any town in which he is stationed, but what is there here? Desert and sand and a sun that would make me look like a Moor if I ventured out without a veil. The insects are terrifying and poisonous and the women hate me.' Anna repressed a smile. The screams from Dulcie's house had brought several armed men to rescue her from what had seemed at least rape by the leader of the Moors, but had been caused by the presence of one scorpion, quickly crushed beneath an iron heel. The pretty face was slack and already shiny with sweat, and Anna felt a reluctant twinge of compassion. It was a country that taxed the strength and sanity of even the strongest of men and if their women followed them, then only the most resourceful could survive.

'I have arranged for the wives to meet during the heat of the afternoon, to sew and talk and to bring their problems to us. This is the biggest and coolest room in the compound except for the chapel, and we can give them wine and water or a drink made from fruit. This will be after dinner tomorrow and all wives of officers should attend,' said Anna, firmly. Her natural authority and the fact that she was the wife of the senior serving officer in the garrison made even Mistress Dulcie bow to her wishes if there was no way of avoiding them. 'I have arranged for boys with fans to cool them and we have received fresh supplies of oranges and figs and dates,' she added, as an incentive.

Dulcie brightened. 'I can talk and give advice

71

but I am not good with the sick. The sight of blood makes me faint and the smell is like St Paul's during the plague.' She shuddered. 'I came here to escape the dangers in London and the possibility of the plague coming back and now I find that there are discomforts of which I had never dreamed.' She sighed. 'Do you not miss home, Mistress Bennet?'

'Of course. I miss the books and shops and the clean linen in abundance, and the company of scientific brains such as those of men we entertained during the short time after our marriage, before my husband was sent here.'

'I shall not stay.' The small chin set firmly and Dulcie set down her cup as if that made everything clear. 'I shall return when the next ship leaves from the Mole and wait for my husband in Kent where my father has his estates.'

Anna made no comment either to persuade her to stay or to urge her to leave, as she had heard this vow at least five times at regular intervals and knew that the fear of scorpions was outweighed by the jealous thoughts that Dulcie had when handsome Muslim women, and men, waited on her husband at table.

A servant placed a bundle of letters on the small table by Anna's side and told her that a ship had brought more of her goods and many books. 'Books! Would you not rather have fresh silks and some of the Indian cottons now fashionable with the ladies in London?'

'There will be clothes but that can wait until later. I must see if Lady Marian has sent the books I ordered and the lens I asked her to find.

I left a list with her when we had no time to buy everything we needed and she promised to ask a friend who knows more than she about such matters, to act for us.'

Her impatience to see the books filtered through to Dulcie, 'I'll come back when you unpack the *pretty* things,' she said, pointedly. 'Please send word when you do so as there is so little of interest here for me to see.'

'Tomorrow or the next day,' said Anna. 'Not today as I have to see some of the native women this afternoon, and that would not amuse you.' She remembered the hospital and reluctantly left the parcels of books still bound in hessian. 'Will you walk with me to the hospital?' she asked, knowing that this would send Dulcie home faster than anything she could say as an excuse to rid herself of her vapid company, but she couldn't resist going into the study to see how many parcels there were.

Dulcie followed her and stood before the portrait hanging where Daniel Bennet could see it when working at his desk. 'I have never had my portrait painted,' Dulcie said, enviously.

'It is a copy of one that we had painted by Mr Lely to give to my kind guardians as thanks for all they did for me while I was growing up, and the deep love I hold for them.'

'Do they paint many copies? Who would buy them if they knew nothing of the subject? Although it is pretty enough to grace any wall,' said Dulcie with an air of condescension.

Anna frowned. 'It is a strange feeling to know that strangers will have the copy. There is only one other at present that went to a friend of the artist in Amsterdam.'

'To the Netherlanders! But we are at war with them!'

'We signed a treaty at Breda this year and even if the privateers do not seem to keep the peace, we are no longer at war with the Dutch, at least for a while, though these times are uneasy and it is difficult to know one's friends.'

'I would rather stay friends with the French,' said Dulcie. 'They have good manners and know how to flatter in the most diverting way.' Her eyes were dreamy. 'I have met members of their diplomatic when I was staying with my parents, and remember one man who charmed me greatly. My husband did not care for him as he was jealous of his pretty compliments and his thick dark hair.' Anna smiled, knowing that Major Meredith had thin mousy hair that could not be hidden under periwigs in the heat of Tangier, and any man, like Daniel who had a fine head of his own hair, was the envy of his brother officers.

'And do they take wives with them to England and the Court of St James?' asked Anna.

'They travel and leave wives at home, unless they have a posting with an Ambassador at a high level and remain in London or Amsterdam or the Danish capital for long periods.' Dulcie laughed. 'My handsome Frenchman was gone before my husband could object more than usual that I was dallying with him.' There was a note of regret in her voice. 'He was young and had beautiful hands and eyes and I often wondered if he had a mistress as well as the wife he left in Paris.' She seemed to savour even the sound of his name. 'He is called Le Comte Marc Lefèvre, and he moves between Paris and London or did before he was sent to the French colony in Guinea. He might be there by now and I may never see him again.'

'That must be a relief to the major,' said Anna, smiling. 'The world is full of such libertines and men of dangerous charm. I recall such men.' She stopped. The hospital needed inspection and the smell of savoury dishes told her that Daniel would be back for dinner soon if he could leave the Mole, and this was no time to remember Sir Rollo Fitzmedwin and his dangerous charm.

The beds were clean and the men looked more comfortable when Anna went into the ward but the corporal in charge was nowhere to be seen. Two old women squatted by the door, the only ones willing to risk being with the notorious corporal, and the soldier who had talked to her earlier was also missing. Anna went into the kitchen at the back of the room and saw that a thick soup of lentils and onions was bubbling ready for the men, stirred by an army cook who went each day to make sure that the sick men were fed.

'Where is the corporal?' she asked. The man stirred vigorously and pretended not to hear. She repeated the question, standing so close that the steam of the soup reached her cheek and the man had to take notice.

'He went out, ma'am,' he said. He glanced at the slit window and then back at the soup.

Anna followed his glance and saw that there was activity away by the gate leading to the outer defences where the graveyard was situated. 'There has been a death?' she asked. The man nodded, fearfully, as if he would be held responsible. 'Who died?' She had seen the two men who might have succumbed, but they still lay sleeping on pallets by the door. There was no sign of the surgeon who would certify death and the cause for the records, and she assumed that he was present with the chaplain at the graveside, at the customary hurried funeral as soon as possible after death in the hot climate where corruption came fast in already decaying bodies. She started in surprise as the surgeon came into the kitchen to inspect the food.

'Did your man die?' asked Anna. 'Daniel told me that a man was badly hurt and you were with him for hours by the Mole.'

'No, he lost a leg, poor wretch, but will do once we bring him here in the cool of night, but he is better in the breeze by the water under the palm trees until later.' He tasted the soup and approved it. 'I amputated and tarred the stump and he will live unless this wretched heat gets to him and he has a fever.'

'Then who died? I came through the room and saw no empty pallet since this morning early when I ordered the corporal to make the place sweet as the women he had misused refused to work with him.'

'Corporal!' The surgeon shouted. He went into the ward and looked round. The only man missing was the one recovering from a fall and he

76

had seemed healthy enough. The surgeon walked past each of the pallets. 'You're right, ma'am. There is no patient missing who might have died, and I am bound to give the cause of death before burial.' He eyed the red-faced cook with speculation. 'Come my man, you know more than you have said. Who is so kind as to bury another of my mistakes?' He laughed. 'Unseemly haste even in this heat it would seem.' He set his face in a more serious mode. 'Come now, I haven't all day. Have you anything to say or do I have to see for myself?'

The cook pulled the boiling cauldron to a shelf away from the fire and said nothing.

'Someone has been digging a grave over by the wall. The gate is shut now but I saw men with spades and heard the sounds of work,' insisted Anna.

'We had casualties during the night and perhaps they dig future graves,' suggested the surgeon. 'It is a good thing that they do as we learned to our cost when we had corpses enough but no graves and no diggers and the foxes and vultures defiled good Christian bodies with no rites read over them, almost as I remember in London during the plague.' He saw that Anna was alarmed. 'We will examine what rubbish is being buried, ma'am. Come with us, cook, and tell the women to feed the sick and do what must be done for them.'

The heat struck like a hot iron as they walked slowly across the beaten earth and through the wooden gateway to the rough burial ground filled with rocks and coarse grass and a few wooden crosses at the heads of sand-covered mounds. Anna drew back as they approached the pit being dug and the Arab servants rested on their spades to watch the Englishman pull aside the cotton shroud that encased a body ready for burial.

'What is this? Eh, man, what is this? What in God's name has happened here?'

Anna saw the face of the man to whom she had spoken only hours before now; the man who had laughed and told her about the corporal's behaviour, even though he knew that what he said might lead to the flogging or worse of a fellow soldier.

'He fell again and died, and you were not here to examine him, sir. I heard you would be at the Mole until tonight and knew that we must hurry to get him buried,' said the corporal. Anna knew that he was lying and one glance at the grim face beside her told her that the surgeon believed not a word of it.

'Guard! Bring two men and shackles. I smell murder!' He stripped the body and turned it over. A jagged wound in the back with blood seeping from the gash told all.

'It was an accident! He came at me and I fought him off!' The wretched man fell to his knees and vowed by all the saints that he was innocent of murder. 'As the blessed Virgin is my witness,' he began again after the surgeon thrust him away.

'He came at you backwards and fell on your knife? with a hip that made him limp and walk with a crutch? If you don't hang for murder, you will for popery! You heard him, ma'am, calling on

78

the symbol of the Catholics!' The weeping man was dragged away to the gaol in heavy iron bonds and the surgeon told the servants to go on with the burial. 'We have enough witnesses once I get the men in the beds to speak, and you, ma'am, you saw the body and heard what the wretch said. He denied nothing but the way it was, and that was impossible. A stab in the back is not self-defence and never could be.'

'What will happen now?' Anna asked in a small voice. She was shaken by the terror in the man's eyes far more than at the sight of the body.

'He will come before the colonel in the morning and then be hanged,' he said as if she should know. 'We can't be lily-livered over this, ma'am. We must show the Arabs that justice is done even to our own and we give no quarter for murder, treachery or thieving.'

Chapter 5

The messenger from the Navy Office tried to keep his feet still and not trample mud all over the floor. The Verney House was quiet and he had waited for over half an hour to see Lady Marian or Mr Edward Verney but they had not returned from the house on the Strand where Alice was now living, five weeks after her husband left for the Indies.

Rain had fallen in cold monotony all day and the roads were once again muddy and slippery and his boots were clogged with dirt, and he wasn't sure if the news he brought would be welcome or not. He listened and heard the stable-hands, calling that the carriage was coming and five minutes later, Mr Edward Verney strode into the hall, looking like thunder.

'Never ask me to go there after dark again! It's bad enough in daylight but with the dark and the rain, the going is far too treacherous.' He saw the man standing awkwardly twisting his hat in his hands but didn't at once notice that he was a stranger. 'The cellars of the burned houses make for more accidents than the last war with the Dutch,' he asserted. 'Twice, coming home, the wheels slipped and we were nearly flung into cellars and Sam must see if the offside horse is lame.'

He became aware of the man. 'Who the devil

are you, sir? Can't a man come home at night without having strangers waiting in his house?' The fact that Alice had been in a stupid and fractious mood had made him ready for argument and this clerk seemed just the right object for his rancour.

'I come with news of Sir Vincent Clavell, sir.' The man spoke softly with a glance at Lady Marian who was pausing at the foot of the stairs.

Edward glanced up. 'Come into my study where we can talk. You are from the Navy Office?' The man nodded and Edward flung off his surcoat and left it on the floor for the servant to pick up and brush before putting it to air. 'Wine,' he barked; 'And biscuits. My daughter was too concerned with her own vapours to give us a good supper and her new companion wouldn't know a kitchen if she had to live in one!'

The man coughed. Rich men frightened him and he dreaded the reaction of the powerful businessman to his news. He sank on to the wide bench that Edward indicated and waited while candles were lit and the fire stirred and Edward was sipping wine with his back to the fire and an expression of relief on his face.

'Now, sir,' said Edward.

'As far as we know, Sir Vincent is safe, sir, but the ship ran into squalls and foundered on Scilly. A fast cutter on the way to Plymouth brought the news and we hope to hear more within the day.'

Edward smoothed his chin and nodded. 'No loss of life? No likelihood of the ship having to return to Chatham? I suppose the repairs will be done quickly and the journey continued.'

'I brought the news that came and I know nothing more, sir, but the Navy Secretary insisted that you be told before another night passed.'

'I am grateful and I shall send a note in the morning.' He became aware that the messenger was wet and cold.

'Sit closer to the fire, my dear sir.' He poured out a generous amount of wine and pushed the biscuits towards him, his natural kindliness surfacing again. 'No, that's not good enough. We both need something more.' He summoned the maid and demanded cold pie and mulled ale, and the clerk warmed under his better humour and the influence of good food and drink. He told how the news had come and how the captain of the cutter was sure that he had seen Sir Vincent on shore with a body of men who were trying to pull the ship clear of a sandbank before the ebbing tide. 'If the repairs take long, the officers may come home to wait in comfort. If he came and you had not been warned, it was thought the shock might be too great for the ladies.'

'I am very grateful,' Edward repeated. 'I think you are right and until we hear more, I suggest that the news comes to me alone and not to the house on the Strand where Lady Clavell now lives. She has vapours enough without this news to make her wonder if he will return soon or be away for far longer than he anticipated. Report to my offices in Lincoln's Inn.' He laughed. 'It is more convenient and you will not be so wet.'

As soon as he had gone, Edward took down a map of the coast of England and the islands. On paper, it seemed quite near and yet, in bad weather, with the winds and tides stubborn and the time of year unfriendly, it could take many days of sailing to reach Scilly, and many more days for news to come to the mainland. The cutter would come quickly, but even so, news would be delayed, especially if the next ship to leave Scilly for home was slower and more cumbersome.

Marian called from her boudoir as soon as she heard him walk up the stairs. 'Not bad news. Edward?'

'Nothing but news of ships, but no loss of life,' he added.

She sighed. 'I wish that you had no part in that trade. We are at peace with the Dutch and yet the King turns a blind eye to privateering but soon might have to condemn it, and we'll all have our fingers burned.'

'None of your private fortune is invested in ships my dear, and most of mine has been withdrawn. I saw the signs long before they were clear and now that an amnesty has been declared, for men who ran to The Netherlands to have the right to return without pain, it shows that we shall have peace and trade and exchange of culture again.'

'I hope you are right, Edward. There are many men of good family who fled from the Court to further their fortunes in the Low Countries. They will be glad to return.'

'Perhaps,' he said, shortly. 'The king has an eye on their money. There is still a great need for loans to the Crown and we also need the brains of men who have skills to offer in the way of architecture and planning of roads and sewers.' He felt the need to talk quickly so that Marian couldn't ask awkward questions and he knew that talk of planning and sewers was not the bedtime conversation for a lady.

'Do you think that Sir Rollo will be pardoned?' she asked, suddenly wide awake. 'He was a rascal but quite charming and unforgettable.'

'Nothing was proved. There was only the word of wicked Mary Creed, and even if she was a searcher during the plague, and as such an authority she swore to the magistrate that he killed a watchmen, we know from our own bitter experience that she was evil and hated anyone connected with us.' He shrugged. 'Her testimony is worthless now as the Devil claimed his own in the fire and Rollo could return safely.'

'Would you receive him, Edward?'

'Yes. He was wild and bad enough but the times were violent and terrible, and even if he had killed to escape a sealed house bearing the red cross of the plague when he was whole, would not any man have done the same?' He gave a short laugh. 'We can be forgiving now that Anna and Alice are safely married, and no further burden on us to protect.'

'Alice looked ill,' said Marian. She smiled. 'She does not know why but I think that when Vincent returns he will have good news.'

'You jump to conclusions, madam.' He was still annoyed at the lack of comfort that his daughter had offered them and was not prepared to accept excuses. 'Women's talk,' he muttered and left his wife to sleep in peace.

Edward slept fitfully and rose early, uneasy that he had kept the news of Vincent's shipwreck to himself. It would be far more of a shock to Alice and Marian if they heard about it in the new coffee house or when they were visiting, but when he left for his office, having a great deal of work to do, he saw that Marian was still asleep and he had no time to wake her, to explain and then to calm her down, and later, it seemed less urgent, so a few days passed with no more news and he assumed that the ship was once more on an even keel and heading for the Indies.

There were other matters to take his attention. The last of the booty taken in his final sortie into piracy had been sold and his share in the ship also, but he had to reinvest his money quickly before the Crown agents saw his profits and suggested that he invest with them. The iniquitous poll tax made law early in 1667 was bad enough and it had taken all the skill of learned lawyers to pare down the levy to include only his private house and office and not the other residences in the country and the minor companies that he owned.

Alice, too, was a constant worry, as her new duenna was blind when it came to visits to places to which Vincent would never take his wife, and as long as the woman trailed behind her, Alice thought she could go exactly where the fancy took her. With Sarah Clavell, Vincent's sister, a few months younger than Alice and as yet unmarried, at least she had another female to complete her outings and Sarah seemed very domesticated. The two young women giggled together and whispered in secret but Sarah insisted on taking linen to be bleached each week and included fine linen that had become yellowed by usage from the Verney household, thus freeing Lady Marian from having to send her servants across the river to the marshes, where the linen was hung to dry after treatment with a mixture of bleaching agents including fine white wood ash, called lye.

Sarah set out each time with a boy carrying the bundle of linen, a maid to help him and another girl to accompany her to the ale-house where she rested until the last batch of linen, left the week before, was carefully folded and wrapped and the account paid. Alice, now very sick each morning, never ventured across the river and Sarah seemed to enjoy the task, returning flushed and bright-eyed as if it was an adventure, and insisting that many well-known ladies of quality went there with their servants and did as she did, and rented a room for a few hours so that she could recover from the barge on the Thames.

Marian compared Sarah to Alice and wondered how two girls of roughly the same age who had been so much alike in the country, now seemed different, and she had to try not to wish that Sarah was her child and not Alice. 'Alice will settle down once she has a baby,' she said, often enough to convince herself, and at least her activities were less now that she couldn't be sure of her stomach, when travelling by coach or after exertion. Debbie smiled whenever she heard Alice wailing that it wasn't fair, that life had no right to treat her so and that she hoped the baby would die, but later, each day, Alice began to feel better and to eat ravenously, and her health was blooming.

Alice seldom spoke of Vincent but often, Marian disturbed her when she was looking sad or puzzled as if she tried to find an answer to a problem, and at these times, Marian forgave her all her tantrums and sent Debbie with savoury dishes and syllabubs from her own kitchens, to the big house on the Strand that never seemed like a real home.

'I shall go riding as soon as the sickness is better,' Alice vowed.

'The curricle is less jolting than the carriage, and the air will do you good,' said Marian.

Alice looked defiant. 'I mean on a horse, madam. I can't ride in a carriage up and down the park like an old lady. Time enough for that if my husband burdens me with more children and then goes to the other side of the world each time.'

Marian asked Edward to speak to her but it was Sarah who persuaded her that she must not do anything so rash as Vincent would be horrified. 'He has given his word that you may go to Court, Alice,' said Sarah, wistfully. 'I wonder if I shall ever be allowed to do that?'

'I shall insist that I need you with me, my dearest Sarah and we shall have the richest of gowns and the best linen imaginable, with fine lace from the continent and ribbons made of pure silk.' They dreamed and discussed their dresses and the impact they would make on society.

'You shall choose a handsome man to be your husband, Sarah. It is good being married. I miss Vincent so much,' said Alice with the superiority of a married lady over a slightly younger spinster, and Sarah smiled, as if she didn't object to being patronized, and continued to amuse Alice, help Lady Marian and to make sure that the linen was bleached regularly so that it was noticed and remarked on by many of the visitors to the two houses.

On a fine but frosty day, Alice was restless and feeling full of energy and decided that now she was well again, she could enjoy the short journey across the Thames to the marshes for a day. Secretly, she had suspected that there was more of interest than linen and the smells of the laundry to take Sarah there so often and she needed to see new places and find out what took so long each week.

'I have a notion to come with you, Sarah. The day is fine and I am well and the air will be good for me.'

'Ladies in your condition must be very careful,' said Sarah, firmly. 'What would my brother say if I allowed you to risk a fall on the slippery plank from the barge?' She looked severe and slightly apprehensive.

'What nonsense,' said Alice, with a petulant tilt to her head that boded ill to any who thwarted her. 'I am as fit as you are and have more colour in my cheeks than you, miss.' She regarded Sarah with curiosity. 'Why do you refuse to let me share this outing? We share everything as sisters and yet you do not wish me with you now.'

'It is your health that I consider, dear Alice, and the smells and humours of the river are not good for ladies with delicate stomachs.'

'I shall come with you.' Alice called to her maid and was ready before Sarah could instruct the boy to put the bundles into the carriage. Alice said no more but was silent on the short drive to the jetty. The other side of the river seemed close in the clear air and the flat barge was ready for the carriage to be driven on to it. 'We stay in the carriage and have no slippery planks to walk,' said Alice with a touch of sarcasm. 'I am over-whelmed by your care of me, Sarah, but I see no danger, and no discomfort in this venture, and I think the inn will provide good food and rest and a change of scene.'

Sarah was tense and pale when they reached the inn and sent the servants on in the carriage with the linen, as Alice vowed that she would die if she had to wait another minute for a warm posset, and if the company in the inn was no better than it looked, she would rest in the room provided.

'You wanted to see the marshes where they hang the linen,' said Sarah. 'We can be there in five minutes and come here later.'

'You said you considered my health,' com-plained Alice. 'I need something warm inside me and to get out of the wind.'

'And so you shall have something. Sit by the fire and I'll take our cloaks up to the room and ask the landlord to make a really hot posset.' Firmly refusing that Alice should stir another step, she caught up the cloaks and ran to the

89

stairs, after giving the order to the landlord, and five minutes later, she came down, breathing fast and looking relieved. She sipped the hot spicy drink as if it was she who needed it more than Alice and began to talk normally for the first time since they set out for the marshes.

Alice laughed at the antics of a small dog brought in by a man selling laces and pins, and bought far more than she could use in a month. She turned, smiling, to see how Sarah reacted to the dog. Sarah was looking at the back of a man leaving the inn and had no time for performing dogs, however beguiling. The expression that Alice surprised on her friend's face was a mixture of love and agony and Alice watched the man pass by the window to fetch his horse. She wrinkled her nose in an effort to recall where she had last seen him and then remembered.

'What brings Master James Ormonde here?' asked Alice, with a sharp look at her friend.

'Mr Ormonde?' Sarah replied as if the name meant nothing to her, but her face seemed to grow tighter and her hands trembled as she held the pewter mug.

'He has no bundle of linen and so no cause to be here when he could be riding in fairer fields.' Alice laughed. 'He should have left his lace with us. It was not fresh, as if he had ridden far and fast to keep a tryst.' Her voice was teasing and unkind. 'A man far too handsome to be wasted on maids bringing washing. But as he has no fortune, he must take what offers.'

Sarah called for food and suggested that they didn't need the room for resting as Alice was finding enough to watch in the main room of the inn, but Alice insisted that after dinner, they must rest and she could see if the innkeeper kept a clean house, with comfort enough for Sarah when she came to the room alone; and after eating far more than was good for her and noticing that Sarah picked at her food with no appetite, Alice yawned and insisted that she must rest.

Reluctantly, Sarah led the way up the stairs that she had mounted so often over the past few weeks and opened the door to a big room with a huge four-poster bed in the middle of the sanded floor. A fire sulked in an iron grate and the air was musty. On the table was a bottle of wine and some small pastries and a paper propped up by the bottle.

Before Sarah could object or take it first. Alice snatched the paper and unfolded it. 'Are you sure that this is the room?' she asked, with an innocent air. Sarah nodded dumbly and watched helplessly as Alice read the note intended for her. 'This is intriguing. Sarah. Someone has used this room as a place of assignation and sets out his passion in very fair words. It is signed with one letter only. Who could it be? Perhaps it isn't as it seems, but a note left for you by someone afraid to approach and yet dying of love for you. I have received such notes and I find the best solution to unwanted attentions is to do this.' Quickly she tossed the paper into the fire and Sarah watched it curl and die in the flames. 'Signed J, but nothing more and I know of nobody who we receive at home except old Sir James Belfont with the initial J, and if Vincent would not receive him, then surely he is not welcome?'

Sarah was weeping softly. 'Dear, dear Alice, you will say nothing? I love him with all my heart but I know that he will never find favour with my brother. He is of good family and as good as many who come to the house,' she said, brushing away the tears and looking defiant. 'He wants me to run away with him but how can I when Vincent rules my life and only gives me an allowance that could never support two?'

'You must wait,' said Alice. 'When you are eighteen, you can expect your own fortune and do as you please if you are of the same mind.'

'I cannot wait. I can never live without him,' Sarah declared with feeling. 'When I saw him leave today, I nearly cried out and it was as if a knife pierced my heart.'

Alice smiled. This was amusing and very romantic. 'I will keep this our secret and never come again to this place unless you ask me.' She sighed. 'It must be so romantic to have a lover and to meet in secret. I am a married lady with a child coming and nobody to keep me warm in bed. Married, with no husband, and you have a lover.'

Sarah looked shocked. 'You have a husband who is your lover, too. He adores you and you alone. You could never be unfaithful to Vincent!'

'No, of course not.' Alice turned away and put a hand over her swelling and tried to think that her encounter with the French diplomat had been a bad dream. It had never happened. It was impossible that in half an hour or less, she had been seduced or near raped in some wondrous way that had left her bemused and longing for those same arms to hold her again.

They lay on the bed and talked, and Alice learned that James Ormonde had been ordered to leave his father's estate when he made his decision to be an actor with the King's Company. Sarah seemed very relieved to be able to confide her troubles to her dearest friend and when they left for the barge, they were both in excellent spirits. 'We go to the play in a few days time and Mary, the chief orange seller, will bring me a note, and later collect my reply.' Sarah shrugged. 'I hate my secrets to be known to such women but I pay her well and she is discreet or loses her money, and James swears that she would never give him away.'

Twice, Alice almost said something of the French count but something made her decide that no other person must know what had happened between them now or ever in the future. To know another's secret was power, but discretion about her own was safety.

There was an air of excitement about the house when they returned. Debbie rushed out to the carriage and helped Alice to alight, then led her into the hallway and sat her in a chair as if she might find her legs too weak to hold her upright. Lady Marian hurried down the stairs and Sarah, who had intended staying in the carriage waiting for Alice while the servants unpacked the clean linen for Lady Marian, before the carriage took the two young ladies back to the house on the Strand, decided to join the others in the hall.

'My love!' said Lady Marian. She looked flushed and had not changed into her gown for receiving company. She seemed to make an effort to compose her face and hands and led Alice to a seat. 'Such news and enough to make your heart beat too fast as mine is doing now.'

'What can you mean, Mother?' said Alice in an agony of impatience and irritation. From the expression on her mother's face, it might be several minutes before she came to the point of the news, whatever that was. It could be nothing more exciting than an invitation to share a box at the theatre, but somehow, Alice knew that this was more important. Sarah stood waiting but shared none of the tension. Her thoughts were far away and she barely heard what was said.

'Sit down, Sarah. This concerns you, too. Deborah! Make tea and bring it into the drawing-room.'

Alice glanced at Deborah and raised her eyebrows. The price of tea and the fine white sugar needed for it had made even Lady Marian keep this precious luxury for only special occasions.

'Please, Mother, tell us what is amiss. I shall die of curiosity if you keep it from us a moment longer.'

Lady Marian took a deep breath. 'We have news of Vincent!' she stated, triumphantly.

'And where on the high seas could he write notes to be delivered to London?' asked Alice, in disbelief. 'Or did a passing ship take on the task and bring mail from all on board? Vincent told me that this happened at times and that he would endeavour to send word if this opportunity arose.

Where is my letter, ma'am?'

'Better news than a letter could bring! A fast horseman brought word from Plymouth to the Navy Office that the ship foundered on Scilly and was dragged ashore for repairs but on putting to sea again was found unseaworthy for a long voyage and had to return to England.'

'Vincent is coming home?' The ecstatic question came from Sarah and not from the man's wife. 'Oh, this is good news, ma'am. I have so much to ask him and I have missed him sorely.'

'My dear! This is shock, even if it makes you speechless with delight,' said Marian with an air of slight disappointment. 'Drink your tea and it will revive you, and then you must go home to prepare for his return, tomorrow.'

'Tomorrow?' Alice was confused and filled with a nameless fear. 'So soon,' she added in a feeble voice.

'Now you must go home and rest, Alice. I'm sure that Sarah and Miss Charity will see to the servants and tell them what is needed and I shall prepare a supper for us all to welcome him, tomorrow. Sam will meet the stage at Tyburn and bring him here and then take all his baggage home while Vincent sups with us.' She embraced the two girls as they prepared to leave. 'Alice, I am almost as happy as you are. He is a good husband to you and we all love him, too. How happy he will be when he hears that you are with child. I know it was his dearest wish.'

'He will go away again,' said Alice as if to reassure herself that he could not stay long in London.

Marian laughed. 'Enjoy his company while he is here and it may come that he no longer hankers after the sea, once he knows that you will be a complete family.'

Alice hardly saw the carriages that they passed on the way home and Sarah had to tell her to wave to friends and to smile. 'They will think you have had bad news and not this wonderful message. We must make sure that the servants unpack for Vincent while we sup with your family, Alice, so that when he comes home, it will be as if he never left it.'

'It can never be quite the same,' said Alice, quietly. 'I feel as if he has been away for a very long time and that much has happened in that time.'

'Much has happened. You found out that you had taken with a baby and we have Miss Charity with us and have much to tell him about the places we have seen while under her charge.' Sarah giggled. 'He may say that she has allowed us to go to the theatre too often but I know he wants us to be happy.'

'And what of Master Ormonde? Do you intend telling your brother that you have a lover? I shall say nothing, my dearest Sarah, but tongues wag and you will have to be very careful.'

'I have made up my mind to see less of James for a while, but to tell Vincent that my heart is set on marrying him. He has so much wealth that he will indulge me in this as the Ormonde family were once of great eminence,' said Sarah, hopefully.

'I fear his family had strange loyalties and were

strong for Oliver Cromwell. My father condemns them as traitors to the Crown and their business has never flourished since the time when Royalty was restored.'

'Why must the sons who were not even born when the Protector was in power suffer from the sins of their fathers?' said Sarah with passion.

'People forget until they choose to recall what suits them,' said Alice with surprising wisdom. 'I fear that Vincent is very much against any hint of allegiance to Oliver, and might not take to a brother-in-law who acts at the Drury Lane theatre.'

'If we were married and Vincent gave us substance, we could live quietly in the country if that would suit him better. I'm sure that I can persuade Vincent that my happiness lies with James,' Sarah said with an attempt at certainty.

'You look pale,' said Alice. 'We must rest and then choose what to wear when Vincent returns.'

'Would you not rather meet him here alone before going on to your parents?' asked Sarah. 'I can send a message to Lady Marian and leave the house to you and Vincent until you have been together for a while.'

'No!' Alice blushed. 'I prefer to meet him there and it is kind of my mother to make everything easy. We shall have time together later and I am not yet ready to be alone with him. I feel strangely distant, but I suppose that women do feel like this when they are pregnant.' She laughed at Sarah's shocked expression. 'We were married for such a short time before he went away. I feel diffident.'

'You were married for six months with no sign of a baby and had plenty of time together to become acquainted!' Sarah replied. 'It was a long enough period for any woman to find out that she was no longer shy in the marriage bed.'

'Sarah!' Alice cried in sudden alarm. 'Are you unwell?'

'It is nothing. The excitement and what happened this morning have given me palpitations and I feel a trifle faint. I think that tea does not agree with me.' Sarah smiled and her colour returned. 'There, I am better and we have much to do, Alice. I shall tell Miss Charity the good news and make sure that Vincent's dressing room is clean and his linen is stacked neatly in the press. He took so little with him that he can walk in and it will seem that he has never been away.'

'He will have very white lace and linen bands,' said Alice, with a wicked smile. 'He might even believe that I shall be a good housekeeper.'

Chapter 6

'You have good news?' Pieter Van Steen tried to appear unconcerned but the pile of letters and important-looking documents on the wide table made him unable to hide his curiosity.

'Good news indeed, *Menhir.*' Sir Rollo Fitz-medwin laughed softly. 'There were times when I wondered if I would ever rise above my fate and be able to pay my way but now, my revenues from France and Switzerland and England have arrived and I can once again be affluent.' He smiled at the man who now looked uneasy as if he wondered what the Englishman would do next.

While Rollo was almost dependent on the Van Steens since his marriage to their daughter Helena, Pieter was in a position of power and could decide what the young couple did, where they lived and who they had as guests, but the air of relieved flamboyance and the sudden change in the fortunes of his son-in-law was upsetting. No longer would he have a docile aristocrat at his beck and call, able to dangle the title before his envious business friends as if he owned the right to do so. The set of the firm shoulders now told him that the new independence might have repercussions.

'I have invited friends to supper,' Pieter said in a placatory voice. 'We will have good wine and food and much talk. Helena will be pleased at your good fortune and we must celebrate.'

'We will celebrate this well,' said Rollo, 'And tomorrow, my wife shall buy clothes befitting her station.' He became animated as the infinite possibilities of his wealth were dawning on him. 'I shall make the builders hurry and order the furnishings of the house and have my own establishment.' He saw the expression on Pieter's face. 'You have been more than generous, and I shall never forget everything that you and your family have done for me,' he said and Pieter smiled.

'But now, I am my own man again and can provide for my own family.' He glanced at the huge painting that now had pride of place above the heavy serving table by the wall. The faces of the solemn family which included the portrait of Helena dampened his mood. 'Clothes,' he said as if to himself. 'Clothes will work a miracle, and she shall be painted by the best in Holland.'

He returned to his business and spent the rest of the day ordering clerks who spoke English and Dutch to make out letters and receipts and to make a start catching up on the neglected papers. He read letters from friends in England, long in coming and yet still fresh enough to amuse and interest him. Rollo sat back in a high-backed wooden settle, against the draught, and read that the treaty with the Dutch was welcomed by all but the faction led by the Duke of York and his followers who hated the anti-Catholic feeling in The Netherlands.

'You can come home whenever you feel so

inclined, my dear friend,' wrote Alan Denzil. 'Send word and I will see that they make shift for you in any of your estates. I have kept faith with your family and very quiet about your whereabouts and so the Crown has taken very little after your father died, but come soon or the King may enquire too deeply into your affairs and expect more investment in his vain forays. Your father gave me the power of attorney before he died and the care of the estates, but time has made this trust a burden that you should share, and surely, you miss the country of your birth?'

'Is something wrong?' The gentle voice broke into his thoughts. 'My father said that you have news to make you happy and yet I find you sad.'

'Not sad, Helena. Just overcome by the goodness of my friends. This man, Alan Denzil, was a squire in my father's service and a good friend when I was young and idle.' She smiled. 'Yes, I know it is only a few months – nearly a year since I left England but I feel that I have grown apace, and the peace of this house has made me passive.' He pushed aside the papers and walked across the room. 'From this window, I see the smooth water of the canal, the slender trees and fine houses on the other side and there is a feeling of being enclosed in peace, but a peace that is soft and without life, like being rolled in a Dutch pancake,' he said to himself. Helena waited, hoping that he would speak to her in Dutch again, and not understanding his English words.

She just smiled. 'You will come to dinner now?' she asked at last. 'My father and mother are seated.'

Rollo bit back an impatient retort, and forced a smile. Next week, next month or whenever he could have the house finished and ready for occupation, he could eat when he liked, drink what he liked and meet whoever he found interesting.

The family looked up as they went into the room and Pieter bent his head to ask a blessing on the food. The serving maid passed round thick pewter dishes and served soup from a wide Delft bowl of fresh blue and white which matched the ranks of china displayed on the dresser. The meat that followed was well cooked with vegetables but had none of the presentation for which Rollo yearned now as if he had recalled other food, other tables and other refinements; but as usual, he praised the dishes, and the wine, which was served more frugally than suited his mood.

Rollo made his excuses as soon as was polite and returned to his papers. From one package he took a box that held two medallions. 'Even with the peace signed, and the amnesty in force, it is well to have some proof of the signing,' wrote Alan. The Breda medal was finely wrought in copper, and the second one in gold. 'I have bought several to lay by, in copper, silver and gold. In time, they may be valuable, and if the Dutch sail into the Medway again with guns afire, then we can look on them as curios, and wonder what happened to treaties. With the engraving done by Jan Roettier and the face of Britannia from a likeness of Mistress Frances Stewart, we have the best of both nations, happier than if our engravers had done the work and a Dutch face had appeared on the back.'

Rollo called for Helena and gave her the gold medallion. 'Engraved by a good Dutchman and sealing the peace between our countries,' he said. 'Such unions are to be encouraged,' he added with a laugh and kissed her on the lips. Helena blushed and drew away, glancing towards the open door anxiously. 'Come to bed,' he suggested and then shook his head. 'I know! It isn't seemly to lie with my wife during the day when honest men work!' He held her close and kissed her again. 'Soon, in our own house, we shall lie in bed all day if that is what we want.' Helena smoothed down her bodice and her smile was almost frightened.

'My father,' she began.

'Your father is a good and worthy man who I respect and I shall do nothing to offend him,' he assured her. 'But I am not like him. When we live away from here, life will be different for me and for you. Tomorrow, I shall take you to buy clothes and fripperies and engage a maid to tend you instead of having the services of the kitchen maid.'

'I do not need a maid. I can dress myself; I am not a baby. Only ladies in high places have maids and women of ill-repute have extravagant clothes,' she said as if repeating by rote what her mother had told her.

'I shall not dress you like a whore! You are a lady! You are *Lady Fitzmedwin* by right of marriage and as such you have a position to fill. When we go to England, you will be treated as my wife and must dress well to please me.'

'England? But I am Dutch and this is my home!'

He took both her hands in his and looked into the pretty but troubled face. 'Have you no urge to see my country, to be with me in my own estates and to be a member of London society?'

'I speak so little English and know nothing of your life there.' She sounded fraught. 'I am a good wife and obedient? I can arrange a household and look forward to having our own home, but I am familiar with The Netherlands only and have heard terrible things about England.' Rollo gave a wry smile and waved a thickly engraved giltedged card before her. 'What is that?' she asked.

'This is an invitation to sup with the British ambassador. He has taken his time to accept me but news of my renewed fortunes works wonders in high places and now we are once more, acceptable, and to be cultivated.' He frowned. 'Such attentions might be good or not, but we must go and show how we prosper.' He laughed. 'Have you never seen inside that house? I went as a humble supplicant when I came first to Amsterdam and was received badly but now, we shall walk in through open doors and be greeted with smiles and oily palms.'

'What shall I do?' Helena was almost in tears.

'Waste no time. Go to where it is best and have them do your hair in puffs as they do now in London. Tell them to come to the house before we leave for the soirée the day after tomorrow, to make sure all is well with your appearance as there is no time to engage a lady's maid now, and we must buy clothes tomorrow.'

'I can take one of my sisters with me to choose a gown,' said Helena.

'To your dressmaker? Do not bother either your sisters or your mother. I shall accompany you and you must wear what I choose.' Excitement and a sense of dread as to what the women would choose as suitable attire for an almost royal occasion made him sound harsh. Suddenly he felt as if the heavy wooden panelling and precisely patterned tiled floors were imprisoning him. The house smelled of cooking and cleaning, of beeswax and cabbage soup and he longed to look out of a window and see the Thames, ever moving, ever noisy with craft and men shouting and the ripple of the waves against the piles, even if men walked about with swords to hand after dark and link men to see them past the broken burned ruins of the City at night.

'May I show this to my father?' Helena spoke diffidently.

'The medallion? Here, take the other one and give it to him. You shall wear the gold one on a chain to the soirée and we shall be living proof of a warm and happy alliance.' He was teasing her but she coloured again with pleasure, and darted away to take the medallion to her father.

'I have heard a little about the names of people you will meet,' said Pieter, when later, he sat with Rollo after thanking him for his gift. Rollo smiled politely, aware that nothing that happened in Amsterdam could pass ignored if Pieter Van Steen wished to know about it. 'There will be many Netherlanders including Orangers and the Southern factions, and Johan Kievit, who fled from Rotterdam to England and some say is a renegade.' Rollo raised an enquiring eyebrow, and Pieter felt important. 'He was once burgomaster but we heard little of him until the negotiations for the Treaty began and I suppose we have him to thank for much of that, so he is now free to return, just as you are free to face whatever made you leave England, my son.' Pieter looked solemn. 'Helena has told me of your plans tomorrow, and she is worried. She thinks that you may take her away from us and live in England.'

'Of course I shall return to oversee my estates and Helena will come with me, but we are of two countries and I have come to love much of what I have seen here. Helena will be free to come and go as she pleases. If I am busy with my squires and business, she must go where she may not be bored,' he said, easily.

'A wife must stay by her husband. There have been whispers that you left England because of a duel over a woman, another source says you are wanted for murder and others say you were in debt but that is not so, as today has proved. All these rumours were not important until there was a possibility of your return to your own country, but now it concerns us all.'

'Do you not want your daughter to be accepted by the highest in the courts of both countries, Pieter?' Rollo smiled as he sensed the battle in the man's mind.

'I wish her to be happy with you and to stay

with you at all times as a good wife must, but I do not think she would be happy in your other world.'

'Then I think I know more about women than you. What woman would prefer a coarse gown and the smell of cabbage to silk and the sweet scent of French perfume?'

'I know my daughter and I know that she has had a life free from intrigue and acrimony. Our daughters make good wives and mothers and look for nothing more,' said Pieter, firmly.

'She is Lady Fitzmedwin now, and if as you say she is a good wife, she will do as I wish.'

Pieter left abruptly and Rollo turned back to his papers, and sent his servant to the studio by the Damrack to say that he would be coming to look at pictures. He walked quickly along the canal bank avoiding the puddles and mud between the cobbles and saw the value of the thick broad shoes that everyone wore. The dusty studio was deserted except for Willem de Graeff who was busy with his brush cleaning.

'Have you time for wine?' he asked, and poured a surprisingly good hock from a green bottle. 'I hear that you have enough money to buy anything you see here!'

'Good news travels fast,' said Rollo wryly. 'I shall have to remember who were my friends when I had nothing. Invitations come now from people who despised my situation and waited cautiously to see what change might occur in my fortunes before giving me a hand: but how did you hear this?'

'*Menhir* Van Steen is clumsy when his spies are

out. They tell more than they gain and everyone in Amsterdam now knows that you have estates in many parts of England and Scotland and immense wealth. You have been invited to the Ambassador and to all the other important soirées.' He grinned. 'Your personal shadow came here to learn what was said between us the other day, ready to report on your conversation over the paintings.'

'The Devil he did!'

'He wanted to see the pictures in the back room but I refused and he couldn't find the master to ask him. I winked and hinted that they were pictures of a certain nature and that you were too shocked to see them. He seemed disappointed. I think that we are a sober race with many undercurrents of passion that never surface in respectable houses, but the whores by the canals supply the answer, and such paintings find homes in the most austere of establishments.'

'He didn't see Anna?'

'You have thought of her since you came here?' Willem looked serious. 'Be careful, my friend, you have the look of a man with an obsession and you live in Amsterdam where such passions are frowned on. Also, you are married to a daughter of a prominent house and all eyes will now look with curiosity to see what you do.'

'I have learned patience as any man must in prison, even with such a fair jailer and good friends. I also know much more about true values and although I shall return to England with joy, I am not the man I was when I fled. My father died and I am left with such a mountain of work that I fear without the help of my best friend in England, one who has stood by me in all this, I might have lost everything.'

'When do you leave?' Willem led him into the back room and unveiled the portrait of Anna Maria Bennet.

'What?' said Rollo, after a full minute. The painted eyes seemed to dominate the room and to look on him with a certain reflective compassion. She was almost flesh and the elegance of uncontrived grace made each hand, each fold of her gown beautiful, and yet there was none of the exuberance of satin and lace and puffed hair that appeared in Lely's most famous pictures of women in the Court and from prominent families.

'I asked when you leave. Come away and drink, my friend. You are in no state to return with those dreams in your eyes.' He covered the picture. 'I have bad news. The master will not sell as he values it for teaching. There were three copies. One here and one with the lady and her husband and one in the studio in London, being finished.'

'Then I leave as soon as possible,' said Rollo firmly. 'I must engage a man used to travelling or one who can arrange my passage in comfort with my wife. I need servants, and more than servants, I need a friend with whom I can talk and pass the time. One who can advise also when I am asked about Dutch concerns and policy.' He regarded Willem with speculation. 'Do you know of such a man?' Rollo laughed. 'Is there a man who has the same interests and tastes, who loves art and would like to see the studios of the great English painters and sit at the feet of the masters?'

Willem looked disbelieving then wary. 'What would you want from me?' he asked.

'Nothing bad,' Rollo said. 'I want that other copy bought without anyone knowing for whose house it is destined. If I can never have her, then I must have that.' He tried to hide his emotion and laughed more loudly than he needed. 'When I am in London, no doubt I shall meet other women, more beautiful, more pliant and forget her, but the painting will be a reminder that all women are not loose and easy and mine for the picking, or so subservient that they bore me.'

Willem took a large sable brush and held it like a sword. 'I am at your service, *Menhir*,' he said. 'Pay me enough to get to England and I ask no more. Once you have found your own servants and companions, leave me with enough to pay my way for a year and then forget me. I will buy that picture if it is possible, or commission another copy.'

Rollo grasped the paint-stained hand, then wiped his own on a filthy rag smelling of turpentine. 'I shall need pomade and scent enough if I stay here,' he said. 'You must leave the studio and become sweet and clean before you travel with me.' He gave him money to buy clothes and to visit the barber and pay for his lodging until he was ready to leave Holland. 'And now, I must take my wife to buy a gown. Where does the wife of the French ambassador buy dresses if she cannot get them from Paris?'

'Little Helena in such clothes?' The idea seemed amusing.

'If she comes with me, she must get used to all manner of new things and ideas,' said Rollo.

'Make sure you go to a good wig-maker, too. Without a lady's maid who is skilled with hair, a wig hides many disasters and is fashionable in France and England and even the cities of Germany.' He made a list of establishments that would be useful and Rollo began to realize that he had been kept on a very close rein since his marriage and he had heard of none of them except as places not frequented by the solid citizens of Amsterdam.

Helena opened her eyes even wider when she saw the lilac silk dress. One after another, gowns of all colours had been displayed before her and Rollo had curtly dismissed them all as too theatrical for her. He explained yet again that the dress was to be worn at the Embassy and at last the vendeuse, a French refugee, understood what was required.

The dress slipped over her shoulders and Helena tried to pull it up to hide the swell of her bosom but the dresser tugged it even further down to show the half moons of her breasts. 'I cannot wear it!' Her pale shoulders emerged smoothly and her slender neck looked bare. 'I need a shawl,' she said, hopefully.

'*Nee Mevrouw,*' the woman said as if scandalized. 'Jewels only and perhaps a fan. Now we shall see if this is what your husband likes,' she said, propelling the reluctant girl out into the salon.

Helena's fine hair had slipped from the huge puffs that the hairdresser assured her was the

111

fashion in all the salons in the cities of Europe, and Rollo had wisely decided that the white wigs were too pale for her complexion so to add to her confusion, an edifice of blonde hair was placed over her natural hair and Rollo nodded his approval. Helena looked ingenuous but very pretty and he was satisfied that he could take her to the reception on his arm and not be ashamed.

'You will not leave me alone with these people?' Helena begged when she could find no excuse for hanging back and arriving too late to be noticed at the reception. Rollo pressed her hand and urged her to walk faster up the wide shallow stairs from the octagonal hall.

'We stay together until you find another lady with whom you are comfortable and then I must meet many people,' he said, firmly, but his urbane smile gave no hint of the apprehension he felt at Helena's first introduction to the life of a nobleman's wife, and he swept her along to meet the Ambassador and his wife and all the other dignitaries lined up to receive guests.

At last, they were clear of introductions and at liberty to take a glass of wine and to survey the gathering. Rollo was pleased with the quiet dignity that Helena had shown and her pretty appearance and was aware of many pairs of eyes viewing them with curiosity. His own clothes, long stored but now immaculate once more, sat well and comfortably and he smoothed the soft velvet of the gold encrusted sleeve and let the fall of lace flow over his wrists as if he had never worn fustian and heavy knitted stockings.

The sound of many voices speaking in many

languages made him smile, recalling other occasions when he had been bored by such company, but now revelled in his emergence from the dark chrysalis of badly lit houses with few windows and the sober life of the average eminent Hollander. Helena glanced at him from time to time, as if he was a stranger and even called him *Menhir* twice until he corrected her. 'They will think you are my whore and not my wife,' he chided her.

By the huge mirror that reflected the whole room and gave guests an excuse for prinking and patting coiffeurs and lace as they spied un-observed on friends and enemies, a man stood stolidly watching the growing crowd. He was dressed in the best quality worsted but his style was modest and his clothes drab in colour. Only the exquisite lace, in points sitting from neck to shoulders and the fine leather shoes showed him to be a man of note, and the Quakerish garb made his strength more apparent than any peacock-hued silks would have done.

'Who is that?' Rollo asked.

'That is Michiel De Ruyter, our famous admiral,' whispered Helena, in awe.

'And the younger man with him? His son?'

Helena nodded. 'His son, Engel,' she said simply but he sensed her disapproval.

'He at least can show a little taste,' said Rollo. 'That coat has the cut of London or Paris and the shirt is of the best design.'

Helena pursed her lips and looked too much like her mother. 'They say that he drains the family of wealth with his frivolous ideas and his

113

household of servants and hangers-on, as if he was of the Royal house or at least a burgomaster in his own right.'

'Money is for spending, my dear,' said Rollo. He glanced at the chain of sapphires from which hung the gold medallion resting on her bosom. 'Or would you rather wear a daisy chain round your throat?' He was teasing her, remembering her gasp of pleasure when she saw the sapphires.

'My father says that jewels are a good investment and last,' she said with dignity but as she lost her reticence, she began to talk to two ladies who were brought to meet her and found them easy and amusing. Rollo watched the man by the mirror and marvelled how a man so plain could have routed so many British ships and outwitted the navy under the eyes of the forts at Chatham and the Medway and stolen the *Royal Charles* after ramming the cables across the river. He must have gained many honours and much wealth in the process, and yet if rumour was correct, he lived as simply as the Van Steens and had only two servants. The son made up for it, Rollo conjectured, then wondered if Engel De Ruyter would feel differently when his father died and he inherited the responsibilities as well as the means to an easy life.

More and more, Rollo thought of his estates back in England and felt a growing need to see to his own affairs. Matters that he had dismissed as beneath his care now were important and the husbandry of his farms and woods and parks called for his personal attention.

He turned to watch the company and amused

himself by guessing from which countries the guests came. The French were voluble and well-dressed, with luxuriant wigs and fine manners, but Rollo searched the crowd for English faces.

'Sir Rollo Fitzmedwin!' The man's face was familiar and Rollo struggled to put a name to it, without success, but the voice was English and the handclasp warm. 'I was at the Court of St James's and then Whitehall in the King's service, sir.' He shrugged. 'We are sent anywhere that the King needs diplomacy and the need is great. My name is Samuel Beaumont and I am now here to smooth out details of the Treaty.'

'How is that done with a body of men who give nothing away and have the greatest suspicion of any who are not Dutch?'

'We use many methods. Johan Kievit paved a path and even the puritans have weaknesses. Merchant families have to gather considerable wealth before they can merge their families by marriage with the powerful Regent classes and Rentiers. They know that the prosperity of the Seven Provinces depend on the success of overseas trade and now piracy is frowned on except when they can vow that the ships carried the flag of Denmark or France and were hostile, other means must be found to further their progress.' He sipped his wine and looked into the clear red depths. 'Men can be bribed without losing face, and it is simple to find those willing to help us.'

Rollo quizzed him, asking how this came about in a country where the people were honest, looked after their sick and old and the fatherless in the best conditions in Europe and preached moderation and frugality.

'If a man calls on a burgomaster, a clerk or a merchant who could be of use, and the man has many family commitments, like seven children and an extravagant wife, after the wine has been poured and the many pictures on the walls have been admired – did you ever see such a country for paintings? – the visitor asks to see the children and playfully places a jewel in the hand of the youngest. The conversation continues, but about nothing uppermost in the minds of the two men, and when the visitor leaves, the jewel is ignored and is taken from the child after the man leaves and is kept, unless he is not open to bribes.'

'What more can you tell me as amusing?' Rollo laughed and felt a kind of elation to be among his own again and to hear gossip.

'You see that ravishing creature over there? The Eurasian?' Rollo nodded, having found it difficult to ignore the voluptuous body and fine chocolate brown features of the woman with a Dutch army officer. 'We ought to follow the example of the Netherlanders. They have a practical approach to the sins of the flesh and allow long-service men to marry women from the colonies and bring them back here if they are not totally black.'

'Marry them?' Rollo was amazed. 'If they are of rank, it could be so.'

'They have less trouble with their troops than we do. Less rape and so less hostility among the servants and slaves.' Samuel sighed. 'The Cheese-eaters may be a careful race but they are practical. Their troops and sailors are the best fed and shod of any in Europe and so attract recruits without recourse to the press gangs. They also get paid,' he added drily. 'We have had two mutinies and much rioting at home when the men were not paid and refused to sail and some have stolen away to Holland and France and now fight for them. If we were invaded now, we would face English as well as Dutch and lose even more who need money to keep families alive. Mr Pepys at the Navy Office does his best but is embarrassed by lack of funds from the Royal purse.'

Rollo saw a man watching them who nodded to Samuel and then turned away to watch them more discreetly by means of the mirror. Rollo held out his hand to Samuel. 'Are you not about to press a jewel into my hand?' he asked, shrewdly.

'You have enough wealth to make bribes impractical,' said Samuel calmly. 'But we would like your help. You speak Dutch and French and have *entré* to the Court of His Majesty Charles and have a Dutch wife. When you go to London, very soon, we have letters that must be placed in the right hands by a trusted courier and not by someone who has opened the seals and noted the contents.'

'Why not a trusted illiterate servant?'

'Such men do not travel in huge yellow carriages with an entourage of servants and immediate access to people of importance,' said Samuel drily.

'And in return?'

'The assurance that any accusations against you in London are now forgotten completely.'

'My accusers are dead and I am innocent,' said Rollo. 'But I welcome the official acceptance of that. I want one more thing.' Samuel stood tall and braced himself as if facing difficulties, then laughed when Rollo explained. 'There is a portrait I wish to buy but without seeming to want it. I promised the commission to an artist who may come with me to London, but you, Sir, must do this more privately and send it to my house in London.'

'What lodging is this? Your house on the Strand was burned in the fire, destroying much that you valued and they say, your accuser.'

'I have taken a house in Pall Mall,' said Rollo shortly. 'Bring the papers a week today and I will see to your errand.'

Chapter 7

The walls of the outer ring of defences opened to the horsemen who made a bodyguard to the impressive figure on a white horse, and the jingle of silver bells on the harness made soft music as the representative of the King of Morocco alighted.

From the shelter of the deep white arch of the main building, Anna watched as her husband and the other officers greeted the emissary with dignity and concealed their impatience. For two hours, they had waited for the party to arrive and the tight uniforms were hot under the fierce sun. True, Daniel Bennet had ordered everyone into the shade until the guards on the fort saw the outriders and gave them warning of the arrival, but many men now had red faces and signs of discomfort.

The loose robes of the Moroccans flowed and seemed to create their own coolness and the man with whom Colonel Daniel Bennet was to have talks seemed at ease, and as he saw the sweating men waiting, he had an amused glint in his dark eyes, and took his time in walking to the entrance where Anna waited. She saw the brief expression and couldn't refrain from a twitch of her lips as if she, too, saw the humour of men overdressed and overheated in that climate.

'I am honoured to receive you in person,

Sherif,' said Daniel. 'May I present my wife, Anna Maria Bennet. Anna, this is His Excellency Maulay al-Rashid.'

Anna lowered her gaze under the deep scrutiny and dipped slightly in a brief curtsey. She wondered why the sherif himself should honour them when there were far more elaborate forts and embassies in the towns of Fez and Meknes for such an illustrious sherif to visit, but Daniel had said that the visit might be a sign to neighbouring villages that raids on the fort must stop for a while as the British had been of service to the sherif.

Captain Giffard, under orders from King Charles, had, with the aid of two hundred volunteers, gained the town of Dila for the dynasty of Alawite, thus making the dynasty appear safe for the future.

The formalities over, the two men sat together under the slowly wafted fans held by four Arab boys. Anna clapped her hands for refreshments and sat apart from the men, knowing the customs of the country and not wishing to offend, although he had seen her unveiled. She reflected that as a Berber, the sherif would be used to seeing the women of his followers unveiled, unlike those of more rigid communities, and she relaxed, enjoying the conversation and the presence of a charismatic man of good education. She was surprised to find that Daniel knew the man far better than she had supposed, and now, they talked and laughed as old friends, although from time to time, al-Rashid made a comment about privateering that made Daniel look serious.

'I have an edict from our Sovereign forbidding all such piracy against Moorish vessels,' said Daniel. 'Ships putting in here for victualling and water come under my command and that of the fort at Larache and I represent the Governor.'

'And what of Spain and France? Do you object to receiving goods from their ships?'

Daniel smiled. 'French silks and wines are welcome and Spanish leather has no equal. The Dutch are now at peace with us and still plunder the French and Spanish. They give us free passage in the Channel and have our protection in the Straits.'

Al-Rashid sipped the mint tea that Azziza had made in the Berber fashion, then imperiously commanded one of his men speaking in an Arabic dialect that came from his Berber heritage and was incomprehensible to either Anna or Daniel. Men appeared in the room, bearing bales of silk and large pots of olive oil and wine. Others brought sweetmeats and nuts and fresh fruit from the oasis that was dangerous for the British soldiers to visit.

'You have our friendship and we have your help,' the sherif said with a smile.

'What is it you want al-Rashid?' asked Daniel, more bluntly than was polite.

'You have prisoners in your compound who pine for the Rif mountains and their women.'

'We treat our prisoners so well that perhaps they do not wish to return,' said Daniel, but he knew that the sherif spoke of two men who were relatives of his family, caught spying before the

Moroccans had become more peaceful. 'We would, of course, require assurances that we can proceed with the building of the Mole unhindered? It is but four hundred metres as yet and needs twice that length to make a secure harbour and haven for all shipping in the Straits.'

'If you will excuse me, I have sick men to attend,' said Anna. The sherif rose and gestured towards the bales of silks. His disappointment was barely hidden. 'I shall come back soon,' she said with a smile.

'If these were taken to my harem even the birds' song would be drowned in the laughter and excitement, but you, Madame, ignore my offerings.'

'I mean no offence,' said Anna, quietly, 'And these things will be put to good use, especially the oil and wine which I can use in the hospital.' She gathered up a pile of leaves and a jar of unguent and started for the door.

'You have servants to tend the sick, and beautiful ladies do not soil their hands.' He looked at the simple gown of turquoise cotton and her Arab slippers which she had firmly refused to change in his honour, saying that if his family wore them, then why should she cram her feet into Spanish leather and wear clothes unsuitable for the climate? Her arms were bare of jewellery and the simple gold chain at her throat was all she favoured.

'My wife is more serious than most women and loves learning more than frippery,' said Daniel. 'She understands more than most men and has a talent for healing the sick.' He spoke almost apologetically and for the first time, Anna wondered if her husband would not rather have married a woman more simple and eager to take his advice in all things.

Their passion was still the same and moments of tenderness, though rare, made her feel that she could never love another man but her skills were taken for granted. She found that more and more work was thrust upon her in the hospital, leaving less time for reading and relaxation and visiting the surrounding countryside now that there was less threat from marauders.

'These books are yours?' Anna nodded and left the men together. Outside, the sherif's men sat in the shade and chewed dates. They stared at her as she passed but made no sound and she went swiftly across the compound into the building where the sick lay. Ayesha greeted her warmly and took the leaves into the kitchen to boil and make a poultice, then asked why the sherif was with the colonel.

Anna shrugged. 'They talk of prisoners and silks and he brought enough olive oil and wine to last for a very long time. I cannot stay long as we shall eat together and I must be there even if this is not the custom with your people. My husband insists that we conform to your ways when we visit and that visitors must do as we do when coming to us, with the usual exceptions of diet of course, and real taboos.'

'My Lady will be beautiful in the new silks. I can bring a woman to make gowns for you and if you would like to try one, she can make a djellaba to wear at leisure when the heat is too much.'

Anna looked at her plain gown and laughed. 'I have forgotten how to dress,' she said. 'Come, show me that wound we treated yesterday.' She opened the jar of soothing ointment and watched the linen bandage being rolled back. The deep gash made by a piece of iron as the man jumped down from his camel had festered and brought the man close to death, but now, the wound was clean and his body heatless.

The man lay back and watched the faces of the two women bending over him. Ayesha made little crowing noises that seemed to comfort him and he didn't flinch today when Anna touched him. Gently, Anna cleansed the wound afresh with warm oil and dried it with spirit, knowing that the tissues were partly insensitive from the injury and the man would not jump at the contact with the spirit.

He gave a cry and she smiled, telling him that it was good to feel the lotion as it meant he was recovering. Ayesha came with a linen pad in which the boiled leaves and seeds of fenugreek mixed with charcoal steamed, and made the man look apprehensive. Ayesha spoke to him brusquely, and although Anna could not understand all the words, she gathered enough to know that he wouldn't dare object!

To ease the application, Anna smoothed some of the unguent on to the wound and then Ayesha slapped on the poultice, holding it firmly even when the man wriggled. After a few seconds, he relaxed and managed to smile and Ayesha laughed, binding the limb firmly and taking away the soiled dressings.

A sudden silence in the room told Anna that someone had entered, and as she turned, the sherif took up the pot of ointment and sniffed the contents. Ayesha made a deep obeisance and stood away from the bed, and as the new corporal saw his commanding officer, he stood rigidly to attention, and Daniel Bennet watched Anna's face.

'What is in this?' al-Rashid looked at Anna.

'It is made from Alkene, or as we call it in England, Spanish Bugloss. It has many curative properties and it is something I can obtain here as it grows in sandy rough soil.' She sighed, glancing round the now crowded room with the pallets almost touching. 'We have many who would benefit from herbs from my garden and from the apothecaries in London, but I am learning from Ayesha, and many of the soldiers and slaves gather plants for me to see and identify in case they can be used.' She gave a wry smile. 'It is to their advantage to do so as we have managed to save many limbs and to help some with other conditions.'

Al-Rashid glanced at the other men on the pallets and saw that they were not all English soldiers, and the man who had endured the poultice was an Arab prisoner. He spoke to him, and the man, after a cautious glance at the stern face, said that he had been saved by the English lady and her servant. 'My life is yours, oh mighty one, if I can go to my people.'

'Your life belongs to the one who saved it,' was all the consolation he received. 'Never forget.' He walked slowly from pallet to pallet and Anna was

125

amused to see how puzzled he became. 'You care for all men, *madame?*'

'All who need medicine,' she said, simply. 'All men are the same when they are sick.' She laughed. 'I know when they are better because they begin to grumble, but here, I understand little of what they say and so escape their displeasure.'

'I came to see your husband but also to find out why so few of my people object to being here and few prisoners escape. You grow food and have goats and sheep, I have seen, and there are palms with dates and fig trees. Perhaps you grow too independent.'

Anna sensed his change of mood. 'If there is a stable fort here, surely even if the British leave it will be of great value to you, and we are teaching many things of value to your servants.' Daniel smiled slightly and turned away, noticing the affect that Anna had on his visitor. 'I am learning, too,' she added. 'If only I had books that would tell me what plants are safe to use and what are their properties. I have some but not enough.'

'You must come to my oasis where the mosque has a library of many hundreds of books. There are wise men there who will teach you and you may take notes of our plants and be given some to use.' He turned to Daniel. 'When you release the prisoners, come with your guard and be my guest. The air under the trees is sweet and we have more rain than many places and grow many things.'

A huge dish of rice with many small pieces of goatflesh and lamb, mingled with spices and

126

decorated with leaves and flowers was ready with fruit juices and fresh water from a sweet well. The sherif motioned to his taster and the meal began, taken in a leisurely fashion and Anna was surprised to see how well the meal was presented by kitchen servants who had once been surly and unwilling, and when the sweetmeats had been offered, it was arranged that she should go with her husband the following week to study in the library attached to the mosque.

'I shall have to look to my wardrobe,' Anna said, when the last of the mounted men vanished over the desert.

'Do you have the dress you wore in the painting?' asked Daniel.

She turned to him, her eyes misty. 'Does that dress bring back memories?'

'It became you well and the sherif saw the painting and remarked on it,' he said, carelessly. 'He is a man of great intelligence and has been to England. Many of his children have been painted and he regrets that he cannot allow an English painter to portray the faces of his wives.'

'And yet he likes to look at other women in portraits,' suggested Anna.

'I heard that he has a collection of erotic paintings of slaves and prisoners and others from France and The Netherlands, and of course, many of his harem are not wives and so can suffer no disgrace if he has their pictures for men to see.'

'They can suffer!' Anna became indignant. 'They are women with feelings and if the custom forbids men to look on them, then they suffer as much as any in a higher situation.'

'You are in Tangier, my love. This is a very different kettle of fish, and slaves are for barter and sale and depend on the sherif and those like him for their lives.' Daniel spoke easily as if unconcerned and turned the conversation to their visit. 'We must take token gifts of English pottery and silver chains, but the sherif does not want us to take gifts to the harem. He knows how little we can bring from home and is in the mood to please us, not to demand anything. Besides,' he added with a grin, 'the contents of two rich merchantmen of the Spanish fleet has filled his needs, and we shall buy from him many leather water-bottles for our men to take into the desert.'

Anna lay on her bed during the worst heat of the day and tried to sleep. Daniel had gone back to the men working on the building of the Mole, with no firm idea when he would return. The long afternoon lay ahead and her head ached. Books were too heavy to hold and the flies were troublesome as one of the screens was torn. She gave orders for its repair and dressed again, envying the loose light garments worn by her servants. Azziza came with the message that Mistress Dulcie Meredith was waiting to see her and Anna tied back her hair quickly.

'You may make tea, Azziza, and go to the hospital to see if I am needed.' She saw the crestfallen expression and realized that Azziza and the rest of the servants were agog to see what lay neglected in the bales of silk. 'Ask Ayesha to come if she can and you shall both stay and advise me as to what I do with these gifts.'

Dulcie was looking cooler and her hair was damp from a bath. The sudden rains that fell periodically on the coast filled the tanks but water was still precious and from her complacent expression, Dulcie must have used a week's ration in her bath. She saw that Anna was regarding her with suspicion and her hand went instinctively to pat her damp hair. 'I had no invitation to meet the sherif,' she said, 'So I had to amuse myself this morning.'

'It was business that the men had to discuss and women were not wanted,' said Anna.

'I saw you walking with the sherif in deep conversation,' Dulcie said, pettishly. 'Isn't it time we had an entertainment here and invited him? Handsome men are not easily come by, and we need diversion.'

'Azizza has made tea and we have some gifts from the sherif that you might like to see,' said Anna, knowing that this would take Dulcie's mind from the sherif and there would be no need to tell her of the proposed visit to the oasis.

Even Anna was impressed with the lengths of silk and cotton that emerged from the bales, unwrapped by the Arab women with much hissing of approval. Dulcie was enchanted and envious but brightened when she was asked to gather the wives of officers and non-commissioned officers so that Anna could give each of them a length of cloth. 'You choose first before they come,' Anna offered generously. She counted the lengths and found that she would be left with four that she could use and there were several pieces of bright cotton cloth that she could wear as cool working dresses, and she bowed to Ayesha's suggestion that one length of silk should be made into a djellaba.

When Daniel returned, late and after dark, the bales had been cleared, the trinkets given to the Arab women and the silk-embroidered slippers lay on a stool before Anna packed them away.

Anna called for food as soon as Daniel had sluiced his head with cold water and changed from uniform into a loose cotton shirt and trousers. He watched her as she ate and saw the signs of strain in her eyes. He was guiltily conscious that Anna had given up much for him and that he was a poor husband. The admiring eyes of the sherif had shocked him into looking at his wife with renewed interest and concern. The portrait seemed to reproach him and yet he could see no other way of living. His books lay unread and his duties took all of his attention and Anna had the company of Arab servants and the simple minds of the other wives.

A pile of herbs lay where Ayesha had left them and after eating, Anna lit an extra candle to consult her book so that she could identify them. She gave a gesture of impatience. 'I cannot understand. The descriptions are bad and the words are unfamiliar. Perhaps these herbs are good but I can never use them until I know for certain that they cure and not poison. I trust Ayesha as she knows I help her people as well as our own, but when wilted, one leaf looks like another and so I cannot be sure.'

'The Moors and Berbers have their remedies,' said Daniel. 'They know what can be used.'

'They have so few plants to use and I long for the treasures I find on a walk only a few yards from our home in London, and from the baskets of women from the country.'

Daniel walked about the room and then stood gazing out through the screen into the impenetrable darkness. 'You will have to learn new skills,' he said, his emotion making his voice harsh. 'I have had word to stay here for another year.' He gave a short laugh. 'We do too well, you and I, Anna. We have letters praising our work and our diplomacy and we either stay here or go to the old Dutch colonies of Guinea.'

'Have we no choice?' Her voice sounded tired.

'That is our choice. Tangier with all its dust and unrest even if the sherif is friendly, or Guinea with its disease and death that would put a load on any skill with any medicines that you could find the world over. This place is not as bad, I think.'

From the desert, they could hear the whisper of sand and the rush of wind, and servants ran to put shutters over the open windows. The night air grew cold and the wind howled against the walls of the fort. Anna stretched and poured wine, her energy returning with the cold, and Daniel kissed her gently when she offered him the glass. Together, they lay and revelled in the cool and he caressed her body and sent her shivering into delight. His body was scarred from his earlier wounds and her fingers found the marks on his back and smoothed them as precious.

'Tangier, Guinea, or the ends of the world, if we

131

can be together, it is enough,' she said, but in the tristesse after they had made love, and Daniel was asleep, she listened to the storm and the heavy rain that lasted for an hour, the heaviest she had known since they came to the settlement, and wondered if she could bear this life for much longer. Quietly, she left the bed and dressed, called softly to the guard to escort her and pulled a heavy cloak over her head as she bent to the last of the rain.

A woman sat by the open door of the hospital, swaying half asleep on her haunches and from the pallets came soft moans and snoring. The oil in the earthenware lamps smelled strongly and the smell of discharge was even more pungent.

The man at the end of the row tossed and muttered in his sleep; the sweat induced by one of Ayesha's potions now left him cold and Anna called the woman to cover him after stripping the shirt and replacing it with a dry one.

The man with the amputated leg was groaning and pulling at his stump as if to tear it away. He cried that the absent foot was full of pins and needles and there was no rest from it. Anna took some of her precious supply of laudanum and mixed it in a drink of orange juice, squeezed from some of the fruit left that day by the sherif, and helped him to drink it all, but she knew that there was little she could do for the man. The phantom foot would trouble him for months if he lived that long, but she could smell the sweet sickly odour of corruption and knew that the wound was badly infected.

The woman followed her, now fully awake and

aware of what she must do, and Anna went back across the fast-drying dust to her bed. She went over the events of the day and wondered if there were any books in French or English or even Dutch, her half-forgotten second language, that would open more than the pages for her.

Morning came fresh and cool for long enough allowing Anna to eat bread and drink the first draught of the day with her husband, and he took his time over his food. 'The paid servants will see that the prisoners make good the wall that collapsed yesterday and there is little I can do until it is finished. I must write letters and send them by the next ship that calls. Is there anything you want me to ask that they can send here?'

Anna smiled, faintly. 'I have enough silks to fit a bride and trinkets and slippers that I cannot wear here and my books came on the last talley. But what are books without the means to make all the things I would do if I was in London? I sent a letter to the doctor who is the brother of Edward Verney and he will send me what he can, and ask an apothecary to furnish me with instructions as to the usage of some things with which he is not familiar.' She sighed. 'The doctor-surgeon here is a saw-bones with a heart but little time for herbs and less time for the dying. His supplies are bad and there is very little laudanum left to kill pain and bring dreams to console the poor wretches who must die.'

'Did you go out last night again?' Daniel looked angry. 'You know I forbade it! Can you not rest apart from those wretches? If there is nothing that you can do, then leave them to the women

133

and make more shift to looking more like a lady!'

'A lady like Dulcie?'

He reddened. 'Of course not, but she at least dresses to please and spends her time waiting for her husband's return. Twice last week I came home weary and you were dressing foul sores and making the Arab children wash their eyes with salt water. However, your interests have at least made the sherif invite us to his palace on the oasis, a singular honour and one that will impress Whitehall.'

'It will make Whitehall even more reluctant to give us leave to go home,' said Anna sadly. 'Sometimes, I feel as one of the slaves must feel, so far from home.'

'Our home is together, Anna, and we have so much to share.'

'If we could share it.' Anna sighed and glanced towards the piles of books that lay on a low table. 'You are too tired to read and to study and even the stars now have lost their interest for you. Last night, the sky was hung low with many that I have never seen, even through the lens.'

'You should sleep and not watch the sky,' he said, curtly. 'I am a soldier and this place takes all my energies. When we go home, you shall have pretty things and leisure, with servants to spare your hands.'

Anna put her hands behind her, suddenly remembering the time when she was in the country and her hands had roughened with work on the farm and Sir Rollo Fitzmedwin had held her hands and she had been ashamed at their roughness. 'If I work, I have rough hands,' she

134

said. 'I cannot sit all day eating Arab sweetmeats!'
But she saw in her picture her hands, smooth and
elegant and was glad that there was only Daniel
and the servants to see them now.

She sensed his disapproval and smiled. 'I shall
lave my hands in oil and wear only my finest
when we visit the Sherif. Ayesha is having some
silk made into a haik for me.' He raised an
eyebrow. 'It's like a djellaba but more elegant and
some are made in Paris for wives of diplomats
serving in Arab countries. If you think it suitable,
it will be a compliment to the Sherif for me to
wear it.'

Daniel was non-committal, but laughed. 'Keep
out of the sun or you will indeed look like a
Moroccan. Maybe your dark looks make you
popular here. There must be more than Dutch
and English in your blood. Spanish, perhaps or
Italian? When I am posted to the Spanish Main,
you can claim kinship there, also.'

'And you could never be mistaken for anyone
but an Englishman,' she retorted, but he had
gone to write his letters. Have I changed? she
thought as she sorted out clothes for packing and
a pile for mending. I love my husband and know
every piece of his mind and body and yet I have
never felt so far away from all I love.

The morning passed and she was still pensive,
and slightly ashamed of her thoughts. Daniel is
my love, she told herself again and again and it
should be enough. We have shared pain and
passion and learning and he gave me so much
when we were in London and the Surrey farm,
and now, he is the Colonel, hard with his men,

loving with me but rarely tender, and I long for my garden. She closed her mind to the flattery of other men who once she had regarded as a threat and beneath her notice, like Rollo who had tried to abduct her.

Restlessly, she recalled a similar expression in the eyes of the sherif, who had many wives, many concubines and could have nearly any woman he wanted.

And later, when a horseman came riding fast and the guards shouted but let him through, she waited for Daniel to come home, neglecting all her duties and handling the single beautiful ruby that glowed in its gold setting, feeling trancelike and light, but desirable, not for love of the Sherif, nor Rollo, but that she knew she was still beautiful.

Chapter 8

'Vincent has been shut away in that room with my father for long enough,' Alice said. 'Why can't they talk to us instead of discussing the state of the nation and the amount of shipping off the English coast?'

'You didn't make him very welcome, my love,' said Marian, mildly. 'I know how you felt, but men do not know the feelings of us women at these times and tears, even if they are of joy, are misunderstood.'

'I was overcome,' said Alice. 'But I am better now and need to see him.' The locket containing the miniatures of them both hung about her neck and she had put on her blue silk dress, making sure that hers was brighter and prettier than the one that Sarah chose to wear, and yet Vincent had not reacted to her tears as he would once have done, but frowned and told her to compose herself; that he wasn't drowned and that he had a great deal to do and would appreciate a private talk with Mr Verney before they sat at table.

'It was unfortunate,' Marian agreed. 'There was no time for him to hear your good news and I know I promised that you must be the one to tell him, so he is still in ignorance.' She rose from her seat as the two men appeared in the doorway. 'Come, Edward, we cannot keep the servants waiting. The food will be quite spoiled.'

Vincent went to his wife, with arms out-stretched. 'Why didn't you tell me! Your father has just told me the wonderful news and I am overjoyed.' He embraced Alice in front of the family and kissed her on the lips. Alice clung to him for a moment, so that he would not see the tears of chagrin. It was to have been *her* moment, *her* triumph and not a piece of news flung at Vincent as incidental to his homecoming as the state of shipping!

'My dearest girl,' he said, with a return to the tenderness he had shown before he left for the voyage. 'This makes all the suffering of the past few weeks bearable. It also makes up my mind that I no longer wish to go to sea. I shall go to the Navy Office and hand over my command and we can leave London for the country and live in peace until you are safely delivered. My estates need attention and I feel glad to be home.'

'You must have time in your own home first,' said Alice in alarm. 'You have missed so much of the Season and theatres, and you need amuse-ment.' She glanced at Sarah who looked almost as dashed as she did. 'I am healthy but restless,' Alice went on. 'I need amusement or I lack sleep. Sarah and I have an excellent companion in Mistress Charity and we can leave you to see to your horrid ships and business in the City.' She wrinkled her nose engagingly and laughed, once more the child bride who must be indulged.

'We shall see,' he said, patting her hand. 'Now, Madam, I am famished and so excited that I could devour a whale.'

Vincent sat close to his wife, gazing fondly and

laughing at anything she said that was even slightly humorous and Alice was reassured that he felt as loving as ever and that she didn't have some kind of mark on her face that could tell him of her one sin. Sarah ate little and her eyes seemed too large for her face, but it passed unnoticed as everyone knew of her love for her brother.

'I shall sleep here and tidy up our belongings ready to be taken home tomorrow,' said Sarah at the end of the long meal. She looked at Lady Marian and smiled. 'If you please, Madam, I would like to stay for a few more days and leave my brother alone with his wife.'

'You show a deep sensitivity,' said Marian, approvingly. 'I am sure that you are right. Stay for as long as you wish Sarah and make this your other home whenever you need to be in London and the others are in the country.'

'My dearest Sarah!' Alice tried to hide the panic in her voice. 'You are our dear sister, and Vincent and I could not drive you from your place with us.'

Vincent looked pleased. Two such loving and innocent young women did more to soothe his unrest than anything in the world, but he wanted to be alone with his wife. 'I am grateful, Sarah. You are the most understanding of women and you must come and go as you please, always sure that we love you and want your company.' He took Alice by the arm. 'Come, my love, it's late and we must go.' He bowed to Marian over her hand and clapped his father-in-law on the shoulder. 'We must talk again, as more has happened than I thought possible. I shall need your advice over the selling of my ships and the reinvestment of my capital. I cannot thank you enough for your care of my finances and hope that you will continue to help me.'

Edward looked flattered and went with the couple to the carriage, where Alice was then swathed in rugs and shawls as if she might die of cold. She glanced at Sarah almost enviously and then settled down into the soft cushions.

Miss Charity had waited up for them and now helped Alice with her outer clothes, wishing to make a good impression on her employer. 'I made sure that all was ready in your rooms,' she said. 'A good fire burns and there is wine and cordial on the table.' She simpered as if preparing for a bride and Alice dismissed her with scant thanks. Vincent had eyes only for his wife and led her firmly up to the bedroom, his pulse quickening as he recalled her passion and response the last time they were together.

He dismissed the maid who hovered sleepily by the door and kicked the logs in the grate into flame. The room was warm and shadowy and he gently kissed his wife and removed her clothes, one by one until she stood in her transparent shift by the fire, then knelt naked at her feet and pressed his lips to the dented navel. Alice shuddered with growing desire and knew that her body showed no guilt and her lips gave no sign of any other kisses.

He caressed her body and entered her carefully as if she might break even though Edward had assured him that the medical men said there was no danger after the first few weeks, and Alice was released physically and mentally and shriven from fear. Content, she lay in the crook of his arm and slept and Vincent thanked the god who had returned him to his wife and his son-to-be.

'I want you to be examined by Dr Verney,' said Vincent when they were dressed and ready to start the day.

'He visits the sick in the hovels outside the City gates,' protested Alice, 'And his linen is yellow, which shows little care from his house.'

'He is Edward Verney's brother and one of the cleverest doctors I know,' said Vincent, firmly. 'He cared for the sick during the plague and healed many, never suffering himself nor did any of his family, and he is a member of the Royal Society. We must fetch Sarah to come with us and abide by anything he says for your well-being.' He kissed her again. 'You are too precious to leave anything to chance, and I shall be easy if he tells me that you are well.'

Alice blossomed under his care and lapsed once again into the girl-bride, exacting promises of treats and knowing that she could have anything the besotted man could provide for her, so when they set off with Sarah to the austere house and waited in the badly heated salon, Alice was in good humour.

Dr Verney welcomed them heartily. 'Come into the other room that is warm and comfortable. I waste no fuel in here as patients are inclined to return and wait for far too long if they are warm, and I have many to visit.' He enquired after Lady Marian and if there was news of Anna. 'I sent a

141

book and some samples made up by my apothecary, and hope to send more now that we know what she wants.' He sighed. 'How she must miss the help we can give to people here. She finds some herbs growing that she recognizes, but longs for the ones she knows are effective.'

Alice tossed her head, resenting any mention of another person when it was she who required his full attention, and Dr Verney smiled, knowing her well from infancy. He glanced at Sarah and smiled again, kindly. 'So, I have two young ladies to examine,' he said.

'No!' Sarah backed away. 'I have come to keep Alice company. There is nothing wrong with me.'

He gave her a keen glance and shrugged. 'As you wish,' he said, and led Alice through into his medical room.

'Are you unwell, Sarah?' asked Vincent, suddenly concerned and convinced that he had been neglectful of his dear little sister.

'I have the vapours but nothing more,' she said, and wished that she felt less frail.

'You are pale and I think have lost weight,' he said, thoughtfully, and when Alice came back, triumphant in her good health, Vincent insisted that the doctor should look at Sarah and prescribe a tonic. She protested, nearly in tears, but the doctor agreed that she was pale and rather hysterical and might need a potion. Sarah followed him into the other room and the others waited for what seemed a long time, before Dr Verney returned and said that Sarah was dressing.

'Has she the wasting disease?' asked Vincent, in

142

alarm. 'I thought she coughed twice in the carriage and her looks are like that of a girl in decline.'

'I think that she is worried, which could show in this way but I would like to see her again in a month. I have asked for a tonic to be made and will deliver it in person when I bring the herbs for Miss Anna.'

Sarah emerged from the room and her eyes were red with weeping. 'Dear, dear Sarah!' cried Alice. 'Were you frightened? Dr Verney has said you must take a tonic and you'll be better. Come now, we shall take you home and put you to bed.'

'I am not ill,' said Sarah, with spirit. 'It is nothing. It is the time of the flowers.'

'I would like to see Lady Marian when I call,' said Dr Verney.

'Then come back now and have dinner with her. We can leave you there on our way home with Sarah, and Vincent is taking me to dinner with some of his fellow officers and their wives.' She smiled. 'Sarah can stay quiet with Miss Charity and rest.'

Dr Verney collected books and a box of dried herbs and a bottle of laudanum to be added to the books that Lady Marian had commissioned from the old bookshop where Anna used to buy her scientific literature, now housed in Duck Lane after being burned out of St Paul's churchyard. He placed his bundles on the floor of the carriage and asked after the health of Vincent. 'No injuries from the wreck, sir? And no time for scurvy in the men?'

Vincent told him of sailors who died as the ship

foundered and more when they fell from the rigging and the mast snapped. 'It was a sorry day and one that I would hate to repeat. It made me aware of my own mortality and now that I have a son on the way, life is indeed precious.'

'You are blessed with a healthy girl for a wife, your own safety after many trials and now we know that our fears about you were unfounded,' said the doctor, devoutly.

'Fears for Vincent, sir?' Sarah looked anxious, and Alice mildly curious. Many men caught the pox or some milder disease during the Grand Tour of Europe or during their rowdy youth but she had no doubts about her husband. He hated dirt and would never go with a whore, but would have confined his adventures to bedding servant girls from his own estates.

'I thought it nothing of consequence when you mentioned it, sir, but there have been men who after contracting mumps have been rendered unable to sire children. Praise God that this is not so with you.'

'Mumps?' exclaimed Alice. 'That is a disease of babies, not men.'

'That is so,' said Dr Verney, patiently. 'But as with many conditions, if this attacks an adult, it comes worse and the suffering is more.' He smiled. 'The good sea air on your ship and your natural health must have sent the disease packing. I believe that fresh air mends more than it kills, and you must make sure that you drive daily and walk some distance each day now that you are over the sickness, Alice.'

'I have come back at the right time,' said

144

Vincent. 'No green face and a lie-a-bed wife to greet me but a beautiful and healthy young woman, well over the tedious part. Why, Sarah looks as if she is the one in your condition, not you,' he said in a teasing voice.

'Leave me with the Verneys,' said Sarah. 'I mean to stay for at least another week and you can be together,' she said, with a forced laugh. 'I will help you carry your bundles, Dr Verney and tell Lady Marian that you will be with us for dinner.'

Alice waved from the carriage and was glad once more to be alone with her husband. All thoughts of the French nobleman fled before her new-found happiness and she revelled in the power she held over Vincent, who hung on her words and was ready to indulge her. He even wanted to decide on names for the baby but she remonstrated and said that it would be a girl. Sarah followed the doctor into the house and tried to walk past him into the drawing room, but he took her by the arm and sat her on a settle in the hall.

'Now, young lady! It is best if I know first and then we can plead your cause more fully. My brother is hard about such matters and you will need my help if you are not to be disgraced.'

'How can you know?' she wailed. 'I have been sick this week and not seen my courses but I am the same!' She tried to smile. 'It needs but a tonic to bring back my flux and all will be well.'

'Who is this vile wretch who has brought shame on you?' The doctor patted her arm. 'Don't be afraid to tell me, my dear. You are as one of the family and we must know.'

'No vile wretch, sir,' she whispered. 'He is the man I wish to marry and when Vincent returned, I wished for time to ask his blessing and support so that we could marry.'

Lady Marian came from the drawing room and saw them seated with bent heads as if mourning a death. 'Something is wrong? Alice is sick and you hesitate to tell me?'

'No, Marian. Not Alice, but Sarah, and it is a sorry business. Is Edward there?'

'He is in Lincoln's Inn or the Navy Office,' said Marian. 'Tell me what is wrong. Sarah my dear, you look ill.' She called to Deborah to put a warming pan into the bed and make up the fire in Sarah's room. 'No, not a word until this young lady is in bed and then you can tell me what is wrong.'

With a pleading glance at the doctor, Sarah was led away in tears, and Debbie pursed her lips and wondered how Miss Alice had not heard the retchings early each morning.

'Now, Marian, I don't know what to do. Edward must know and of course, her brother, and the pity is that he is fond of her and would not want to turn her away.'

'Turn her away?' Marian stared and then her eyes clouded. 'No, I cannot believe it. Are you sure? Sarah is but a child.'

'Almost the same age as Alice and now sharing even this experience as they shared all else,' he said, dryly. 'She refused to tell me the name of the man but Edward will get it from her.' He paced the room. 'She is dependent on Vincent and he is her guardian, but worse things happen at sea, ma'am!' He blew his nose, loudly. 'They can marry and leave London, if that is what Vincent wishes, and there are enough bastards in the Royal house to make it the fashion if he does not give his consent.'

'Vincent must know.' Marian called for Sam to send him with a message that she wished to see her son-in-law at once. 'No, wait. I shall go with you and Dr Verney and then see my husband in his office.' Sam exchanged solemn glances with his wife Debbie, and shrugged. Babies were conceived easily and with pleasure and mistakes could be remedied by hasty marriage as happened in the kitchens of every big house, when the master objected to flagrant fornication.

'Won't you have dinner first, My Lady?' asked Debbie. 'I have given Miss Sarah a draught and she is calm and sleepy, and Sir Vincent might be less angry after his own good dinner.'

Marian Verney nodded, slowly. 'You are right Debbie and the doctor needs his dinner now, so we must talk quietly and try to think of a solution.'

Dr Verney showed her the parcel of dried herbs and the laudanum, and checked the books that Marian had acquired for Anna. 'If we go to Edward's office, I'll have a word with Roger Carter, his head clerk,' he said. 'He will know what ships leave for Tangier and the fastest way to reach Anna.'

'Of all my charges, Anna was the most virtuous, as Kate never suffered the passions of love and Christopher married young. Kate lost one man at sea and her grief kept her pure until she married her pleasant vicar,' sighed Marian. 'I thought when Alice married Vincent all my maternal worries were over but Sarah has been like one of my own and my heart aches for her.'

Dr Verney helped himself to more fowl and wine and broke the fresh bread that Debbie set at his side. A dinner such as this was a rare indulgence and he made the most of it, as his was a more frugal household. Marian paid the account for the books from James Allestry of Duck Lane and Sam brought the carriage round to the door.

The paintwork was immaculate and Sam looked mature and solidly good looking in his fine livery. Marian smiled. Surely Edward and Vincent couldn't be hard on the poor girl. It would be good company for Alice and her own baby to share this with Sarah. The sharp wind made her sit back in the carriage and as the horses picked a way through the uneven pavings and Sam avoided driving close to burned-out buildings where the cellars were hidden under a thin layer of paving or wooden cobbles, and could collapse under pressure of wheels, she wondered again at their own escape from plague and fire. For months after the inferno, houses had smouldered and sometimes burst into flame, and the streets were warm to the feet and molten glass made hard slippery beads that threw many horsemen.

The fields had lost their coating of fine ash and now lay fallow until the spring, with stunted brown tree stumps and the remains of hovels, raked clear of the fire breaks and left to rot until the great new plan of the new London could be put into being. Edward was not in his offices but Dr Verney saw Roger Carter and gave the parcels into his keeping, knowing that he would carry out orders in a meticulous fashion.

Marian braced herself for her meeting with Vincent and when they reached the fine new house in Pall Mall, only a few houses away from the mansion built for Nell Gwyn as a sign that Royal favour had not deserted her even after her liaison with another courtier and her brief retirement from the theatre in Drury Lane, Sam wheeled the horses expertly to set the carriage at the door.

'Lady Marian?' Vincent was in his shirt sleeves as if he had just left his bed and had not finished dressing. Alice came down the stairs wearing a full gown that had been thrown on hastily and her hair was over her shoulders.

'My dears!' In spite of all her resolution that nothing would make this interview hysterical, Lady Marian Verney burst into tears. Vincent looked shocked and Alice sat on the settle by the fire and wished that she had eaten more before Vincent took her to bed. Hurried eating and too much wine now lay acid on her stomach and she was in a bad mood. How could they come into the house bringing such an air of unrest when she needed peace and her husband all to herself!

'The fact is, my dear Vincent,' said the doctor, bluntly. 'Your sister Sarah has a lover who has impregnated her.'

'I don't believe it. You lie! What malicious tale is

149

this?' He searched each face for comfort and found none. 'Who?' he said in a strangled whisper. 'What wretch has done this to my dear sister? Alice, what do you know of this rape?'

'Rape, Vincent? Not that. I believe she is fond of the man but has not said his name,' said Dr Verney, but Vincent was too filled with rage and shame to hear him.

'Come, madam!' he shouted. 'You are her friend, her caring confidante and you must know.' Alice shrank away from him, frightened of the man she now saw under the loving husband.

'I know nothing,' she exclaimed. 'But I think that Sarah wants to marry and begs your consent.'

He looked at her with derision. 'A likely story my dear, and does you well to protect her, but you know more than you say. Who is this fine fellow she couldn't wait to bed until I came back? Had I been away a year, there would have been two children in my household instead of one! No time for my consent then, no time for weddings with my blessing!' He caught Alice by the arm. 'Or was there a plan to steal away into the country and have the child taken by a woman ready to adopt it before my return?'

He turned away and Alice saw that he was weeping. Cautiously, she put an arm round his shoulders to comfort him and to show herself that she was not in his bad books. With a soft moan, he buried his face in her breast and she could hear his words only dimly but with an inner clarity that burned like fire. 'I would as lief believe that my own dear wife was unfaithful to

150

me as I would believe that Sarah was not deflowered without her consent?'

'You will not consent to her marriage?' asked Alice, softly. 'Would it not be better?'

'To whom?' He saw her face. 'You do know. You know the name of the man and she has confided her distress to you. Tell me, before I go and shake it from her!'

'It is young James Ormonde,' she whispered, unable to know if it was better that Vincent thought that his sister was raped or wooed.

'One of Cromwell's sty! He did this to spite me and my family. Do you know, ma'am, that he has been seen with John Desborough, Oliver's brother-in-law, lately come back from Holland and examined in the Tower before being released as no longer a threat to the Crown?' He looked down at his state of undress. 'Wait. I shall dress and use your carriage, ma'am, and you shall come with me.'

Alice followed him upstairs. 'Where are we going?' she asked, in alarm.

'You have tormented me to take you to Whitehall and that's where you shall go, madam. I should beat you for your part in this. You should have told me as soon as I returned, but my love for you and our child forbids it.'

With fingers that refused to button and a mind that couldn't recall where to find her shoes, and unwilling to call her maid, Alice sobbed as she managed to dress, her throat hot as if she had been running. She caught her hair up into a snood and added a hat with soft feathers that dipped a little over her face and hid her reddened eyes, and drew on a cloak lined with fur and fur mittens.

Vincent had not as yet appeared and Lady Marian was sipping a tisane to calm her nerves. Dr Verney sat with his face in his hands and outside, Sam hoped that they would come out soon to prevent the horses from taking chill, and when Vincent came down the stairs, soberly dressed in full uniform with his medals and orders showing his rank and private status, Alice wanted to faint. His face was grim and he didn't seem to see any of the company as he strode out to the carriage.

'You are seeking an audience?' asked Dr Verney. Vincent nodded, curtly. 'Do you not think it wise to cool a little and to ask Sarah what happened?' he suggested, mildly, but Vincent refused to answer and sat in one corner of the carriage and let the ladies shift for themselves. 'A message first to beg an audience might save the ladies much discomfort and waiting and the Court might be away,' Dr Verney added, hopefully.

'His Majesty will receive any with a just petition and I am high in his regard,' said Vincent. His smile was savage. 'He will have heard of my return and know that I am leaving the service and selling more shipping from my merchantmen. The Navy Office is looking for bargains, and I may have just such a one to offer.'

Alice sat silently in her corner and felt the cold even through the thick fur, and she dared not ask questions as anything she had said had only added to Sarah's downfall.

They passed number seventy-nine Pall Mall,

and saw carriages gathering outside the house, and Alice wondered if the king might be visiting Nell, but Vincent saw nothing but his own hate and when they reached Whitehall, and the request for an audience was received, Alice knew that something terrible was about to happen.

Refreshments were brought and Vincent was treated with great respect and after only a short wait, was told that the Duke of York would receive him. 'Alone!' said Vincent and followed the officer along corridors and through salons into the offices of the Duke.

Now, the waiting was longer and Alice looked about her at the rich hangings and tapestries but felt none of the elation she had anticipated when the delights of the Court had been told to her, and in the heated chamber, her hat was hot and her mittens kept slipping to the floor from her lap. Lady Marian was uneasy and gave up making small talk with the doctor, and even news from Anna describing the country in which she now lived and the wonderful architecture of the Moorish palaces and the beauty of the people, seemed empty and meaningless as they wondered and waited for Vincent to reappear and, when he did, none of them knew what to say.

'I've kept you waiting, ma'am,' he said, formally to Marian. 'I beg your pardon. I am grateful for your company and now can return you to your family, but first I must see Sarah, so if we can leave now?' he added, politely, and walked out to the carriage where Sam was busy removing blankets from the horses.

'Did your meeting go well?' Dr Verney ventured.

'I was received cordially and given all the assistance I required,' said Vincent, but his expression forbade further questioning.

'We could have stayed at home,' said Alice, piqued at his attitude and the fact that she had been introduced to no one.

'I needed you where I would know that you could not see Sarah nor could you send any message to another party until I had seen the Duke.'

'But I have no idea of Master Ormonde's lodging and I do not know the man,' protested Alice. 'How could you think I would do that?'

'You are fond of Sarah, my love, and so am I. What I do now is best for all of us but it could have failed if you had breathed a word either to her or to any other person.'

'What can you mean?'

'We are home, Lady Marian,' he said. 'My apologies for putting you out and I beg your further indulgence in asking to see my sister in your boudoir if she is dressed for bed.'

'First take a glass of sack Vincent. You are so pale.'

Alice poured the wine herself and sat by his side. 'Is everything to be settled and Sarah to stay?' she asked.

'My dear girl, there was never any idea that she would be turned away. Sarah will stay with you and together you will bring up your children. I have taken steps to make everyone know what I can do if crossed and shamed, and Sarah can be

154

proud again.' He drained his glass and made for the stairs and Alice smiled with relief. Lady Marian smoothed down her dress as if to shake off something unpleasant and Dr Verney shrugged into his surcoat. 'I will expect to see you both in a month,' he said and hesitated, as Vincent appeared at the top of the stairs and called him.

'My sister is having hysterics and needs something to calm her,' he said.

Alice jumped to her feet. 'Not you, Alice. Later you will comfort her and let her tell you how hard a man I am.'

'What have you done?' she whispered.

He smiled but the venom in his eyes made her shudder. 'Even as we speak, Master Ormonde is on his way to the Tower on a charge of rape, where he shall cool his heels until I see fit to discharge him from my accusation. Let's hope that his friend, John Desborough, left it warm for him.'

Chapter 9

Willem de Graeff set down his bag on the leather trunk and told the boy to watch it carefully. The skyline was filled with swaying masts and pennants and the water of the Amstel seethed with activity.

Quickly, he walked along to the house on the Herengracht where Sir Rollo Fitzmedwin was living with his wife's family. The tall narrow houses were almost finished where the Herengracht had been extended to finish the graceful sweep to the north, and the white figures on the frontal elevations of the roofs showed coats of arms and signatures of merchants' businesses, elegant against the stepped gable stones of dark reddish brown. Willem glanced upwards, more to see if there was anyone looking from the high windows than to admire the twin dolphins poised for ever like figures on a vase, or the figure of the yawning man that signified that the owner of the house was a druggist.

A barge on the canal beneath one of the houses, laden with heavy furniture, lay sluggishly tied to the enormous gold topped bollards as men hoisted each piece on ropes over the heads of anyone fool enough to walk under the swaying load on its way to the upper windows. The permanent hooks jutting from the gables, held rope pulleys to bring the heavy furniture into the top rooms by the only means possible as the doors were narrow and the stairs too steep and angled to allow free passage.

He raised the bronze door knocker and let it fall and the door was opened by a girl wearing a tight leather bodice and full woollen skirt. Her wooden clogs were more suitable for a servant than for the younger daughter of the house and she blushed when she saw Willem. '*Goedemorgen, Mijnheer,*' she said, shyly, and he laughed when he saw her surprised expression.

'No paint today, Juffrouw Marijke,' he said. 'I have given up washing brushes and am now a gentleman! I came to say goodbye before leaving for England.'

'Is it safe to go there? My sister is frightened but her husband insists that she must go with him.' She stood back to allow him to pass and then called the servant to tell Sir Rollo that he had a visitor. 'You will take wine?' she asked, hopefully.

'There is no time. I leave on the tide and must take some papers for Sir Rollo. He has a fine house built and it now waits for furnishings. I am to tell his servants what must be brought from one of his estates and give orders for more to be made in London,' he announced, proudly.

Rollo appeared from an upper room. His linen shirt was spotless and even though his jacket was dull and his britches of an even darker shade, he looked impressive. 'I will walk to the boat with you, my friend,' he said, and gave a leather case to Willem. 'I have furnished you with papers to prove that you are acting for me. Go first to my

157

notary and to my estate manager and squire at these addresses and they will make everything smooth until I come in a week or so.'

They left the house and walked along the edge of the canal to the bustling square beside the Amstel. Gangways were already being lifted from some ships as the wind teased the pennants and begged to take them to sea, and the sailors pulled at sheets and anchors and shouted if their ropes were fouled by other boats. Rollo stood with one foot raised on a low bollard and gazed at the scene. 'I have relieved you of one commission,' he said. 'I have asked the secretary of the ambassador to make that purchase and it will be delivered to the house on Pall Mall to await my return.' He glanced at Willem who was watching him thoughtfully. 'I think you will agree that it is best so, as then you can know nothing of this matter. However, find out where Mistress Anna Bennet is living and how she fares. Word will spread fast enough of my return and I would like to know how I might be received in many of the houses I have listed, including that of her guardians, and my distant relatives, the Verneys.'

'You are related to the lady?'

'Not by blood. She is a distant relative of Lady Marian Verney and I am connected with that family but twice removed, by marriage.'

'I will do my best, and take time to visit studios. Gossip there will tell me a lot that the clerks and notaries dare not say.'

'God-speed, Willem. Don't get so drunk that you forget your position as my emissary, and try not to let the ladies fill your time. You look human now that you have good clothes!'

He watched the young man swing his bag over his shoulder and pick up his wide bag of canvases. Willem grinned. 'The English like scenes of the sea and I have some of the Amstel, and of Volewijk complete with the gallows just to warn them if they ever feel like attacking us again.' Two boys carried his trunk up the gangway and he followed, pausing to wave from the deck before disappearing into the maw of the ship.

Rollo waited for half an hour, deep in thought and hardly aware of his surroundings. One ship cast off and was rowed clear of the moorings, the shouts of the overseer sharp, and the groan of oars, badly placed, fading over the green water.

The ship carrying Willem followed and Rollo felt a tug of longing as he saw it leave for England. He frowned. Helena had been emotional about leaving and so they had postponed their journey for a week or so, but Rollo knew that the papers he had to deliver must go to England soon and there must be no more delay. If he was to make full use of the fresh esteem in which he was held by important people, and the fact that he was now free from any accusing voice, he must take his wife to his home or go without her.

'Have you finished with your dressmaker, and is your shoe mended?' he asked, with more irony than usual, when he found Helena in her room.

She blushed. 'I am ready next week,' she said, firmly. 'But I could not leave today. I shall be very ill on the boat and must have medicines to take with me.' He sighed and shook his head but smiled and Helena knew that he was not really angry. 'Could we not stay until the weather is warmer?'

'I thought you liked the cold. You have told me so much about the canals freezing and the sliding on ice and parties in the ale-houses with big fires and hot ale,' he teased her.

'This year we have not had cold weather,' she said, with a disappointed glance out of the window.

'Then come to England before the ships are encased in ice and cannot leave harbour; or was that what your prayers were about?' She turned away and he saw her shoulders heaving. 'Come, my love. We have to see the new house and get many things chosen before we leave, so that when we return, all will be as we like it and not as other people arrange it for us in our absence.' Already, the family had tried to give them ugly and heavy pieces to help furnish the new house, and even Helena now saw the beauty in well-carved and simple lines and elegant mirrors to make more light in the dim corridors where no windows could be, as the houses were joined and had windows at the backs and fronts only.

'There isn't time to do everything before we leave,' protested Helena. 'It is our first real home together and I would like to make it good; and very slowly,' she added.

'We have talked of this, my dear. You know that when we go to England it will be for several months and perhaps a year or more? I can send an English servant who knows my tastes to furnish the house here. In England, you will have an even larger house with many windows, and many hearths, and all the time you need to choose fine hangings and chairs. There are amusements for a lady and many friends I wish you to meet.'

'Willem has gone to do that for you,' she said, sulkily. 'He can speak English and know what people are saying, but I understand so little and at the reception I sat like a fool while you talked.'

'You sat with three Dutch matrons and talked for hours,' he said. 'When I called you to meet my new friend, you did very well and used the right phrases that I taught you. Every day you must learn more and by the time you live among the English, you will pick up words quickly.'

'Live among the English? I am a Netherlander and my home is here. I thought that you dared not go back and so felt safe, but now, I am frightened of being alone in a strange country.'

'You are now Lady Fitzmedwin and my wife,' he said, sternly. 'I want you with me as I am very fond of you and I shall be proud to show you to my friends.' He tried to sound sincere, but her dress of dark green did nothing for her complexion and made the milky white skin which had looked so vibrant when Helena wore the right colours, now look pallid.

'I am ready,' said Helena. 'As you say, there are many things to do if I am to be ready to cross the sea with you, so soon.'

Rollo ignored the dignified sadness and stood aside so that she could precede him from the house. They walked in silence along the canal bank and the one hundred yards further along the Herengracht to the new house which was as yet barely furnished but showed signs of great

161

elegance. The tiled floors were bright and clean and the heavy doors glowed with polish. Pictures, chosen by Helena with great pride, showed seascapes and scenes of the old harbours, and a few of the country with fertile fields and small figures clogged and dark-capped. Rollo had chosen these but Helena thought them too ordinary and preferred the ships painted on a background of waves that looked more like ruffled silk and puffy crimped hair than water, none painted completely by any of the famous artists, but bearing their names. Piles of pewter dishes awaited washing and arranging on the long dresser in the kitchen and again in the main living room where the Delft china was already arranged, some following the Chinese mode and some blue and white. It was increasingly Dutch, comfortable, clean and signifying an air of prosperity but with the doors from the back rooms closed, claustrophobic and dark.

A chill wind made Rollo close the door as soon as he opened it and he demanded candles, which met curious glances from the workmen still engaged on the finishing, and a shocked refusal from Helena. 'It is day! We need no candles.' She saw his expression. 'Well, perhaps tallow, but good white candles are expensive and there is no need of more light unless I am sewing, and the servant can sit by the window at the back.'

'You shall have more than one girl to serve you, Helena. We agreed that rooms must be built for them and that you no longer will do any work in the house. The whole house must be well-lit and beautiful and the salon must have huge candelabras such as I have in my houses in England.' Helena smiled. 'We shall not live as frugally as your parents do. I have money enough to satisfy every whim and you must ask for anything you want.' He spoke sincerely, out of the real affection he felt for his wife, but most of all because he knew in his heart that but for the Dutch family, he might never have survived to go back to England.

'I need very little,' said Helena. 'I want to live here in this beautiful house and to have you with me. I am a good wife,' she said, firmly. 'As yet we have no children, but when we do, I shall be a good mother.' She sat on one of the chairs in the half-empty salon and gazed at a picture of her sisters. 'I know little about the ways of the world and about paintings, but I can make a home comfortable.'

Rollo wandered into the kitchen and eyed the blue and white tiled wall against which the kitchen fire would be put and he kicked a wooden wash tub viciously. If he was not careful, this house would be exactly like the one in which he had lived with Helena and her family and from which he was escaping. The narrow confines were not just of plaster and brick and the style of the house. This was broader than many in the whole of the Herengracht and the envy of even the highest in the land, but the sight of Willem leaving without a backward glance, carefree and eager for adventure, made the house seem to contract and grow even darker. In his house on the Strand, he had been in his kitchens only twice in his sojourn there, but here,

163

domesticity was inescapable.

'I will tell the servant to come and help you and to escort you home. I have business at the Waag.' Rollo stepped briskly along the cobbled path and breathed deeply. The seven turrets of the old weigh-house cheered him. There were castles like that in Germany and some parts of England, with many doors and windows and airy light. Even if this was a place of business, the meeting home of the Guilds and where the surgeons held anatomy lessons, at least it was imposing and stood alone, not hemmed in by other similar buildings. The sights and sounds of pedlars and merchants, servants and chair-men and the distant cries from the ever present water, made him think of London and his need to go back, to see the familiar places, to eat English food and laugh at English sallies.

Rollo relaxed. There was much to remind him of home here. The steeple of the south church or Zuiderkerk was graceful and the Montelbaan Tower was like one of the clock towers destroyed in the Great Fire. If only it was the Thames on the other side of the square, Vauxhall to walk in and not the placid paths by the endless canals; a view of distant hills and rolling downs or the sweet chestnut woods of home.

He drank klare with some Dutch acquaintances, all curious as to his plans. They shook their heads over the thought that Helena would make an English lady and had no reticence in voicing their opinions as they ordered more of the Dutch gin.

'Leave her to her family, *menhir*. She has your

name and rank and a fine new house and that is enough for any Dutchwoman.' Hendrick grinned. 'Leave her where she is happy, at least until you have prepared the ground. You have had a fire and much trouble and many of your friends may not remember you. Keep two houses, two lives. A wife here and what you like in England with no hurt to Helena if she knows nothing. All men who have your opportunities do this and everyone is happy.'

Rollo laughed and shook his head. 'I am a faithful Dutch husband.' He said it with amazement. The heady memories of youthful conquests now seemed a century away and lack of opportunity in his changed fortunes had stifled his sense of adventure, until now. The dark clothes and lace collars around him now looked like garb worn on the stage to set a tragedy. 'I am due for dinner with my father-in-law and he does not like to be kept waiting.' The men watched him leave and he knew that for the next hour, he would be their main topic of conversation. At least, the Sir Rollo Fitzmedwin they knew had done nothing to blot his name while he lived in Holland whatever they suspected of the man who had come to them in need, and he walked slowly, trying to think what was best for Helena, best for him and if he might find Anna Maria Bennet again. 'Bennet!' The name stuck as he muttered it. Anna Maria Ruyter sounded better and he recalled her dark beauty and her intelligence, her response that showed the passion as yet unleashed and the pride that forbade her to take a lover without marriage. He sighed. She loved Daniel Bennet who in his own way adored her

165

and knew her mind better than any man when it came to learning and the thrill of books.

Pride and memory made him quiet at dinner and Helena glanced at him anxiously, wondering if she had made him very angry by refusing to travel with him today. She brought tea into the living room when the men settled to their long clay pipes and tobacco, and sat apart, waiting for her husband to speak to her.

Rollo tapped the ash from his pipe and set it on the table. 'I must go to England very soon and this delay worries me,' he said. Helena blushed scarlet and her father eyed her with reproach. 'A ship sails in two days time and I shall be on it,' Rollo asserted, and avoided looking directly at his wife. 'I have made every effort to persuade Helena that she will be happy in London and she can come home whenever she feels the need, but if she is not ready, then I go alone and settle my estates. This will take a long time and I shall not come here until I am satisfied with my business in London. Once there, His Majesty has the power to use me in any way he sees fit, which could mean a place at Court or with an Embassy. The fact that I speak and know Dutch might lead him to send me to the colonies where Dutch and French and diplomacy are needed.'

His father-in-law looked impressed and nodded, soberly. There would be much to tell his friends when they gathered to gossip and exchange opinions, and from Rollo's face, he could not tell that he was deliberately making his stay in England stretch as far as he might want it to go.

'You understand? If I go, it is none of my doing

if your daughter refuses to go with me. I love Helena and want her with me, but if I go alone and have to stay for a year or more, unless you bring her to London, we shall not meet again for a very long time.'

'I could not go to Batavia, or New Amsterdam! I am sick going across the Amstel and know nothing of French or Spanish and little English.' Helena took the tray of cups and tea pot and left the room, her face red and her eyes streaming.

'I am sorry,' said Rollo, simply. 'Tell me what I must do, *mijn vriend*. I have responsibilities to my wife, my king and my estates.'

'You have agreed to take papers to London, I am told,' said Van Steen. 'Matters of state must take precedence over the moods of my daughter. Go, with my blessing, but send word soon and come back for her when you can. The house will keep her occupied and she has great status as your wife, so you can go and feel no longer in my debt or in the debt of any of my countrymen.' Rollo nodded gravely but suspected that they would be delighted to keep their daughter and all she had gained by her marriage, and let him go with a sense of relief now that he was no longer malleable and lacking money except for what he had realized from the sale of the valuables with him when he fled from England.

'You could take Hans with you,' suggested Pieter. 'He would take care of you in every way if you were willing. He understands English and is a faithful servant.'

Rollo smiled blandly but refused the offer. A faithful servant to the Van Steens maybe, but a spy to watch every movement as he had done over the past months, and report back to Pieter Van Steen. 'Would you have me bring English retainers here, to quarrel with your servants and make us all unpopular?' asked Rollo. 'I doubt if Helena would like it if I appointed a major domo from my home.'

Hastily Pieter withdrew what he had first thought was something that Rollo couldn't refuse, and after summoning the whole family as if to a wake, he sternly told Helena to do everything possible to pack her husband's effects and to send him away happy, so when the dark figures grew smaller and the wooden ships moored by the docks faded, a week after Rollo had announced his intention of leaving, he wondered if his relief was not matched by that of the Van Steens, after days of delay before the ship could sail, when all goodbyes had been said, all tears shed by the women and all flattery had become repetitious and stale.

As if to make up for the lack of wind and wallowing seas, the ship picked up speed and ran with all sails set for England, making good time and leaving Rollo with a sense of intense excitement as he saw the dim green shores rise before him and real hills come into view. He had left his carriage for Helena and he knew that this was the one gift that reconciled her to losing him, and made Pieter a very happy man, as none could point a finger at his daughter and say she was deserted.

English voices came as a shock and the soft southern accents fell as music to ears that had concentrated on the more guttural tones of the Netherlanders. On board, Rollo had changed into the subdued but elegant clothes he had worn when he left England and his appearance caused no more than the glance awarded to any man of substance coming off a ship.

He hired a coach and had his baggage piled on the roof and took the more valuable pieces with him inside, making sure that his sword was at hand and a loaded gun at his side for the drive to London, taking it for granted that the plague and fire and the aftermath of misery had bred a new strain of cut-purses and highwaymen. The official papers were safe under the seat in a special sealed box, and he leaned back and breathed the air of home.

From Woolwich, he went by barge with his valuables around him after a night in a comfortable inn, and had the bulk of his baggage sent on to the house in Pall Mall and a message to Willem at the inn where he was staying by Whitehall Stairs, that he was to move into the new house at once to guard the goods.

The face of London had changed, with huge gaps through which buildings long hidden from the river could be seen and the sad legacy of the fire was everywhere. Swathes of land, bought from the owners of burned property at a low price now made way for the architects, and Wren's vision of a few wide roads instead of the tumbling houses and narrow lanes of the City of London was coming into being. As Rollo passed the site of his old town house, he stared, memories filling his heart with misgiving. Had he really been sealed up there accused of being a plague victim on the word of an ignorant Searcher? The boat went on, oared by many hands and came to Whitehall Stairs where he called a hackney carriage to take him directly to the Palace, where he kissed hands of the Duke of York and handed over the papers given into his trust by the English ambassador to Amsterdam.

Rollo sank back into yet another hackney and sighed with relief. His responsibilities were over and he was free to meet Willem and find out how London was doing, how well Willem had arranged his affairs and if his friend and squire Alan Denzil was in the City.

The mansions on Pall Mall were enormous and imposing and young trees were everywhere, planted with care and an eye to the future, with walks laid out to the river and up into the fields, and carriage-ways to Tothill Gardens and Palace Yard. He smiled, revelling in the sights and sounds and was suddenly reluctant to meet his friends so soon. His messages might only now have been delivered and he couldn't kick his heels waiting in a half-furnished house for the men to arrive, so he ate in a tavern by the Navy Office and listened to what was said around him, seeing no familiar face and feeling vaguely foreign. He brought out money to pay and found Dutch guilders mixed with his English coins, realizing from the surly look of the inn keeper that such currency was under suspicion and the men who tried to pass it off in the ale-houses must be Dutch spies or worse. He walked through the City, almost lost at times as old landmarks had disappeared, and after being showered with mud from a passing curricle, he wished he had stayed off the ground, but nothing dampened his elation at being home.

Soon, he told himself, I will present myself to the Verneys and see Anna. His pulse quickened. If Daniel was still a colonel, he might be anywhere but in the capital and Anna might be living with her old guardians, but first he must talk to Alan and Willem. The front door of the house was open and Rollo stood back and gazed up at the beautiful façade of the house he had ordered but never seen. 'You've done well, Alan,' he said later, when they met and could discuss the estates.

'I had a good price for the freeholds of the land burned on the Strand and from other rents you had in the stews. Your farms are in good order and making a profit, and money invested, except that lent to the Crown, gives a good return.' Alan completed his report, with Willem listening with awe, wondering how Pieter Van Steen would react if he knew the exact extent of the wealth of this young man.

'You don't need me,' Willem said, frankly. 'I am a simple artist with few ambitions and this house is terrifying.' He glanced almost fearfully at the spread of the staircase and the high wide windows and the leaded bookcases that reached from floor to ceiling in the new library, as they inspected the house. Rollo raised an eyebrow over the books.

'Every gentleman in London has a library even if he can't read,' said Alan, drily. 'The older the books, the better educated you will seem and I bought these when they were being sold cheaply after the fire. Some still bear the signs of smoke, but there are very interesting ones amongst them.' He laughed. 'Every dotard at Court now pretends an interest in the stars and in science since His Majesty goes to the Royal Society and watches dissections and the making of lenses. It became more fashionable than wenching. The King plays tennis and now that the Dutch hope to drown him at sea, he spends time on his new boat given to him as a gift from your other country, Rollo.' He laughed. 'They say he sails it himself, pulling ropes and trimming sails like any pressed man, but it is but a yacht and so can be crewed with no more than thirty men, and our boatyards are making copies so that they can race.'

'What of my friends?' Rollo asked.

'It depends on what you want,' said Alan, bluntly. 'I have passed my first fling and many were sobered by the fire and loss of property and the loss of relatives with the pestilence, and men like Routh are riddled with the pox. Some have a care for their estates now and have married and a few foreigners are now favourite at Court and toadies who have lent money and so have a place with the mighty.'

'Is my money lent in that way?'

'Only so much as will keep them from your heels, and that in stocks that show least return.' Alan frowned. 'I hear that some make demands that they would never have dared do from Oliver.'

'Demands from the Crown?' Rollo looked interested. 'I sensed a mood of tolerance when I met the Duke,' he said. 'Is the exchequer so low?'

'Sir Vincent Clavell has had a man clapped in chains in the Tower for raping his sister, with no trial as yet and no redress, until Clavell withdraws his accusations.'

'He is not at sea? I knew him and his contact with another family, Lady Verney and her husband Edward,' said Rollo, attempting to sound only faintly interested. 'Distant relatives.'

'Clavell married their daughter Alice and she is pregnant, so Vincent will have his own child and another bastard to care for if he doesn't turn the girl away to one of his estates in Scotland or Ireland.'

'And what of the others in that family?' Rollo asked casually.

Alan shrugged. 'I know nothing more as I have been out of the City for a long time. Call on anyone you once knew as they are all interested in your return if only to lay ghosts. They will want to know that you have been received by the Duke and then all doors will be open again.'

'Are there rooms prepared for me here or shall I lodge at the inn with you, Willem?'

'We can camp here tonight and be more comfortable than the inn as I slept with a lice-ridden traveller last night who snored, and there are no small rooms. Make your calls, *menhir* and I will make shift to have a bed and food ready in an upper room. Will you ride or go by hackney until your own carriage is ready?'

'I must brush the dust from my shoes and find an enclosed carriage, as I suffered more from the streets here than from any canal bank in Holland,' said Rollo, and took half an hour to make himself neat and soberly dressed in a way that would have made his wife smile her approval, but finally, almost diffidently as if the dream might be better than the reality, he was driven to the front door of the house that had once held so many hopes.

'Sir Rollo!' Debbie paled and sank back against the wall. 'Lord, Sir what a fright you gave me. We thought you far away or dead,' she told him with thoughtless candour.

'I am alive and wish to see your master or Lady Marian if she is at home,' he said, formally. Debbie did her best to bob a curtsey but her advanced pregnancy made it impossible and she hurried away to find if Lady Marian would receive a visitor.

Marian came downstairs with her linen cap awry and threads cut from her tapestry clinging to her skirt. 'Rollo, my dear boy!' she cried, and he smiled with real pleasure that here was one person at least who welcomed him back. 'Come into the study,' she went on. 'The fire is better there and we can talk comfortably. Debbie, bring wine and some of your almond biscuits: but you will sup with us, and see my husband when he returns from the City?' He hesitated. 'Come now, we can send messages to any who think they have a prior claim on your society,' she said, warmly. 'Tell me about your new house, which has made everyone wonder as you have not been to see it and some said it was bought in your name for quite another person, to save Poll Tax which could not be claimed with you out of the country.'

'You heard that I was alive and had a free

pardon for sins imagined by my enemies?' he asked, cautiously.

'Many rumours,' she said lightly, 'but nothing that matters now you are here. Edward will be anxious to see you about some business regarding sale of land to the Crown for new roads as he heard that your agent had made a good deal with the Office.' She put a hand to her cap and blushed. 'Go into the study and pour some sack for both of us and I will join you presently. I must send word to Edward that you are here and ask him to come home early.'

Rollo stood inside the door and stared at the painting that hung there. In the original oils, the glow was intense, the skin vibrant and warm and the eyes beautiful beyond any he had seen in Holland.

'It is lovely,' said Marian ten minutes later. 'Fi, Sir, you have pretty manners. You need not wait for me to take wine. A copy went to Holland and one has just been sold to an anonymous buyer, but one connected with the Embassy, and the only other one has gone with them to Tangier.'

'Gone with whom, madam?'

'My dear Anna has gone with her husband to Tangier on the orders of the military and stays there for many months to come. She writes that she needs books and herbs and the means to treat the sick and wounded, but I feel that she will die there if she works in the heat and dust of the desert, far from us and from everything that makes life good. I have her letters here. Stay and read them while I tell Debbie that we shall need the venison sent by Lord Chalwood.'

Chapter 10

Lady Marian Verney looked sad. Her pleasure at seeing Rollo for whom she had felt a certain affection even when she was told of his bad character in the past, had driven all other worrying thoughts from her mind. 'My husband will tell you more but we are a household with mixed blessings and sadness. Alice is well, expecting her first child and Christopher and Kate live happily in the country, but Sarah, Vincent's sister, is ill because her brother is unyielding in his vow to ruin her lover.'

Rollo listened with growing interest. 'So much has happened since I was in this room and I find London much changed. I came by way of the City and was lost twice as there were no churches, no Exchange, and houses of many of my former friends have vanished.' He asked about Alice and her new home and about Christopher who was breeding fine horses in Surrey, close to the manor where Marian's aunt and uncle lived, with the expectation of Christopher becoming their heir. 'I did many things that give me cause for regret now and I would like to be on better terms with all your family,' he said.

Marian waved a deprecatory hand and smiled. 'That was a terrible time when death was everywhere and it seemed that the forecasts of the mad Simon Eccles were true.' She put her hands together on her lap and sighed. 'We are not yet free of such prognostications. Did you hear that he ran naked through the palace at Whitehall with a dish of fire and brimstone on his head, crying that Sodom and Gomorrah were destroyed by fire and so shall this place be. He cursed the Royal house and there have been many murmurings against the Crown since that day.'

'He should be hanged,' said Rollo, but turned away.

'Mary Creed, our servant who did such terrible deeds and murdered our dear Lottie, made the same forecasts, but God punished her.' Marian went on, unaware that Rollo was having his own bad memories. She told him about family matters and about the fate of people he had once known, but said little of Anna and Daniel, knowing that once, he had tried to seduce her ward and might not want to be reminded of her although he had been taken with the portrait.

'I have brought with me some fine Dutch paintings, ma'am, and hope you will accept one. Nothing can compare with that portrait,' he said, quietly, able now to have the excuse to gaze at it again. 'In my opinion, Mr Lely is the finest of artists and some of the Dutch paintings are too heavy and dour, but I have one of the harbour at Amsterdam and one of a room in a typical Dutch home.' He said nothing of his marriage but told her that the Netherlanders had been very good to him and he now had two countries to love.

'Say little of that to Edward,' Marian advised.

'He still smarts over some of the humiliations wrought by their Admiral De Ruyter at the Medway.' She smiled. 'It's just as well Anna changed her name and he can forget her link with his family however slight it might be.'

'She is happy, ma'am?' He studied the painting again. 'Such good painting of the hands, don't you think, ma'am?'

'She is working too hard and all her letters speak of disease and herbs and other unhealthy things. She says nothing of what she wears and of what functions she attends now that the new Governor is expected and the Embassy is being refurbished.'

'One of my ships put in at Tangier and the captain said it was a sorry place for women. Most of the men have Moroccan concubines and it is worse than the posts in Guinea, where, in the absence of their wives, they have some recourse to prostitutes; at least the Dutch have this, and are allowed to marry Eurasians which makes for better feeling with the natives.' He shook his head. 'I must learn not to confuse the two nations.'

'You have changed a little but you are not wholly Dutch! I still see the man who came here and visited us in the country, even if your dress is more sober and your face tells me that you have learned patience in exile. I know that Edward will want you to stay here if your own house is not ready.' Marian spoke on impulse, needing another man in whom she could confide her thoughts about Vincent Clavell and his cavalier treatment of the unfortunate James Ormonde.

She knew of Rollo's wealth and sensed that he had power that might help Sarah to obtain the release of her lover, even if she had no idea how this could come about.

'I brought a Dutch artist with me who wished to see Mr Lely's studio and perhaps study under him for a while. As you commissioned the portrait of Anna, could you give him *entré* to the studio? Any task that I can do for you in return I will endeavour to carry out, ma'am, as he is partly servant, partly friend, and a good fellow who deserves to be accepted.'

Marian told him about the man arrested and asked if anything could be done. 'I fear for Sarah and her child and surely, the man isn't such a bad match? I cannot plead with Vincent as he has taken himself to Scotland and left Alice and Sarah under the care of Mistress Charity, their duenna, a good soul but slack in her duty over two young women, and I fear for them. They attend the theatre without escort and frequent certain places where no respectable married lady about to bear a child should be seen. London is full of cut purses and worse and the ways at night are dangerous.'

'If I can escort you to the theatre, ma'am, and they wish to join you, I can take on that pleasant duty while Clavell is away, but I doubt if he would be pleased with my company as we parted on bad terms.' He walked to the hall and made his adieus, promising to call again later when he had given more orders to his servants and asked Willem to join him for supper at the Verney mansion.

The mention of Alice and Sarah made Lady Marian uneasy. It was impossible to ignore what was going on even though her daughter was married, had her own establishment and made it clear that she neither needed nor wanted interference from her mother. 'Debbie!' she called and told her that there would be visitors for supper and that she wanted Sam to take her to visit Alice. 'Are you well, Girl?' She saw that Debbie was red-faced and her hands were puffy and she walked as if dragging a heavy weight instead of a baby in her womb.

'I have asked the girl to prepare supper, My Lady,' Debbie said, calmly. 'I think my time is close and Sam has sent for the woman I shall have with me when I am confined. Everything is ready and I have taught the girl well. You will find nothing to annoy the master and I shall try to be as quiet as possible.'

'And the nursery maid is there to look after little Lottie?' Marian took the girl into her arms. 'You are family, Debbie, and you must make sure of a healthy baby for Sam's sake as well as yours.' Together, they wept as they recalled another birth, a baby called Lottie who was also the namesake of the eldest of the Verney daughters, Kate; the baby born to Lottie, Sam's first wife, during the plague.

'I am very strong, My Lady. Sam takes good care of me, and Lottie will have a playmate soon.' Debbie put a hand to her side.

'Tell Sam that I will go by curricle and the groom can drive me,' suggested Marian. 'He is to stay here and I shall collect my husband from his

180

offices on my way home. No, I say it will be so!' she said as Debbie protested. 'Sam is to be your messenger and help and ask for anything you need.'

Marian put on her cloak of velvet and tied a silk shawl about her neck to prevent the draughts of the curricle from giving her stiffness in her shoulders. It was a relief to leave the house with a real excuse for seeing Alice, who was eager to know when Debbie would be delivered.

Alice listened with a hand to her mouth as if it was she about to go into labour. 'Does it pain a great deal?' she asked.

'Yes, but it is over so soon that it is soon forgotten,' said her mother. 'Each time it is less, and quicker.'

'I shall have but one baby,' asserted Alice. 'I feel heavy and my clothes no longer fit. I crave for sour things and then have heartburn, and Sarah refuses to get out of bed until dinnertime and goes out nowhere unless we go to the theatre, but spends her time weeping over that stupid man.'

'The good Lord gives children and they come with marriage,' said Marian, lightly. 'We have to take what He gives us and rejoice.'

'I am not very fertile,' said Alice, complacently. 'It took over six months to start a child and if I feed my baby and not have a wet nurse, I shall not fall a second time for many months.'

'Yes, Dora. You may bring tea,' Alice said. Marian eyed the new servant with interest. The girl was as neat and colourless as a mouse and as quiet.

As soon as the door closed behind her, Marian

181

asked, 'Do you need another maid? Margaret is very good with your clothes and you have two girls in the kitchen and two more for cleaning, as well as sewing maids and laundry girls for rough work.'

Alice handed her a cup of tea and heaped white sugar into her own. She scraped the bottom of the Japanese cup so vigorously that Marian wondered if either the delicate porcelain or the tiny gold spoon would survive. 'I told her to go,' said Alice. 'She was always spying on everything I did and began to be insolent as if she had a right to more than I gave her.'

Marian laughed. 'My dear, all women with child have such fancies and some weep more than usual. Many have a hankering after odd food and believe their husbands no longer love them, while you have taken a dislike to one who served you well and was the best girl with a smoothing iron that I have seen.'

'She has gone and I never want to hear her name again,' said Alice, stubbornly. 'I have forbidden the servants to admit her again under any pretext, and if she came here when my baby is born, I know she would put a curse on it.'

'Alice, my dearest girl, you must calm yourself! She has gone and you have another maid. You have no cause to have the hysterics over one servant.' Marian made a mental note to tell Dr Verney that Alice was fanciful and needed calming medicines. 'Are you going to the Court Theatre?' she asked, to change the subject of conversation.

'We shall see *The Merry Wives of Windsor* to

cheer Sarah and to give us diversion.' Alice chuckled. 'Poor Miss Charity was shocked by the play against the Royal Family, and bustled us home after it was over as if we might be arrested for seeing it!'

'I'm glad that she did,' Marian said, sternly. 'It is a play that Vincent would forbid you to see and it has been removed from the playhouse. Mr Lacey who acted the principal part was arrested and has now been sent packing from that theatre even though he did not write the play. It was, I hear, scurrilous and does nothing to make the common people love and respect their sovereign.'

'They have bastards so why does Vincent need to do this to James Ormonde when he and Sarah wish to marry and make all right again with the church?'

'Had you no success with him? I am disappointed that Vincent should be so hard. He loves Sarah dearly and yet brings her such pain.' She watched her daughter carefully. 'Vincent went away in a hurry. What did you say to him, Alice?'

Alice began to cry. 'He was so condemning and righteous and I asked if his love was not twisted. Was he not in love with his sister in a way that should be for a wife, and had he not married me because I was like her? He was very angry and I said that his anger showed his guilt. He would not be so if it didn't touch him deeply.'

'You must see Dr Verney soon. You are far too fanciful and your words must have hurt Vincent very much.'

'I have written, begging his pardon,' muttered

Alice, 'But also begging forgiveness for Mr Ormonde, who Sarah dearly loves. I sent the letter as soon as he left and it may catch him at one of the stages. I look for every stage that comes to London and hope to hear soon, for the poor man languishes and writes such sad letters that Sarah shows them to me and we weep together.'

A sound from above made Marian realize that it was time to leave. 'I have an offer to escort you to the theatre,' she said. 'Sir Rollo is back in England and made his courtesies to me today, much changed in demeanour and yet handsome. He will call on you when I come tonight, and you can decide if you want the shelter of his box at the playhouse.'

Alice smiled, her mood changing fast. 'His box would be better than the pit or the smaller boxes and his presence would make Sarah feel better. Do you think he might fall in love with Sarah and save her from ruin?'

'No, he is just a friend, and to take another man's burden is not likely. Stop scheming and enjoy his company.'

'Go before Sarah wakes. She sleeps so much I wonder she has any waking time,' said Alice. 'Come tonight and bring Sir Rollo and we shall drink coffee from these cups and with these sweet little spoons.'

Marian sat in the curricle and tried not to think that Alice in her careless way had arrived at the truth of Vincent's affection and jealousy for his sister. 'Drive faster,' she called to the groom, 'I must see how Deborah fares.' If it is so, she

184

thought, then that love is far more dangerous to James Ormonde than any save that of a lover.

Edward Verney looked cross. It was a cold day and the curricle was the last type of vehicle he would choose to travel in after a hard day bargaining. 'Where's Sam? You know his first duty is to me and he must bring the carriage.'

Marian tucked a fur rug round his knees and handed him some mittens. 'Debbie is close to her time and I told him to stay,' she said, firmly.

'Time was that we had none of this and no servant was allowed inside the house with a child, nor was any servant allowed to live indoors with his wife.'

'You allowed Mary and Joseph Creed to live in and they were bad. Sam has been a loyal friend and suffered for us when he stayed to look after the house with Lottie when we left for the country, so I feel as if he is one of the family.'

'He must be recalling that time,' admitted Edward. 'I hope they are comfortable. Has she a good woman and a wet nurse ready?'

Marian smiled. He tried to hide his feelings under a brusque manner, but she knew how much the couple meant to him. 'It is all arranged,' she said and wondered how men thought a house could be managed if they left everything to the last minute. 'Debbie will lie-in until she is strong and then the nurse will care for Lottie and the new baby and be ready to receive Alice's child when they visit us, so there will be no need for you to be upset by crying children.'

'Have we had word from Anna?'

'Not today,' said Marian. 'I told her that Debbie was near her time and she asked me to buy a present for the baby, so I shall write and tell her that I bought binders and a soft shawl.' She glanced at her husband with caution. 'We had a visitor, and he is coming to supper with a friend from Holland.'

'Holland! Are you mad, Ma'am? That perfidious country has nearly ruined our shipping and many a good man died at the forts by Chatham and the Medway. Because of them we have to pay a band of troops to be rushed to any place where we fear invasion, and it is said these Trainbands often take the law into their own hands and do more harm than good.'

'It is Sir Rollo Fitzmedwin who called today. He is free from exile and has been received by the Duke of York with important diplomatic papers from Amsterdam.'

'Rollo? So he escaped with a whole skin, did he? I wager a woman saw him comfortable and hid him from the worst until he could put a nose above ground.' Edward sniffed. 'Young mountebank,' he said, mildly. 'What does he want from us?'

'Nothing but friendship, Edward. I know he was wild before he left England and many say was wicked, but he's changed. He's more soberly mannered and has offered help with Alice if she insists on visiting places of which we disapprove,' Marian said, with a hint of pleading in her voice.

'Well, at least he can't do harm in that bed,' Edward said coarsely. 'And even Sarah isn't very inviting just now. Why can't Vincent stay and look

186

after his own stable?' He helped Marian down from the high step and she went inside the house and down to the kitchen before taking off her cloak. The nurse was sitting at the table drinking porter and Sam walked aimlessly about the room. Little Lottie glanced up from her rag doll and smiled in such a way that her mother seemed to be behind the child's eyes. Marian choked back a tear and asked if all was well.

'Yes, My Lady,' said the nurse and Marian saw that she was clean and tidy and seemed to be efficient, and that Lottie liked her. 'The midwife is there and it will be only an hour or so. I have water ready and Sam put the cot close to the fire, with warm clothes and clean rags.'

The cook who had taken Debbie's place for a while asked for Marian's opinion of the soup and fowls and Marian left the kitchen with a warm feeling of friendship with her servants that she suspected was rare in London houses.

She called for her maid and changed for supper into a more elaborate dress and jewels, knowing that they would go on to the theatre with Rollo and the two young women, and when Rollo appeared, with Willem looking slightly abashed at the luxurious surroundings, she was elegant and composed and Edward had got used to the idea of having one of the hated 'butter-boxes' in his house.

Rollo smoothed down the heavy silk jacket that fell neatly over dark green britches and picked out the purple and ochre of his shirt. His natural hair was smooth and thick and tied back with a wide purple ribbon, and Edward eyed him with

187

envy, suspecting that his wig maker had not tucked in all the sharp ends of thin wire that helped make the shape of the periwig he now wore. Willem went at once to a picture on the wall near the entrance and soon lost his shyness as Edward warmed to his real interest and showed him the two Lelys in his possession, the one of Anna and another of his wife and daughters done some time ago. He showed Willem small paintings of the manor in Surrey, an ancient castle that had once been the home of Lady Marian's family and a picture by Hals.

Rollo gave him a picture of the harbour in Amsterdam and Willem ventured to present a small one of his own work, a pretty scene outside of the town, where the polders bloomed and the water stretched along by small cottages, so by the time that supper was served and Edward was able to announce that Debbie had a fine son, which called for wine for the servants and master alike, there was a festive atmosphere and Edward had almost forgotten that Willem was Dutch.

From time to time, Willem lapsed into Dutch and Rollo answered him, but it was done quietly and without giving offence. 'What if they ask about Helena?' Willem asked.

'You say nothing of that family. I have not said I am married and it must be so until I change my mind. First I must make my friends welcome me back before they have the shock of knowing I am married to a Dutch lady. The feeling here is not without suspicion of everything from across the Channel and I must tread warily.'

'What can be done?' Edward asked. 'Sarah

Clavell has been seduced and her lover is clapped in the Tower awaiting trial for rape. As far as I can see, she is just as much to blame and she went to him willingly. We had enough whitster bleach in our clothes to dazzle the whole of London, while they took their pleasure!'

'I have been here for only a day, so I can have no impact on the law, but surely this is a high-handed decision?' suggested Rollo.

'Sparked by malice and quite unfair,' said Marian. 'I am fond of Vincent and he showers my daughter with every luxury, but he is hard in certain ways and there is no way of making him see reason; but may we forget this sorry matter and enjoy the play?' she asked.

Sam insisted that he must drive the party in the big carriage and said that Debbie was asleep and likely to be for hours, while the baby was cosseted by the women and he had not had a chance to look at his son for more than five minutes before the baby was whisked away to its cot. He was smiling broadly as if this was his first child and he had never suffered any tragedy in his life. Someone had stuck a long feather in his cap and he whistled as he drove the carriage.

'Take this for ale but stay sober if you are to fetch us again, Sam,' said Edward when they reached the theatre, following the small coach in which Alice, Sarah and Mistress Charity travelled.

Gradually, more colour came to Sarah's pale face as her youth and natural resilience made her enjoy the play except when Mistress Knipp sang a song of broken hearts. The playhouse was full

189

of a merry crowd and Alice listened with sparkling eyes as Rollo amused her with tales of his journey by sea and his descriptions of the wide flat fields of Holland. She was also relieved to hear of the easy birth of Sam and Debbie's baby as if in some way this made sure of her own easy confinement. The two young women ate sweetmeats as both were over the early stages of sickness, and Marian sighed, thinking that if only Sarah could have her heart's desire, the two girls could look forward in complete happiness, once more sharing, as they had done ponies, escapades and all the giggling joys of youth.

'You must stay for some coffee,' said Alice, eager to show off her new habit and her delicate china, and Willem who had been dazzled by the splendour of the dresses, the huge puffed hair creations of the ladies and the excess of lace on the men's clothes, was avid for even more delights as a child let loose in a kitchen filled with forbidden delicacies, so Rollo laughed indulgently although he was tired, and followed the party into the hall.

'My Lady! There was a letter brought by fast galloper from Sir Vincent,' said the new maid. Alice snatched it up and took it aside. She read the words with growing excitement and then thrust the letter into Sarah's hand. Sarah read it quickly, swayed and fell to the floor in a dead faint.

'My dear love,' said Lady Marian, sinking to her knees by the prostrate form. 'Is it such bad news?' The girl moaned and blinked and tried to sit up, but her face was ashen and her hands cold.

'Is it true?' she whispered. 'It is not a wicked lie to tease me?'

'Vincent has agreed that Master Ormonde must be freed and that you can marry. He was touched by my letter and feels remorse at his actions and asks your forgiveness, Sarah.'

'I shall go to the Tower with this letter if I can be of that service, Alice. It may be a few days before the order is completed, but once this is set into action, he will be sniffing at free air,' said Sir Rollo.

'I find it hard to believe,' said Sarah who was reviving fast with the help of some strong spirit. 'I have not had a note from James for four days and I felt that he was in deep despair and could not write, or was ill.'

'Such a day!' exclaimed Lady Marian. 'I am tired and you must rest, Alice, and make sure that Sarah sleeps. So much excitement quite gives me palpitations.' She made Edward call Sam and they left for home, happier than for a long day and when Marian saw the tiny red and shrivelled face that was young Sam, and counted the right number of fingers and toes, she went happy to bed.

Edward sat on the *chaise-longue* at the foot of her bed and pulled off his wig, far too stimulated to sleep and anxious about his ships after hearing that although the Dutch had ceased to pirate merchant vessels in the Straits of Gibraltar, the Spanish continued to do so from Ceuta, the town in which they were still firmly fixed after being driven from most of North Africa. There were tales of other pirates of no one country, banded together for lawless gain, who were savage and took prisoners, subjecting them to torture and mutilation before tossing them into the sea.

His unease made Marian wide awake and they talked until a slender light crept higher over the City and dawn came angry and cold. Lady Marian pulled on a warm wrap and crept down to the nursery, where a sleepy girl sat rocking by the fire and a small head moved restlessly in the wooden crib. Marian whispered to the girl to stay in the chair and gently pushed back the shawl from the baby's face. A son, she thought. A son for Sam and Lottie ... but it wasn't her dear Lottie who had borne this child, but her almost as dear Debbie. She wept quietly for a moment and then wondered if the child that Alice would bring into the world would be very fair. Vincent was of medium colouring but Alice was a golden girl. Sarah was slightly darker as she grew older but was still fairer than her brother. Two little fair heads. Marian decided, and smiled when she went back to bed and fell asleep for a few hours.

She was awakened by the sound of a horse, snorting his disgust at being ridden hard, and Edward shouting for his groom and carriage. Her personal maid pulled back the curtains from the tester bed and said that Mr Verney wanted to see My Lady, and Edward strode in, without apology for waking his wife and walked distractedly about the room.

'Bring tea,' Marian ordered, and the girl left reluctantly as she sensed the tension in the room.

'I want no tea!' Edward sounded angry but there was something more in his voice.

'I know, my dear, but it is plain that you have something to tell me, and the girl was listening with all ears.'

'I'm sorry, my dear,' he said and his wig took on a slightly dejected angle. 'I was leaving for the City when a horseman came and set the hens running. He has word from the Tower. Young James Ormonde is ill of a fever and sent a message for Sarah, and Alice made the man come on to us with the news. I must go there and find out how bad this is, and if it is the plague again. Sarah must not touch him until we know what ails him.'

'I shall ask my brother to see him and then we shall know the truth. Bad things happen in jails and if they know we have an interest in Master Ormonde, he may have better treatment.' Edward left abruptly and found his brother about to leave to visit the sick. 'Have you ever been to the Tower?' asked Edward, fearfully. The grim walls had never filled him with anything but dread and he had heard of damp and cold and rats and ill treatment that made a man mad.

'Once or twice,' said Doctor Verney, calmly. 'I physicked one of Cromwell's relatives and he recovered, so take heart, Edward, I'll see what can be done. Do you know anything about his condition?'

'Only that he has a fever and can hardly see to write. His mind wanders and he has a rash, but that is all the messenger could tell me.'

Dr Verney pursed his lips. 'Not the plague, I think, but probably typhus, the enemy of all in captivity. Some call it the jailfever, as it attacks

193

those wretches confined to dungeons with lice and rats and bad food. No fresh air,' he said, almost triumphantly. 'Fresh air and a draught of sack each day is the best medicine in the world.'

Edward waited anxiously in the carriage, unwilling to pass between those tragic gates or to see the interior of a place where men entered and came out changed or dead. Dr Verney talked to the turnkey and was admitted with the respect due to a man who had received honours from the king for his services during the plague. Few doctors had stayed in London, with a handful of apothecaries, to heal and comfort the stricken during those terrible months, but Dr Verney had never wavered and now was held in esteem by king and commoner. For an hour, Edward fumed at the delay, partly from anxiety and partly because he was needed in his offices and had a meeting soon with the Navy Office, but at last, the huge doors opened and his brother stepped out, briskly.

'As I thought, it is typhus and badly tended. The rash is the usual mulberry stain and his skin is dry and hot. I think he is on the verge of losing his senses and if the bleeding does no good, I fear for him. I have arranged for better quarters and treatment and shall look in on him again tonight. When the turnkey heard that he was to be released, he was uneasy. Master Ormonde as an accused rapist had little sympathy from anyone there, and has marks that show this lack.'

Dr Verney gave the groom instructions to take him to another man who he thought was dying. Edward had to conceal his impatience at the delays that morning and his fear of touching the clothing of a man who had just bled a typhus patient, but gratitude outweighed any other consideration and he tried to relax and to report the latest news about Alice, Sarah, and Sam's new son.

Later, weary from his busy day and unsure of the fate of the last ship in his employ, Edward went home. The shabby coach that his brother used was standing by the heavy portico and Edward hurried into the house. Marian sat, in tears by the table, an untouched cup of coffee near her hand.

'I was too late,' said Dr Verney. 'He was in such a poor way that nothing could have saved him. Now, Marian, who is to tell Sarah?'

Chapter 11

Anna could see that the letters were carrying bad news, and she sighed. Daniel had enough to bear without taking on the worries of the Court in England. She sat on the cushion-covered bench and wished that the dry wind would stop for just an hour, and the heavy clouds brooding on the Rif Mountains would shed some rain and make the ground soft.

High to the south, she could see the mountains, now half hidden in the swirling sand storm that had not reached the fort, but had brought the scarifying wind. She clapped her hands for Azziza and tried to settle to her books with the help of the girl who translated anything she didn't understand, but the sight of her husband frowning and at times even cursing, was too much for her concentration.

'What is it?' she asked.

'They say that Clarendon is in trouble and likely to lose his seal of office.' Daniel Bennet threw down the letters and picked up his mug of water. He took a swig of the half-warm liquid and wiped his mouth with the back of his hand. 'The new Governor is still in London and we have to do our best for another month or so. The King refused our last requests for funds and sees no need for haste.' Daniel sat beside Anna, his face turned to the dull breeze. 'The commanders here are at the end of their tethers, with no real governor and too many officers giving too many different orders.'

'Supplies came for the governor's house and some medicines arrived,' Anna said in an attempt to make it sound easier. 'Dulcie said that the King was sending an envoy to see what progress we are making on the Mole and another to make sure that everything is comfortable for the governor when he arrives.' Anna laughed. 'She is already practising her curtsey and trying on the dresses she wore in London.'

'She'll not need to curtsey to the envoy or the jackanapes they'll send to see that the hangings are the right colour,' said Daniel, bitterly. 'We need more guns and food from Lisbon, more horses and saddlery and men to replace those dying of fever, and more guards for the stores on the Mole. The finished houses are as yet unoccupied and the architect's ideas of shops and places for recreation have been the laughing stock of the workmen who are nearly blown from the jetty on the windward side.'

'There were two more men injured yesterday,' said Anna. 'One died in the night and the other is in great pain. Is there a box for me from Dr Verney?'

'Ask the sergeant. He is unpacking and making a tally of everything that came on the last ship, before thieving hands take most of it. I've put a guard on the whole store with orders to shoot anyone who loots our supplies, whether they are Moor or British, and I hope to put an end to this traffic.'

197

Anna found the sergeant sorting out dark blue tunics for the soldiers to wear while working by the Mole. He inspected his list and handed over a sack and a wooden box, which the servant took into the house. With the help of Azziza, Anna opened the sack and tipped out the contents on to a deal table. A smell of decay met her senses and she sat down heavily, all her pent-up depression and frustration surfacing. What had been a thick bundle of herbs and dried roots was now a mass of glutinous evil-smelling corruption. She felt the sack and found it damp, and the neat letter, tucked in with the herbs and now almost illegible, gave her no comfort. Dr Verney had listed everything with their uses, adding his own wise comments to help her in the hospital.

'I can use nothing of this,' she said to Azziza who was looking at the mess with amazement. How could her mistress bother to have such things sent to her all the way over the sea? There were plenty of weeds growing on the ridges and in the sand dunes. Anna opened the box and found that this at least had withstood the sea spray and the dankness of the hold, and the laudanum was intact, together with three good books that she had requested.

She prepared a draught of laudanum and took it across the compound to the hospital, leaving the rest securely locked in a chest, and not daring to take it to the building where there was little hope of locking away anything of value. It made the dispensing of medicines laborious and took far more time and energy than she had to spare but this was the only way to prevent the inevitable stealing. She turned, away from the sight that met her on the rise beside the mortuary. Daniel had forbidden her to interfere with discipline but she could not look at the brutal floggings of men tied to the hated triangle used on ships and in barracks alike, and the cries of pain were as bad after the steel-tipped cats had scarified the flesh and salt was rubbed into the wounds. She tried to shut out the sounds, knowing that after the flogging, salt probably would heal the cuts and prevent infection.

Every pallet was occupied and many men lay in a kind of merciful coma, past pain, past anything but oblivion. Anna gulped back her tears. One of the herbs would have helped the man with dropsy so bad that his belly overhung his legs and his face was thick and purple. She pressed his arm and it retained the mark of her fingers on the swollen, water-logged flesh. The Arab purges only made him weak and did little to help his condition, and the doctor dared not bleed him again as he had dripped water from the flesh round the cut vein in his arm for days after the last attempt, and contracted a fever.

Ayesha came from the room at the back with a poultice, and Anna helped to apply it in spite of the unwillingness of the man for whom it was intended. 'Haaa!' hissed Ayesha with satisfaction when it was bound into place. 'He is better and will need only four more if it is the will of Allah that he should live.' She saw the cup in Anna's hand. 'You have some sleep for him?' she asked. 'Did the other things come and may I see them?'

Anna shook her head. 'They must have been

stowed on deck or in a wet hold. The herbs and plants were ruined but this arrived safely, and my books.' She sighed. 'I shall ask for more and Dr Verney will send them in a box this time, but the heat during the voyage must kill many plants and some herbs are not as effective when dried. I need eyebright to treat the children with sand blindness, and unguents made from elderflower and other shrubs that do not grow here.'

'My Lady is going to see the sherif soon. He has many plants in his palace.' She smiled, showing good teeth. 'If My Lady wears the haik that was made from the silk, the sherif will want to buy her.' Anna laughed, but there was no humour in it. Daniel had been furious when he saw the ruby sent to his wife by the sherif and had been tempted to send it back, but had not dared to do so and insult the sherif, thus harming their better relationship and risking reverting to the time when the well-trained Sudanese troops had attacked and pillaged the forts and the stores without restraint.

The cook was waiting to serve the food, and that at least was palatable due to Anna's insistence that sick men needed extra nourishment. Anna watched until she saw that Ayesha was supervising the feeding then walked back to her own quarters in the white-walled moorish house beside the small chapel. She ignored the three men who emerged from the church, knowing them to be Irish workers who secretly took the Host from a priest who took confession. The growing numbers of Catholics in the army and the workforce was a constant worry to

Daniel, not because he had any real objection to any man following his own conscience, but because the numbers might prove dangerous if a Catholic purge was begun in England. All over Europe there were men and women who had fled one country or another to follow their own faiths, and the armies of Holland were full of Englishmen and Germans, French and Danes, who swore allegiance to the foreign power. Some dared not return home, but there were several Scottish regiments that were allowed to fight for Britain if Holland was not at war with her, but were on call for service in The Netherlands whenever they were required.

The man who had been flogged was being carried, senseless and face down on a litter, the salt and blood mingling in bright streams on his back, and Anna wondered if he would be brought to the hospital, but she knew better than to interfere with army discipline and stood aside to let the men pass to the barracks.

The governor's house was the most impressive on the compound, its dazzling white walls built of stone and the wide high windows curved and graceful over the shady porches and the colonnaded cloister where a cool walk continued round the entire building. Anna went inside to see what progress had been made and smiled. Daniel would be angry, she knew. Silk tapestries and fine carved furniture had taken space in the ship that could have been used for useful supplies, but she paused to watch the servants polishing and sweeping, homesick for good order and some of the things that she had once felt were unimportant, like airy rooms and precious vases, delicate muslin curtains and new cushions.

She sighed and went slowly back to her own home, aware that this show of wealth was essential in such a country where riches were the hallmark of power and prosperity, and the men they sent, to show the sherif the elegance of the British way of life, must be men who the King held in high regard for their clothes, extravagance and poise, like any of the young men who had eyed her from theatre boxes and in the carriages in Vauxhall gardens. None, she decided would bring anything but false values and even more luxuries, to a place where fresh fruits were a luxury and good water rarer than wine.

She stopped as she entered the house and gasped. A huge basket, woven from palm leaves, lay filled with oranges, figs and fresh dates. She glanced towards the closed door behind which Daniel was working. This latest gift from the sherif would please him as little as the gift of the ruby had done, but even Daniel couldn't say that fruit was not wanted. She filled a bowl with fruit and sent the rest to the hospital for Ayesha to lock in the store and give out to whoever needed it, and when Dulcie arrived ten minutes later, curious to know what the horsemen had brought, the modest bowl that Anna showed to her disappointed her, even when she was asked to choose some fruit to take home.

'You go to the palace, today?' Dulcie said in a tone that showed disapproval and envy mixed.

'We leave as soon as it is cool and stay for two days,' said Anna. 'Ayesha will manage the hospital unless you wish to take over my duties there,' she added, equably.

Dulcie examined a white hand and shrugged. 'You know I would be useless, and I hate the smell of the place,' she said. Anna instinctively hid her own hands, which in spite of her attempts with olive oil and sugar, to rub away the rough skin, remained more like the hands of a servant than of the wife of a colonel in His Majesty's army. 'You will never want to leave,' said Dulcie. 'There are times when I envy the women in the seraglio. They are pampered and given the choicest of food, have clothes and jewels and the company of many other women, and of course have a very handsome husband.'

'Who is shared and can reduce any who displease him to the state of a slave,' said Anna, drily.

'He must like you, Anna. He never gives any of the other officers' wives a single orange.'

'He does it to show that he has all the fruit he can use while we have few palm trees and very little fresh fruit,' said Anna, trying to dispel any illusions that Dulcie could have about his desires, and she prayed that Dulcie would never discover that the sherif had sent her the beautiful ruby. 'I wish we could put off this visit,' she confessed. 'There are two men in the hospital who need my care and Ayesha tried to give them Arab remedies that are right for some complaints but not these.'

'I could go in your place,' suggested Dulcie with great eagerness. 'I have some fine dresses ready for when the governor comes and I can act as hostess to Daniel and the other officers who are going. I can't think why my husband was not chosen and then I could have insisted on joining him,' she said, irritably.

'I do want to go there,' admitted Anna. 'The sherif has lovely gardens in the oasis and many plants that might be of use in the hospital.'

'I can understand you wanting to walk in the gardens but surely you will enjoy the food and the luxurious surroundings. They say that the palace is almost as opulent as the one in Paris, but of course, very foreign-looking.' She glanced at Anna and smiled, slyly. 'Perhaps that's why the sherif prefers you. I stay out of the sun and keep pale but you are almost as brown as a Bedouin woman.' Dulcie continued to eye her friend with malice. 'You dress simply, so you are no Bedouin, and you wear no jewellery to show the wealth of your husband or tribe. I wonder that some of the women can raise their arms for the weight of gold chains.'

'I shall wear jewellery,' Anna said, quietly. 'It will be my duty to make my husband proud of me, and to show that I am from good stock, but most of all, I must find out what plants will grow here that I can use for medicines. I have been studying desert plants and those that grow by water in hot climates, and if I can, I will bring back more fruit for you and some silver bracelets made by the Arabs.'

'The thick ones with tiny bells?' Dulcie clapped her hands.

'I thought I was the Bedouin woman,' said Anna, drily. 'Shall I ask for a place in the harem for you?'

'For all the company I have here, it would be an improvement,' Dulcie said, peevishly. 'I shall go back to England on the next ship, and then my dear husband will be sorry!'

'Not the next ship, Dulcie. Remember? There are two courtiers coming who will want to be well-received and might bring you some diversion, with news of London, the theatres and what Lady Castlemaine has been doing.' She explained what Daniel had told her. 'So, you will need to stay and be the best-looking of the ladies here, with white hands to be kissed and plenty of time for dalliance.' Dulcie didn't notice the edge to Anna's words but laughed, happily. 'I think you should stay here in case the winds blow them here far earlier than we hope for,' said Anna.

'Stay at the oasis as long as you wish, my dear Anna. I will do my duty here until you return. I must go and tell my servant to wash my fine lace shawl and to rinse it in very clear water. Our tanks are full after the storm,' she added, defensively, 'And I have been very careful with water, this week.' She frowned. 'The water from the last well they sunk is brackish and fit only for the animals but it does leave the sweet water for us. How I long to see a calm lake with willows and birds that I can recognize. I hate the desert roads with all those terrible vultures hovering overhead as if willing me to die. Perhaps I do not envy you the journey, Anna. I think I am happier here. I'll go home and make sure we have everything ready for guests.'

'They will stay at the governor's house,' said Anna. 'I went in this morning and saw that it is nearly ready and very fine.'

Anna smiled when Dulcie had gone. At last the woman might be of use, if only to keep the visitors occupied and leave Anna to get on with more important work. She supervised the packing of two fine dresses that she had not worn since leaving England, included the gown she had worn in the portrait and added the silk haik, thinking that this might be suitable attire if she had to visit the women in the harem. Her jewels glinted on the velvet base of the casket with the fire of fine emeralds and diamonds, and the ruby glowed amongst them.

'Azziza, you will attend me and stay with me all the time,' said Anna, firmly.

'My Lady, what if His Excellency the sherif commands me to go and leave you with him? He is my master above the colonel and above my father.' She extended her hands with the palms uppermost.

'That will not happen,' said Anna with more firmness than she felt. 'I am English and married to an officer and we shall be guests in his house. No sherif would violate the trust between guest and host under his roof, as you know, Azziza, so stop worrying and get that baggage out to the boy to load on to the mule. We shall have a guard and escort of twenty men and some of the soldiers from the oasis will come to meet us and take us to the sherif.'

Daniel was dressed in full uniform, the usually tight collar of his tunic showing a certain loose fit as if he had lost weight, but he looked a fine figure on the big grey horse. Anna insisted that she too could ride and so not hold up progress by travelling in a closed chair, and as the evening grew cool and the horse tugged at the bit, she felt as if she was back on the soft downs under a sunset, instead of on the dusty road across the scrub and sand to the distant tuft of trees that gradually opened up to become the oasis.

Men, on Arab horses with coloured saddle-cloths and jingling silver bells on the harness, swept out of the scrub in a circle, fierce and hawklike, making a studied approach, half to impress and half to show a deeper more sinister strength. As the light failed in the sudden dip into night, flaming torches were lit by the escort and when the small column reached the palace, Anna was bemused by the beauty of the dark faces, the white djellabas and the shadows cast by the torches, the sweet music of the harness and the sounds of hooves, and the magic of the blackness outside their immediate circle.

Azziza was taken in hand by a tall woman with bold eyes who eyed Anna with ill-concealed curiosity. 'What does she say?' asked Anna.

'She gives greeting and says that we must wash the dust away and prepare for the feast. I must go to the servants to sleep and she will give you a slave to sleep at your door.'

Anna called to her husband who was being led away by his host. 'I want Azziza to stay with me,' she said, firmly. 'I shall not sleep in the harem even if that is what they want. We are together and I am frightened to be alone with a strange slave.'

Daniel frowned and Anna suddenly recalled

that the sherif spoke excellent English and had understood every word she uttered.

'I beg your pardon, Colonel. My servants misunderstood my orders,' said the sherif. 'They are not used to your ways and thought that you had brought another woman for my house, especially as your wife is to eat with us.' His voice was smooth and yet his eyes belied the softness of his explanation.

Daniel compressed his lips. 'My wife must stay in my rooms, Sherif. She is unused to your ways and came only to study your plants.' He tried to smile, sensing the tension. 'If you wish it, she will dress according to your customs while she is here, but she will need her own attendant who knows about Western dress if she wears the gowns she brought with her.'

Bless you my darling Daniel, thought Anna. It was at times like this that his flashes of understanding made her know that he still loved her and knew her heart.

'Tomorrow, when we walk together in the garden you shall wear the haik for me, *madame*, but tonight I wish to see you dressed as for the Court that I so much admire in Whitehall, where the customs are so different and free and men may look on women and touch even those who are not their property.'

Daniel nodded curtly but seethed inwardly at the inference that they were as bad as the most profligate of the courtiers that the Sherif had met on his visit to England.

'My wife is a lady of strict virtue, Your Highness; given to learning and good works and is a wife that any man would be proud to have. I owe my life to her,' he added, simply.

'A ruby above price?' suggested the sherif. 'At least you must wear my jewel so that I might envy it against your throat,' he said, and Daniel nodded again, knowing that this must be so; Anna must wear the jewel or there would be a deep insult implied.

The heavy rugs hanging from the walls and the soft gauzy curtains over the shuttered windows made an elegant haven that could have come from Versailles. Perfumes that smelled of India and the Orient seemed to filter into her senses and make her vulnerable to the charm and sexuality of the men about her as they stared at Anna, a woman, boldly unveiled and eating with their master and his guest, but not of the harem.

The ease and efficiency of the silent slaves who plied them with lamb and spiced vegetables, rice and exotic fruits, contrasted with the kitchen servant left at the fort and the simple dishes prepared by Azziza and the army cooks. For the first time, she wondered just who would come to prepare for the Governor, and she wished that there was more time to train a cook to make some of the dishes that Debbie could conjure up in the Verney household.

'You sighed, *madame*. Is the food not to your liking? I shall order fresh dishes and more cool drinks,' said the Sherif, who had been watching her eyes become dreamy.

'Please,' she begged. 'Everything is perfect; so much so that I am envious of your cooks and your servants.' She gave a sweet smile and helped herself to more lamb, eating it with the fingers of her right hand and expertly avoiding dripping mutton fat on to her gown. Daniel smiled his approval and vowed to tell her that she was looking lovely, but soon became involved in discussions about the length of the Mole and the need for more storage compounds.

'What would you store, mon Colonel?' The tone was teasing but the sherif eyed him with barely disguised malice. 'Sweetmeats and cloth from the Indies? Or guns and powder from Lisbon and England?'

'In outer compounds, it must be materials for building and repair and furnishings for the new houses when they are finished,' stated Daniel, calmly. 'Your corsairs board our ships to inspect our cargoes, in spite of the orders signed by the Emperor of Morocco and our Royal House which agrees to give safe and uninterrupted passage to both our navies, so I assume that you will exert that right over our storehouses, too,' he added, wryly.

'My ships have been at sea for far longer than we have had the agreement and there have been misunderstandings,' said the Sherif, smoothly. 'They are like seabirds that never come to land and so may not be taught better manners.' He appeared slightly embarrassed and suggested that *Madame Bennet* was tired and they might talk again tomorrow, after he had shown her his garden in the cool of the morning.

'You were very good,' said Daniel when they were in their magnificent room. A slave brought warm scented water in which floated crimson blossoms and Azziza was ready to help with Anna's clothes. Daniel sat at the table and examined his papers, an incongruous touch in the opulence and luxury around him, but he seemed unaware of the soft light from the many oil lamps, the sound of music played in the distance and the subtle perfume that was everywhere. Azziza went to her bed in the corridor outside the door and Anna brushed her hair. Daniel yawned, then came behind her and kissed her neck. 'I am a rough soldier and I shall be so until His Majesty has no further use for me, but I love you, Anna.'

She smiled. 'I married that soldier and followed him here. I want no other husband and no other place than this tonight,' she said, softly. She put her arms round him and drew him towards the heaped cushions that made their bed. They sank into the softness and her body was lulled by the scents and the music and the fact that at last, after many weeks, Daniel seemed as he had once been, young, passionate and demanding in his need for her. He kissed her with lips that could never have enough of her soft lips and flesh and his hands found her body in caresses that made her want to cry out until he took her with such force that she did cry in pain. Hazily, she held him close, in an embrace that made them complete, and so they slept, suddenly and with strange dreams, as the aphrodisiac cordial took effect.

Music again made Anna stir and cover her nakedness, chilled as dawn brought movement and relief from the thought of heat to come.

211

Azziza brought lemon tea and left her to dress and Anna put on the silk haik and bound her hair back in a wisp of a veil. Daniel had left to see his men and to give them orders for the day, and when she had dressed, a girl came, bowed low, giving the salaam of respect and led her with Azziza a step or so behind, to the garden. The huge fretted door gave way to a bright walled garden where fountains and streams made the place cool and watered the many plants and trees. Anna gasped. The luxuriant vegetation spilled over the paths and seemed to mock her own efforts back at the fort to force flowers to grow and leaves to form. The soil was black and fertile and palm trees bent slightly to the breeze that couldn't be felt below the high walls.

'You could be happy in my gardens?' The sherif took her hand and kissed it in the manner of a born European courtier. Anna gazed at him coolly and he placed her hand by her side as if giving up something which he valued but had no right to touch. 'I am confused,' he said with a sudden smile. 'You are English and yet today you wear the robe of my women. I can kiss the hand of *Madame Bennet* but because you wear the haik and have no husband or parents with you, I may not touch the women dressed for Allah even when you have attendants.' He laughed. 'Let me show you my plants and then you shall sit with one of my wise men and talk about healing, while I talk with your husband.'

Anna made notes of names and drew swift sketches of leaves and flowers, with the properties that they contained, and at the end of the long morning had a mass of information culled from plants and books, with the help of Azziza who acted as her interpreter.

At the end of the visit, she had bundles of plants to transfer to the arid soil of the fort and recipes for medicines but she wished that there were more familiar ones. She dressed with care for the journey home, with the grey light bringing coolness for a good hour of comfort on the journey, and the sherif did them the honour of escorting them to their mounts. He showed them a mule laden with bales of silk and more fruit and waved aside any attempt to accuse him of great generosity. Even Daniel seemed to have mellowed during the visit but his mouth tightened when the sherif asked if there was anything that *Madame Bennet* would accept from him as a special and personal gift.

'Yes,' said Anna, her eyes shining.

Daniel glowered. The atmosphere of the oasis must have gone to her head as it had to his own in some curious way.

'Anything! slaves, fine furniture, food, more flowers? I will send for jewels to match your dress and if your husband allows, a eunuch to protect you.'

'None of these things, Your Excellency. I would like two tubs of your good earth for my plants.'

Chapter 12

'I shall never leave this house until the day I die,' Sarah vowed with passion. 'I shall live here, and refuse to be sent away so that my brother can forget I exist and so forget his guilt.'

'You have not seen Vincent and until you do, there is no knowing what he has in mind for you,' suggested Lady Marian.

'He will want to take the baby and send it away and make me marry someone of his choice to make all well in the eyes of the world,' Sarah continued. She waved a crumpled note and then folded it carefully again and hid it in her sleeve pocket. 'I have his last note giving me permission to marry James Ormonde and he can never deny that it was his selfish temper that denied me the love of my life and the father of my child by sending him to the Tower to die.'

'Vincent loves you dearly,' said Lady Marian in an attempt to calm the girl who now stood with eyes blazing and hectic spots of colour on her pale cheeks. 'He did what most men would do when they heard that a sister of tender years had been seduced. Duelling is frowned on and there was no way of knowing if your lover was faithful only to you,' she added, unhappily, but Sarah just stared at her as if she was mad.

'Why doesn't he come?' demanded Sarah. 'Mr Verney sent fast gallopers to catch up with him and yet we hear nothing. Is that what makes for brotherly love, Madam?'

'He has to travel to oversee his estates and may not return for a while,' said Lady Marian. 'If he has taken the boat to Ireland, then we may see nothing of him for many weeks, and you will have to make the best of it.' She smiled. 'If his ship had not foundered on Scilly, you would not have seen him for over a year or more, so this parting is less.'

'*If ... if...*' Sarah's eyes flashed. 'If he had stayed away, I would have eloped with James and had my baby before he returned and all would have been well.' She burst into tears. 'Now, I am a widow before I married and have lost the father of my son.'

Alice appeared in the doorway and shrugged, her pretty face petulant and bored. 'Not more tears, My dearest Sarah? I swear you could drown us all before the week is out.' She sank into a seat and arranged the full skirt about her in neat folds. 'I am tired and my legs ache, and yet in my own house there is nobody who cares about me. All attention is on you Sarah, and yet you do nothing but weep and stamp as if I can do anything more than I tried to do for you.' She regarded her friend with an angry glance. 'I tried to persuade Vincent to let you marry and it was my plea that changed his heart even if it was too late.'

Sarah flung herself into her arms and sobbed less noisily. 'I beg your pardon, Alice. I do beg your pardon most humbly. What would I do without such a friend? I promise to be good now and to think of the baby; the two babies who will be all in all to us.' She smiled through puffy eyelids and asked to be excused while she washed her face.

'Have you any news?' asked Lady Marian as soon as Sarah had gone.

'A message to say that Vincent left for Ireland instead of Scotland as he heard of trouble at one of his estates and fighting between the two religious groups in one village, which means a few barns fired and cottages destroyed before order returns, so the last of our letters still follow him and he will not return just to comfort his sister, especially when he hears about James Ormonde's death and knows now that he was in the wrong,' Alice asserted with a hard expression in her eyes. 'My husband is not as soft as once I thought him to be. He loves me less now that he sees me growing up, and treats me as other husbands treat their wives, pleased to leave me with women and to go away and amuse himself where he wills.'

'Vincent has vast estates and many duties,' Lady Marian said. 'If you were not pregnant, you could have gone with him and I know how much he wanted your company, but Ireland and Scotland and the bad roads and dangerous paths are not for ladies in a delicate condition.' Marian rose and asked for her cloak. 'Sir Rollo was asking after your health and that of Sarah. He will call in a day or so and try to amuse her, but he has much to do in his own establishment and must report to the King and the Duke of York.'

'If only it was he who had to go to Ireland and

that Vincent had never left home to go to sea,' Alice said with passion. 'So many things might have been avoided, and Sarah and I would have been lighthearted girls with no babies to bother us.' She smiled, mistily. 'I remember how we used to ride together and raid the orchards for plums. I had such good times in the country, and then when we came to London we had all the young bloods eyeing us and making us feel beautiful.'

'You would have been in exactly the condition in which you are now, Alice. Vincent is your husband and made you with child before he left, so that would have been the same. The only difference would have been that Sarah might have been kept on a tighter rein and not met James Ormonde in private.'

'They met but a few times,' said Alice. She stared out of the window and saw nothing.

Marian laughed. 'They say that it takes but one bedding to make a child, and that more certain if passion is there and not the simple joy of marriage. Some women have babies more easily with certain men. If she had married someone of her brother's choosing, she might have taken longer to be made pregnant.'

'Then why do whores never have children, or very seldom?' asked Alice. 'They have many partners and some must be compatible.'

'Whores have disease and are made barren by it,' Lady Marian said with little true knowledge. 'I do not know why it is, but some say one thing and some another. I only know that I am to have a grandchild and will love it dearly: a child with hair as golden as yours was when the first darkness faded, and your eyes turned to an even brighter blue than the blue that all newly born have.' She paused by the door. 'Christopher was fair and Kate darker. Peter is darker too, but he is the image of his grandfather, and gets more like him every time he comes home. I must go as he is expected today. He will come to the theatre with us when Sarah is over her grief, and he needs clothes for his tour.'

The carriage was ready and she went straight home from the house on the Strand, eager to see her younger son who had left his school for ever and was no longer boarding at Eton. Edward was there before her, pretending that he had business at home and trying to hide his joy at seeing his young son again. Marian watched the two together and smiled. Peter was serious and quite good-looking but with none of the airs of the Court and no idea of his own importance. She felt relieved. He would do well abroad and she hoped would come home again without any of the puffed-up ideas that young men seemed to get from contact with France or Germany or Holland, but she dreaded losing him. 'Surely now that there is so much unrest abroad, it is better to tour our own country and to visit such places as Scotland?' she ventured.

'I want to see the treasures of Rome and Firenze, madam,' said Peter when they were over the first greetings. 'I paint and sculpt a little and would like to study more.'

'Then we have just the man to advise you,' said Edward, heartily, forgetting his first displeasure at the thought of having a Dutchman under his roof. 'We have a new friend, a good and honest man of good Dutch family who wishes to sit at the feet of Mr Lely and has met Rembrandt in Amsterdam.'

'We are no longer at war with The Netherlands, father. I can go there if he has addresses and gives me letters of introduction.' Peter laughed. 'It would be a good beginning to my tour, as France is not safe, and yet from Holland I can enter freely if I take a French-speaking companion.'

A movement by the door made him turn and pause. 'Sir Rollo Fitzmedwin,' the servant announced.

'Sir Rollo here? Do you receive him, Mother?' Peter looked surprised. 'After he left, all sorts of rumours flew about and I thought he was in exile.'

'He was accused falsely,' said Edward hastily as steps were heard on the polished wooden stairs. 'He has kissed hands with the King and been accepted in all society. He has a fine house in Pall Mall and is invited to all the houses of those who matter now.'

'You came from Holland, sir?' asked Peter as soon as introductions were made. 'I am about to embark on the Tour and would like your advice or that of your friend from Holland. I paint a little and would do more and must see the work of the great masters.'

'Go to Italy,' said Rollo at once. 'Study the old masters before you see the new ones like Rembrandt and Vermeer. Michelangelo can teach more after one afternoon gazing up at his work

219

than any artist living now.'

'I think that Holland is closer to home but might not be as free if our uneasy peace is broken,' said Edward. 'There might not be time to go there after travelling all over Europe. I hear tales from the Navy Office that treaties have been made with the Danes and with France against the ties we now have with The Netherlands. With no true parliament in session, the King does what he wills, and we suffer from it. Our ships are safe now in the Channel but are still attacked in the Straits by Spain and the corsairs, so you would have safer passage across to Holland and then by land to the other parts of Europe, and take your time over your journeys.'

'You are wrong to believe all you hear,' said Rollo, quickly. 'The country that gave me a safe haven is now our friend and we can depend on it being so for years, so leave that visit until you tire of the baroque and the overgaudy paintings of Italy.' He spoke with force as if Peter must on no account be allowed to go directly to Holland.

'Come now, sir, you praise Rembrandt enough, and as for Mr Lely, you said he was without equal. What has Italy to show the boy that we cannot supply? Study the English artists before you leave, my boy, and come with us into the study now. I will show you a painting that will live for ever. Sir Rollo praised The Italian School but he was speechless when he saw this portrait.'

Once more, Rollo gazed up at the picture of the woman who had haunted his mind ever since he last saw her, in spite of his marriage and now his return to the delights of his own country after exile. He had kissed many hands since his return, slipping back easily into his relaxed and elegant manners, to the amusement of Willem who had seen him only in the dull garments of the respectable Dutch businessman, with thick stockings and square-toed shoes that did nothing to show off a handsome calf, but none of the pale, soft and scented fingers had thrilled him by touch or suggestive pressure on his palm. He looked at the painted hands and recalled when they were less white and smooth than were portrayed so magnificently. Anna in a simple country dress with roughened hands from tending the sick captain who became her colonel husband: Anna making butter in the farm dairy in Surrey, and Anna riding with him across the Downs with her hair flying and her eyes bright with exhilaration, and Anna frowning at him when he interrupted her buying books in St Paul's churchyard during the plague.

'You were so nearly mine,' he whispered. 'But I have the copy of this.'

'What did you say, sir?' asked Peter.

'I have seen a copy of this in Amsterdam,' he said, but said nothing of the portrait now hanging in his private sanctum at the back of his dressing room in the new house.

'May I meet your friend, Sir Rollo? I would like to stay at home for a while and see more of Mr Lely's work and that of other artists and then may go, as you suggested, to Italy.'

Rollo was conscious of a great relief. If Peter or any other eager mind sought out the contacts that Rollo had made in Holland, then everyone would know of his marriage. 'That sounds an admirable programme, Peter,' he said. 'I can give you letters and if you take a tutor with you, then you will have the respect of many learned men who will know that you want to learn and not to fritter away your time with carousing.'

'There is such a man,' exclaimed Edward. 'Do you recall our son-in-law in Surrey, my dear?' Marian nodded, and Edward turned to Rollo. 'He is the rector there and his younger cousin is a curate who tutors the children of neighbouring gentry. George Silke would like his cousin to better himself and this might be the opportunity. A man who has travelled can obtain preferment on his return.'

'And how long will you be away, Peter?' asked Rollo, casually. Give me a year before you go to Holland, he wanted to ask. That would be enough time to decide what to do about a Dutch wife and my life here.

'I have told him to go for a year and a half and to write each month, with letters in addition to his own from the tutor, to let us know their progress. After that, if my son shows any bent for science or art, then he can go to one of the universities, at Leiden or here in London.' Edward looked pleased. 'Peter has more the mind of Anna, our dear ward. She has been as a daughter to us and had more brains than many a man.' He grunted. 'More sense in her little finger than any of my own children apart from Peter.'

'They are all happy and married,' said Marian, reproachfully. 'I would not have it different for any of them, and with Alice about to be a

222

mother, I shall want for nothing more.'

Edward laughed. 'She has the fashionable figure; one that is seldom out of fashion in the Court as Lady Castlemaine bears child after child for His Majesty. The pillow is a dangerous place for promises, and she is clever.'

'Gossip I haven't heard, sir?' Rollo raised an eyebrow. 'I am catching up but hear so many rumours that I know not if they be lies or truth.'

Edward paced the room. 'Poor Clarendon gained the hate of Lady Castlemaine and she has been working against him for months. The man has charm and estate and power as Lord Chancellor but gives no favours to the ones she loves, so she plots his downfall and he begins to topple.'

'If Clarendon had not been with him in exile, the King would not be on the throne now,' said Rollo, bluntly. 'He advised patience until the tide turned against the republic when Oliver died and paved the path to restoration.'

Edward shook his head, sorrowfully. 'I heard terrible tales and I believe them to be true. In spite of Clarendon making the treaty of Breda possible by his wise wording of the terms and his persuasion of all parties, which saved England from utter ruin and defeat, just at the crucial time, the young bloods were jealous and wanted him away. My Lady Castlemaine mocked him when the King demanded the Great Seal to be taken from him and given to Sir Orlando Bridgeman, a man who is popular enough but with none of the fibre of Clarendon.'

'It was said that she watched from her windows

overlooking Whitehall when Clarendon left after giving up the Seal,' said Marian. 'Lady Castlemaine has a wall covered in bird aviaries and she stood in there, in her nightgown, looking like a bird of paradise, herself, mocking his downfall. She hates him for marrying his daughter to the son of the Duke of York, and hopes that the King will make the Duke of Monmouth, her eldest bastard, his legitimate heir.' She looked sad. 'I grieve for Clarendon and hear he has left for France. There are so few men of manners and intelligence about the King and yet my daughter still dreams of becoming a lady of the Queen's bedchamber.'

'Vincent will be back again before the baby is born and he may then stay a while and take over his own responsibilities, for I can see nothing good for Alice if she persists in her ambition,' said Edward. 'My task should be at an end once my daughters are married but there seems to be no end to it with Alice. I fear that she connived with Sarah over her lover and once Sarah is over this shock, they will be as thick as thieves in some other mischief again.'

Rollo gave a half-smile. I sound like a solid citizen of Amsterdam, he thought. A year ago I might have wooed the lady myself when her husband was away or one like her, thinking her fair game, and now, I spend my time with older men and try to keep Willem out of the clutches of loose women! 'May I bring Willem de Graeff to call on you again, Lady Marian?' he asked.

'Bring him to dinner tomorrow after you have seen the Duke and tell us the latest gossip,' she replied, smiling.

Rollo walked out to his carriage and watched the faces of passers-by as his coachman took him back to Pall Mall. There was more colour here and more noise than he recalled in Amsterdam except in the square by the old weigh-house where business was done. The coach passed by St Giles Fields and the grassy mounds that hid the plague pit, still avoided by any who passed that way, and he stared fascinated at houses awaiting destruction to make way for new roads, with the faded red crosses marking the tragedy of the pestilence, painted on the neglected doors.

His own new house was bright with gilding and colour, a small army of servants striving to make everything neat and beautiful, with men carrying mirrors and huge candle-holders, swathes of hangings and fine carpets to deck the reception rooms, but Rollo could picture only one woman to grace this mansion, not the simple girl he had married to help him in exile. Willem handed him letters from Holland and opened some of his own from his parents in The Hague and from another artist.

'They tell me that some of your Court plot an alliance with France, *menhir*,' said Willem, in a thick Dutch dialect that he used when annoyed with Rollo. 'Is not our word good enough for you popinjays?'

'Our word and our women,' said Rollo, grinning. 'I hear that you bussed the pretty girl in the ale-house by the Stairs while I was with the Duke. Who was the man keeping himself clean for Marijke, Helena's sister?'

'Is she not clean?' Willem spoke in his normal voice.

'As clean as any Dutch whore but better in bed, I hear.' Rollo unfolded the letter from Helena. 'I can only tell you what I hear. I am a married man, and seem to have lost my taste for whoring.'

'You love a dream, *menhir*,' said Willem, acidly. 'You keep faith with your body but not with your heart, and you will shrivel up if you keep celibate.'

'Come, my friend. I may have news for you tomorrow. Mr Lely has accepted my letter and will consider taking you. Is that better than any minx with the pox? There will be better women and more company for you if you take lodgings close to his studio. You dislike all this, and like a true Dutchman, count the cost of every extravagance you see until it eats a hole into your mind.'

Willem looked relieved. 'I like the family we visited and will go there as often as I'm invited, but all this is too much for my comfort. Find me lodgings and I will move tomorrow.'

'First we drink jenever together and then decide what to do. I shall keep a room here for you and it will be your duty to come here often when I am away, to see that all is well if my squire or agent cannot be in London.'

'You have some really old Dutch gin?' Willem laughed. 'I might have known you would bring the best of Holland with you and leave the worst for ever.'

'For ever?' Rollo looked startled. 'Not for ever. I have a wife and property there and must return.'

'You have already left Helena. How often do you pine for her and long for her in bed? You may go back, but you will never be the same man to them. I have watched you emerge as a butterfly in your fine clothes and fancy manners. Could you wear the fustian jacket and lace collar again, under the straight sober hat?'

'When in Amsterdam, yes, but here, I am English and would look as out of place in Dutch garb as I would in silks in Amsterdam!' He looked annoyed. 'You enjoyed the theatre and the ale-houses, and the fine clothes of the Royal Family when we saw them in Tothill gardens.'

'I saw a pageant, not people,' said Willem. 'One vast circus of painted faces and rich apparel, with mutterings in the crowd that were ignored by the mighty. Such cries of 'A barren Queen', and 'whore' when the Lady with the King drove by.' He frowned and drained the small glass of fiery jenever. 'I walked to Tyburn and saw that the Dutch are not the only nation to flaunt their gallows' meat.' He gave a bitter smile. 'You string them up high but we put them higher from the windows of the Weigh House, on the hooks used for raising goods and furniture, but they die the same death unless they are quartered and drawn.'

'You gazed at one face enough,' said Rollo. 'One face with the Royal party made you forget that you despised all such pomp.'

Willem blushed. 'They say that Frances Stewart does not bed with the King and yet he loves her.'

Rollo smiled. 'Enough to make her the face of Britannia on the Breda Medal,' he agreed. 'It isn't always the lady who falls to our charms that we love the most, and My Lady Stewart is much loved and doesn't fill a nursery with bastards for the King to support.'

A manservant stood waiting for his master's attention and Rollo followed him to a room where many suits of clothing were displayed. He examined several, asking the man what was now worn at Court for an audience and at last selected a richly embroidered tunic of crimson velvet with dark grey pantaloons and pale green stockings. He tried on a wig and frowned, preferring his own natural and abundant hair but bowing to the inevitable, and when he was shaved, bathed and dressed ready to meet the Duke of York the next morning, he was a picture of elegant good-breeding and taste, his carriage shone and showed the mark of his rank and family and the new gold and green uniforms of the footmen and coachman were dashing and opulent as any driving down Pall Mall.

Whitehall was a flurry of movement as the King was in session with some of his advisers, and the Navy Secretary walked past Sir Rollo, followed by clerks carrying bundles of papers with heavy seals attached to them, but Rollo was admitted without undue delay to the offices of the Duke. Rollo took pleasure in the warmth of his reception, still cautious after his time abroad, and waiting to hear if the King had plans for his future.

'Men of rank who speak other languages are precious to our Court,' the Duke said. 'Doubtless, you have duties within your own estates and with the investment of your monies, but we have a prior call on your allegiance, Sir Rollo.' He paused but Rollo made no comment. 'His Majesty requires diplomats of the highest integrity to make a good impression on our overseas lands and the men working there. He needs loyal subjects to report the truth about conditions in our colonies and to suggest ways of bringing wealth to our treasury. You speak French and Dutch and some Spanish. You made an extensive tour when you were fresh from school and know the Courts of Europe.'

'I have not been to France for many years, sir, and in the present climate I would hesitate to think I might be of use there.' Rollo tried to appear unconcerned. France was close to Holland and Helena might be more willing to live there than in England which she considered much more foreign and across a dangerous sea.

'Not France. Any man can sit in that Court and act for us. His Majesty would wish you in another place where we have to send a new Governor. Have you heard of Tangier? It is a sorry rough place on the coast of North Africa with little to commend it at present, but we need to have a governor there with all the elegance and power of any of our diplomatic courts. We have appointed a governor but as yet he balks at leaving England until his palace is ready.'

'What use would I be in such a place?' asked Rollo. His mouth felt dry as if he was confronted with something of great moment.

'You could make sure the palace is ready and pave a way for His Excellency before he arrives to take up his post. There are local rulers who have been recalcitrant in the past but now seem more amenable due to the behaviour of our military men stationed there, but they remain convinced that we are a poor country with no riches to expend on our representatives. Outward show is everything to the Emperor of Morocco and his sherif at Tangier and I hear the Dutch and Portuguese make a fine show in their colonies, even if they live on a spit of land no more than dust. Now we have peace of a kind, we can show what our Court can provide.'

'Their allegiance was made necessary by force of arms, sir?'

'Partly, but they know that we treat our prisoners with justice as good as we mete out to our own men and the women are safer than they were when first we took them prisoners and made them slaves and whores. The bagnio where we keep prisoners is not full of starving wretches and many are exchanged for our men who are imprisoned in the bagnios of the sherif. Besides, we have a garrison of fourteen hundred men and three hundred slaves working on the Mole there, which is the reason we bother with that strange and alien land. All these to guard three hundred people living there but we have made trading profitable for many of the tribes, so there is less trouble.' He watched the pale face of the young man and sighed. 'It is not a popular place for soldiers or clerks or courtiers and His Excellency is blenching at the idea, but we shall be grateful for your presence there, just to arrange the more pleasurable of the routines and the comfort and supplies of food for the Governor's Court. You may have good sport there, shooting and hunting what game there is in the desert. There must be something!' The Duke looked uncomfortable, convinced that the picture he painted of life in Tangier was very short of comfort and pleasure and a young man would be bored and frustrated there. 'Take your own servants if you wish and a friend or so. Even a mistress if that is necessary and you cannot stomach Berbers.'

'I can think of no place where I would rather be, Your Grace,' said Rollo, firmly. 'If you will give me leave to arrange certain matters I shall wait on your orders.'

The Royal Duke looked at him as if he was mad and seemed at a loss for the words that he would have used if he had met with a very natural resistance to his orders. 'So be it, Sir, and accept our profound gratitude for this show of loyalty. We wish you to leave in six weeks time and come here first for papers and details such as we know of the place.' He smiled, graciously. 'When you have done what you can, we may send you to France or Rome in comfort, or give you leave to live on your estates if you have no longer a love of London.'

'Is the Mole finished, sir?'

'No, it needs as much again and then may be of great use to bring supplies and act as a haven for ships in the Straits and in the Mediterranean Sea.' He sighed. 'I am a sailor and love the sea. I would come with you if I could but affairs of state make the Court uneasy if I am parted from these shores and in any danger. The young men go abroad and leave us to worry. My Lord of

Monmouth has left after his illness and seeks the amusements of the French Courts, but we remain to keep the throne safe.'

Rollo bowed low and left the presence, his mind confused as if he dared not believe the orders he had been given. Tangier, with its desert and hardship, its heat and disease, and its one priceless jewel, the wife of Colonel Bennet, his beloved Anna was there waiting for him. He walked by the river, telling his coachman to pick him up in two hours time by Whitehall Stairs and the ale-house there, and he sat brooding over his ale and thinking of his future. Anna was there but would she receive him after their parting? Had she ever known that he was on the point of abducting her before he had to flee the country? Her face had shown her attraction and if he had stayed, would she have given up the idea of marrying her colonel and settled for Sir Rollo Fitzmedwin?

The river ran fast after heavy rain and the small boats tossed by the sides of the small jetties, awaiting custom. Clerks with bundles of papers and seamstresses with new gowns in wooden chests embarked to take the tide and the quicker route to the City by water, instead of venturing over the rutted and badly repaired roads that still hampered travel by hackney carriage after the fire.

Rollo ignored the glances inspired by his rich clothes that showed him to be a courtier of substance, and went back to his carriage. Six weeks, he thought. Six weeks to plan what I must do, for this post and for my approach to Anna.

Chapter 13

The cry of a baby came from the back rooms where Debbie and Sam lived. Debbie closed the door and went up to the boudoir, easy in her mind that the nursemaid would look after her baby and little Lottie Kate. Her dress hung in ill-fitting folds but there had been no time to alter them after the baby was born and she had been glad to wear extra layers of clothing during the cold weather.

Lady Marian looked up and smiled. 'Debbie! This is a surprise. Are you sure you are well enough to climb stairs and begin your duties again?'

'You are so good, My Lady. I am well enough,' said Debbie firmly. 'Most women lie-in for only ten days but you insisted that I lay by for three weeks, and now I am ready for work.' She sat on the stool that Lady Marian indicated and smiled. 'I came instead of the new cook so that I could ask what you would like for the master's supper when the guests come.'

'How are the babies? I must come down today. I haven't seen them for over a week and yet I wished to do so.' Lady Marian sighed. 'Miss Alice and Miss Sarah have taken up much of my time and Sir Rollo is a frequent visitor and will be until he leaves for Tangier.' She laughed. 'He has changed more than I thought possible. He seeks our company and asks about every member of our family and eats with us nearly every day.'

'Miss Anna is in Tangier, My Lady. Does Sir Rollo know of that?' Debbie looked very curious. 'We all thought, that is the servants gossiped, that he was in love with Miss Anna and tried to seduce her.' She spoke with the freedom of a friend as well as a trusted servant. 'He was a bold fellow before he left for Holland. All the girls liked him and he liked far more than was right!'

'And now, Debbie? Does he kiss the maids behind doors?'

'No, he teases them and once or twice has pecked a cheek but that is all. Henrietta tries to see him whenever he comes to the house but he doesn't take her to bed.'

'Exile has made a sober man of him or as sober a man as one with his charm and looks could ever be. He becomes more gallant with the ladies but none of the ladies with young daughters have been fortunate to catch his eye, and all at the theatre watch to see to whom he hands favours, but he is impartial, enjoying the company of ladies and a mild dalliance, but no more.'

Lady Marian put down her hairbrush and looked at Debbie more carefully. 'Is that your best gown, girl? It looks as shapeless as a rag and you must not wear it when Mr Verney is here.'

'I'm sorry, ma'am, but the seamstress has quinsy and lies in bed at her home. There has been far too much household linen to mend while I was lying-in, for any time to be spent on my own dresses, and if I am to take up my duties now, I shall be hard put to find time for sewing.'

'Do you know of a girl, who would come in? I have thought for a time that we need another girl to see to the linen and take the lace for bleaching.' Marian looked sad. 'Sarah made a good habit that I find hard to break but she will never go to the marshes again on that or any other errand.'

Debbie began to speak, then hesitated. 'I do know of a woman who would like to come here, My Lady,' she said, almost reluctantly. 'Perhaps you would like me not to mention her as she was once in Miss Alice's house, and was dismissed.'

'Margaret?' Marian smiled. 'She would be excellent. She was dismissed by a whim of my daughter when she was ill with morning sickness and thought that all the world was against her. Tell Margaret to come tomorrow and start on your dresses at once. She was a good worker and one that I wished was here long ago.'

'Thank you, My Lady. I'll ask Sam to tell her when he calls for Mr Verney to bring him home. She can stay downstairs where Miss Alice will not be tried by seeing her face, and I know she will work hard and serve you well. She lives with her widowed mother just five minutes away from here and could come in each morning, when the sewing light is good.'

'I shall not mention this to Alice and you must keep it to yourself, too, Debbie. My daughter is prone to many strange moods and I have fears for her mind when the baby is born.'

'She is so young, My Lady. This sorry tale of Miss Sarah has done nothing to comfort her. If my Sam had ever been as hard as Sir Vincent then I would have given birth to a monster,' said Debbie, sadly. 'She needs her husband now and she needs to see his sympathy for Sarah, or both babies will be born to sadness.'

'Sir Vincent had a hard time as a boy, being nowhere near the inheritance of those estates until his brothers died, but now he has wealth and power, he revels in it and is less than the amiable son-in-law I hoped to have.' Marian looked pensive. 'He will come back if he has a son, I think, but he will leave Alice alone for many months whenever the mood takes him.'

'I will make sure that everything is ready for tonight My Lady, and keep out of the way when Mr Verney is about until I look respectable. The dresses I wore before I was pregnant are too tight and these are too loose, but I bless the day I met Sam. He is a good man and a loving father.'

Debbie hurried down the back stairs as the carriage made a shadow over the window, and she called to the cook that the master was home and would be hungry. The two babies were asleep, the baby boy in his crib and Lottie lying where she drooped over their rag dolls and the rattle that Sam had made from a hollowed piece of wood filled with acorns. Debbie sighed. Soon, Sam would come in and kiss her, look at the sleeping children and demand his dinner. Soon, they would be able to sleep together again and be husband and wife and live out their contentment. Her eyes misted with tears. 'God is good,' she whispered. 'Nothing more can happen to hurt this house or this family ever again.'

'We shall miss you, my boy,' said Edward Verney when he stood with Rollo by the fire waiting for the rest of the invited guests to arrive for supper. 'We have come to depend on your visits to hear all the gossip of the Court and what is happening in Pall Mall.'

Rollo smiled. He recalled the suspicion and anger in the older man's face when he thought that Rollo was a rake and a mountebank. 'I shall be loath to leave you, sir, but it comes at the right time. I believe that my presence within your walls would embarrass you once Sir Vincent returns and knows I am here.'

Edward stared at him and then looked bemused. 'I forget, sir,' he muttered. 'I forget much that happened when the world was a sad and bitter place and many things happened, now best forgotten. You have been the perfect knight since your return and have done much to ease the tension with Sarah and Alice. They look on you as a brother who amuses them and sees to their care, and I would trust you with either of them alone. It is almost as if you are a married man who has no inclination to stray.' He laughed, mistaking the flush on Rollo's cheeks for embarrassment, and not for the sudden fear that Edward might have heard rumours of his marriage to Helena. 'Not marriage, then, but a passion for a mistress far away in some foreign land?'

'A man may have many passions, many preoccupations, sir,' said Rollo, 'None of them about women or marriage. I have collected many books to take with me as I hear the culture of the

Africans is indeed alien and I suffer from *ennui* without entertainment. I may be gone but a short while but His Majesty will have his say in that. He could keep me away from England for many months and I shall need occupation.'

'You have changed, and it is not all because of your exile,' said Edward, bluntly. 'I can no longer recognize the insolent buck that made many matrons fear for their daughters, including my wife! Youth must out and slake its lusts but the shadow of the Tower must have had a sobering influence.'

'I am free of that accusation, sir, and the simple life of Amsterdam made me know what to value in friends and possessions. I came back to find my squire Alan had kept faith to the last ear of corn on my estates, and my fortunes are intact, and you made me welcome.'

'You will meet Anna, no doubt,' said Edward, eyeing him with ill-concealed curiosity. 'I believe that Tangier is a small place, with the British enclosed within a kind of prison wall.'

'Not as bad as that, sir. I have maps of the area and it shows compounds, and farms and stores spread over an area like a small village, with walls to keep out the sand and the marauding tribes. They have horses and camels and livestock and a hospital for the sick and wounded.'

'Anna has written about that,' Edward said, and showed her last letter to the man who now took it eagerly. 'She finds the life hard but does her best to tend the sick even with few medicines and none of the herbs she used here.'

Rollo laughed as he read the last of the letter.

I wish they would send more for the sick instead of some painted popinjay to smooth out the cushions for the Governor's palace. Rich tapestries and fine furniture may be good for show and to impress the sherif who dangles riches in front of everyone as bribes for services or just for allegiance, but I would rather find a surgeon and more physic on the next ship that calls at the Mole.

'She sent to my brother for plants and laudanum but they perished on the voyage through bad stowing and so she must wait for more, packed in wood and straw to keep out the heat and damp, but the hold or deck is no place for such perishables.' Edward put away the letter, pulled at the skirt of his coat and made sure that his periwig was straight. 'I hear carriages,' he said, and a few minutes later, the shouts to the groom had faded and the sound of voices preceded the company.

Rollo frowned. It was a rare thing to have Edward in this mood to talk about Anna and to show him her letters, and there were so many questions he wanted to ask but must not show too much interest in the answers. He straightened his shoulders and smiled in the practised way of the courtier, kissing hands and paying compliments and being amusing. Alice looked very pretty and her high-waisted gown flowed over her stomach and was elegant in the fashion made popular by Lady Castlemaine who seemed hardly ever without a child in her womb. Sarah looked pale and her growing mound made her seem even thinner in contrast, as she had none of the softness that Alice showed in face and hands and in the lovely translucence of her skin. Her eyes still showed her deep sorrow and bitterness, as if the memory of James Ormonde was eating away her substance and her heart and her hatred of her brother ruled her mind.

'Dr Verney says that we may have our babies at the same time,' said Alice. 'My dear Sarah and I can comfort each other and lie in the same room.' She turned to Rollo. 'I have brought gifts for Anna. If you could take them for me, I would be sure that she receives them. The carpenter has made a box that will secure them against the journey and I know that my mother and sister Kate will ask you to take their small gifts, also.'

Rollo steadied his hand round the slender stem of his wine glass. 'Any service,' he murmured. 'Dr Verney might like me to take his offerings, too. I shall have a cabin, small but adequate, where I can see that these things come to no harm.'

'Even Daniel Bennet cannot turn you away if you bear our gifts,' said Alice, with a calculating smile. She glanced at him in a knowing way and he realized that Alice knew that his desire for Anna had not faded.

'I shall deliver them, madam,' he said, stiffly. 'After that, I shall have my duties with the governor's business.'

She looked disappointed, and went over to talk to Willem who was trying to appear more sophisticated than he felt in such company. 'Tell me about life in Amsterdam,' she asked him, with an air of innocence. 'How did Sir Rollo fill his time and what happened there to make him dull?'

'Dull, *Mevrou?*' Willem looked across to the velvet seat where Rollo sat with Lady Marian and the daughter of a ship-owner who wanted nothing more than a closer contact with the handsome young man. 'Sir Rollo lived as all the Dutch live, with less excitement than London offers but with good solid fare and good ale, and the old jenever that Mr Verney likes so well.'

'He had a mistress there?' Alice said suddenly as if to surprise Willem into some admission that he would not want to tell her.

'No, madam!' Willem regained his wits. He glanced at Rollo and set his mouth firmly. 'Rollo is my friend and patron and did nothing in Holland to cause a single eyebrow to be raised. He pays me well to study here and I owe him my future.'

'And acts mighty dull as if he is enchanted in another place,' said Alice. 'He is too old for me and for Sarah but is useful as an escort and one who satisfies my father with his care of us.'

Willem grinned. 'You are not looking for a lover, madam?' His glance travelled over her maturing body. 'Another month or two and you will be unable to risk a liaison. None misses a slice of a cut cake but after, there is danger.'

Furiously, she flounced away and Rollo came across to his friend as soon as he could tear himself away from the infatuated girl with Lady Marian. 'You annoyed the lady?' he asked.

'She was too curious about your life in Amsterdam, Rollo. That one is dangerous. I suggested that she wanted a lover before it could make another baby, and she was angry.'

'The devil you did.' Rollo tried to contain his amusement. 'Thank God that you have all the coarseness of a Dutch artisan, my friend! She will ask no more questions.'

'You found me lodgings, Rollo? I find it impossible to work in that huge palace you built. The servants grumble if I spill a little paint and the light in the room in which I sleep is not good.'

Rollo wrinkled his nose. 'It is time you found a sty to stink out with turpentine. I have rented two rooms with a good skylight which you can unlock tomorrow and then tell me what you need for furnishings. It does nothing to sever your duty with me,' he asserted, to stem the burst of gratitude he knew was threatening, and sent him to find some more Rhenish wine.

Marian saw that all the guests were well-supplied with sack or wine or ale and the servants in full livery passed dishes of sweetmeats and savouries among them. 'My heart went out to the poor wretch,' one man said with a cautious glance to see who was listening. 'I believe he would have been happier as plain Edward Hyde and not the Duke of Clarendon. Envy, my dear sir! Envy and the malice of men and women lacking his great attributes have caused this impeachment. I never thought I'd see the day when the King gave consent for his plea for mercy to be burned at the Gibbet by the public hangman. His Majesty would do well to study who was loyal when he was cast out of his own country and did much to bring him back to favour.'

Edward looked uneasy. 'Flattery and the love of women who mould the royal heart and mind now rules the country. There are murmurings in the Navy Office that the lack of funds cannot go unheeded for ever and that privateers no longer bring such good spoils for the privy purse. I have given up such traffic and am now content to let other men deal in slaves and human suffering. They say that many blacks are like us and have feelings of love and hate and gratitude. Many men swear by their loyalty and intelligence and some have been given Christian burial in this country. If they have souls, I want none of that trade and neither will I have black footmen for my carriage or I would lose Sam my coachman.'

'What of Eurasians?' asked his friend.

'Sir Rollo says that many Dutch and Portuguese marry such wenches as they find in the colonies. They make shift with what they can find and it is said that necessity is the mother of invention and the father of the Eurasian! Many are beautiful in a foreign way and learn fine manners but some have ideas above anything they have known and refuse to pick up even a handkerchief, and wash only when they have to appear in public with their men.' He sighed. 'Come and see the portrait of our ward, Anna, who is serving with her army officer husband in Tangier. She deserves a gentler life but bravely sits there with her husband and tends foul wounds and the fluxes caused by the heat and bad food. When the new governor goes there, civilized company may be more available, but the country is hard and there are few white women with whom she can have social contact.'

'Hard indeed, sir, and my wife would refuse to serve in such a country, but Colonel Bennet is a very fortunate man for many reasons. If I and others like me who had no opportunity to make the Tour, had women like that, we could pursue adventure and explore strange lands,' said the portly businessman who had seldom ventured from his home in Chelsea as far as Greenwich or Reigate. Edward smiled. It was the men who sighed over faraway places who would be alarmed if faced with the opportunity to visit them.

'My daughter Alice is another who would like to travel. Her condition forbids it now, but she may well go with her husband when he returns from his estates and the child is born,' said Edward. He watched Alice with growing apprehension. She was blooming and even prettier now, flirting with the last guest to arrive, the son of the English Ambassador to France.

'And have you seen the French Court?' she asked, her eyes bright with interest that the young man found flattering. 'Is it true that the clothes are finer than any we see here, and the food is exquisite?'

'I was there as a child before we fell out with the French and my father decided to stay there with my mother and aunt and left us children with tutors and servants and my old Grand-dam to care for us, but I remember fine buildings and beautiful women and men dressed in so much lace that they frothed like the cow parsley growing in the hedgerows.'

'Sarah and I used to deck ourselves with it and pretend to be at the Court of St James,' said Alice, wistfully. 'But we are grown up now and fancy real lace, real beauty and polished manners such as the French have.' She took a small orange and peeled it slowly, taking the peel in one piece as she unwrapped it from the top of the fruit and she had a winding stream of golden peel. 'Do you see your father's counterpart?' she asked, casually. 'I suppose there is a Frenchman for every Englishman, each in the other's country?'

'I know nothing of the new diplomatic circle but I met Le Comte Marc Lefèvre before he went back to Paris and then on to Guinea.' Mr Hoxton looked important. 'I rode with him once and spent a night playing cards with his party. My French is good but I lost my money,' he added, ruefully. 'The French have no hearts. They knew I was a novice but played to win everything I had, but my brother who is older came in and forbade me to continue. He won some money again and the French were annoyed.' He sighed. 'I long to join my father and learn to fence and to play at cards and to do everything I have been denied by not making the Tour. My father says that I might be abducted if foreigners knew I was the son of an important man and he dares not send me away.'

Alice sighed in sympathy. 'This Count Marc? Is he tall and very dark with bold brown eyes and a scar on his cheek?'

'Yes, Lady Clavell, he is like that. You must know him well to describe him so.'

245

'He came to see my father and we met, briefly,' she said. 'It was of no account. He was gone before I saw him close.' She lifted the orange peel and smiled. 'Now who shall be my lover? The shape of the peel as it falls will tell all.' She laughed as if it was a great joke and Mr Hoxton began to peel his own orange, carelessly so that the peel broke in half. 'You will have half a love, a girl who does not return your attentions, and will play you false,' said Alice.

She tossed the peel over her shoulder and turned to see what form it took, then caught it up swiftly before he could see the letter L that it made on the polished wooden floor.

'What was it?' he asked.

'What could it be but a V that shows my husband is faithful to me,' she said, lightly, but her breath came fast as if she suffered a great shock. Was it possible as the witches swore, that to mention a man with whom a woman had been close, it conjured up his image and his influence for good or evil? She almost felt the strong hands and smelled the French pomade and male smell that had come, through the stupor and the passion he had inflamed in her body.

Supper was announced and Alice was scolded for eating oranges and so losing her appetite for the good venison pie and the salmon served cold on a bed of lamb's lettuce. She picked at some fowl and ate an oyster or two, more to satisfy her mother than to serve any need she had for food. Sarah ate little, but this was usual and she was never upbraided for it. Sorrow was her excuse and the slight cough that went with her loss of weight was put down to fatigue. She drank more of the milk straight from the cow and Lady Marian looked on helplessly as Sarah would listen to no one about her health.

'You drink too much milk, my dear,' she ventured. 'Many believe that unless the milk is cooked, it brings bad lungs and bloody fluxes. I shall ask Dr Verney for coltsfoot for your cough and a plaster if it gets worse.'

Sarah smiled in such a way that Marian felt old and ignorant, and Sarah ate a little venison, as if it had been her intention to eat when the mood took her.

Another shout for the groom made Edward look at the timepiece by the wall. 'My brother comes late, as always,' he said. 'Bring more sack and another dozen oysters, girl. Where is Debbie? She looks after us better and sees what we lack on the table.'

'She will be back at work tomorrow,' promised Marian. 'Her dresses were a disgrace so she keeps away from the drawing room until they fit again. One will be ready to wear tomorrow and we shall have our own Debbie to serve us as we wish.' She smiled, pleased that the mending and making would be done well and that Margaret would be of use to her. She saw Alice talking in an animated way and hoped that her bad moods were passing. In time, she might be told of Margaret being downstairs and might even want her back again to work for her. I'll keep this to myself in case it upsets her again, Marian decided. The evening was going well and it was as yet only midnight. Some had settled to cards and some to dancing and the rest sat and talked and drank more strong wine and settled the problems of the whole world.

Willem was slightly tipsy on jenever and Rollo sent him home in a hackney, unwilling for wine to loosen the man's tongue and make him boast of what he knew of Holland, and the fine house that Menhir Fitzmedwin had built for his wife on the Herengracht. Rollo remained sober and sat with Dr Verney while he attacked a good supper with all the hunger of a man who had eaten nothing since noon and then only a piece of bread and meat.

'Mistress Verney does not come here with you, sir?' asked Rollo.

'My wife comes from Puritan stock and their influence will never leave her if she lives to be a hundred. She is a good wife and mother and will do anything to help the sick, but she despises the show that my brother finds essential to his life.' He helped himself to more salmon and filled his glass again. 'There are some things which can be changed and some that can't,' he said between mouthfuls. 'Women's hearts set on something can never be changed and the influence of a church is hard to break.' He attacked a slice of pie with his knife and speared a piece on the end which he waved about until Rollo thought it would fall on to the floor. 'Marry a wife and you accept a lot that you would rather leave with her mother,' said Dr Verney, briskly. 'If you can change something, then do but bow to what remains and let it be. I come here as often as I like and there is no acrimony because my wife never comes except for weddings and funerals and the birth of a baby. Marian visits us to bring treats at times and my wife loves her, but she is as out-of-sorts here as that young Dutchman must be in your new house.'

'So, if I married and my wife didn't wish to travel with me, I should leave her at home?' Rollo filled the glass with more sack. 'I was thinking of Vincent Clavell who has done that, and others of my acquaintance.'

'Best left behind and they probably breathe sighs of relief to be left so,' asserted Dr Verney. 'Now Anna is another matter. She follows her man and serves the sick. She might find she'd be happier back here after a while. Even I felt the strain of the pestilence and was glad to have done with it, even if it won me a handsome pension from the Crown. Anna is made of fine steel but steel can snap. I read her letters with anxiety and pray that she may come home before the horrors eat into her soul.'

'I am leaving for Tangier soon, sir. May I take anything of use to her, from you. I understand she needs herbs and plants.'

Dr Verney eyed him with interest. 'You may take her what I can cull and what you can get from the apothecaries and herbalists my boy, but see her, make her smile, tell her stories of London and the countryside she loves. Anna never did need jewels, even when she wears them well and with the confidence of good breeding, so leave such trifles behind if her family want to burden you with them. Get that artist of yours to paint pictures of farms and green grass and young calves, and take them if they are small enough. I will see that you take the right herbs and if you carry them under cover, they may survive better this time.'

'I have ordered some from Covent Garden, and they are to be wrapped in small packages so that no one plant or seed touches another kind, and so if some rot, some will be whole,' said Rollo. He flushed under the scrutiny of the doctor. 'I have read her letters and wish to help,' he said, stiffly. 'I knew her when the family were in Surrey and I admire the lady.'

'Take care of her, Rollo. I doubt if you are the man to do it, but see that she comes to no harm while you are there.' Dr Verney plucked a piece of cheese from a bowl and bit it into two. 'There are better things in this life than misery caused by strict rules, as Sarah found, but she, poor girl, might not enjoy the love of a child for very long.'

'What can you mean?'

'She has a disease of the chest which coltsfoot will ease but not cure and her child might take its toll of her strength. But that is Sarah. Anna should have happiness in her future and if she has to change, her life, well, I have seen too much suffering and misery because of the bigots who pass judgement without knowing what they say, ever to want her to suffer when she could live and smile again, here or wherever fate takes her.' He heaved himself to his feet and staggered slightly. 'Too much sack but a well-padded stomach,' he said, with a tipsy smile. 'I talk too much when I am in my cups. Take no notice my boy and come for the herbs when you can.'

Chapter 14

'Camels, My Lady!' said Azziza. 'Many camels.'

Anna heard shouts and running feet as men took up positions on the walls of the main compound and on the fort. She caught up her gown and struggled into it, feeling vulnerable when half-dressed, and yet unwilling for the growing heat of the day to take over. Women gathered together in the middle of the main inner compound where they would be safer from any firing or an invasion of the fort. Since the greater friendliness of the sherif and other representatives of the Emperor of Morocco, there had been no attacks on the fort or on the men building the Mole, and the sense of threat had lessened to such an extent, that now there was almost panic when an unfamiliar incident happened.

Daniel Bennet shouted to his sergeant to control the men and to show no sign of aggression. 'I see no arms and they look like servants and not soldiers,' he said. He climbed to the top of the tower and shaded his eyes with his hands. 'Put away your arms but stand ready with swords to form a guard of honour,' he said. 'We are being visited by the sherif.'

Anna hastily brushed her hair and changed her gown for another of finer cut and quality, and Azziza brought fresh water and Attar of Roses made from the blooms of damask roses grown in the oasis. Azziza smoothed hands oiled with jasmine lightly over Anna's hair to make it shine and to protect it from the sun, but Anna drew away, suddenly feeling as if she was a woman of the harem being prepared for a visit from her master.

'Prepare cool drinks and tell the cook to expect many men for rice and meat and dates.' She smiled. 'If the sherif is with them, then you can try the new dish I taught you and bring it when we eat.' Azziza hurried away, bursting with importance as she gave orders and made pastry from the fine white flour that had come on the last ship for the governor's stores, insisting that it was she who was honoured and no man must touch this English dish of almonds and fruit in a pie fit for only the highest. Anna smiled. It would be a strange dish in London but one adapted from what was available, and very palatable, if over-sweet in the Arab way.

The line of dust and slowly moving beasts came nearer and faces could be made out among the white robes and bright saddlecloths. The leading camel had a canopy under which the Sherif sat with jewelled sword and golden chains and all the pride of his race. Anna stood back with the other wives as the procession came through the open gateway under the arch to the barrack square. Daniel and the other officers stood to attention, and then Daniel, as senior officer on duty at the fort, stepped forward to greet the sherif who was now standing, surrounded by his bodyguard of Sudanese soldiers.

The women stared, half in admiration, half in fear at the polished black faces and the tall fine figures of the men who served the Sherif and now parted to let him greet the Colonel. The bodyguard went back to the shade with the camels.

The camel drivers unpacked huge hampers and sacks from the beasts and set them down until they were told what to do with them, and Daniel tried not to appear confused.

'I have brought what *Madame* Bennet requested, Colonel,' said the Sherif. Anna was conscious of the curious glances and the expression of fury on Dulcie's face as he spoke rapidly to Daniel's interpreter. 'Soil, *Madame*. I bring dirt like any slave and ask only where my servants shall lay it down for your plants.' He was laughing, fully aware of the impact his visit was making and amused at the thought of any woman wanting earth instead of precious gems, to grow plants to treat the sick and unworthy and the infidel.

Anna bowed and stepped forward. 'I was grateful for the two baskets I brought with me from the oasis, Your Excellency, and I have had a low wall built of stone to protect that and any more I could find in the hills.'

She called to Azziza to show the men where the earth must go and to find Ayesha who had more knowledge of such things and would oversee the operation, and when she turned again, Daniel had led the sherif away for cool water to wash his hands and feet and for refreshment in the new reception rooms of the governor's house.

Ayesha made the men fill huge pots of coarse clay that could be kept in the shade of the covered walks and the rest of the soil was piled up into the bed made by the new shallow walls in the hospital compound. In one pot, she planted green shoots from her own store and smiled. Kaif would serve at times instead of the medicine that the English used for sleep and pain. It brought peace and forgetfulness and was pleasant even for those not in pain, but with memories of better times than these.

Anna made arrangements for a meal, with the help of Dulcie who now became animated and anxious to make the visit a success. Dulcie's husband hovered close to the sherif and the other officers began to see that this could become the pattern of their lives if the Governor came and diplomatic relations were good in North Africa, but Daniel chafed at the waste of time. He had promised to visit the workmen on the Mole to decide if a ship should be sent to Lisbon for better supplies, with an officer to make sure that the stone that was required was sent this time, and not the inferior material that crumbled under water.

The well-tried method of pier-building, using blocks of masonry held together by cement and iron strengtheners on a bed of loose rocks embedded in sand, had done well if the right stone could be obtained. Many thought it might be better to adopt the methods employed in Genoa in the harbour there, when wooden chests filled with rubble were sunk instead of solid blocks, protected by ironshod wooden piles in echelon on the seaward side; but those who favoured the new method had never seen the storms and turbulence of the Atlantic sea and the heavy currents swirling round the half-finished Mole.

From time to time, Daniel watched his wife, who seemed to blossom in the company of the sherif, and with Dulcie, displayed all the hospitality and dignity of the governor's representatives. 'It's what they both need,' he murmured, and felt a twinge of conscience that he was depriving his wife of everything she had once found pleasant and harmonious. Even Dulcie was quite different when flattered and treated as a beautiful woman, complimented and made to laugh and left fluttering on the edge of dalliance.

The hot afternoon lost its flame and the sherif prepared to leave for his own home. 'First I must see what you have done,' he said as if asking a child to show him a favourite toy. He watched the men planting fresh roots from his oasis in the black soil now neatly raked over the bed, and shrugged.

'It will help the sick and wounded of all who come here for help, Your Excellency,' said Anna, quickly, but even after the caravan of loaded camels had deposited all the heavy baskets of earth, it looked a small bed and not as imposing as the sherif obviously expected it to be. 'I have kept some for plants from my country that do not like full sunlight and would wilt if planted outside,' she added. She smiled up at him, her eyes shining. 'It is the perfect gift and one that I shall remember all my life,' she said, simply. He kissed her hand and she saw that he was moved by her words, but a moment later, he called harshly to his men and was helped on to his canopied mount, without another glance in her direction.

'Earth, when he would have given you rubies?' said Dulcie later. She looked completely puzzled. 'I can't understand you, Anna. I would have asked for more silk and some of those pretty Arab slippers.' She sighed. 'But what a wonderful day! I feel as if I have just come from the theatre or from the Court and been treated as a lady of rank again.' She reached for another sweetmeat from the bowl that Anna had filled only half an hour earlier and which was now half empty. 'I know,' she said, and put it back again. 'I shall grow fat and then even my husband will not desire me.'

'You could take a sheik for a husband if you grow fat,' said Anna, smiling. 'I am worth but few camels.' Dulcie looked at her slim figure with envy and pushed the dish of sweets further away. 'There will be plenty of entertaining when His Excellency the new governor arrives with his entourage,' Anna said, consolingly. 'I met Lord Middleton once and he is a very amiable man, with few vices as I recall from what I heard.'

'His envoys arrive with the next sailing,' said Dulcie. 'A sloop from Lisbon came and the captain said that it had called in at the port for supplies and would leave there in a day or so. The new rooms are magnificent and even the Sherif was pleased to praise them.'

Anna yawned. 'I am weary and yet I have to see

two of the sick men before I sleep. Ayesha called me as soon as the sherif left and we plastered one of them but they are very ill with a fever.'

'I wonder you do not succumb to some foul malady,' said Dulcie. 'I shall go to bed smelling of sweet scents and hope that my husband notices me, while you will bring nothing but the stink of the hospital in your hair.'

Darkness settled over the distant Rif Mountains and the strange cries of desert animals made the silence quiver. Anna called for a guard to escort her over the empty spaces beyond her own house, and carrying several medicines, she walked to the hospital. A flash of lightning over the hills did nothing to break the dryness and she was glad to know that the plants from the oasis would have time to settle before bending to the force of a storm. Apart from her siesta, Ayesha had not slept for many hours and Anna hurried to find her and make sure all the treatments were finished before sending her firmly to bed.

'I am your servant, My Lady,' said Ayesha, surprised that any who owned her service would consider whether she slept or not. 'I can sleep here on a pallet and be ready when that one dies. He is of the Faithful and I must pray to Allah for him.'

'Pray now, and leave him. He will never hear or respond and you will have done your duty,' said Anna. She walked round the room and settled a man in pain with a soothing draught. She spoke to one of the soldiers wounded in a fight with another soldier and due for punishment as soon as he was fit for the lash, wondering when she must say that he was well again. Now, she gave him work to do among his fellow patients and hoped to persuade Daniel that he was of more use to her than lying groaning with bleeding weals on his back.

At last the room was quiet but for a few snores and groans and the sighing of the wind outside. She sat with Ayesha for a while, drinking tea made from hibiscus flowers and sugar. 'The sherif was generous, My Lady,' said Ayesha.

Anna saw that the woman dared not say otherwise but had something on her mind. 'What plants did he bring?' she asked.

'Plants for the harem, My Lady. Flowers to dull the senses and to make for love; plants to keep a woman's womb from filling and scented flowers that will perfume a bath or skin or make the hair shine.'

'No herbs of healing?' Ayesha shrugged. 'None of the plants I saw in the books I studied?' She closed her eyes. 'How can I fill the good soil with such things when I need herbs that will help the suffering?'

'You must not destroy them, My Lady. The Most High Sherif has spies who will tell him everything that you do. He will ask you if they thrive and if you have used them, knowing that I am familiar with their usage.'

'I have no use for them, Ayesha. I do not use such herbs.' The glimmer of a smile that was swiftly hidden made Anna stare. 'What have you given me when I was unaware of it? Has Azziza put herbs in my food?' She paled, realizing once again how much fell to chance in this harsh country, and how easily she could be poisoned by cooks or servants preparing her food. She remembered at least two women who had aborted their babies after Ayesha had given them bitter drinks, and she had wondered, with some relief, why she had not become pregnant since her marriage. Dulcie said it was due to the heat and the fact that men were less fertile in hot climates, but now, she had seen the glint of superior knowledge in the smile that Ayesha couldn't hide.

'I could have poisoned you, My Lady, but you are good to us and your husband is just. The other men are as men everywhere and they are nothing.' She spat on the ground as any good Muslim might do on the shadow of the infidel. 'The women they sent from England save our women from degradation and there are whores in every oasis, so this we understand, and the wives of the soldiers are good for money and business, so they live.'

She spoke with a chilling sense of reason and without rancour. The foreigner was within her country so must be exploited and tolerated for as long as it was acceptable. One day, the Emperor would lift a finger and all would change, but until then, she was a servant of the wife of Colonel Bennet and so had a certain status and had learned from her mistress things that would serve Allah when the foreigner had been driven away.

Anna looked at her half empty cup. 'And what is in that?' she asked.

'Nothing to harm you, My Lady. I drink of the same cup and there is nothing but a little Kaif to make you dream and to forget that there are sick men and that the desert will be there tomorrow and tomorrow.'

Anna called the guard and was escorted back to her rooms. Daniel was not there and had not returned from the Mole, so she ordered men to ride out and find him, following Daniel's own decree that if one of the officers stayed late and didn't return after dark, an extra escort should be sent to the Mole, in case of treachery among the local men.

She lay awake or rather in a half-sleep induced by the Kaif that Ayesha had given her. Her brain told her she should be anxious about her husband, but her body was relaxed and she felt no fear. How often had this happened? she wondered. There had been times when she had been angry with the dirt and lack of care shown to patients, and afterwards, she had calmed down and thought that she was being overzealous.

'In England you would be burned as a witch, and I'm not sure if that shouldn't be your fate here,' she said, into the darkness, but she recalled whispers about herself when she had once walked in the City of London and was named Anna Maria Ruyter, eyed with suspicion as a foreign Dutch spy and a papist, because of her dark eyes and colouring.

Daniel returned with the men she had sent to find him, weary and annoyed that she had obeyed his own orders and sent men to the Mole. 'There is much to be done there and we need more supplies. If we have nothing to shore up the latest rocks, they will be swept away again during the next storm. I have men working by the light of torches and fires and still they can not make all safe.'

'At least the sherif will not harass the men now,' said Anna, calmly.

He glanced at her, angrily. 'Not until he finds it less amusing to bring earth for a garden and remembers that you are only a woman.'

Anna felt her head beginning to ache and she was now wide awake. 'At least he treats me as a woman is treated in England if she has rank and good looks,' she said, with spirit. 'I have no fears that he will forget that I am your wife, Daniel, and I think my presence here has helped you more than you will admit; or ever know,' she added, thoughtfully.

'Then, madam, you will feel quite safe if I leave you for a few weeks?' His anger was mixed with guilt and Anna knew that he hated to tell her that he was going away. As always, he resorted to taking this high-handed way of saying something that he knew was not right or acceptable to her.

'Where do you go, Daniel? Has the sherif invited you to the oasis?'

He strode about the room, still fully dressed. 'I have to sort out business in Lisbon where our agents are buying masonry and iron and to negotiate for corn, and oats for the horses.'

'There are civilian clerks to do such work!' said Anna.

'There are, madam, but as they do nothing but savour the delights of the city, I must go and make sure that we have what is ordered and that no more money drips into the wrong hands,

261

before the new governor arrives.'

'When do you leave?' she asked, faintly. 'Can I not come with you?'

He pointed to the boxes that she had not noticed in the dim candlelight. 'I sent word to have my bags packed but you were not here, I suppose? My valet knew what I would require and I am ready to leave within two hours, when the cutter is cast off from the Mole. They say the wind is fair and we shall make good speed.' He saw her anxious expression and the sad dark eyes and took her face between his hands. 'I am sorry,' he said, awkwardly. 'You married a soldier and I must give the King my service. You will have two men with you wherever you go and the major for support in all you want for the hospital.'

'Cannot Dulcie's husband act for you? A major would take almost as much influence, with your letters, as you would if you go in person, Daniel.'

'And leave his wife to any who set eyes on her?' Daniel gave a short laugh. 'No, I am needed there and you will be safe, with Azziza and two guards.'

'Am I less of a woman than Dulcie? Perhaps I should accept the offer that the sherif made, of a eunuch to guard me!'

With difficulty Daniel controlled his voice. 'You were splendid with the sherif and he respects you. I know you to be a good and faithful wife and I have no fears for your fidelity. Soon, you will have the company of men and women of your own kind and I rejoice that you can have more amusement when they come.' He saw her tears and hastily embraced her. 'I shall be gone for no more than a month or so, and by then you will be busy arranging soirées with the new envoys and their wives. I must stay to see the ship despatched and follow by fast cutter which might even overtake the ship. One ship from England is in the offing and may well carry these new faces for you to see, Anna.'

'Who are these men, Daniel?'

'The envoy representing the governor is Sir Rufus Allin, a man of little consequence and one who will leave things much as they are.'

'I have not heard his name,' said Anna.

'Few have,' said Daniel, drily.

'And the other? The man who will oversee the house and the social contacts.'

'I have no idea. Enjoy their company if that is possible and make use of them. Open our house to them and if possible establish them amiably with the sherif.' He called and two men carried the baggage to the mules that waited outside.

'I must come with you to the boat,' said Anna, impulsively. Daniel hesitated, then nodded and shouted for another horse, and Anna pulled on a warm mantle that fell to the hem of her gown.

'The men will escort you home and I have given orders as to your safety,' Daniel said when they were riding through the darkness. He seemed subdued and uneasy. 'I hate to leave you my dear but I must. There will be packages and letters from home in the next cargo and you will find plenty to fill your time.'

'I am not a child,' said Anna. 'I cannot be bought by oranges! I am a woman without my husband and you offer me letters from friends.

What if you remain in Lisbon or go back to England? Do I tend the sick for ever or take a lover? Am I less in need of you than any woman of her husband? You smile at Dulcie and her little adventures but say nothing of my needs.'

'You are not like Dulcie. You are my wife and are conscious of your position. No man would dare to try to take you against your will and this is not the Court of St James where lax conduct is the fashion. I have no fears on that score, madam.'

'The Court of St James seems to come closer with that ship approaching,' said Anna when they stood by the Mole and Daniel's baggage was loaded on to the sleek cutter. She smiled, bitterly. 'I once said that I would follow you to the end of the world but I never thought that I might be left there, alone!' She watched Daniel's hard profile as he looked out at the lights on the ship, anchored and awaiting dawn and the men to unload her. The sherif has given me plants to make me desirable and to inflame my own desires! As a favour, she thought with a smile tinged with irony. They will flourish in such good soil but be wasted.

'Goodbye, my own darkling darling,' Daniel said in a husky voice. He kissed her with passion and released her quickly, and Anna watched with her hand to her cheek as he went on board. He had called her that now for the first time since a time in Surrey when he wanted her desperately but resented his own desires. Would he ever change? And if he did not, what was there for her?

264

Her hand felt rough on the saddle leather and she turned her back on the Mole and the boats moored there, ignoring the huge ship that was now threading a way to a safe haven near the shore. Anna gave the order to return sensing the disappointment of the guards who wanted to see the ship into harbour and talk to the sailors, but she was in no mood to indulge them and to stand waiting for perhaps two hours for the gangways to be put down. She stared at the rim of light beyond the Rif range and felt very tired. The bucks from London could wait. Dulcie was welcome to see to the honours and there would be far too much time spent in their company later to make the first meeting a hasty necessity, let alone a pleasure.

The sleepy servants were lighting fires and some were gathering the camel dung that had dried since the Sherif's caravan left the compound. Anna smiled. The dried dung was invaluable as fuel and far more use to her than the plants she now saw recovering from transplanting into the dark soil. Word spread that the ship from England was about to tie up and the kitchens in the new palace sent out fragrant smells of spices and fresh meat and the acrid background of charcoal stoves.

Anna slipped wearily from the saddle and walked slowly to her own house. Dulcie sat in the best chair and was already dressed in a fine silk gown and soft leather slippers. Her hair was carefully curled in huge puffs as she had heard was fashionable in London and she reeked of scent. 'I was in two minds whether to wait here or to ride to meet them,' she said. 'I thought you had done that and I'm surprised to see you return.' She put a hand to the unaccustomed rolls of hair and hoped they were pinned safely enough. Anna gave a tired smile. The thought of Dulcie riding with that hair style was incongruous and the expression of relief when she saw that Anna had not stolen a march on her, was amusing.

'I am tired. Daniel has gone to Lisbon and will be away for weeks,' said Anna. 'I shall go to my bed until Ayesha calls me if she is concerned about a patient.'

'You look worn out,' said Dulcie with satisfaction. 'I shall give orders that you must not be disturbed on any account. I shall see to everything,' she asserted firmly. 'I do not mind to what trouble I put myself if you are unable to take up your duties as hostess, but tell me, did you see the ship and did Daniel tell you anything more about our guests?'

'Only one, whose name escapes me, and the captain of the cutter didn't know the name of the other. Daniel didn't think that either would be a threat to our womanhood,' she added, to Dulcie's disappointment.

'I hope I have not wasted my time. I have been up for hours, ever since word came that the ship was sighted. My husband rode out to the Mole just after you left and must be waiting now. I asked Azziza to make tea but she hasn't brought it yet and said that you have none until the new stores arrive.' Anna ignored the innuendo that Azziza must have some hidden away, but had

266

orders not to give it to Dulcie, who used all hers quickly and then went to the various wives for more when she had none left.

'We can drink orange juice and water or some of the Arab tea that Ayesha makes so well,' said Anna, drily, wondering if Dulcie had tasted some of the Moroccan woman's concoctions.

'I had something she made and I was sick,' said Dulcie. 'I wonder if she is a witch and wants to poison us all.'

Anna began to remove her clothes. 'Tell Azziza to pull the blinds and to leave me to sleep,' she said. Dulcie left as soon as she knew that no tea was forthcoming, and Azziza flitted about the bedroom, making all tidy and taking away the soiled and dusty gown that Anna had worn on the horse.

Sounds that would normally have made her rouse herself, now faded into deep sleep and Anna slept while men hurried with horses and camels to fetch the stores, and sergeants and corporals barked orders to guard the influx of valuable food and equipment. Her dreams were strange and distorted and when she woke to drink some water, they merged with the sounds in the compound, and she didn't really return to full consciousness, but drifted away again in a lighter, more refreshing slumber until past noon.

'Azziza?' she called at last. 'Bring me tea and bread.'

'My Lady, they have come!'

'Who has come?' Anna sipped the hot tea and nibbled a piece of flat Arab bread flavoured with caraway seeds.

'The Lords from England and their servants. So fine, so much silk as if they were dressed for the seraglio and love.' She giggled. 'Even the sherif does not deck himself so when talking to his wise men.'

'They will find tight tunics and collars hot here, even in silk, and velvet is like a hot blanket under the sun,' said Anna, smiling at the vision of red-faced men turning almost apoplectic in the heat of the day. She felt cool and refreshed by her long sleep and called for a fresh cotton gown of deep rose pink. She put Arab slippers over her bare feet and brushed her hair until it shone in long swathes, caught up into combs at the back of her head. 'I must go to the hospital at once,' she said.

'Mistress Dulcie asked for you, My Lady. She asks you to dine at the governor's house today.'

Anna laughed. 'I have other things to do. She can enjoy the company of the men without me. Send a message that I am not rested and will see her later and even give her some tea!'

Azziza looked shocked but went to do her bidding. Anna walked through the heat to the hospital and forgot visitors, Dulcie and absent husbands as she helped a man struggle for breath and made poultices for fresh wounds from accidents at work on the Mole. Two men carried the dead body of the man with dropsy to the shed where the doctor would examine it later before burial, and Ayesha wailed the grief of her tribe for one of the faithful.

Dulcie sent a message again and this time, Anna felt a twinge of guilt. It was discourteous to ignore the visitors even if her duties took up her time. 'I shall send someone to escort you here for supper,' she read.

On an impulse, Anna put on the dress she wore in the portrait and was ready when Azziza came and hissed that there was a fine gentleman to see her. She picked up her shawl as the night grew cool and went into the lobby. Her guards stood by the door waiting to go with her at all times as their master had ordered, but between them, dressed in dull blue silk of a modest cut and muted finery stood the man she had never thought to see again.

'Mrs Bennet – Anna. Your servant, ma'am,' said Sir Rollo Fitzmedwin.

Chapter 15

The last hogshead of rhenish wine was rolled down the plank into the cellar and Edward Verney stood back, satisfied that it was safe. He consulted the list and found that Sir Rollo Fitzmedwin had been extremely generous, as supplies of Bleichert wine were hard to come by and it needed much influence to obtain it from the shippers. 'I shall miss the boy,' he said.

'We shall all miss him,' said Lady Marian when he returned to the drawing room, his periwig dusty from his inspection of the cellar. 'He left no gifts when he went to Tangier but ordered these to be sent two months after he left, to keep his memory fresh in our hearts.' She smoothed out the silver lace and the gold ribbons in the package now open on the table. 'He sent clothes for the new babies to await their arrival and something for Kate and Christopher as if it was their anniversary days. He met Kate again when she came for Mothering Sunday but he hasn't seen Christopher since our days in Surrey.'

'Christopher was ill-pleased to hear of Rollo's return, but that set of harness was far too good to be refused and I think that if they met now, or rather when Rollo comes back to London, they could meet on an amicable basis.' Edward frowned. 'He's changed and has given me no cause for regretting receiving him into our home again, but I wonder how deep this care goes?'

'What do you mean, Edward? He has brought laughter and company such as we have not seen for many a day and has taken away much of the anxiety I felt over Alice and Sarah. He has been tireless in amusing them and visiting friends and he worked hard over his books and Alan Denzil swears that he knows everything about his estates now.'

'He has changed.' Edward ran a hand over the sore patch on his chin, where the morning pumice had caught the skin painfully. 'I sometimes wonder why. I know the threat of the Tower must have affected him and he has spent a long time away from all he held dear, but there are younger, more amusing households to which he would be welcome, and many at Court who now strive for his favours. I would like to know what happened in Holland to make him so, and to know with whom he spent all that time, when the peace was only fragile and Breda hadn't been ratified.'

'He had means enough to live, with all the jewels he took with him and the revenues from Switzerland and France.' Marian let fall the soft silk and smiled.

'He had the jewels,' Edward admitted, 'But he said that his revenues came late and only just before he left for England. Someone was interested enough to take a handsome face as surety.' He shook his head. 'We did the same. Now that he has gone, I can think more clearly. His charm and presence blinded us to the reasons behind his actions. These gifts speak of future favours he wants from us or he would have

271

left with thanks and mutual regard and sent us letters, and perhaps visited us on his return.'

'You have all the suspicious mind of a businessman, Edward. The young man is sincere and charming and has taken a lot of trouble to convey our gifts to Anna.'

'To Anna! Yes.' Edward strode to the window and stared at the circular drive that had been newly covered with gravel of the best quality. 'And how will he be received there, Madam? Tell me that. Colonel Bennet has no love for him and Anna was attracted to Rollo, when Daniel was away and she had no hope of marrying him. You may think I notice nothing of what goes on under my nose, but at the wedding in Surrey when Christopher took his bride, Rollo had eyes for Anna and for Anna alone, and she was not indifferent.' He gave a short laugh. 'Women melt at weddings, into tears or lust, and if he had not fled that night because he was accused of murder, tell me what might have happened, Madam!'

'That is in the past and a part of Rollo's youth. He has gone with gifts, and Anna is married and living in a small community where every eye sees what happens. As the wife of one of the senior officers in Tangier, she will have no time for an alliance with a courtier. She is serious and concerned with the sick and as the months pass, will be even more so.'

Marian folded away the silks and ordered chocolate laced with sack, knowing that Edward would stay and talk if he had something to drink. 'I have heard nothing from Anna for longer than I care. I know that Daniel left for Lisbon just

272

before the envoys of the new governor arrived. This letter came on the same ship that brought them there so she had not met Rollo and the other man and his wife. We can but wait for the next ship and hope that all is well.'

'You have enough on your mind, my dear,' said Edward. 'Vincent should come home and see to his own stable! Those two young madams make me mightily impatient. Alice has a fancy that the two babies will be born at the same time instead of when the good Lord decrees. It is as if she can make it happen so, and will take no other opinion. She had a room prepared to take two beds and cribs for the babies and enough clothes for six babies.'

'She takes raspberry leaf tea and makes Sarah take some too, so that they will have easy births.' Marian poured out chocolate from a slender pewter jug and handed Edward the dish of almond fingers. 'I am worried about Sarah. Each day she looks more pale and her skin is almost transparent and her spirits are low. I sent confits and Dr Verney gives her horehound and coltsfoot and now orders lungwort for her cough, but she is no better. Their time is near and as Alice thrives, so Sarah wilts before my eyes and I think she will die.' Tears fell on the almond biscuit and Edward touched her hand, awkwardly. 'I know that your brother is the best doctor she could have, but I do fear for her, Edward,' she sobbed.

'If it is God's will, she will live,' said Edward without much conviction. 'I must go now. I will call in at the Strand on my way home and bring you the latest news, but today, stay here and

273

build up your strength or you will fall sick, too.'

Marian waited until the carriage left and the house settled down. She picked up the silks and lace and took them to show Debbie. More and more, Marian visited the nursery and longed for her own grandchild to be there if only when Alice was visiting. Debbie picked up the pail of soiled linen and handed it to the nursery maid to take away and covered the baby with a clean sheet. Her dress now fitted well and even if Debbie was plumper than before her marriage, she looked trim and every inch the housekeeper in charge of everything beyond the back stairs in the Verney household.

'Margaret is a good worker,' she said when Marian commented on the dress. 'She has altered all my clothes and now makes new covers for the chairs in the small salon, using the tapestries you gave me to have made up, instead of handing them to the woman who did the stool covers and brought lice into the house.' She laughed. 'There is always gossip when Margaret is here. I think she imagines the half of it, but she is shrewd and somehow learns secrets that I would never suspect were there to be learned.'

'Does she gossip about us? I wouldn't want her here if that was so. Lady Mortimer sent off her lady's maid when she was told that everyone in the ale-house knew of the price paid for every-thing new and even the colour of her ladyship's bedcurtains!'

'I have been firm and she knows better than to venture beyond that door, My Lady. When I told Sam about her, he was angry and said we wanted no second Mary Creed here and he would see that she never found out anything about us that could hurt us.'

For a moment, the two women looked strained, recalling the days when Mary Creed had brought so much unhappiness to the family, then Debbie smiled. 'Margaret has her cap set at Henry Crag who works for Sam, when there are more visitors with their own horses and Sam and the groom are hard-pressed to tend them all. He hopes to be taken on for good and Margaret fancies the rooms over the new stables.'

'I had no idea that she was so concerned with us,' said Marian. 'I'm glad you told me, Debbie. Good worker she may be, but she is not the kind I would want for a personal maid and from what I have seen when I come down here, she is far too sure of herself for a woman in her position.' She bent to look into the crib and touched the tiny hand curled over the sheet. 'The linen is whiter than it used to be, after Sarah set the habit for bleaching, and if Margaret does that and the making and mending, she has no call to put her nose into any other business here.' She regarded Debbie with affection. 'You manage so well, my dear, and have brought Sam much happiness. The maids are quiet and you keep the babies out of sight and sound of Mr Verney, so I'm sure you can manage one sharp-tongued woman who is not even a member of our household but here on trial to see if she suits us all.'

Marian left the nursery and peeped into the kitchen where a maid rolled pastry and another scoured the pots with silver sand. Sunlight shone on the glowing pewter and silver and the warm air showed no dust on the sunbeams. The comfort and orderliness soothed her and she tried not to think of Alice and her tantrums, and the reluctant feeling that perhaps this time, on the matter concerning Margaret, Alice had been right. There was something about the woman that made Marian think of a bird of prey about to pounce, but while waiting for the right victim, preened its feathers and showed its colours to impress any who looked at it, and so convinced the world of its innocence. She shook off the feeling but avoided the sewing room and went up to her boudoir.

Debbie prepared coffee for herself and for Sam who now had a liking for it, and as it was cheap, drank that more than ale while waiting for his master to summon his services. She carried the tray into their own rooms and set it down until he came from the stables. He was laughing and she knew that he had as always, taken a peep at his son on the way to her. He kissed his wife and fondled her, and Debbie felt as if she had everything she wanted from life. Her body was back to normal and Sam was as ardent as he had been before the baby was born. She caught her breath as he stripped off his tunic and sat in shirtsleeves to drink the coffee and take his short time of leisure.

'We save money by drinking coffee,' he said. 'I bought the harness from old Mr Downs and sold it when I'd polished it and mended it as new, for a fair profit. Mr Verney has put our money by and it earns its keep.' He sipped the hot liquid with satisfaction. 'I'll have a bit of meat or pie, Debbie. I have to be at Lincoln's Inn and then to take the master to his brother, and I want to buy you something pretty, so I'll have no time to go to the Old Swan.'

Debbie blushed, knowing that this was her present for being a loving wife again, and after last night in the deep double bed, they had decided that they could not deny themselves but must accept whatever children the good Lord sent them.

'It's natural and I'm a man, Debbie,' Sam had said as he lay exhausted and Debbie felt as if heaven had opened its gates again. 'But we must save as much as we can for the day when you must leave Lady Marian and tend our own house or lodging, and then it will be of concern to nobody but us if we have six children! Mr Verney has promised me a piece of land at the back of the field and he will have a house built there for us to rent, or if we have enough, to buy. It won't be tied to the stables and the work but free for us for ever.' His honest face shone and he kissed her again. 'I want three more at least and each one more like you, Debbie. They'll all grow up together; Lottie's child and yours, and none to say the difference in my heart.'

'Take your new livery, Sam. That tunic has lost a button, but you can leave it for mending as you go. Margaret has gone to see to her old mother, but she will find it and mend it as soon as she gets back.'

'I'll send Henry to fetch it tomorrow,' said Sam, laughing. 'You wait! He'll ask anyone to go instead of him as he thinks she's after him.'

'And so she is,' said Debbie, 'I know that look and she will get him if he's not careful. He could do worse and she would see him comfortable.'

'Not such an armful as my Debbie,' he said, and hugged her hard.

'Well, see that you never try to find out!' she said, but kissed him again and then pushed him towards the door. He slung the new livery tunic over his shoulder and said he'd wash before putting it on, and opened the door to leave. Margaret stood back as if she had been close to the door, and Sam brushed past her without more than a grunt of recognition. He grinned as he knew just how thick the door was and that if she had been prying, she would have heard nothing, but then paused, wondering why he had imagined that she wanted to pry. She was kind and efficient and made the maids laugh with her tales, and there was no harm in her.

'You were quick,' said Debbie.

Margaret smiled. 'Mother was sleeping and the woman next door was there sitting with her, drinking my ale! I could tell you a thing or two about that one, but she is useful and so I let her think I never notice how much ale she takes.'

'There's some coffee left, Margaret, if you like it. Sam had to go out and has had something to eat so I made this early. Take a cup into the sewing room with you. Sam left a tunic to be mended, which he'll need tomorrow, so do that before you go to the marshes with the linen. I have a bundle from Lady Clavell here to take at the same time and there will be a big bundle to collect from last week. The boy can go with you but if he can't carry it all, take the new little maid and show her what they do with the whitster bleach.'

'I like going there. It makes a day out for me and the other women are friendly and we tell each other such tales as you'd never dream were true!'

'How many are true?' asked Debbie, drily. 'I hate listening to gossip and I know that Lady Marian would not like you to talk about this house, Margaret.'

'I would never do that,' said Margaret, a little too quickly. 'There are some I know about and know more than they think I know, but not Lady Marian. I would never dream of saying anything to hurt her.'

'You'd be hard put to find anything like that here. Lady Marian is the kindest, most considerate of mistresses and I know of nobody who could say less.' Debbie walked towards the bedroom door, hoping that Margaret would leave her alone, but the woman followed her, glancing about as if to memorize every detail of the furniture, the hangings that Debbie had made herself and the unmade bed with the mattress lying out over the sill in the fresh air.

'I'll help you make the bed before I start on the sewing,' Margaret began.

'No,' said Debbie, turning pink. 'I am changing sheets, today.' But Margaret had picked up one end of the feather mattress and heaved it across to the bedstead.

'There. I'll take the dirty sheets for washing, on my way,' she said. She spread one out, showing the wet stain left from Sam's lovemaking and she giggled. 'He has his oats now, does he? Some say you shouldn't for much longer than this.'

'That has nothing to do with you, Margaret! I am married and am healthy and that is all there is to it!' Debbie tried to laugh. 'If you catch Henry you will have more than this to show on your wedding night, if you are a virgin still after all these years!'

Margaret gave an exaggerated sigh and her eyes glinted with malice. 'That's true,' she said. 'I am a virgin and hope to be until I marry, not that I haven't been sorely tried by several who shall be nameless.' She saw Debbie's smile and her face tightened. 'There are some who have a lot to answer for when they have husbands away and yet the sheets are soiled. You can smile, Debbie, but I know more than anyone thinks. I use my eyes and ears and see things what you would pass over and not know to be important.'

'Other people's business is not important to me,' said Debbie. 'Go now and get some work done before you cross the river and I must tidy here before I see to the dinner as we have four extra mouths to feed this noon.'

'Who is that?' asked Margaret.

'It's none of your business,' replied Debbie, caustically. 'Just as what people do in marriage beds is none of your business, too!'

Margaret took the cup and opened the door. 'You'll see. Time will tell and then you'll all wonder what went on under your very noses.' She looked back, her face alive with excitement. 'At least your baby looks like you, but I wonder what some babies will be like.'

'Like their own mothers and fathers, I suppose, unless the mother has been frightened by a monkey and bears the signs,' Debbie said, good-humouredly, but when Margaret had gone, she made up the bed pensively and wondered what the woman had meant. Most of her tale-telling was due to her own colourless existence when away from the great houses, and many women took gossip and the chance to know more than their companions as life-blood to their impoverished minds. I like to gossip but not to cause unhappiness, thought Debbie. I would never hint at something wicked that someone had done, and if all Margaret has to go on is rumour and her own highly coloured suspicions about someone she obviously does not like, then this could be dangerous.

The babies were being fed as Debbie went up to Lady Marian and she felt a twinge of discomfort as her own breasts reacted to the sight of her baby being suckled by a wet nurse. Lottie Kate sat watching, chewing a crust and helping herself to pieces of meat from a plate and Debbie longed to take over both the children and leave the work of the house to others; but this was not the time and she knew that she couldn't bear to leave the kind family that was more than just a kind employer. If I was alone in a house with no other women to talk to, I might get like Margaret, she thought, but she smiled, as if that wasn't really possible.

'My Lady?' Debbie stopped and appeared embarrassed.

'What is it? Has Margaret told you something that I should know?' Marian sighed. 'These people say that what they must tell is for the good of someone or has to be told to present a clear picture of justice. It is never just because it gives them a sense of their own importance to be the first with news. Now what has the woman in the new ale-house done? Or is it the latest about the Duke of York now that he is recovered from the small pox?'

'No, My Lady. Margaret hints with such dark looks that I fear that she does know something of importance and will cause mischief with it sooner or later.'

'There is nothing she can do. My conscience is clear and so is that of your master. What we do, is our own business and she has no other place of work so she will be thinking of someone of whom I have never heard, you can be sure. The darker the looks, the less she knows,' Marian added, comfortably.

'I fear for Miss Alice,' said Debbie, bluntly. 'She hints of strange things but will not say what. I know that Miss Sarah will have a bastard through no fault of her own, so that is no longer news and I know that Miss Sarah will care for it with love, if Sir Vincent will allow her to keep it, but she nudges and winks as if Miss Alice has something to hide.'

'Many have asked if all is well in that marriage because Vincent is away for so long, but we explain that he had to see to his estates, and they are as far-flung as Ireland and Scotland, Cornwall and the Fens. He knows of his wife's condition and will come back as soon as he can.' Marian laughed. 'Margaret has noticed that Sir Rollo has been very attentive to Alice, as he has been to Sarah and me and half the ladies in London, with no thought of lechery, but Margaret smells intrigue. She is a silly woman and you must take no notice of her.'

'Do all children look like their fathers and mothers?' asked Debbie as she took the heavy silk dress and hung it to air and slid the fresh one over Marian's head and shoulders.

'What a strange question. Little Lottie is the image of her mother and your baby has Sam's nose and eyes and your sweet mouth, Debbie.' Marian reached for perfume to scent her arms and hoped that Edward wouldn't notice that she wore a patch to hide a pimple on her chin. The fashion was widespread but Edward refused to accept that any respectable matron wore patches and only painted actresses and whores flaunted them.

'The wife of the baker had a child with red hair,' persisted Debbie. 'Neither she nor her husband have red hair and everyone gossiped about them. It is said that the baker beat his wife as soon as she was able to stand, after the baby was born.'

'Did Margaret tell you this?' Debbie nodded. 'If Margaret expects the baby to have Rollo's eyes, then there must be miracles, for he was not here until Alice was over the morning sickness, and well on into her term!'

'I know that. Miss Alice is a married lady and has nothing to hide, but supposing I was having a baby and suddenly someone took me without my leave and added his seed, would not the baby be changed?'

'More old-wives tales, Debbie. Some even say a fright at seeing a two headed mule will cause the baby to have two heads, or a hump on the back if a snail is found in the bread, but I have never seen such a thing.' Marian frowned. 'I cannot believe it, but I keep Alice away from cripples and the blind and make sure she is well-fed and warm at all times when I am with her. I wish that her duenna was as firm and could forbid her from taking the air at night when it is damp.' She pinned a huge pendant emerald on to the yellow silk of the dress and leaned back so that Debbie could brush her hair. 'My brother was not like me,' she said, slowly. 'He had dark hair and brown eyes, and even though I have dark hazel eyes, I am not really dark, and when I was young my hair had blonde lights in it. Edward is of medium colouring and we often wondered how Alice came so fair. My mother was worried in case people pointed a finger at her, as my brother was so unlike the rest of us, but she found an old portrait of an ancestor with flowing dark hair and dark eyes who my brother resembled to an uncanny degree four generations later, so your next child might be like an old grandfather or a cousin long gone, Debbie.'

'My family perished in the plague,' said Debbie. 'So Sam must trust me and take what comes as I must trust him with other women.' She laughed, knowing that her dear Sam would never bed another woman while she was alive.

'Dear Lord!' exclaimed Marian. 'Hurry Girl, we have talked and not seen the time.'

'All is ready, My Lady, and the girl will serve sack and ale until you go down. It will take Mr Verney a few minutes to settle them and show them the picture.' Debbie smiled, knowing that every visitor had to be shown the picture of Anna, more because it was painted by Mr Lely than for its sentimental value, and Marian made her entrance like the Grand Dame she was becoming.

'Letters from Vincent and from Anna,' said Edward. He glanced at his guests who showed no sign of moving on and sighed, knowing that the letters would have to be put aside for a few hours, then talked business as they ate and Lady Marian wished them further. She excused herself and went into the study where the letters lay on a silver tray. Eagerly, she opened the one addressed to her and sat by the window to read it. She glanced up at the portrait and smiled. It was as if Anna spoke to her and her picture brought her close.

'I received your gifts with much pleasure,' wrote Anna. She went on to tell Marian of the good soil that she had been sent by the sherif and of various happenings within the compound but made no mention of Sir Rollo Fitzmedwin. Marian frowned and read the letter again. Knowing Anna so well, she felt that apart from ignoring the presence of what must have been the most handsome guest that Tangier had received for months, there was an undercurrent of desperation in the words. 'Please God Daniel comes back soon,' were not the words of a wife parted from her husband for a few weeks and in no apparent danger. If he had ridden into battle, a wife might have voiced such a sentiment, but not Anna who was resilient and had lived under such hard conditions for long enough to accept her fate calmly.

Marian sat in silence and knew that Anna must have met Rollo as she mentioned the fact that the wife of the envoy to the Mole and the government of Tangier was a mild and pleasant woman who had left three children in Kent to follow her husband until she was satisfied that he would not catch cold, bring a concubine into the house or fall off a camel. Marian sighed. Anna must have been worried that Daniel would object to her receiving the man who he had once thought to be his rival, and her own feelings might have been mixed.

The letter from Rollo was almost as lacking in content, but he pleaded haste to catch the ship returning to England. 'This is a strange country, and arid, but your ward makes a garden and there are palm trees. Tomorrow, I visit the Sherif and find shade in his oasis but now, there are stores to supervise and many preparations to make for the day when Tangier once again has a governor.'

The afternoon wore on and the maids were not back from Lambeth Marshes. The guests went to their various homes and Edward joined her in the study. 'Was all well with Alice?' Marian asked. He nodded and read his letters. 'Did you see her and Sarah?' she persisted.

'I saw Alice and my brother was with Sarah. She is sickly and so thin he hesitated to bleed her but gave her physic to clear her system instead. What is this, madam?' He waved the letter from Anna. 'No mention of Rollo? Has he got off on the wrong foot so soon?'

'It must have been a shock to see him after all this time and to know that he is alive,' suggested Marian. 'There has been little time to see each other as the letter had to go on the ship returning to London. See in the other letter. Sir Rollo was in haste and pleads our understanding that he will write more later.'

'You are right,' said Edward, his face clearing. 'My friends brought good news about the last of my ships and now I am free of such risky transactions forever but must make haste to invest in stocks before the treasury think I have loose money seeking a precarious home! I shall go to my office now and find Roger Carter and we must work out our needs.'

Marian took up her tapestry frame and sat with it in the light from the window overlooking the driveway. A hackney carriage drove past the window with Margaret the maid and the serving boy in it. Marian called to Debbie to meet them and to inspect the linen and to find out why they were so late. She settled down to her gros point and when Debbie came with her tea, she saw that the girl was flushed and annoyed.

'What is it? 'Marian asked.

'I'm sorry, My Lady, but Lady Clavell knows that Margaret works here now and is very angry. Margaret called in the house on the Strand with their clean bleached linen and was seen from a window.'

'I gave orders that the woman must never go there! I also gave orders that she must bring the linen back here quickly and not waste two hours over gossip in the kitchens of other houses!' Marian was furious, partly because the woman had disobeyed her express orders and partly through a guilty feeling that Alice had found out and would take her to task over it in no uncertain terms.

'One lace collar was torn in the press, My Lady,' Debbie said.

'Lace collar? What does one lace collar matter when Margaret has put us all out of joint?'

'She is in tears and swears she meant to save us all time and meant no harm, My Lady.'

'Listen to all she says and tell the other maids to report any gossip from her lips about my family,' said Marian. 'If I hear one word out of place, she can go and never be seen here again, so warn her that you will find out if she gossips even if it is in the last tavern across the City of London!'

Debbie stared, amazed at her mistress's vehemence. Margaret was a gossip and a trifle malicious but surely there must be something to hide if My Lady took on so badly about one slip.

'I beg your pardon, Debbie. It's none of your doing. I am angry because Alice will be very cross with me and I hid the fact that I took in the woman that she had turned away.'

The two women looked uneasy. 'Yes, My Lady,' said Debbie.

Chapter 16

The smell of hot wax and the sound of Arab music made a curious combination and the glittering room seemed somehow unreal. Anna walked forward and was greeted by Dulcie who laughed and led her towards the new envoy seated by the arched window talking to Major Meredith. The two guards fell back and stayed outside the door and Sir Rollo Fitzmedwin followed her, still wondering if she would ever smile at him.

It was unfair, he supposed, to meet the lady without any warning, but he had taken it for granted that she would have heard of his arrival by now and have braced herself to meet him, even if she had no welcome for him. After the weeks of anticipation when he knew he would be with her in Tangier he had almost convinced himself that she would greet him as a long lost friend, even if she did not throw herself into his arms.

The candelabra flickered and shed wax as the breeze from the huge fans wielded by Arab boys set the air moving, and Anna instinctively gave the order to fan less strongly to prevent the dresses and uniforms from being sprinkled with candle wax.

The air grew cooler and the fanning stopped as the servant announced that supper was ready. 'I missed your husband, madam,' said Sir Rufus Allin. He held his arm ready for Anna and left his wife to Major Meredith while Rollo had to content himself with Dulcie, who seized his arm and pressed herself close to his side. In a dream, Anna made small talk and heard nothing that she could remember after that evening. All that she could recall was a voice saying softly, 'Madam, you have walked out of that picture and are even more beautiful than I remember.'

From time to time, Dulcie glanced across at Anna and wondered if she was really grieving now that her husband had left for Lisbon. Anna was so strong and she hardly ever showed emotion, but this inner tension had a dangerous edge as if it indicated something that she had to keep tightly within bounds or let it free and burst into hysteria. Sir Rufus was enchanted with the two ladies who would make all the difference to the social comfort of his wife and he talked of London and the theatre to amuse Anna, taking her silence for absorption in all he said.

'The other wives will help Lady Sophie,' said Anna when he asked what there was to amuse her during the day when he would be busy on matters of State. She looked at the slightly overweight and certainly overdressed woman and knew that she would have the vapours if she was asked to look in at the patients in the hospital and to help Ayesha. 'Dulcie will welcome a companion, and the wife of the lieutenant is well-born and amiable, fond of fashion and tapestry and is very good with children,' she said, rather helplessly as she could think of nothing to add to these mundane amusements that might be suitable for the occasion, but the envoy beamed as if Anna had mapped out a very full programme for his wife.

'And you, madam? I hear that you work among the sick.' His smile faded as if about to hear of a death and she smiled, faintly, sensing a drawing away as if she might carry some infection.

'I do my best with so little that I can use to help, but tomorrow, I shall unpack the baggage from home and see if they have sent anything of use this time. I hope that the men can bring my stores quickly,' she said. 'Some might rot if left in the heat.'

'They have sent all my wife's clothes and her favourite chairs and a hip bath,' Sir Rufus said, complacently. 'I gave orders that this must be done before nightfall even if they used flares to light the way.' He frowned. 'I was told to bring a hip bath but is it safe, madam? We wash our faces and when the weather is really hot we sponge our bodies, but immersion surely can be dangerous?'

'It was a good thought,' said Anna. 'We all use baths here and some of the men turn hoses on each other to get cool.'

Sir Rufus paled at the thought and then said that it might be a good example to the natives, but he would make his toilette in private.

'The Moroccans are very clean,' Anna said, firmly. 'I had to revise my thoughts about them and I have made friends with many of the Arabs who know a great deal and have an ancient culture.'

'No fear of violence, my dear?' he asked,

quietly. 'I had the Devil's own work cut out to persuade my wife to come with me. The thought of wild natives crushed by our might has haunted me for days before we came here, as who knows what villainy they plot?' He firmed his chin and the loose jowls quivered. 'A show of strength and plenty of guards and discipline must have made this place safe, and that is due to your husband and the officers like him. Never be soft with these people, my dear, and you'll have peace.' He glanced towards the arched open windows at the dense blackness of the night as if he feared to see faces or worse outside.

'My husband is hard but just,' said Anna. 'We have a peaceful compound and have earned the respect of the people here. If you show firmness but justice you will fear nothing, Sir.'

He eyed her elegant gown and laughed. 'Ladies don't know about these matters, my dear. How can you know what they do behind those walls where the huts are and where they sit round fires and talk in strange tongues?'

'I do know, Sir Rufus. I sit with them at times and talk and we exchange our learning. I have learned much about herbs and healing and they have learned from me, so much that they trust me.' She laughed more freely than at any time that evening. 'I do not visit the sick in this gown, Sir Rufus. I dress simply in cool cotton and sometimes wear the haik that the women wear when it is very hot. Lady Sophie might find it pleasant to have some made.' She looked away to hide the amusement in her eyes at the thought of Lady Sophie condescending to dress like a

Berber woman, and found that she could no longer avoid meeting the gaze of the man for whom she felt such conflicting emotions. Rollo ventured a tentative smile with none of the bold stare with which she was familiar from other times, and she smiled too, her amusement softening into a kind of intimate but muted welcome, of two people with little to say but a great deal to share.

He's harder, she thought, but not with the hardness of Daniel, who was soldier first, and husband after that with anything left from his duty to the Crown. He's suffered, too, she decided, and wondered where he had lived since he left so abruptly from the manor house in Surrey well over a year ago. He smiled with his eyes and she glanced down, aware of their brightness and his pleasure at seeing her. She sensed danger but shook herself free of the idea. I'm a married lady in a position of trust, she told herself. My husband is away and that makes it all the more necessary to be prudent with other men.

Dulcie had no such inhibitions and smiled coquettishly, with her hands touching his arm at every chance she had. She helped him to morsels of meat and selected the finest of dates for his dish only, and her gown began to show patches of sweat under the arms.

He said I had stepped out of the portrait, Anna reflected. We were not in Daniel's office where it hangs, so how could he see it? She remembered the original in the Verney mansion and knew that he must have seen it there in London, but he had remembered her gown as the one in which she had dressed that last day in Surrey, when he left forever, or at least into exile, with no word of farewell, no touch of the hand, no kiss.

At last, when Lady Sophie yawned and moved her feet restlessly in her tight shoes, Anna felt that she could leave without seeming impolite. She called for her guards and took leave of her new hosts and gathered up her shawl. Rollo eyed her guards with astonishment. 'Is this necessary, madam? I would be honoured to escort you to your own home.'

'My husband insists that I have two men with me wherever I go outside my house. He is away and cannot protect me, so this is what he decreed.'

'The influence of Africa must be great, madam. Does he treat you as if you live in a seraglio?'

Anna blushed. 'I am given much freedom and have no need of guards except at night when shadows make me nervous, but Daniel shows his care of me even when he is away,' she added, proudly.

'Do your guards forbid you to have visitors?' He raised an eyebrow and she was cross as if he thought that Daniel treated her like a child.

'I am free to do as I please,' she said with a tilt to her chin. 'Goodnight, Sir Rollo. I have no doubt that we shall have to put up with each other's company for many a day, but I would like to be alone now.'

Dulcie came closer. 'Come to dinner to-morrow, Anna. Sir Rollo must visit us first and see the lovely Arab silver we have collected.'

'I'll come if I can, Dulcie. I have to see the hospital women and to ask Ayesha if the poultices did any good. I shall go there early and try to be ready at noon to see you.'

'I have messages from your guardians, and many gifts,' said Rollo. 'May I bring them to you at the hospital?'

'Sir Rufus will want to unload all his baggage first,' said Anna.

'I have my own men with me and they are even now bringing loads to my quarters. All that might perish in the heat; and many more things that I insisted must be brought to you, Anna, even if Lady Sophie cannot find her favourite shawl.' His eyes were bolder now and she drew in her breath when he used her name with easy familiarity.

Dulcie laughed. 'Anna has all the gifts,' she said. She could see the handsome man taking more interest in Anna than in her and she was spiteful. Until Anna arrived Rollo had been so courteous and had even hinted that he found her attractive and could flirt with her if she allowed it. 'You have arrived too late, Sir Rollo. We have an admirer who showers Anna with gifts and has sent her rubies.'

Anna blushed, with anger and not with confusion, realizing that Dulcie had known about the ruby for a long time. Servants gossiped here even more than in England and she might well have known that it was impossible to keep anything like the gift from the sherif a secret. 'The sherif is generous to us all,' said Anna. 'You have enjoyed his silks and fruit and perfumes, too.'

'No, Anna. It's you who have been generous. He gave you the presents and you, in your goodness, gave them to others so that we could all share your good fortune.' Dulcie smiled, like a cat who sees a mouse trapped and can wait for the kill.

'If my dear aunt and uncle have sent me gifts then I shall be anxious to see them,' said Anna. 'I shall go to the hospital at dawn, Sir Rollo, before the heat is too intense. Come there when you can or follow me to my home and bring their gifts to me.'

'If I may suggest,' he said, stiffly. 'Any letters you may want to send should be ready tomorrow. The ship turns to Lisbon and there may not be another for weeks.'

'Thank you,' she said. 'I will write tonight before I sleep and say that I shall write more when I have leisure and have seen the contents of the mail.'

'And shall you mention that we have met?' he asked.

'If you bring gifts from them, then they surely know that,' said Anna. She smiled and left the hall with her guards and Rollo turned to smile at Dulcie to make sure that she did nothing to harm Anna, but missed the soft sighing of her skirts and the jasmine in her hair, as she vanished into the darkness with the men carrying flaming torches.

'And who is there with something amusing to say? What does a lady do during the day?' asked Sophie. She looked into the delicate cup at the mint tea and pushed it aside. 'Is there no tea from China or India? Have I come all this way to be deprived of creature comforts?'

'We have tea when the ships come from England and Lisbon but it is used quickly and we need more to be sent,' said Dulcie, with a glance at Sir Rufus who was taking in everything she said as if it must be Bible true. 'We also need more French wines and other civilized necessities. The Arabs never drink wine as it is forbidden by their religion and so we suffer,' she said, plaintively. 'I have told my husband that if I have no better supplies or amusement, I shall leave for England on the next ship!' Major Meredith smiled, knowing that Dulcie would never leave without him, but Lady Sophie looked alarmed.

'Pray do not say that, my dear! I have come here with some trepidation but now I have a sense of intense relief having met you. I feel we have so much in common, and you must see to it that we have what we need for our simple pleasures, sir,' she announced to Sir Rufus.

'There is wine for the governor's cellars and more on the way,' said Rollo. 'It takes up much space but I have been told that this must be so until we are well-stocked and His Excellency takes over the house.'

'It is good to know that you share my feelings, Lady Sophie,' said Dulcie. 'Anna is dull and thinks only of the hospital which is no place for ladies, when there are slaves and Arab women to care for the dying.'

'And does she care for the soldiers and civilians of the town and fort, madam?' asked Rollo, politely.

Dulcie flushed. 'Yes, she does that and some make a good recovery,' she admitted. 'But she grumbles all the time that she could do more if she had the right medicines.' Once more she tried to paint a dim picture of Anna to make Rollo lose interest. 'She dresses plainly with her hair tied back and spends all her time talking to the women in their own language and teaches them our secrets of healing. They give her local plants and herbs but I believe them to be poisonous and that she should not trust them.'

'Are any of the local sheiks less fierce and warlike than I have heard?' asked Sir Rufus.

Dulcie smiled. 'You must ask Anna. Al-Rashid, the sherif who represents the Emperor of Morocco, is charming and very handsome. He brings many camels laden with gifts,' she added, and thought it unnecessary to say that they were carrying bags of soil. 'He eats with us here at times and makes a royal progress. He invited Anna, with her husband, of course, to his oasis but none of the other officers' wives.' She stole a glance at Rollo who looked polite but uninterested. 'She even wears the flowing robe that the women of his harem wear and so pleases him,' Dulcie said with a shocked expression that made Sophie gasp.

'She has never been inside the harem?' Sophie settled herself again forgetting that her feet hurt and her dress was too tight.

Dulcie shrugged. 'I was not there, but there were hours when the sherif was talking with the officers and so I imagine that she must have visited his many wives. They say that he can have

298

any woman he desires, and I am glad not to have been invited to that dangerous place, even if my husband was present. Anna walks with the sherif whenever he comes here, alone, and he goes with her into the hospital to see his own people.' To her disappointment, Rollo appeared to be unimpressed. 'Ayesha, a woman who works with Anna in the hospital said that the sherif had offered a big black eunuch to Anna to guard her, but Colonel Bennet saw no need of it. It does show that women are in grave danger from these men,' said Dulcie.

Pink spots of excitement showed in Sophie's cheeks. 'I expect I shall have to go there with Sir Rufus,' she said. 'I am immune to the wiles of such men but we must go well-guarded, and first Sir Rollo should go there to make sure it is safe. You must come with me, my dear.' She held up a hand. 'I insist. It is your duty and I shall be easier with another well-bred lady to accompany me.'

'I have letters of introduction to the sherif,' said Rollo, drily. 'I found many who had met him on his visit to Europe and the Court of St James, and during his time at the University of Leiden, in Holland. He has the manners of a French courtier and speaks many languages. You may find him dull as Mistress Anna Bennet is dull. They both have good brains and much interest in books.' He smiled. 'He is however, a very fine figure and you will enjoy meeting him, Lady Sophie. I feel that you may well attract him as he prefers ladies who are not so thin that they break in half.' He made a gallant bow. 'It may be that you need a eunuch to guard you in this country,

My Lady.' Sophie fanned her reddening face vigorously, and Rollo made his escape before she could decide if he was teasing her, or if the men of this country might be as exciting as she began to imagine them to be.

Rollo walked out into the night. The sky seemed to hang lower than at home and the stars were brighter. The smell of camels and the dry scent of dust made an oddly disturbing impact as if Africa was telling him that this was no ordinary country with familiar smells, customs and people, but a place to which he must bow or be rejected. He listened to the night sounds, of animals groaning, distant shouts of men changing a guard on the ridge beyond the fort and the wailing of a woman mourning a man lately dead.

How could Anna bear to live here? How could she have married the stern captain and followed him here when he was made colonel and even more rigid in his army ideas and discipline? He looked at the flickering light from the windows of the house where Anna lived, and as he came closer, a man rose from a sitting position on a rug and Rollo saw the flash of white teeth in a dark face. Whatever Daniel Bennet might be as a husband, he must inspire loyalty and have great trust in his Arab servants and soldiers to allow a man to sleep across the door of his wife's house when he was away. Rollo frowned. Perhaps the sherif was right to offer eunuchs. The lights still burned and showed dimly through the gauze curtains which kept out flying insects. She would be writing to the Verneys, he thought, but as yet she had nothing of which to write, as the baggage was still packed. He laughed, softly, feeling like a boy again, looking up at the window of a girl for whom he had a sudden infatuation. He recalled his first conquest, a virgin, well-guarded but cunning enough to evade her maids when he sent a note to meet him under her window. His smile died. This was not like that. His desire for Anna had deep roots in her rejection of him without marriage and her love for Daniel.

He went back to the huge house where his quarters were remote from the governor's and so private. He wrote his letters and called for a man to take them to the ship, telling him to collect any from Mistress Bennet on the way. The letter to Edward Verney was slim, and to Holland it was even slimmer, but he wrote of the colour and sounds of Africa to Willem, and thought that of all people, he was the one he would like to be with him now.

Rollo lay half asleep and wondered if he had brought the right gifts. The sherif had given Anna rubies and he knew that al-Rashid had wealth enough to bring only the best. Anna had been to the oasis and if Dulcie was not lying, had received many camel loads of gifts from the sherif, publicly, which many might believe were gifts for a mistress. Such men in this precarious peace might have the power to arrange a distant posting for any man who stood in the way of a seduction of his wife by a powerful ruler. He had heard of men in service, living in the colonies, who had died and left wives and children who were taken by the ruler with all lands, and been absorbed into the seraglio of the sheik or potentate. It was as good a reason as any for Daniel to insist on guards for his wife.

He tossed restlessly although this bed was more comfortable than the cramped cot on the ship and when he dreamed, briefly, it was of Helena looking at him sadly. 'God's Death!' he said and flung back the coverlet. He called for water and for ale and washed all over as he had learned to do in Amsterdam. He dressed simply in a white linen tunic and silk britches of dark blue, with silk stockings to match and buckled shoes. As yet, the sun was only a thread over the desert but he caught up a hat to guard him from the later heat, and, refreshed and curious, he ventured out into the well-swept compound. Sheep and goats were being driven out through the high arches that at night were closed by stout doors barricaded with stones. Horses stood in the shade awaiting riders to change guard at the outposts, and camels came into the compound carrying more stores from the ship. The smell of spices and meat cooking, the acrid scent of animal droppings and the smoke from fires fuelled by camel dung and cactus was an assault on the senses that was unfamiliar but appealing. Even now, when night had not quite relinquished her hold, Arab music whined and brought a primitive accompaniment to the cocks crowing on the dung hills.

Men stared, and women drew folds of their robes close to their faces as if unsure if they should be veiled, or if this stranger was a part of the fort's manning. Rollo smiled and addressed them in English, French and Dutch with varying success, but when he was then ignored, he knew

302

that they accepted him as no threat, but he suspected that servants were similar the world over and there would be much discussion and curiosity about the newcomers as soon as they were free to gossip.

He asked to be shown the way to the hospital and was taken by a man who thought that Rollo must be a doctor from the big ship, and insisted on showing him a weeping sore on his leg before Rollo could explain that he was a diplomat with the new envoy. It was a relief to find someone who spoke English but as soon as the doorway to the hospital was before them, the man turned to the group of Moroccans who followed like tame geese and a babble of voices showed that all the previous conversation was being relayed and dissected, with possible lavish embellishments, and many dramatic waves of the hands.

The thick white walls made dense shade within the doorway and the narrow windows let in a meagre light but kept out the sun. Rollo blinked and recoiled slightly and his head spun with recollections of St Paul's in London during the plague when the crypt was used as a pest house, but he quickly recovered, realizing that this place was clean and the men well-tended, and any slight stench was from wounds turning gangrenous or the fluxes of dysentery. A woman in a white djellaba came silently towards him and looked as if she was in charge. 'Is Mistress Bennet here?' Rollo asked.

Ayesha made an obeisance and shook her head. 'My Lady has returned to eat and to bring what she can for us,' she said.

'You lack food?' Ayesha shook her head. 'What then?' he asked.

'We have no cures and little comfort,' she said, simply, the palms of her hands pink against the dark skin of her arms as she gave a gesture of near despair. 'The sherif sent much earth to grow plants but the plants are not for the sick and those that My Lady had sent, withered or fell rotten as they were dead when they arrived here.' She sighed. 'Many camels brought the good black soil from the oasis and yet we have nothing but Kaif and some laudanum and some of our purges. It is the will of Allah, but when we had the herbs from England that My Lady brought with her, Allah was good and made many better.'

'Al-Rashid sent *earth?*' said Rollo. He smiled.

'His Mightiness, who is my father and my mother and blessed of Allah, also sent gifts such as a woman would like and accept before giving pleasure, but she gave them away and kept the earth.' Ayesha gave a grunt of disbelief. 'She gave even to me, rich cloth and sweetmeats and fruit for the dying.'

'Thank you. What do they call you, madam?'

'I am Ayesha who cares for all here and serves My Lady well, as Allah wishes, to serve all men who are sick, and the women, in their own houses.'

'Thank you for serving her, Ayesha. I have brought medicines and more comfort, and today, if you have the soil raked and watered, we may plant herbs from England and Holland and France.'

He glanced at the sick men and wished that he

304

could spirit Anna away to more wholesome pursuits but strode back to her house amid the now noisy and busy groups, about the business of the day. Two of his own men stood in the shade with a barrow of chests and a hessian-covered box of fine oak carved with leaves and flowers and fruits as if it held a cornucopia. Rollo nodded to them and they followed him to the door. The guard admitted him and in a minute, Anna came to greet him.

For a moment, they stared and said nothing, then Rollo said brusquely, 'I'll waste no time on pleasantries, madam. I am pleased to see you again, but I have with me gifts that you might want to see.'

Anna blushed and drew herself up tall as if she had expected another greeting and found this one strange. The men brought in the boxes and Rollo showed her the gifts from Marian Verney and Edward, from Alice and Sarah and from Kate and other friends who wanted to send love and kindnesses. The books, Anna glanced at and put aside and the small package of drugs from Dr Verney was hastily unpacked and the two big bottles of laudanum brought the first smile to her eyes, but she looked dejected when she had seen the silk scarves, the pretty fans and soft bodices of fine cotton that were items she needed but were not enough.

'You are kind to bring them safely, sir,' she said. 'I hope they were not a labour. I know how limited space is on a voyage and you had your own baggage.' She called to Azziza to make tea and to bring bread and goat cheese, then asked politely if Sir Rollo would prefer coffee or ale. 'I must eat now and then go back to the hospital. Last night two men fought and are now weak from loss of blood. Ayesha cannot stem the flow from one man and we need to bind more tightly but cannot in case we cut off the blood for ever.'

'You are too late, ma'am. I am from there and they carried a body away as I left. There was nothing that any human hand could have done to save him, and Ayesha begs you to stay and rest a while before returning.'

Obediently, Anna sat and sipped her tea, her dark hair soft and shining and her gown pale and without ornament, deliberately demure as if to tell Rollo that she cared nothing for her appearance or for any opinion that another person might have of it. He seemed not to notice her clothes but gazed at her face as if to imprint it on his memory, hungry to see what he had not forgotten but which might have altered.

'I have ventured to bring a few mean things of my own, madam,' he said when he pushed aside the platter of cheese. He called to the men outside and they carried in the chest and set it down at Anna's feet on a low table. She traced a carved leaf with one finger and looked up at Rollo with a smile. 'It was carved to my orders, ma'am, and is lined with cedar wood to keep all sweet within it.'

'It will look well in my bedroom,' she said, politely, but made no attempt to open it.

'Open it, ma'am. It has secrets,' he said, and drew in his breath as her fingers touched the gilded clasp.

Anna pushed back the lid and gasped. Row on row of bottles, all gold topped and very fine were laid in velvet slots, each labelled with the name of a medicine in a concentrated solution. Other sections held dried herbs and packages of seeds and the powdered bark of medicinal trees. Her hand trembled over the dried foxglove that would have saved the man with dropsy for at least a few more months and might have saved his life, and she could see no more for her tears.

'Sir! This is more than I can bear.' A great rending sob tore at her and made him want to hold her close but he dared not touch her.

'It is nothing,' he said, lightly. 'If it pleases you, I am glad, but it is but a handful of seeds.'

Chapter 17

'Willem has offered to escort you Alice, and it is better to take Peter with you, too.' Lady Marian looked at her daughter with enough anxiety to make Alice cross and even more determined to attend the Duke's Theatre Company at the Lincoln's Inn Theatre.

'I missed the first performances of the farce and if I am to lie-in with this child, I must have something amusing to think of when I have no diversion other than a screaming baby.' Alice moved slowly, the weight and girth of her pregnancy making progress difficult down the stairs and out to the waiting carriage. 'I see you had it all planned Mother. There was no need for you to trouble yourself, Peter,' she said ungraciously to her brother sitting in the carriage with Willem de Graeff. 'Are you sure that you wouldn't rather I took the midwife with me and a wet nurse and another maid? Why don't you come, Mother and then all the world would know that my delivery is soon and clear a way for me!'

'If Sarah was well, I would come, my dear,' said Marian, firmly. 'But I shall stay in your house until both the babies are safely born and you are in no danger.'

Alice hugged her mother with a sudden fierce intensity. 'Forgive me, madam. I am on edge and need this diversion, and I am glad that Peter has not left for Holland.'

She was helped into her seat and faced Peter who eyed her with a degree of apprehension. 'Why have you changed your mind?' she asked. 'I heard that you were to go to France and Italy before Holland.'

'Willem has been good enough to give me lessons in Dutch and has talked so much of his country that I feel I shall be more at home there than in Italy as I know nothing of the language, unless Latin is useful there. I shall visit the University of Leiden and perhaps stay for a term to perfect my Dutch and to see the paintings of Van Dyck and Rembrandt and Velasquez.' He glanced at Willem with affection. 'I shall have contacts among his friends and be able to write to you about everything I see. Dutch lace is beautiful and I shall send some for you and for Mother.'

'My friends are simple people, Peter, and you must take up some of the invitations from business contacts of your family too or I shall be accused of getting you into bad company,' said Willem. 'Mr Verney might not approve if you spend all your time with artists.'

'With Mr Silke, I shall not stray far and he shares my interests so we shall be on the best of terms,' said Peter with satisfaction. 'We leave next week and I hope that I see my nephew before I go, Alice.'

The theatre was crowded and hot for the time of year and Willem was relieved when Alice was sitting comfortably in the box where she had a good view of the stage and of the people in the audience. She looked with distaste at the people in the pit. 'I never saw so many common people in the pit as now,' she said. 'They seem to be able to afford more than a few pence for a seat in the gallery.' She sniffed. 'We shall see maidservants and clerks sitting in the four shilling boxes next.' She accepted an orange and leaned forward to see who was in the Royal party but there were none from the Court as yet, and the play began.

'Mr Dryden is famous for his plays,' explained Peter to Willem who had no idea what he was about to see. 'This one is called *An Evening's Love* and is one of his latest and most popular.'

Alice felt a twinge of wind pain and wondered if the title was a little too apt for her in her condition. She stared at the actors and heard little of what was said on the stage. An evening of love? or A morning of love? What of a few minutes of violent and passionate love that had no warning, no time for regret? She wondered where the French count was now, far away in Guinea, and his face was more vivid in her mind than the face of her husband or her mother. She could remember the way his hair fell and the darkness of his eyes, and the short upper lip, and the cleft in the chin below the sensual mouth.

The orange was sour and made the bile rise in her mouth. She wiped her mouth and wondered if Sarah had more blood on her handkerchief today. She had complained of back-ache earlier but had slept since dinner-time and seemed rested when Alice left for the theatre.

The audience in the pit were laughing and

310

shouting as the play got under way and they had finished remarking on the well-designed scenery. Alice relaxed and began to laugh at the actors, enjoying the play more than she had expected. She laughed aloud and then clutched her side. 'Is something wrong, Alice?' asked Peter in alarm.

'No, it's gone now. I must not laugh as heartily, it would be better to see a tragedy and keep from merriment,' she said, but her belly was tense and she knew that this discomfort was not caused by the wind or the laughter.

The actors bowed and took time for refreshment and the audience talked and shouted and ate sweetmeats bought from the orange girls. Alice turned pale and felt as if her waistline would burst. 'I want to leave,' she said, with dignity. 'I know that we sent the carriage away until the play ends but you must bring a hackney carriage to the door, Peter, and Willem will help me to it.'

To her relief, the shabby carriage of Dr Verney was at the front of the house on the Strand when the hackney carriage set down its load and Willem held Alice by the arm to help her into the house. Hurried footsteps above them told Alice that Sarah was ill and she went up the stairs as quickly as she could to the room prepared for the two mothers-to-be. A maid rushed past them on the stairs and then hesitated. 'My Lady,' she gasped. 'Miss Sarah is near her time and the master is expected tomorrow.' She hurried on down to the kitchens and Alice clung to the balustrade, partly to ease the pain and partly to collect her wits. Vincent coming home now? She

311

gave a bitter laugh, and as the pain eased, went into the bedroom.

'Alice?' Lady Marian looked flushed and anxious. 'Sarah insisted on going to bed in here but she will disturb you, my dear. I shall ask for the bed in the next room to be made up for you, so that you can sleep.' She suddenly realized that Alice had been away for only two hours. 'Are you well, my dear?' she asked.

The next pain was sharp and Alice breathed deeply and bit her lip. 'I told you that Sarah and I would have our babies at the same time,' she said, breathlessly. 'Send my maid to undress me and ask Dr Verney if he would be good enough to–' She clutched at the bedpost and the sentence was never finished.

Lady Marian and the maid undressed her and put her to bed. The woman chosen by Dr Verney to deliver the babies examined Alice and said that she would be delivered in about four hours time or thereabouts. Dr Verney came too and nodded his approval. 'A good healthy girl like you Alice will have no trouble.'

'And Sarah? Is she well and will her baby live?' whispered Alice, glancing at the still form on the other bed as Sarah fell into a fitful doze.

'If it is God's will,' he said, gravely.

'It must live,' muttered Alice through her next pain, and over the hours, she tried not to scream as Sarah was doing and bit on the towel to break the tension of each pain.

Dawn made the candles pale, and the oil-lamp that was smoking badly was needed no more. Alice felt cool water on her face and wanted to be rid of what was pushing at her and causing pain. Water flooded the bed and she glanced across at Sarah who lay naked and limp. The cry of a baby came from the other bed just as Alice made a great effort and pushed and for a moment Alice thought it was her child, but her pains were still vigorous and she strained again.

Hastily, the midwife wrapped the baby that Sarah had brought into the world and placed it in one of the cribs by the big four-poster bed on which Alice lay. She thrust both cribs close to Alice's bed to give her more room to tend Sarah who was moaning and bleeding steadily. The baby was still covered with blood and mucous, but the midwife left it to hurry back to Sarah. She made sure that the afterbirth had come away and cast anxious glances at Alice all the time she waited for the bleeding to abate, until she was sure that Sarah was safe. The baby was crying softly and giving no cause for alarm so she ignored it and hurried back to Alice, approaching the bed from the other side, which was easier for delivering the baby.

She called the maid to send for Dr Verney and turned with relief to Alice. 'Now then, my pretty,' she said and hoped that Dr Verney would be generous after all her work. One sleeve of her cotton gown was torn from Sarah's frantic clawing and her hair hung down as the pins fell out, and Alice was heavier than the emaciated girl on the other bed.

Alice gave a shout and felt the baby slither between her legs. The midwife took the baby and slapped it soundly to make it cry and then wrapped it as she had done the first. 'Now we wait for another pain and get rid of the afterbirth,' she said, soothingly. 'Hold your baby, My Lady,' she said. A feeble cry from the other bed made her look up sharply and she saw blood on the pillow as Sarah coughed and moaned.

'Go to her!' said Alice. 'Go, Woman, she is bleeding.' The midwife hesitated. 'I have no pain now,' lied Alice, and held her breath to hide the rising tide of discomfort. The midwife ran round the bed to Sarah and raised the girl's head, leaving Alice holding her own swaddled infant.

Alice shook away the clouds from her mind and looked at her baby. She felt a wave of love for it and knew at that moment that no other baby would ever be as dear, but she struggled half out of bed and dragged the other crib closer. The next pain was brimming up and she had little time, but she held her breath to delay the contraction and grabbed the other bundle of clothes until it lay beside her on the bed. She pushed her own baby into the crib and gave in to the next pain, groaning to attract the attention of the nurse.

At that moment, Dr Verney came into the room, summoned by the maid. He went to Sarah and the midwife came and pressed on Alice's flaccid stomach to expel the afterbirth. 'There now, it's all over and you have a lovely baby. Let's see what it is.' She unwrapped the clothes and held up the naked male child. Expertly, she tied off the cord and wrapped him in a binder and clean sheets. 'Put him to the breast, My Lady. It will help you if you tend to bleed after this is over,' she said. 'And then have a good long sleep while we clean him.'

'What of the other baby?' asked Alice.

The midwife smiled. 'This is the one you should care about, My Lady. This your son and heir, born to a proud position.'

Alice struggled to sit up but was pushed down again by the thick hands. 'You must treat them alike,' she insisted. 'My baby and the baby of my dearest friend will be brothers for ever. My husband will be here soon and he will be angry if that baby is neglected, even if it is a bastard! It is his nephew, and his sister is dear to him!'

Dr Verney bent over the bed. 'Calm yourself, Alice,' he said, sternly. 'I shall see that Sarah's child has every care. It is a fine boy but strange-looking. I never saw the child's father but some say he had foreign blood, or it may be that Sarah was ill while she carried him, but he isn't like Sarah, or Vincent or anyone I know.' He picked up the child that Alice held to her breast. 'Now this one will be a Clavell. Do you mind that it is more like Vincent than you, my dear?' He smiled. 'Vincent will be very proud as men like to think that it is all their doing and the labour is nothing.'

Alice felt exhausted. 'I shall feed this baby and not let it be taken by a wet nurse,' she said. She looked at the blue eyes and the thin film of fairish hair and knew that she must learn to love it as her own or be ruined. If she fed the baby, then surely love would follow. Many wet nurses became very fond of their charges and hated to lose them once they were weaned, and in this circumstance, there was a bond with Sarah, her dear friend, and with her husband as Sarah's brother.

She woke to a sense of foreboding that was in the whispers about her bed. 'My baby?' she asked, in alarm. She looked about her and saw that the bed on which Sarah had lain in labour was gone and the other crib was no longer there.

'My dear!' Lady Marian sat by the bed and twisted her wet handkerchief in her hands. 'I don't know how to tell you. Sarah has paid for her sin and is now out of her misery and ill-health and past caring about this world.'

'Sarah is dead?' Alice looked across the room. 'Where have they taken her?'

'She is in a room by the back door, awaiting the funeral women.'

'And what of her child? Has he been washed and wrapped in clothes as rich as mine?' Alice was bright-eyed and flushed. 'I shall adopt him as my own and care for the son of my dearest friend, as if I bore two babies today.'

'Hush, dear, you will drive away your milk and make yourself ill of a fever,' said Marian.

Dr Verney came to give her laudanum and Alice still tossed and cried for Sarah. 'Promise me that I may have the other baby too!' she cried and Marian nodded, helplessly, wondering what Vincent would have to say, when he returned.

'Alice and Sarah were as sisters and this has happened at a bad time when Alice is nervous,' said Marian later, when Edward Verney came to the house. 'I have never seen her so determined about anything.'

Edward grunted. 'Determined? When has that miss ever not been determined to have her way?'

But he admitted that it was good to see her love for the dead girl and her care for the child who had caused her death.

Alice was asleep when Vincent arrived to a house of joy and mourning mixed. He was delayed and arrived the next day, and his annoyance at a night spent in a bad inn after a wheel split on his carriage gave way to joy as he heard that he was a father. The groom burst out with the news, hoping for a gold piece but Vincent rushed past him into the hall of the house. Then he saw the surcoat and hat of a man in the hall and recognized Dr Verney who was coming down the stairs with an expression that told of sorrow and not the pure joy of healthy birth.

'What is amiss, sir?' Vincent demanded. 'My wife! Tell me what of her?'

'She is well, sir and you have a son, but your sister has also been delivered of a son, and God took her as the blood flowed and her strength was lost with the baby.'

'Sarah is dead?' Vincent looked at him stupidly. 'That is a lie, sir! My sister would not leave me! She couldn't die before I saw her again.' He sat down and hid his face in his hands, and the doctor thought that tears had unmanned him, but when he looked up his face showed a degree of deep shock and disbelief, but his eyes were dry.

'She had been ill with the lung disease and grew smaller as the baby grew bigger and took its toll of her strength, but she died happy in that she had borne a son and we must praise God for

317

that end,' Dr Verney said.

'Praise God for the bastard that killed my beloved sister? Tell me, does this thing live?' Vincent shouted. 'It shall be sent far away and forgotten and no one shall mention it again as long as I live!'

'You have cause for rejoicing and not for bitterness, Vincent,' said Dr Verney. 'Up in that room, your wife sleeps with your son close by her side.' He sounded reproachful and Vincent flushed.

'I had not forgotten, but this death touches me deeply, sir. I will go to my wife.' He walked up the stairs slowly as if his thoughts were not yet with Alice, and heard a baby cry. He bounded up the last few stairs and into the bedroom, his whole manner changing. Alice stirred on the bed and the baby snuffled at his fingers in the crib and Vincent gazed with wonder at the tiny face, the curled fingers and the soft hair that was already thinning, before growing into curls, as his had done and Sarah's had done as infants.

'Alice, my dear love,' he whispered, and she woke and stared at him as if seeing him for the first time. 'Alice, you have given me the greatest gift a man can have and I kneel in reverence,' he said, his eyes filling with tears.

The wet nurse came and picked up the infant to show him, smiling her pride as if she had given birth to the baby herself. The baby nuzzled close, smelling the milk but Alice raised her head and demanded to be given the baby. 'I shall feed him. You are here to feed James,' she said.

'But, My Lady, the doctor said it would be as

318

well if I took the baby for a while as I have enough for two or more.'

'Give him to me,' Alice demanded. 'This is my baby. They are both my babies and I shall say what happens in this house.'

'Go now. I will speak to you later,' said Vincent and smiled as if he knew all about the vagaries of a new mother's mind. The baby settled quietly in the crib and Vincent bent to kiss his wife, tenderly, but she turned her face away.

'So you are home, sir,' she said, flatly. 'You are home again after leaving your sister to die.'

'I sent my forgiveness and the order that she could marry,' he said, red with anger and embarrassment.

'You sent too late, sir. James Ormonde died in the Tower and Sarah turned her face to the wall. I saw her grow sickly from that day and the cough came from that moment. She was my dear sister and her baby is as my own.'

'I cannot have my sister's sin with us to remind me Alice,' he said, trying to sound firm.

'You should thank God that you can in some measure repent of the evil thing you did and raise her son as your own.' Alice twisted the sheet between her fingers and her face grew pale as if the blood drained away from her vital organs. 'If you had not been hard, sir, Sarah would now be a laughing bride and mother and she and I would have shared all things as we had done since first we met and loved each other.'

'I tried to make amends,' he said, weakly. 'I sent word as soon as you wrote to me and showed me that I was unjust, and I can take no responsibility for her illness. She must have had the seeds of consumption in her before she became with child.'

'All seeds do not grow, and she was strong enough to fight whatever tried her, until her heart broke and she no longer wished to live!' She looked at him with scorn. 'She loved James Ormonde, Vincent. She loved him more than she loved her brother, and that makes you mad! She would have gone to him and given him many children and left this house for ever.' Her lip curled in contempt. 'I knew that your love for her was great, but you were jealous that any man would touch her in a way forbidden to you!'

'I loved my sister, dearly, as a sister,' he exclaimed. 'But you are my dear wife, Alice, and I have come back after months of longing for you. You have given me a son and I am your slave,' he added, unable to bear her coldness and afraid that she might turn away from him forever. There was something strong about her that he had never encountered before this day, even though she looked weak and unable to speak above a whisper. He took her hand in his and found it tense and cold. 'I will do anything for you, my love,' he said.

'Take that Book,' she commanded. He picked up the weighty bible from the table and brought it to her side. 'In that crib is a real Clavell, with your nose and hair and he will have your firm chin,' she said. 'Sarah had a child too and you must swear on the Book that you will adopt her baby and bring them up equally as your own, but with this baby as your heir.'

'And if I cannot do this?'

She sank back, exhausted. 'Then I shall beg leave to live on one of the country estates with my two children and never see you again.' She gave a weak smile. 'Even your promise that I should go to Court and perhaps become a Lady of the Bed Chamber does not make me change my heart. You need not have affection for the boy, and we can send him to school when he grows bigger, but he must have all the privileges of our son, just as Monmouth has the King's favour and the other royal bastards have rank and position.'

'I swear that it shall be as you wish,' said Vincent. 'I also swear that I shall never go away without you again unless it is your will.' He picked the baby from the crib and handed him to her. 'Here in this room are all I hold dear,' he vowed.

Alice smiled, and held out her arms to him when he had taken the child back again, and she was sobbing, with tears of weakness and relief. He held her closely and kissed her wet cheeks, wondering how he deserved a wife so full of generosity towards a baby who could never fill her heart as her own baby must.

'I must see to Sarah's mourning,' he said. 'I will give the best quality rings so that everyone will know of the love we had for her, and the Dean of St Olave's in Hart Street is a relative who needs my charity and will take the services for her, if the Church tries to forbid burial in consecrated ground. Lady Marian will help me buy mourning clothes with hoods for the servants and black bands for friends who come to condole with us.

There shall be black hangings in the main rooms and black horses from my estates to take the carriages.'

He felt her relax in his arms as if a child heard a fairy tale to help her to sleep. 'Full mourning with your hatchments displaying arms to be hung from the hearse and the windows here,' Alice said, dreamily. 'A great reception here and she must be buried at night with torches as is the fashion now.'

'As you wish, my love,' he said and heard the soft breathing as she fell asleep in his arms. Vincent moved away softly and left his wife to the nurse who had looked in once or twice and clucked at the tension she saw in her mistress's face but dared not interrupt the exchange between husband and wife. He went to the library and found Dr Verney eating cold pie and drinking sack and looking very tired.

'I shall go home now, Vincent,' he said. 'I can remember no time since the plague when I have been so drained. You have good women to tend Alice and the babies and I shall be here tomorrow. Lady Marian has gone home to rest, too. We have all lost sleep and been anxious and sorrowful but now you are here, we can take our rest. I shall call on my brother when I leave here to set their minds at rest and then sleep, and my other patients will have to make do with my assistants.'

He yawned and nearly fell asleep in his carriage but delivered his messages and left Marian and Edward together.

Marian looked pensive. 'Alice has her own way

in everything, and he could not object when she was about to go mad with the milk fever if he refused.' Marian gathered up the sewing that she had not touched since she sat down with it after dinner. 'In a way Alice is right,' she said. 'If Vincent had been less adamant over poor James Ormonde, Sarah might be alive now.'

Alice lay in a near sleep for three days and both babies had to be put to wet nurses. Dr Verney gave her soothing potions, and camomile with feverfew to lessen her fever and to raise her spirits out of melancholy, and when she recovered, she had the two babies brought to her and held them one on each arm as her twins.

Vincent sat on the edge of her bed and gazed at the face of the fair-haired child. 'He has the look of my father and I remember that my mother said I had hair just like that, and so did Sarah, thinning before it grew into curls,' said Vincent. He ignored the other baby but Alice was content to know that Vincent would keep his word and let it lack for nothing. 'Shall we call our son Richard Vincent?' the proud father suggested.

'Anything you wish, my love,' said Alice in her most docile mood. 'And the other we should call James, I suppose,' she said, carelessly as if it was of no great importance. She recalled the tales told her by maidservants when she was a child about spirits coming back to avenge wrongs and thought that Sarah would want her child called James. I shall look after them both, Alice vowed and in time she hardly believed it possible that she had not given birth to the two children.

Peter left for Amsterdam and life in the Verney

household returned to normal. Willem came as a frequent visitor but became more and more withdrawn as he knew that sooner or later his promise to Rollo must come to naught when Peter met the men who had known Sir Rollo Fitzmedwin as the husband of Helena Van Steen. He cursed himself for making Holland sound too inviting and for teaching Peter to speak Dutch so well. He read the last letter from Rollo again and sighed. It was plain that Rollo had met the woman in the portrait and the fact that he said little about her showed that he had not found joy in that meeting. It was just as well, thought Willem. If Anna found out that Rollo had a wife in Holland after Rollo had seduced her, she would feel badly deceived. If she was a loving wife with no thought of love for the handsome Englishman, then all would be well, but Rollo had charm and a way of making anyone who talked to him believe everything he said, and Willem distrusted the obsessive look in his eyes when Rollo gazed at Anna's picture.

Marian took great pleasure in the two babies and begged to be allowed to take them home to show Debbie, but Alice demurred, knowing that Margaret was still working at the house and missed nothing. She tried to forget the woman but could not. She recalled the knowing look when Margaret tidied the bed and refolded the disarranged clothes in the bedroom on the day the Count had been with Alice. Even if Margaret had seen him only fleetingly and not in any part of the house where Alice had been that day, he was the only man who had been there since

324

Vincent left on his ill-fated voyage.

Each day James seemed to look more foreign and Richard Vincent more like Vincent and Sarah, and as the summer turned warm, Vincent took Alice for drives in an open carriage and she turned her thoughts away from the nursery for longer periods, although she crept down to see the babies and held James close to her heart each time she was alone in the house.

'You will bore all your friends,' Alice told her husband when he insisted on showing off his son to any who could bear it. She smiled and kissed him. 'I am well again and I shall take James with me into the country tomorrow and let mother take Richard to show to Debbie and the other servants. I know of a woman who will give me something for James now that he teethes badly and cries so much, and Richard will need it soon, so I will bring back a good supply for him.' She sighed. 'I long to travel with you and think I may leave the babies with the new nursemaid and under my mother's care, and go with you to Norfolk where you say you have urgent business.'

'Are you sure that Richard will be safe if you leave him?' Vincent asked, anxiously.

'You are as ill-at-ease as an old wife,' said Alice, fondly. He had been very loving and generous since his return and she knew that he would never go back on his vow. 'I will take Richard to my mother tonight and leave him there while I go into the country tomorrow,' she decided, and had Richard dressed in palest blue to make him seem even more fair.

'Send the nursemaid with him and tell her to

325

keep him free of all draughts,' said Vincent. Alice smiled. It was time that more people saw the boy and more servants had something to gossip about. Talk had filtered from the servants' quarters that many would have taken wagers that Sir Vincent would never sire a child, and while Richard resembled him so much, this was the time to impress this likeness on their memories, however much the child might alter as he grew.

Lady Marian was delighted and led the way to the nursery as soon as Alice arrived, with two maids and the nursery maid. 'Debbie, we are to be trusted with the son-and-heir tonight and for a whole day! Is the other crib aired and has there been a fresh supply of linen warmed and put in the press?'

Debbie beamed and held her hands together as if she had never seen such a wonderful child, and the other servants when summoned, said again and again how like his father the child was.

From the corner of her eye, Alice saw Margaret waiting in the background as if uncertain whether she was included or not. Debbie tried to stand so that Alice could not see her and Lady Marian looked annoyed. 'How long has she been working here at night?' she asked, in a low voice. 'You should have told me Debbie, and surely you knew that she would not be welcome here now!'

'Her mother is worse and so she comes in the evenings after the old woman is asleep,' said Debbie. 'I will send her into the kitchen until you are gone, My Lady. I didn't know she was in the room until I saw your face and turned, and there she was as large as life and bold! She can't bear

326

to miss anything but I am sorry for her as she has a hard life with her mother.'

Alice held the baby on her arm, the long blue robe soft on the purple of her sleeve and the black pinner that was all that remained of mourning clothes. 'Margaret!' she said as if she had just noticed the woman. 'I hear that you are well-placed here and serve Lady Marian well.' She gave a smile of such sweetness that two of the maids smiled at each other and said how beautiful motherhood had made Lady Clavell. 'I was out of sorts with the sickness when I dismissed you but I am glad to see you well,' she added. 'Now tell me.' She stepped closer to the woman and held the baby high for all to see. 'Tell me who this child is most like.'

Margaret blushed and her eyes showed her acute disappointment. 'He's the image of Sir Vincent, My Lady,' she said in a low voice.

'I shall leave him with you, madam,' she said to her mother. 'No, I'll not wait for refreshment. My husband needs my company and now he is back, we are as two lovebirds in a nest, and cannot bear to be parted.'

Chapter 18

'My Lady?' Anna stooped to avoid the sagging doorway of the black woollen tent and held the pot of comfrey ointment in her hand.

'Yes, Ayesha? I have finished here and I think she will have some relief from the pain now.' Anna frowned. 'I cannot stop these practises but could not the women who abort their babies use what milk they have for others as they do at home? This woman left her abortion for too long and has all the milk of a normal birth, so is sore and tense and likely to suffer until we dry it up. The unguent will sooth the soreness but she must not drink more than a few cups a day or the milk will flow and even the tight binder will not stop it.'

Ayesha shrugged as she did when Anna said something that was impossible to contradict but which showed her foreign thoughts in a land where Allah had marked out customs that must not be broken. She held out a hand for the ointment. 'I will take it, My Lady. Your servant came with a message that the English Lord has called and awaits you,' she said.

Anna smiled, faintly. It was barely light and most of the men and women now living in the governor's house would be asleep and none would surface to meet each other for another hour or so. 'He is not a Lord,' she said. 'I left a message with Azziza that I would return for food at dawn when I had finished with the sick men and treated these women.'

'But My Lady! He is not to be refused! Go to him, My Lady, or he will be angry and never bring us medicines again.'

'He brought enough to stock an apothecary in London,' said Anna, laughing. 'So he must give me time to use some of them!'

'Men are impatient, My Lady.' The dark eyes flashed with laughter and something deeper. 'He rises before dawn to greet you and you stay with the women?'

'I have work to do and he is idle,' said Anna. 'I am married and my husband is away, so it is not fitting that I spend hours alone with another man.'

Ayesha gave a despairing sigh. 'The good colonel is away and will be away for a long month or many months and may never return if he follows the path of war. The English Lord is handsome and looks on you with favour, and yet you come here when he calls and use his gifts but give nothing in return.'

'He is pleased that I value his gifts and use them to heal the sick,' said Anna, but she looked pensive.

'He is a man, My Lady,' said Ayesha. 'He smiles at the Lady Meredith but his eyes are with you and his heart, My Lady, is alive for you alone.'

'He will leave for England soon,' said Anna, 'And I shall wait for my husband. Come! I must see that the plants are watered before I go to eat.'

'It is done, My Lady. I do that, and yesterday

saw that in only a few days since they were planted, the shoots revive and the seeds will soon show growth above the soil.' Ayesha smiled. 'See them now My Lady, and drink tea with me if you do not want to meet the English Lord.' Anna hesitated but the dark face was devoid of cunning. 'Tell me more of the new remedies, and I can use them when you are not here.'

They walked back across the rough ground and into the compound where the guard lounged after duty at the fort and now drank ale on the raised terrace of their quarters. Some stood as Anna passed and all murmured respectful greetings to the women who had done so much to take the fear from fever and wounds. Anna had dismissed her guards from day duty as she felt no threat from either the soldiers or the Arabs, as Ayesha had told all her countrywomen that Mistress Bennet was blessed of Allah, and to be obeyed. They went into the back room of the hospital and Ayesha took the boiling pot from the small fire that she kept burning night and day to boil water and to heat poultices.

Anna opened the cedarwood box and gazed at the contents for the hundredth time. Her heart was full as if she was caressed by a loving hand and she knew that a great deal of time and care had gone in with the herbs and drugs. 'He is very rich to bring you these things, My Lady.' Anna took the steaming cup and sipped, oblivious to everything but the fact that Rollo had done this for her. He was not the man to think of the sick and to trouble himself over men in pain. She knew better than to give him credit for that, as few men of her acquaintance were gentle and ready to comfort the afflicted, but took disease and death as acts of God, until they were laid low with wounds or infection. Daniel had suffered but as soon as he was well, he had little sympathy for other mens' suffering, when he should have more feeling after sharing that pain. She frowned and for a moment Ayesha looked anxious, but Anna went on sipping the fragrant Arab tea and picked up one after another of the bottles and showed the contents to Ayesha through the thick square bottoms of the glass.

The tea was soothing and she left the hospital feeling light-hearted. Ayesha tipped her own tea away and smiled, hoping that she had done something to show thanks for the mercies brought by the English Lord, and for his great generosity and bounty to her people.

Rollo stood as Anna entered the room and inclined his head in a stiff bow. 'You are late, ma'am,' he said. 'Surely you rise earlier than this?' He smiled, knowing that she had been up for hours.

Anna called for food and cool drinks and asked him to join her. 'What makes you lack sleep, sir?' she said when Azziza left them alone.

'Al-Rashid sent word that he will call today and meet the new envoy, and Lady Sophie summons us all to dinner,' he said.

Anna looked surprised. 'I was told this yesterday as were all who are invited,' she declared. She laughed. 'Are you making sure that I have no excuse to forget? I have that unfortunate reputation.'

'You do forget,' he said, smiling, but his eyes were steady and made her look away. 'You forget that London exists and that there are people who miss you and long to hear your voice. You forget the past when we were carefree and the kingcups bloomed and the countryside ripened and gave us its fruit. You forget that once I held you close and kissed you.'

'*You* forget, sir,' she whispered. 'You forget that I am a married lady and that I never gave in to you even when we were alone on the downs.'

'You forget your own feelings, Anna. If I had not fled that night, you would have been mine,' he said, and set his mouth in a hard line.

'I married for love,' she said, simply. 'I have a duty to my husband as any married lady has and Daniel needs me.'

'And leaves you here in this terrible place, that has the decay of an over-ripe peach that smells of heaven and has worms inside!'

'You must go,' she said and tried to hide her tears. 'I have work that fills my heart and now that you have brought me so much, I can rejoice again, and be happy in your friendship.'

'Because I have brought you joy? Because I cared enough to scour London for these paltry offerings? Because I have your picture in my house where only my eyes rest on it? Because now, you know that I have never loved a woman as I love you? You know it in your heart and you are not indifferent to me, Anna.'

His hands took hers and drew her gently closer. His head bent and his mouth rested on her cheek and he swayed with her in a chaste but heady embrace but his lips didn't venture to hers and his arms were firm and comforting rather than passionate. He held his breath as he did when gentling a frightened and unwilling colt and felt her heart beat against his breast.

Anna felt a strange languor and a sense of unreality. Her brow was moist and her hand trembled, and she knew that she was ready for love, but she drew away as Azziza called to one of the other servants to bring fresh bread for My Lady and more dates and oranges. Rollo mouthed an oath and walked away while the food was brought, and Azziza regarded them with curiosity, wondering why Mistress Bennet didn't deck her hair with flowers and wear fine clothes when her lover called to see her.

'I have been asked to ride out to greet the sherif,' said Rollo. 'Why not ride with me? He will be here soon, having left the oasis before first light and we can stay on the ridge and wait for him.' He laughed. 'You love to ride and I promise that no harm shall come to you in my care, Anna.' She blushed. 'I accept that you are virtuous and without any love for me, and so I shall escort you and be your slave; but not your eunuch!'

'I must change,' she said, in sudden alarm. 'Daniel would be cross if he knew that I greeted the sherif dressed as a peasant.'

'But he would be relieved to know that you dress so when I call, madam?' suggested Rollo, drily. He looked pleased. 'I think that I prefer it so,' he said. 'If your husband thinks of me as a threat and not the sherif, then he knows your heart. I will wait while you find your habit and I have ordered two fine Arab horses that I had sent from Meknes where the emperor has a huge bagnio of prisoners and uses them to tend his stables.'

'I wish I could ride more often,' said Anna when they galloped to the top of the ridge with the escort to greet the sherif. 'My guards are common soldiers with no love of horses and would be poor company, and Dulcie rides only in the parks at home and hates the fiery Arabs they breed here.' She glanced at the Berber woman sent to attend her, who rode as a man and sat effortlessly on a beast that seemed about to throw her off but obeyed every touch of the reins. 'I must order more women to come with me and we can ride with just one guard. The sherif will not let harm come to any of the ladies of the fort and the women have spirit enough to keep away any who disobey.'

Rollo eyed the fierce-looking woman with mock alarm. 'I would as soon meet the Devil as cross with such women,' he said. 'At home, they would be for the ducking stool or the gibbet for witchcraft, just for the looks they give.'

Anna's head was clearing and she remembered Ayesha giving her something sweet to drink. 'They know a great deal that many witches would like to know,' she said. 'Ayesha is a wise woman and has such a love of herbs and a knowledge of their properties that she could do much harm as well as the good she does with her simples, and in the harems, they use plants to make pleasant dreams and a longing for lust, even among the women captured and unwilling to be taken.'

'I must cultivate a friendship for this Ayesha,' he said.

'Why, sir?' Anna looked confused. She knew now that the drink had been laced with something to please him and wondered how deep Ayesha's gratitude would go to the English Lord.

'Why, surely it is better to be friends with the Devil than be poisoned,' he said, calmly, then changed the subject abruptly. 'What news did you have from England?' he asked. 'Your family sent a sheaf of letters and you must have read them by now.'

'Such news,' said Anna. 'Alice will be delivered soon and so will our dear Sarah, even if that birth might bring sadness. I await the outcome with impatience, but you said that Alice was well?'

'As blooming as a rose, Anna, but with none of the gentler perfume of the jasmine,' he replied. Anna looked away. 'Sarah is not well and all the care given her may not save her as Dr Verney says that a baby is like a plant that grows on other plants as a parasite, and will sap away all for its own needs.' He saw her distress and continued. 'Your brother Peter has grown apace and is ready for the Tour.'

'Not my true brother alas, but as dear,' said Anna. 'He has left for Holland now that your friend has taught him so well and he is eager for a chance to speak the language and to see the great painters.'

'The Devil he has!' said Rollo and his horse reared under the involuntary kick in his flanks. 'I thought he would go to Italy first,' he added, but knew that his action had alarmed Anna.

'There is no plague or violence in Amsterdam, is there?' she asked.

'None as yet,' said Rollo, grimly. He rode away as if to look over the next ridge and then came back with his face composed. The cutter that had come fast on the wake of the ship bringing the envoy and Rollo, had brought letters from Pall Mall as well as from the other houses, sent to the docks from the Post Office to await the next boat leaving for Tangier. The letters from Helena now lay in his pocket and he tried to convince himself that Anna might not hear of his marriage, but knew that this was impossible if Peter should arrive in Amsterdam soon and find all the friends that Rollo had made during his sojourn there. If she finds out that I have lied, or even if she accepts that I never said I was not married but hid the fact from her in that way, I might as well leave now and destroy her picture, all memories and all hope of possessing her, he decided.

The distant cloud of dust came closer and the shouts of men announcing the arrival of the Sherif, al-Rashid, rang out against the rocks and the dusty cactus by the track. The horses were melodious with silver bells and harness couplings and bright saddle cloths were luxurious enough to make a lady's bedcover or to hang on the walls of a castle above the dining table of a king. Anna made sure her feathered hat was firmly pinned and followed Rollo as he galloped to meet the sherif, with her Berber woman beside her and her guards following with set faces that showed their fear of horses.

She reined in as Rollo finished his greeting and the sherif smiled at his welcome. 'And I am honoured Mistress Bennet that you come also to escort me to your home.' He eyed the smooth line of her thigh under the simple riding habit and Anna blushed, aware that this mode of dress was alluring in a way that the more practical and modern way of dressing like a man while riding was not, even if many thought the new way was provocative and unladylike and more sexually daring. She held the reins lightly across the silver-chased pommel and sat tall.

'I am in your debt, Your Highness,' she said. 'The soil you sent is good and we have planted many more herbs that Sir Rollo brought from England.'

'I sent one of my servants to your hospital for treatment and he is better, after my wise men could do little for him. He is a good craftsman and I was loath to lose him,' said the sherif. He rode with Anna and Rollo and looked across the necks of the horses at the Englishman, assessing his worth and strength and anxious to know his relationship with the lady. 'How did you know that Mistress Anna needed plants and how did you know what to bring?' he asked, with a sulky look in his eyes.

'I knew Miss Anna long before I came here, sir. We met when we were hardly more than children,' Rollo said lightly. Anna suppressed a smile. Diplomacy was one thing but this was stretching the truth. 'We rode together and visited the same houses,' Rollo went on. 'I know

Colonel Bennet well and we share many mutual friends.' He glanced at Anna and saw her amusement, then steeled himself for her dismay or condemnation; he couldn't know which. 'I brought many medicines on the instruction of a doctor in England when I asked for his advice, knowing that Mistress Anna needed help, but we haven't met for a long time, almost two years, and we have had little time to exchange family news. We have much to tell each other. Since we met, Colonel Bennet has married this lovely lady and I married a lady I met while bereft of friends and country.' He saw Anna tighten her grip on the reins but she gave no other sign of shock.

'What is your wife's name, sir?' she asked.

'Helena Van Steen,' he said. 'We married when her family was good to me and I had no hope of returning to everything I held dear. The world was a bitter place and I found solace in Amsterdam and with a gentle girl and her family.'

Al-Rashid shouted to his men to spur towards the fort and announce his coming. 'I see that you have no need of my eunuchs,' he said with a laugh. 'Your old childhood playmate will protect you and have no need of guards.' He whipped up his horse. 'That is if Sir Rollo is a good Dutch husband and not a scion of the English Court.' He gave Rollo a searching look and saw that Anna seemed calm and disinterested, and yet did not smile at his remarks.

Married? Rollo married to a Dutch woman? Anna looked at him but he seemed to have trouble with his bandolier, empty now in deference to the sherif but well-made and emblazoned

338

with his crest. Was he joking to make sure the sherif saw no cause for jealousy, after his obvious care for her? She rode faster and when they reached the governor's house, tossed the reins to the groom and walked quickly to her own house to change out of her habit. Why am I sad? Why shouldn't he be married? I married Daniel and Rollo knew that this would be so even before he left England. Why wonder if she is fair or dark, bright faced or solemn, and if her body is lithe and supple and free of blemish?

She tore her smock and smothered a cry of impatience while Azziza brought a fresh one, and angrily threw down the dress she had chosen to wear to dinner with the new envoy and Lady Sophie and the sherif. She chose a new gown of soft cotton of a fabric so finely woven that it flew out like silk from the web, making the many colours of the rainbow envelop her in a mist of pastels. It was fabric sent in the first parcel from the sherif and made into the gown by the servant who also made the haik, so it had a curiously Eastern line that clung and left her body and clung again as her movements dictated. The high waist under her breasts and the soft pinner of lace made a picture that almost surpassed the one hanging where Daniel had put it with so much pride.

It was almost noon and Azziza was excited at the prospect of attending her lady while she dined at the governor's house in such illustrious company. Men stared and women smiled as Anna walked slowly through the heat to join the party where Dulcie sat by Lady Sophie as if she had priority over Anna, and looked on acidly as the sherif took Anna's hand and kissed it, motioning to the seat by his side and ignoring Sophie's expression and the annoyance on the face of the envoy who had taken it for granted that his wife would sit by Al-Rashid. From where she sat, Anna could see Rollo only in profile and they could not watch each other's expressions.

Al-Rashid amused her with tales of his family and his many children and she warmed to his genuine pride in his many sons and his knowledge of horses. She spoke of the farm in England where she had spent so many months during the Great Plague that had killed so many before the Fire of London, and he watched the changing expressions and the softness of her glance as she talked of the family she loved.

'Your herbs did nothing to save the City, madam,' he suggested.

'Some helped,' she said, simply. 'Many men and women braved the sickness and helped some to health but there were many different signs of the pestilence and many remedies that suited one but not all. Some say that prayer helped and some that strong spirits washed away the signs but no one knows how it began and how it ended.'

'We have scourges of fever and many die, but it is the will of Allah and we accept this as we accept death when it comes, and birth and the changes of the moon,' said the sherif. 'It is written.'

'And yet you send me men from your oasis for medicines,' said Anna, with a smile.

'Allah sent you to us and we use what he sends.'

The sherif leaned over towards Sir Rufus. 'Mistress Anna might well be the answer to peace in this land,' he said. 'With her, we have something that we need, and she makes good feeling grow between us as nothing brought by force or diplomacy can do.' Sir Rufus looked pleased and then he frowned. Sophie was not happy and he felt that Anna had far too much influence with the sherif for the peace of his own household.

Rollo twisted in his seat to see her face more clearly and Anna saw that he was eating little. Sophie made a mess trying to eat in the Moroccan way and resorted to using a spoon, but Anna ate with her right hand as Al-Rashid and Rollo did, instinctively doing what would please their guest. Sir Rufus picked up a ball of rice in his left hand and the sherif looked shocked and Anna longed to whisper that he must use the right hand for Allah and leave the left only for all unclean purposes. To her relief, Sir Rufus followed his wife's example and used a spoon and the tension settled, but it was clear that only a thin line between custom and courtesy existed and could be broken at any time by a careless lack of knowledge over local sensitivities.

The meal ended and instead of taking a siesta in the opulent room prepared for him, the sherif insisted on visiting the hospital to see how his favourite silversmith fared, and Rollo had no chance of talking to Anna alone. Ayesha bowed low and made obeisance as she backed away from the sherif, then drew herself up and talked freely as if to an equal when he asked her questions. He inspected the cedar-lined chest

341

and picked up one after another of the bottles and packets, clearly fascinated by what he saw and heard. 'When your husband dies in battle, you will join my household, madam,' he said. 'I shall not take from you but give you land and wealth and you will talk with my wise men and women and give me these things. You shall be my second wife and be held in great honour.' He held a bottle in each hand as if he could not let them go, and Anna wondered if he would insist on taking the chest back to his oasis.

A man moaned and he waved a hand, dismissing Ayesha to go to the man. 'I have a duty to my King,' said Anna, gently. 'I am honoured that you should think so highly of my skills but if I go back to England, I can be of greater use to you by sending more of our medicines and by telling you of our latest discoveries in surgery and learning.' She smiled. 'Ayesha is skilled in my ways and learns quickly. When I go home, take her into your service and give her everything she requires and you will profit by your generosity, Your Highness.'

Reluctantly he replaced the bottles and lowered the lid of the chest, then admired the carving and asked the names of the fruit and flowers carved on the sides. Voices from the compound made him sigh and walk away from the chest. 'I must take a rest as we start for the oasis as soon as it is cooler. I had forgotten that I had invited the envoy to stay for a night with his women. Lady Sophie says that she must have a lady-in-waiting as she is the wife of the King's representative.' He smiled and spoke as a European, with true knowledge of the Courts of Kings. 'It seems that Mistress Dulcie makes a good foil and companion and so has been chosen for that task.'

'Are they leaving today?' Anna couldn't hide her surprise.

He laughed. 'You are not as most women. They would know before it was spoken and talk of it, but you see only your work and think of your husband who leaves you with men to desire you and yet not take you.' He walked swiftly to the governor's house, followed by four Sudanese warriors who sat in the shade and waited for their master to emerge as the sun lost its brilliance and force.

Anna made tea and reclined by the gauze-covered window of her room, sensing the heat outside but feeling cooler as a breeze from the sea came over the warm earth and stirred the hangings. She slept briefly and woke to commotion and the hoofbeats of impatient horses. Hastily, she pulled on her smock and the gown she had worn that morning before she changed for dinner with the envoy and went out to bid them a safe and pleasant journey.

Dulcie sat high on a large but placid horse, dressed in a bright habit that looked hot and so tight that it made her face red, and Sophie sat awkwardly on her mount, having been persuaded to ride and not be carried by cart and so make the procession slow. Dulcie looked triumphant. 'I'm sorry that we shall have none of your company, Anna, but Lady Sophie asked for me to accompany her.' She sighed with mock regret. 'You will have so much to do here while we eat fresh fruit and those delicious sweetmeats that

343

the sherif's women prepare for him alone, and of course for his honoured guests.'

Anna tried to appear envious but knew that Azziza had unpacked a basket of choice fruit and other gifts as soon as the camels following the sherif's party had arrived. 'God speed,' she called, and turned back to her own home.

Azziza came from the kitchen and asked for some of the fine white sugar that Anna kept locked up as the women were almost addicted to its sweetness. 'I have ordered food enough for many, My Lady,' she said.

'I am alone tonight with you and the servants. Make sure that Fatima has food and a good bed if she is to sleep here but I am not expecting anyone to sup with me.'

Azziza smiled. 'The English Lord said that you need the protection of a gentleman and he will eat with you, My Lady. Fatima will sleep on the terrace and I shall go back to my family when you have been served.'

'The English Lord has gone to the oasis,' said Anna, and then recalled that she had not seen him with the party.

'He is here, My Lady. He writes to his friends in England and his wife in Holland, and then comes to you.'

'How did you know he had a wife?' asked Anna. The girl smiled. 'Many letters on the ships to Lady Fitzmedwin who lives in Holland. One of the sailors reads English characters and it was thought she must be his mother but now we hear that he is married.' She raised her hands in supplication. 'May Allah relieve his loneliness

344

and make yours less, My Lady.'

'You may go,' said Anna.

'You have not changed your gown, My Lady. You are not beautiful as you were this morning.'

'I see no need to change my gown,' said Anna. She saw the expression of disbelief and said, coldly, 'He is as my brother. I have to see Ayesha before I eat. Call Fatima to go with me across the compound and I shall be here for supper at nine by the clock.'

Ayesha seemed surprised to see her but led the way to the worst of the cases. She brought poultices for the wounds and then insisted that Anna must go home for food, but first must drink with her.

'I shall go now, Ayesha. I need no drink and I shall have fresh tea made in the English fashion from my own kitchen,' she said, with a meaning glance at the bubbling pot that she suspected contained an aphrodisiac concoction.

'As My Lady pleases,' said Ayesha with a glint of humour. 'Go in peace and Allah be good to you.'

The house was lit by many candles and the food seemed better than even Azziza could arrange it when Rollo came and sat with her. Anna managed to smile at his almost boyish contrition that he had said nothing of his marriage to her. He helped himself to dates and wine and filled her glass again. 'I was over-whelmed when I saw you again, Anna. I am married, but by cruel necessity. I am fond of my wife but I have loved but one woman.' Anna looked at him directly and found no deceit in his face, only a great sadness. She moved from the table and snuffed a guttering candle with her fingers. 'I have a beautiful house in Holland and one in London. I have a wife in Holland but no woman to warm my hearth in London and I felt as if I was an alien there,' he said, with a cautious glance to see her reaction. 'I walked over the land that I remembered so well and found all changed after the fire. I found many of my friends missing from the sickness and many who now live on their estates to escape the Court and the attention of the treasury, which is ever hungry for gifts and loans as the Royal coffers grow empty.'

'You have many friends and there was no need for you to leave Holland,' said Anna.

'I saw a painting,' he said. 'I saw a wonderful vision of a woman wearing the gown she wore when last I saw her in her living, fragrant, desirable flesh.' Anna caught her breath. 'I was speechless and vowed that I must see her again. I also made it my business to search for the copy of the painting that was still unsold and asked an agent to buy it for me. I have it in London now but each time I looked at it, my arms ached for you, Anna, my heart was cold and empty and I yearned for your smile, the touch of your hand and your love.'

She went further away and lit more candles as if she was afraid of the intimate shadows in the room. She pulled the shutters over the windows and then pushed them back again to admit the air and snuffed two more candles that were now mere wicks swimming in wax.

'Sit here,' he ordered, gently. 'We are lonely and

346

far from those who could give us the solace we crave.' She sank on to the cushions heaped in Arab fashion by one wall and saw a moth fly into a candle and burn. 'I married because I was desperate and lonely and needed a woman, and you, my darling Anna, married a man who you thought needed you and who you could cherish in sickness and in health, enjoying matters that interested you in the same way. Did either of us find what we wanted?'

She sat with her head bent, as if she waited for a blow to fall but had no courage to fight. 'I married for love,' she insisted.

'And now? Where is he? Why didn't he take you with him? As a senior officer he had the power and the means. If you forget him for a while, he will never know or suffer and if he does know, then I am waiting to take you forever and to leave everything I have in Holland; wife, property and reputation.'

'You could not,' she said.

'I wanted you when he would not accept your name and would not fly in the face of his army discipline. I wanted you as a woman to be cherished, pampered; to make sure that these hands should never be roughened by toil or sorrow for others.' He kissed the roughened fingers as if caressing a smooth lily and his lips found hers, gently and with a certain diffidence as if he couldn't believe it was happening at last. Anna gave kiss for kiss and all the pent-up frustration of the past few weeks melted away in their first embrace and the joy of his skilled hands and body.

347

Chapter 19

'He's a horse of a different colour!' said Edward Verney. 'A piebald if ever I saw one. Who would suspect that he was married and to a Dutch woman?'

'He knew that you might have prejudice, my dear,' said Lady Marian in an effort to make him more reasonable. 'He was the picture of courtesy and had a real affection for us all, or he would never have come here so often,' she added.

'There's more to it than that,' muttered Edward, but he read the letter again and smiled. 'When he comes back, if he ever does, what a shock he'll have to find out that we know about his marriage.'

'Peter was sure to find out as soon as he contacted the men to whom Rollo sent letters of introduction, so I can see no cause for your suspicions, Edward. As soon as Peter reached Amsterdam, he would know and be bound to mention it to us in his next letter.'

'Rollo had no idea that our son would start the Tour in Holland,' said Edward. 'If that was so, there could have been a year or more, with Peter touring Italy and France before Peter found out about his marriage, and by then who knows what that young monkey had in mind to do?'

'You cannot turn from him now, Edward. Remember his care over the gifts we sent to Anna and that beautiful chest he designed to take all that the apothecaries assembled for her. Anna wrote that she was overwhelmed and already uses some of the potions, and that many of the seeds have taken in her garden.'

'Ha! That's it! It's Anna who is the fish he wants. We were just sprats to catch a mackerel. He made a set for her when we were with your uncle and aunt in the country and was a dangerous buck in those days. I knew he couldn't have changed all that much.'

'You are being absurd, Edward,' said Marian, crossly. 'You were as much under his spell as any of us and he never once made any advances to either Alice or Sarah and there were many other pretty girls who looked on him as if they could eat him. I am very fond of the boy and now that he has sobered, I wish that he and Anna could come together. Daniel is a dry stick compared with Rollo and I think neglects his wife shamefully in the name of duty to the King.'

'Well, there's little we can do about it. They are in Tangier, our son is in Amsterdam and we are here in London and I have work to do.' He called for the maid to tell the coachman to bring the carriage round in ten minutes time. 'I have to visit the Navy Office and I will call in at the Post Office in Lombard Street to see what is for us as soon as it's sorted. That will save time if we have anything from Anna. A ship came in last night from Lisbon and may have mail from Tangier on board.'

'Send it home directly Edward, if there is a letter,' said Marian. 'Anna says so little and I fear

349

that she is ill from over-working in that terrible place. It's time that Daniel went back to fetch her home instead of staying on to see to supplies in Lisbon.'

'He'll take the next cutter if he hears that Rollo is there making fancy speeches or more to his wife,' said Edward, grimly.

Marian watched the carriage leave and went back to her tapestry, but the needle drew blood and she put away the silks and woollen threads and sent for Debbie to give an account of the linen used during the week.

'Since Master Peter left and the baby no longer comes here, we use less, My Lady,' said Debbie. She sighed. 'It was so good to have the other baby here and I wish that Miss Alice could have brought Miss Sarah's baby to the house, too.'

'Alice has been careful of her husband's feelings, Deborah. She made him promise to treat the child as one of his family, as indeed it is, but he hates to look at Sarah's baby and so be reminded of her sin. I thought it unwise of Alice to take them both so far away while she accompanies her husband to visit the estates but she was anxious that all the tenants and farmers should see the son and heir and of course, Vincent is besotted over the child and was willing to give way to her as his pride wishes the same.'

'The paint was hardly dry on the painting of Miss Alice and the baby,' said Debbie. 'The student who finished the background was here even after they left, but now it is very pretty, and all the servants have peeped at it, and say how good a likeness it is of them both.'

'Sarah's death made Alice realize that nobody is immortal,' said Marian, solemnly. 'I think she wants a picture to treasure if the Lord ever takes away her child.' She sighed. 'No picture was painted of Sarah's baby and he is a very handsome child. He reminds me of someone, but it must have been of an uncle of James Ormonde who I met at a soirée some years ago. Likenesses have a habit of coming from generations back at times.' She glanced towards the door and said softly, 'Now, you must promise to keep this a secret, Debbie. I asked Willem de Graeff to have a miniature painted of the child. It's strange but I have a great affection for baby James as if he was my own flesh and he has such wicked smiles that I think he will be very intelligent. Put out good wine and sack, and some of that horrid firewater that the Dutch drink, as Willem promised to bring the finished miniature to me today, now that it is set in its frame.'

Marian gazed out of the window overlooking the distant city and knew that she missed her visits to the house on the Strand. It was natural for Alice to want to leave the house that had so many happy and unhappy memories linked with Sarah Clavell, but with her regained figure and enhanced good looks, it might have been more likely that Alice would pester her husband to keep his other promise and allow her to achieve her ambition to be a lady of the Royal household. Possessive motherhood changed a woman, Marian knew, and she felt nothing but relief at the change in her daughter, and longed for cosy afternoons discussing her grandchildren with her once Alice returned.

Willem came into the drawing-room, no longer with a hangdog look as if he had no business there and had not been able to find the entrance used by the servants. He was beaming. 'I called for the miniature at the jewellers as you asked, Lady Marian, and they have done it well.' He opened a velvet-lined box and Marian picked up a rainbow of diamonds that surrounded the tiny portrait of an infant boy. She gasped. 'The diamonds are as fine as any I saw in Amsterdam or The Hague,' he said. 'I made sure they knew that I had knowledge of such things and checked each one before it was set.'

'You have done well, Willem.' She made him sit and help himself to whatever he fancied to drink and he tossed off two small glasses of jenever. 'Now tell me why we were not enlightened about the marriage of Sir Rollo with a Dutch lady.'

Willem choked on his third glass and rummaged for a handkerchief to wipe his streaming eyes. 'I knew you'd find out as soon as Peter reached Holland,' he gasped, and hoped that by now, Rollo had prepared himself for this disclosure.

'I know he was afraid that we might object to her, but we became fond of you, Willem, and now are convinced that all Dutch are not bad,' she said, kindly. 'Tell me, do you know the lady?'

Willem smiled with relief. It was not his affair now to hide anything, so he talked of his home and of Amsterdam and the Van Steens with growing enthusiasm. 'I am selling my own paintings now and when I return I shall be able to

352

offer for the sister of Rollo's wife. I found that many English like the views of the sea that I paint and that there are many prints made of original works which bring in good returns. Mr Verney introduced me to such a company and they want many of my paintings.' He gave a rueful smile. 'I sit with the other students under Mr Lely but I shall never be a portrait painter.'

'When do you see Holland again, my dear?' Marian asked.

'I promised to stay until Rollo is back in London and he talks now of this being soon as his duty in Tangier is finished.'

'And then? You go back to Holland with him and be reconciled to life in Amsterdam after the pleasures of London?'

'I shall return but I have no idea of his plans,' he said, firmly. 'London has been good to me but I yearn for the canals and the fine fields over the polders and the masts of ships seen over the rooftops wherever I go in the town.'

'We shall miss you. When you marry, bring your bride here to stay and see something more of our beautiful country. My son in Surrey has fine horses and would welcome you, and my daughter who also lives there would be good to your wife, even if they do not speak the same language.'

'I had a letter from a friend who knows the Van Steens well,' said Willem. He neglected to say that the letter was from Marikje, Helena's sister, who was not encouraged to write to a poor artist. 'She talks of a fine German girl who travels all over Europe with her father, a diplomat with *entré* to all the Royal houses and seats of government in Europe and beyond. Helena has met her and may be persuaded to come to England with this Eleanor when next her father is summoned to Whitehall.'

'A German baron came to London last year. Now let me think of his name.' Marian frowned. 'Eleanor? Yes, he had a very handsome daughter who came to the theatre with him and we met briefly. She agreed to visit us but they were recalled when the treaty was safely signed and they had other duties.'

'Was it Baron Franz Paul Dusola, ma'am?' asked Willem.

'That's right! Have you met him?'

'Only when I was washing brushes and his daughter was sitting for one of our painters,' he said with a grin. 'I hardly think that is sufficient to claim friendship.' He thought for a moment. 'Rollo met them after he had his revenues restored and all Amsterdam suddenly realized what a fine fellow he was,' he added, drily.

'And you say that Helena met them?' Marian had a look about her that either meant she was planning a huge dinner party or a major campaign of some kind.

'Yes, she was there and the Lady Eleanor laughed at her fears of travelling, saying she had visited every country in the civilized world and knew Europe like the back of her hand. I remember that Rollo tried to persuade Helena to come to England with us, quoting what the lady said, and making Helena quite cross.'

'Why should Helena change her mind now? Does your friend think she will come here?'

Willem looked away, awkwardly. 'Marikje, Helena's sister, has persuaded her to come and if they travel with the Baron's daughter, they will feel safer than with a boat full of coarse sailors,' he said, remembering what Marikje had written.

'Is Marikje your sweetheart, Willem?' Marian asked, smiling. He nodded. 'Then write to her and say that I shall be pleased to entertain any of Rollo's family until he returns from Tangier.' Marian gave a sigh of contentment. 'If only Anna could return with Daniel, we could have such a grand reunion of Anna and Daniel, Rollo and his wife and now you and your little Dutch sweetheart,' she said. 'If only Alice was here with the babies, all would be complete and I would not be left to my tapestry for hours.'

'Rollo has his own fine house in Pall Mall,' Willem ventured to suggest. 'Helena will want to stay there.' He imagined life in the great house, with his own small room at the back where he and Marikje could be alone.

'If the lady speaks no English, she would be lost in such an establishment,' said Marian, firmly. 'She must stay here until she knows the servants in the other house and knows the ways of housekeeping here. Besides, she will want to be taken everywhere and see some of our lovely countryside.'

'You are very kind, as always, Lady Marian,' said Willem, knowing when he was beaten. He grinned. It was as well. If he took away Marikje's virginity he might find it hard to return to Amsterdam and make any kind of living there, with a raging parent making everyone turn against him; and he knew now that he wanted to marry the girl.

'Write today,' Marian said firmly. 'If you would give kind messages from me and my husband to Helena's family, that would be civil of you, Willem as I speak no Dutch.' Her mind was in a pleasant whirl, anticipating the visit and wondering what Rollo would say when his wife greeted him on his return to England in a week or so. 'Write also to Rollo and remind him of the Baron and his daughter. I expect that Helena has told him about her decision, and it seems that he has been summoned home by the Duke of York to other duties now that the governor's envoy is established and the house is quite ready for the governor's arrival.'

'I wonder if he knows, My Lady. The last ship that carried mail for Tangier from The Hague was lost to the corsairs and Marikje said that many letters were lost. Helena found that her letters went unanswered and it was safer to send them to Belgium first and then on to Tangier. Dutch ships are still at risk in the Straits and it is not certain who does the piracy in those waters now. Also, Rollo has to stay in Lisbon on Crown affairs for a few days on the way home, and may not have news from Holland until he reaches London.' He laughed. 'I know more about Rollo than Helena does just now and I know more about Helena than Rollo does. If I was a dove, I could carry messages to them faster than the mail does, and safer.'

'Edward said it takes but two days to travel from Amsterdam to London by sea, in a fast ship with many galleys and fine sails. Write at once,' she urged. 'And if she is here before Rollo receives her messages, then at least we can take care of her until he joins her.'

Marian looked serious. 'We heard from Daniel some time ago and Edward was worried that his health was bad. Dr Verney told us of the terrible fevers that men have in Africa and in the countries in the Mediterranean Sea. Daniel has suffered in this way after duty in Guinea and Tangier but God has been good to Anna and she seems to keep free of such maladies.' She glanced at the folded paper, sealed with Edward's name on it. 'This is in his hand and Edward asked me to open anything that came from Tangier or Lisbon, in case a message must go back urgently, but I hesitate to do so.' Reluctantly, she broke the seal and read the contents, her face showing her mixed emotions. 'Daniel has been very ill and has been summoned home to London.'

'Will your Anna come home, too?' Willem asked, quickly. From the lack of comment about the lady, he had gathered that Rollo was either well over his obsession with Anna or more likely, he was so involved that he could no longer mention her name in a letter to his friend.

'Poor Anna! She is all alone in that terrible country, at the mercy of foreigners! If Daniel comes home she must pack everything and come too. It's too bad,' she added, crossly. 'A lady should never have to make all those decisions and travel alone. Daniel should have managed better!'

'You can but wait, ma'am, and you have

enough to occupy you with Helena and Marikje if they arrive first,' Willem said. His mind was in a whirl, and he desperately wished he knew if Rollo had any idea of his wife's intention of coming to England. He also wondered if Rollo know that Daniel Bennet would be in London when he returned. Willem breathed again. Of course! Rollo was calling at Lisbon and would hear all about Daniel on his way home. He grinned. 'Rollo and Daniel Bennet might sail together from Lisbon if Rollo catches up with him before he leaves,' said Willem, and hoped that the ship would be big enough to contain two such men with one love for the same woman.

'I must write to Anna at once. Come, my dear, we shall sit together over our pens and you shall have dinner with us after taking the letters to the Post Office. I'll ask Debbie to tell Sam to give you a good horse and the letters may go on the next tide if a ship is ready to leave. I shall tell Anna that we are to have Dutch visitors and also that we must know what ship brings her back when she is ready.' Marian smiled. 'It will warm my heart to see Anna again. I am sorry that her husband is sick, but if it brings my Anna back home safely, then I cannot wish him well enough to return to Tangier!'

She called for Debbie and gave orders for dinner and for a fast horse to take Willem and the letters, and instructed Willem to call in at Edward's offices in Lincoln's Inn Fields and leave a message that Daniel was returning. She dried the ink on her letter and folded the paper, sealing it with hot wax and her own family seal.

If Daniel is still in Lisbon you could take a ship there and come back together, Anna. Bring a servant or two to help and protect you and I shall be overjoyed to have you under our roof once more, until you settle in your own home.

She saw Willem leave and wished that she could add more to the letter but it was too late. She had suggested servants, and then recalled that Anna now had black or brown servants of such a nature that would upset the ordinary calm of a house in London. With alarm she recalled that Lady Witner was given a negro slave boy, by a relative coming back from Africa with parrots, slaves and silks and a bad dose of malignant fever, and whenever Marian visited the house and was greeted by her friend, the massive boy, now fully grown, loomed up behind Lady Witner like a menacing shadow, dressed in the full livery of orange and black that had never seemed so outlandish as when worn by this magnificent black.

She wrote another letter but tore it up. Willem came back and she hurried to meet him. 'Mr Verney was not in his offices but I met him by the docks. The ship leaving tonight on the tide will call at Lisbon and then Tangier, so your good wishes for Colonel Bennet will reach him before your letter to Miss Anna reaches Tangier.' He shrugged. 'A ship bound for Amsterdam left as I watched, and another leaves in two days time, unless I wish to trust my mail to a dirty boat that has the most villainous crew on board I ever saw, and I would have doubts about the honesty of the captain.'

'We can but wait,' agreed Marian, and took pleasure in watching Willem spear his meat on a sharp knife and mop up the gravy with a piece of bread. I miss my son, she decided. It will be good to have Rollo in England again and even Daniel had something to say that was interesting if he was in the mood to talk. She dreamed and planned for the coming visits and soon the house was humming with the news, with the servants guessing what was wrong with Colonel Bennet that he should be sent home, and hinting that as Miss Anna had no children, he might have had the Pox or something in the past to make him unable to give her any. Marian heard the murmurs and wondered again at the miracle of little Richard Vincent's birth after all her fears over Vincent. 'Servants' gossip,' she said to herself and spoke sharply to Debbie who voiced the view that Miss Anna needed another husband to make her fertile.

'White women in hot countries do not bear easily,' said Marian. 'And many women do not conceive at all after living in such places.'

'Margaret says,' began Debbie and then saw that Lady Marian was annoyed at the mention of the woman's name.

'When does she marry?' asked Marian. 'She is a good worker but I shall be happy to see her go.'

'Since Mr Verney refused to take on another groom she is anxious to join the household of Lord Chalwood who has offered a stable-boy's job and a small house out in the country to her husband when they marry. She will mend for the house as she does for us and we shall be the losers, My Lady,' Debbie added, reproachfully.

'I would rather she went. I think she spies on everyone and even if this is her nature, I want none of it. Alice was right about her and I know that she will shed no tears over my losing a good seamstress. Find me another woman who is quiet and minds her own business, Debbie, and I shall see her before she comes into my service. When Alice brings the babies back here, we shall need a good woman and another maid for the linen. A house full of important visitors will tax our servants sorely and I like to keep them contented.'

Edward came home early, full of news. 'Baron Dusola is expected at Whitehall and his party left Holland yesterday.'

'Lady Fitzmedwin is with them?' Marian clasped her hands together. 'We must send Sam to Rollo's house in Pall Mall with a message that she will be inspecting it soon, and then meet the ship and bring her here. Willem must stay here too, to act as interpreter and to tell Debbie what dishes Helena will find acceptable.'

'I have left word with the Embassy that the Baron and his daughter will be welcome here. We must give a soirée, my dear. If Rollo comes soon, we may be able to arrange it before the Baron moves on again to another country.'

Marian changed her dress three times before they left for the docks and insisted that she must be there to greet the newcomers, even when Edward warned her that the breeze from the river was foul and might give her a sore throat, but he was secretly relieved to have her by his side. The Baron was of a very noble family and he might not speak much English, but when the party stepped on shore, Edward's fears were stilled, as the Baron and Eleanor spoke English with only the slightest German accent, and were delighted to be given hospitality with a family before having to endure the draughty rooms they recalled in the Embassy.

'Come home with us, and then you may like to stay in Rollo's house which is ready for you,' suggested Edward, who had refused to have everyone under his feet in his own home for an unspecified length of time. 'Make them too comfortable and they'll be here for Christmas,' he said when Marian wanted them all to stay under one roof. 'Besides, Rollo will want to be with his wife and if Daniel and Anna come home, we shall have more than enough to do here.'

The two carriages were piled up with baggage and Sam ordered hackney carriages to take the rest of the many boxes to the new house on Pall Mall. He swung on to the box of his gleaming carriage and Edward felt proud of his coachman, the spacious carriage and fine livery and the fact that his wife was of noble birth. Marian glanced at the pale face of the silent Dutch woman by her side and saw that her hands were trembling. Impulsively, she took the hand nearest to her and pressed it, gently, smiling with such warmth that Helena burst into tears.

Eleanor spoke rapidly in Dutch and Helena shook her head. 'Tell her that we are delighted to

362

see her and that Willem, an old friend, will be waiting at the house to make things easy for her to talk to us, when you go on to the Embassy to see the Duke,' said Marian.

'Willem?' asked Marikje and blushed. She spoke to her sister and at last as the carriage drew up to the front door, Helena smiled mistily, and wiped her eyes.

'Lady Fitzmedwin!' said Willem, and Helena looked startled as if unused to this form of address. 'You are as fresh as one of our Dutch spring flowers, Helena.' He took her hand and clasped it in his warm grasp. Marikje ventured to come forward and blushed.

Eleanor laughed. 'So that's why the little sister wished to come to England,' she said.

'Would you tell Helena that I have prepared rooms for her and her party and that she must stay there as long as she pleases and not go at once to the house in Pall Mall as my husband suggested,' Marian added, with a slight air of defiance.

Helena and Marikje asked to be taken to change from their travelling clothes into something more suitable for dinner, but Eleanor shrugged away such a suggestion and wandered about examining the furniture, the pictures and hangings with the eye of an expert. 'I am dressed for the day,' she said. 'I shall wear this to see the Duke and if he does not like me as I am it is not my fault.'

Edward took her into the library to see the portrait of Anna, and looked on proudly while she gazed at it in admiration. 'It was done just before she left for Tangier,' he said.

'A Lely, and a fine one,' said Eleanor. 'What a charming subject, and with such grace.' Her head tilted slightly to one side as she looked at it. 'Not wholly English but the darkness adds something deep and sad and those intelligent eyes will haunt me and whoever gazes at her.'

Edward told her about Anna and her history. He mentioned the name Ruyter and the fact that she had been his ward as a distant relative of his wife's noble family. 'She is now married to Colonel Bennet and returns soon from Tangier,' he added.

'A hole as black as Hell,' said Eleanor, cheerfully. 'I have been there once, and found no amusements, no handsome men and no food to suit my father. The sheiks are fine-looking and might have been exciting, but we were there for a fleeting visit and never saw them for more than half an hour at a time.'

A man-servant came to the door and whispered to Lady Marian that it was time for the guests to gather at the dining table. She nodded to Edward who had come back from the library with the Lady Eleanor and Helena smiled when she saw the carefully prepared food and the cleanliness of the appointments at the table.

'Did you think that the English lived like pigs?' asked Willem, with all the superiority of one who had believed this and now wanted to impress Marikje with his air of knowing what went on in the world outside of Amsterdam. He laughed when she looked anxiously at Lady Marian. 'Have no fear. Lady Marian speaks no Dutch and

364

her husband very little. They are good people, rather like your own parents, Helena, and they have a great feeling for Rollo.'

'Have you heard from him?' asked Helena. 'He told me that he would have to come here and not return to Holland for a while, and as he said nothing of when I might see him again, my father was angry and said I would lose him if I did not do my duty and follow him.'

'Was that wise?' Willem said, and regretted it as soon as the words formed.

'Are you afraid of what I might find out, Willem?' she asked, and her eyes were sad and harder than he recalled.

'You refused to go with him when he came here, Helena,' he pointed out. 'If he has changed towards you, then he is not completely to blame, but you bear his name and there is much to entertain you here while you wait for him. The house is very grand and the theatres are good. You will see the Royal family and many fine courtiers and be invited to many houses.' He noticed that Helena was wearing clothes bought from the salon that supplied dresses to the wife of the French ambassador in Amsterdam, and knew that she was maturing and putting aside all her simple garments and with them, perhaps more of her past as she felt her position as the wife of Sir Rollo Fitzmedwin.

'I miss him and I wish to have him by my side,' she said, simply. 'Marikje was anxious to come here and now that the terrible sea is behind me, I am happy.' She smiled. 'My father was impressed when I told him that you were studying with

365

Mr Lely and had been accepted with the Verney family. I shall speak of you again and tell him that you will make a fine husband for Marikje.' Her tone was firm as if she was on a much more influential plane than when she was merely the daughter of the merchant in Amsterdam.

Eleanor listened to Edward and then to Willem, switching easily from Dutch to English and back again and making her own observations. Her eyes missed nothing and her glance alighted on the miniature that Lady Marian wore for the first time about her neck on a thick golden chain. Edward had dismissed it as a piece of female sentiment and a bauble that had cost him dearly. He had not really examined it and certainly had no idea of the good likeness that the tiny portrait had to the infant James.

Marian saw her interest. 'I have acquired this only this week, *madame,*' she explained. 'It is a picture of a dear child, and one who my daughter loves, having been born to her closest friend, now dead.'

She slipped the pendant from her neck and handed it to Eleanor, who gazed at it with a puzzled expression. 'To whom was this lady married?' she asked.

Marian sighed. 'She was to marry her lover but he died and when the baby was born we think she died of a broken heart. He was James Ormonde, a distant relative of the statesman of that name, and a good young man.'

'An Ormonde?' Eleanor laughed. 'I know the family, and a mousy lot they are in colouring. Darker than most in skin but not like this. Tell me

366

what was she like? As the lady in the other picture?'

Marian shook her head. 'My daughter has golden hair and Sarah had hair much like but slightly darker, with blue eyes and fair skin.'

'This is no Ormonde,' Eleanor said. 'I know this face. I have seen it many times in the Court of Louis and in the embassies of Germany when he was there. A fine courtier with a great love of fair women, but as punishment, a wife who bears him daughters and no heir. Tell me, when was he here?'

'I don't understand,' said Marian and Edward looked bleakly at the two women. 'Who do you mean? James Ormonde was the father and Sarah's only lover.'

'You harboured a minx and a liar, madam. I would wager half my wealth that this is the child of Le Comte Marc Lefèvre, and one he would be proud to own as his.'

'He was at the theatre and in this house for but an evening. That is all! He called on my daughter's husband but he was not there and he stayed only an hour at most, or so the servants said.' Marian was agitated. 'You are not amusing, madam! Sarah was as our own child and as honourable. Her lover was James Ormonde and no other.'

'As you say, Lady Marian.' Eleanor tossed the trinket back in a shaft of rainbow light. 'If she had one lover, then why not more? I know nothing of this Sarah but I know women. If she deceived you over one man then she could do so about the Comte, and he can seduce a girl in less

367

time than it takes other men to change a tunic!'
She smiled. 'It is of no importance. My father is
becoming restless and wishes me to leave to see
the Duke. My thanks for your hospitality and I
hope to visit you again before we leave London.'

Chapter 20

'I shall write long letters to Lady Marian and my other friends,' said Anna. Her face felt frozen as if she could never smile again and Rollo touched the corner of her mouth gently. 'Your servants may need help to pack all the things you have bought here,' she said, trying to sound practical. 'So much silver and all that leather will take a great deal of space on the ship.'

'You must come with me,' he insisted. 'I cannot leave you here alone.'

'That is impossible. You said that Helena might visit your house in England and if so, how can we be together there?'

'My Dutch friend Willem told me that, but I have had no letters from Helena for weeks and now learn that a ship was taken by the corsairs, which might have carried them. It is not certain that she will be in London and I shall hear something before I leave next week. A sail was sighted in the offing and now waits for a fair wind to bring her to the Mole, carrying a Portuguese flag and so is from Lisbon.'

'I am anxious to hear from Daniel, too. I have no idea of his plans and without you, I fear that this place will kill me,' she whispered.

'Come, my love. We have to smile tonight at the governor's house. The sherif will be there and all the senior officers and civil servants of the fort.'

He laughed. 'And Lady Sophie tied up in a gown that might have fitted her before she took so well to Arab sweets and no exercise, but I am to be honoured in this way before I leave for the Court of St James and to His Majesty's bidding, so help me to put on a brave show, and perhaps even enjoy each other's company from afar.'

Anna smiled, faintly. 'If I was in London, I would be tempted to paint my face and then hide my pallor and misery behind a mask,' she said. She flung herself into his arms. 'We have had so little. We are only now discovering what might have been and now you have been called away and I have no hope for my future.'

He kissed her with desperation. 'We *must* be together. You shall come to England after I leave and stay quietly until I hear what the King wants from me then we shall go to France and live there away from London and Amsterdam. Trust me, my dearest Anna. We *must* be together, but first, I must settle my affairs and sell property to buy more in France. My land agent will see to it all, discreetly, and Helena has enough in Holland to keep her in comfort for the rest of her life.'

'You loved her enough to marry her,' Anna said, searching his face for a sign that he had never loved as he now loved her.

'I met a simple, loving girl who filled my empty arms and gave me peace after a time of suffering. She and her family were good and I married her, thinking that I might never see England again. I do love her for that and I shall hate to hurt her, but she has her own people and has never shown much interest in England.' He moved restlessly.

'You recall my earlier life when I was profligate and no fit husband for any woman. Loneliness and fear of what could happen if I returned to my home made a man of me, and in a way, I admit that I have Helena to thank for my sobering.' He gave a bitter laugh. 'There was nothing to do but be sober in that household, with her father having me spied on at every turn and using my title to gain his own prestige; until I had news that I would be welcome in London and that my affairs were in order and prospering.' He kissed her lips and then held her away to gaze at her face. 'Now, I feel free. I have given them so much and now I want you, Anna. I want to hold you like this forever and to see your face every time I wake.'

She shuddered. 'I can see no future,' she said, quietly. 'Every time I think of you leaving, it is as if a deep pit yawns and I am standing by its side, helplessly watching you go, and knowing that I can never see you again.'

'We must dress and put on our company smiles,' he said, and shook her gently. 'If we fly to France, it will be but a flutter at Court and there will be many who will approve and envy us. Lord Broukner has a mistress with whom he lives openly in London and takes as his wife to each house to which he is invited. The King has many women, accepted and respected by society; even envied, and the French take it for granted that once married, they take mistresses.'

'I want to be no mistress,' said Anna. 'I am too proud to be hidden in some lonely house to await the arrival of my lover, like a common whore.'

'I will carry you high, like a pennant; a declaration of our love and any who take it on themselves to condemn us will have me to answer them! Many will envy me and so try to decry us, but I have found who are my friends through bitter experience and am content that we shall be comfortable. The treaty with France is being considered and there may be trouble with Holland again if we take sides with Louis, but surely the King will have more sense than to negotiate with France against the triple alliance.'

'Azziza is singing, and that means that she needs to come to help me dress,' said Anna. 'She suspects that when I spend time with you alone we are not talking about books!'

'So the whole fort and the compound know that we bed each other?' Anna nodded. 'Servants talk in any language and Arabs are worse than most,' he conceded. 'I know that Dulcie looks on me as if I was a viper and follows you with a glance that could curdle milk. It is time I left and let you return to normal, until we can be together,' he added. 'Or Daniel might hear enough to bring him on the back of a dolphin or on the wings of an albatross!'

'He had a fever but I hope is better,' said Anna with a worried frown.

'I have a fever that only you can cure but it must wait until after this tiresome ceremony.' He kissed her brow and left hurriedly, nearly tossing Azziza to the ground as he passed her where she was squatting by the door.

'My Lady will wear silk?' suggested Azziza with a smile. 'My Lady will be so beautiful and all the men will desire you.'

'My Lady will wear her best gown,' said Anna, with a lift to her chin. 'She will wear the blue silk, and the gauze and lace pinner and fill the neckline with jewels.'

'The ruby of the sherif My Lady?' Azziza hissed her approval and ran to fetch the rustling silk gown, and later laid the jewel box open at Anna's side. She assisted Anna with the gown and fixed the ruby to the low décolletage and clapped her hands when Anna added diamonds and a fine sapphire necklet and pinned a matching sapphire butterfly into her hair.'

'Rings, My Lady?' she asked as if begging a favour. 'Many rings to show the wealth of the colonel?'

'I am not a Berber woman to wear all my wealth in jewels,' said Anna, and wanted to remove the sparkling array at her throat, but Azziza was entranced and she had no heart to disappoint her. 'Rings!' she said, and put on emeralds and diamonds but hesitated before a simple ring that Daniel had given her when they walked in the fields and the world was young and innocent. She pictured his face, gaunt and severe but full of passion, and his face when he had been near to death and longing for her arms as a child longs for comfort and love. She placed it back in the box and shut the lid.

'My Lady is as beautiful as all the houris in Heaven,' said Azziza. 'My Lord the sherif, who is my father and my mother and blessed of Allah, will desire you and give you honour, My Lady.'

'I think not,' said Anna and smiled. 'I have

refused to be his second wife and to live in his harem because I doubt if my husband would allow it!'

'Your husband the colonel?' Azziza smiled, knowingly. 'When the English Lord goes away soon, then you may go to the sherif?'

'No! When the English Lord goes back to London, I shall go to Lisbon to find my husband.' She stared into the yellow mirror as if another person had made that decision and she had no power to prevent it happening. 'Give me my shawl and ask the guard to escort me to the big house,' she said, in a subdued voice.

Anna breathed deeply and saw the stars above her and a moon that made torches unnecessary. The African night was warm but with a touch of the chill that would surface nearer to dawn after the heat of the day, and when the nocturnal creatures would run across the desert and make the darkness hum with a life unknown during the light hours. She shivered. London had never been as dear as this terrible place, now that she had given her heart and body to Rollo Fitzmedwin, with no reservation, no holding back and with such passion that their union made them both afraid, and dumb with the wonder of their discovery.

Dulcie was wearing a gown made by an Arab woman out of silk brought in from Lisbon. It gave her hair an added lustre and her figure a shape that nature had neglected, as it hung in tactful folds and skimmed her firm hips with charity. Lady Sophie was resplendent in taffeta that sounded like rice on a tin tray whenever she moved, but gave her the regal look that she coveted and already, the two ladies were nibbling sweetmeats and sipping wine brought from Germany.

Rollo stood watching the scene, his gaze gravely bent as Sir Rufus declared that he had a plan for the Mole that would speed the building at less cost. 'Of course, we shall have trouble with the Sherif but that can be overcome with flattery and gifts,' he said, expansively. 'I am not a warmonger and I think he is as near to being civilized as any who are bred in this country can ever be, and so I shall mention it and then ask Whitehall for permission to change our plans.'

'With less monies at your disposal from the Navy Office at home, do you think that this will be sanctioned?' said Rollo. 'I hear that the King is losing interest in the Mole and wishes that we were out of Tangier.'

'That is my concern and now you are leaving, you can have no interest in our doings here,' said Sir Rufus with a bland expression that hinted to Rollo that the base at Tangier would do well without a handsome young man who stirred the hearts of the women and made the portly envoy jealous. Not for the first time, Rollo wondered why he had been ordered home so swiftly, with thanks from the Duke for duty done quickly and completely, leaving him free for other more pressing engagements in London and the Court.

He saw Anna arrive and turned away, suddenly overcome by her beauty and dignity beside the other ladies in the room. Dulcie might bathe her hands in oil and lemon juice to keep them white and soft but who would care if Anna had slightly rough hands when it was so apparent that she was a person of grace and breeding?

Al-Rashid sat on cushions by a low table and watched the assembly, smiling at everyone presented to him as if he was the host and not Sir Rufus. He watched Anna with a smile that made Rollo want to stand between them so that the sherif could not see her, and he walked over to speak to Al-Rashid to make sure that he was well attended.

'I have to take my leave of you, sir,' said Rollo. 'My Sovereign has summoned me to London and I can no longer enjoy your country.'

'I am very disturbed to hear this,' said Al-Rashid. 'You cannot leave me with these people?' He smiled. 'I have no desire for the women, except for Mistress Anna Bennet, and the envoy has no conversation.' He glanced across at the envoy who was drinking far too much wine and becoming red-faced and voluble. 'I think that I shall see less of the people here unless Mistress Anna stays,' he added, with a sidelong look at Rollo. 'I might even feel that I need this fort for the protection of my own people.'

It was a thinly veiled threat and Rollo nodded, without smiling. 'It would grieve her to know you think like this, Your Highness,' he said. 'She has worked hard with your people and given time and health to make the sick well again.'

Rollo flicked the lace from his cuff where it fell over his hand and produced a snuff box studded with pearls. Idly, he opened it and took snuff and brushed the end of his nose with a silk handkerchief. 'A pretty box,' said the sherif. 'French and priceless in its way.' He smiled. 'I know about such baubles and have a collection but none as fine as that.' He held out a hand to take it to examine, and Rollo placed it in his palm. The sherif called for tea and his own servant hurried over with a tray of beaten silver holding exquisite silver cups, filled with hot liquid. The Sherif nodded and Rollo was served with some and asked to sit by him.

'In Holland we have a custom,' Rollo began, and then coughed. 'We have a similar custom of tea drinking but use fine china of a pretty blue and white design that matches the tiles we use in our kitchens.'

'What were you saying?' he was asked. The sherif held the snuff box and turned it in his hand.

'Nothing, Your Highness. Only that if someone admires a possession, then it is as you know, courteous to let it rest where it seems comfortably in the hand of the guest.'

'I shall treasure it and may Allah bless you. I shall pray for His protection over this fort and over the people here.'

'I shall leave with a feeling that I have a friend here,' said Rollo. 'Even if Miss Anna has to join her husband in Lisbon, it will be good to know that the others are safe under your patronage.' Al-Rashid nodded, but more reluctantly now that Anna was mentioned, and Rollo looked across the room at the envoy and hoped that he wouldn't provoke a diplomatic incident through his ignorance.

'You leave next week? I shall send men to guard the ship after your belongings are on it and to make a guard of honour to send you away. I think the corsairs may be away for a while and you will have a safe passage,' the sherif said, opening and shutting the snuff box as a child might when given a gift.

'It is good to have such news. You have good spies, Your Highness.' And more than news, if I think aright! thought Rollo. The corsairs seem to know just what ships come and what they carry.

Dulcie beckoned as soon as Rollo stood to take his leave and to make room for an officer who wished to talk to Al-Rashid. 'You have neglected the ladies,' she said, archly. 'What mischief have you planned with our handsome sherif?'

'No mischief, ma'am, but I have given away a snuff box I treasured, to be assured of the safety of the fort when I leave,' he said, grimly. 'Be very careful. He has charm but he could destroy everything here if he wished and could persuade the Emperor of Morocco that we are not wanted here. I leave you all with some trepidation, and hope that no word is said out of place. Sir Rufus has much to learn about local customs and when Anna leaves, there will no longer be the hospital to make goodwill here.' He glanced at the limp white hands. 'You could, of course learn from her before she goes and take on the sick and wounded. It might make all the difference.' He smiled at her horrified expression and the fluttering of the white hands that had never done a stroke of work.

'My husband would never let me do that! It is

378

not work for a lady!' She smiled. 'You are teasing me, Sir Rollo. Tell me that you will write to me and describe the latest fashions when you reach London. If I give you a note to my dressmaker in Covent Garden, she will make clothes in the latest styles and send them to me here, as it seems that my husband is not as fortunate as you to be recalled.'

He saw the discontent under the bright smile and promised to help her, and hoped that when Anna had gone and the competition was less, she might be flattered by the Sheiks and Al-Rashid. To his relief, many of the guests were leaving as soon as Al-Rashid left for his suite of rooms, and Arab music throbbed to a drum beat that might help the Mighty One to sleep. Anna was talking to Lady Sophie, and men with torches were ready to light her home. Rollo begged to be excused and stood by the door of Anna's house until she came and dismissed her guards, then opened the door and was waiting in her bedroom when she slipped out of her shawl.

Azziza had left cool drinks by the desk and a fresh nightgown for Anna to wear while she sat by the veiled window to drink the last draught of the day. She turned to Rollo and hid her face in his shoulder. 'How many more nights? How can I let you go?' she sobbed. 'Tonight was as it will be if we ever meet again in London. We shall be dressed in fine clothes and be able to smile at each other and talk about the time of year and the food we are being served, but never to touch like this never be close and one, and never to know each other's heart.' She held his hand and kissed it. 'I will go with you whatever you decide,' she said at last when he had released her hair and kissed her throat. 'Tonight, I wanted to cry out that we were lovers and that we were bound together by ties that can never be broken, and then you came over and we talked of cactus and its many uses!'

'My love,' he whispered and carried her to bed. 'I should curse you for making me dependent on your love,' he said at last when they lay still entwined as if they must be closer and closer and never be parted. 'Women were meant to please men and not to send them into this state of permanent desire and slavery. You are right. We are bound by ties that can never be broken even if we are apart; apart for a while,' he stressed. 'We shall share a house and a bed in France and laugh at our fears.'

He saw the thin line of light above the mountains and heard a camel snort across the compound as its master pulled it up. 'The sherif will be leaving,' said Anna. 'Go now and I will see you at noon for dinner.'

Rollo walked softly through the darkness and entered the house by the side door. He heard the camels and horses and the shouts of men as the sherif's party emerged for the journey back to the oasis. The water left by his valet was cool and Rollo washed all over before pulling on clean linen britches and shirt. He heard the horses' hooves recede over the hill and sat down to rest, but was awakened from a doze by fresh sounds. He swung his legs round and stood by the window then hurried down to the men who had come on camels from the Mole.

'News!' shouted one. 'Mail from London and Lisbon.'

Rollo snatched his bundle of letters and told a man to take any that were for Mistress Anna Bennet and to ask her servant to wake her. The dawn air was cool but he was sweating. He went back to his rooms and sank on to his bed, tearing at the seals of the letters as if they contained vital news. His heart pounded with sudden fear and when he read the letter from Willem he let it fall from his hand and stared at the ceiling. Helena in London? Helena installed in the house in Pall Mall and being entertained by the Verneys as their own kin?

I must report to Whitehall, he thought. Until I see the King or the Duke of York I can make no plea for absence from the country unless it is on a diplomatic mission. He reached over and picked the paper from the floor. *I hear that Colonel Bennet is sick and returning to London soon,* said Willem. *I hope I warn you in time, my friend, and that you can arrange your life as you wish.*

He walked slowly to Anna's house as if he had news for her in the papers he held in his hand, but passed unnoticed as everyone seethed with the coming of the ship and the servants had to find out what was on board. 'Anna?' he called. He walked into the room and found her staring into space, her face pale and the letter crumpled in her hands.

'What is it?' he asked, taking the letter from her cold hand.

'Daniel is not coming here. He has been sent

back to England as he is sick and is not fit for work in Tangier. This came from him in Lisbon and by now he will be on his way home.' Her voice broke. 'He will be there when I arrive and there is no escape,' she sobbed.

'Of course there is,' he said, firmly. 'In one way this is good news. We can leave together and make our plans as we sail.' He lifted her face to his. 'We both must act a part for a while. You must be better even than Mistress Knipp at the King's theatre.' She gave a faint smile. 'I have news too, of Helena who has arrived in London with her sister Marikje and Eleanor, the daughter of the baron I mentioned. She is at Pall Mall and spends much of her time with Willem at the Verneys' house.' Rollo set his mouth in a cruel line. 'Have no fear, Anna. I will arrange that she returns home with a good settlement and we can go as we planned to France, once I have settled my affairs.'

'You don't understand,' she whispered. 'I loved Daniel when he was wounded and weak and if I see him again in that state, I shall have no choice but to nurse him again.'

Roughly, he shook her and then kissed her with such savagery that her lip bled. 'I need you! I am sick at heart without you and I have suffered with longing for the sound of your voice and the touch of your hair. When did he ever care enough for you? When did you come before his work and his career in the army? He left you here and for all he knows you might have gone with the sherif and left him forever.'

'He trusts me,' said Anna, unevenly.

'Trust? Was he quite blind to your beauty and

the effect you have on men? Was he right to put that strain on you knowing that men here need the solace of women?'

'I can't think now,' said Anna. 'Could you make arrangements for me to leave? I shall need help to organize our furniture and baggage. I must tell Sir Rufus and Lady Sophie.' She smiled. 'Dulcie will be glad to see me go, but she will be furious to know we leave together.'

Azziza came hurrying into the house. 'Ayesha asked for you, My Lady. The sherif left a message that he wishes you to go to the harem to give medicine to two of his women, but Sir Rufus refused. He told me what is wrong and wants potions from the magic box.' Azziza looked pleading. 'I could ask Ayesha to give them to me and follow the camels. His Mightiness is angry and wishes to have this help now.'

'He hopes to keep you,' said Rollo. 'If you go there now, he can say with truth that you went of your own will, and not even Sir Rufus can then bring you back unless he gives the order to bring you back by force.'

He looked at her seriously. 'Now do you believe that Daniel was wrong to leave you here?'

'Bring me paper and ink,' Anna commanded. She wrote a letter to the sherif, telling him of her recall to London and regretting that she could not come personally to the oasis.

When my husband is restored to health, I will come back, and to show my good faith, I will leave my medicine box with Ayesha who will serve you and the Fort well.

'I treasure that above all else,' she said to Rollo. 'He has wanted it ever since he saw it and now, I have to part with it. It is a part of you, and I love every bottle, every herb but do you agree that if we are to keep the peace, it must go?' She touched his hand. 'A handful of seeds, you said. It was so much more. It was a gift of such love that I never expected to find this side of heaven, and I must give it up.'

'Give up the herbs and keep the love,' he whispered. 'Now we must work and meet again on the Mole in three days' time.'

Chapter 21

The high shrouds supporting the top mast swayed with sickening creaking groans and the men on deck ran to tighten ropes, to batten down shifting deck cargo and to swill away the waste that strewed the scuppers. Anna drew her cloak more firmly around her shoulders and her pale face was indistinct in the depths of the dark cloth hood.

'Are you sure you would rather stay here than lie down below?' asked Rollo. He watched the waves breaking over the bow and wondered how anyone could make the sea a career. 'We leave one unfriendly environment for another,' he said. 'I prefer dry land and can never stop wondering how Vincent Clavell chose to go to sea when he had so much to do with his estates and the company of his friends and family.'

'If all I hear is true, he must regret that now. Sarah was very dear to him, and now he has but her child to remind him of her and of his neglect that led to her seduction,' said Anna.

They leaned against a rail, bracing themselves for the movement of the ship, unable to be warm or comfortable but taking a perverse delight in suffering, so long as they could be together, and the officers on board avoided them as if they sensed the misery underlying the trite phrases of polite comment and the expressions on the two faces. Anna pressed closer to feel the warmth of the firm body that had brought her so much joy, and to stamp on her memory all the small things she remembered now, the way his hair grew long and thick and shining, and the way his mouth could turn from a line of cold derision when he spoke of his enemies or in a derogatory way about Sir Rufus and his staff, to a gentle mobile curve of love that sapped away all her resistance and guilt.

She saw the man he had become, and traces of the youth who had run rough-shod over every will but his own and she knew that he would fight for her to stay with him.

The coast of Africa lay far away behind the mist and droplets of salty foam made her cloak silvery. They were summoned to eat and the crew was surprised that the two passengers showed no sign of sea-sickness but merely looked pale. Rollo crumbled bread in his hands and ate the thick chick pea soup that had been made on shore and brought on board. Spices that he knew he would remember all his life made it palatable, and Anna breathed deeply as if to absorb the scents she had left behind.

'It's fitting that this voyage should be stormy,' she said. 'It matches my mood and makes me know that I shall never go back to Tangier again. The sea in this cruel state will wipe out all I regret leaving, now that we are leaving together, and I think only of what we must face in London.'

Rollo went with her to the small cabin that had been put at her disposal and they sat on the cot.

It was impossible to have any privacy and they just held hands and talked or sat in silence, gazing at each other. 'Trust me,' he said again and again. 'I know that we shall be together even if we have to wait for a few weeks. I must see the Duke and make myself amenable to any duty they thrust on me, if only to earn the goodwill of the Court, and then we may slip away to France and the freedom we crave.'

He put an arm round her shoulders. 'England will be green,' said Anna. 'I have missed the flowers and leaves and the song of birds.'

'France will be green, with vineyards and hills and deep rivers and mighty chateaux where we can escape and walk in the sun,' he said. He glanced at her, sensing that she was sending her thoughts to London far too quickly, and yet blaming himself for taking her mind away from the sick men she had left with Ayesha.

'I wonder if,' she began but he stopped her mouth with gentle kisses, and left her to sleep away a few hours until shouts told them that Lisbon loomed up on the starboard bow, and they could disembark and find a place to stay until they rejoined the ship.

'This country is good,' said Rollo. 'Perhaps when we travel the world, we shall stay awhile and find it gentle.'

'No!' Anna looked distressed. 'They talk of Daniel here and say that he is very sick. They know that I am his wife and so we may not be together here.'

Rollo laughed. 'I thought that might be so and I have ordered a suite of rooms in which are many rooms for guests and for storing baggage and so we can be together and not arouse comment. My valet and your servant will have a place there and this will be a holiday for us all. We leave in a week which will give you time to fashion your thoughts, Anna.'

He eyed her with anxiety. 'I feel like a whore,' she said, softly. 'Already it begins with the arrangement you made and which will be repeated in every city where my name is known.'

He clasped her tightly and kissed her lips. 'My dearest girl, we must be so until I am clear with the King. If Helena had stayed away it would have been different, and if Daniel was not in London then that would have made a difference, too. As it is, I remember him to be a hard man with little humour and certainly no love for me who will make trouble for us if he discovers our plans too soon before we can fly away and leave him no trail.' He saw that she was unconvinced and smiled. 'We have powerful allies, Anna. I made very sure that the Verneys now look on me with great favour and are fond of me as if I was a son.'

She looked up, sharply. 'You did that before you knew I would come to you?'

'I wanted you more than anything on God's earth, and was determined to win you, so I attended soirées and dinners and suppers and musical matinées with them as if this was the most enjoyable way with which I could share my time.' He laughed. 'I am fond of them, but only because you are dear to them and they talked of you. We need their love and support and I believe they will back me against Daniel any day.'

Messages arrived from the barracks and from the king's residence, and at all the functions over the next week, Anna was received warmly as the wife of a serving soldier who had gained the respect of all who met him. An abundance of warm water and clean linen and the fresh fruits of a more temperate country made life pleasant. Rollo stood back, always there to escort her, and giving the impression of the perfect knight who was in attendance to the lady and was just a travelling companion, but at night, they made love with passion and sorrow mixed, and Rollo felt the pain of anger when he could not claim her in public as he wished.

'I am glad to leave,' he said at last when the ship bore them over calm seas under a blue sky. 'Lisbon is too provincial and lacks amusements.'

'After Tangier, it was heaven,' said Anna. 'I was glad to stay to fetch my breath and to hear news of home. Africa is fading fast in my mind, and remains just a flurry of ochre earth and dusty cacti, with white robes flowing under a harsh sky.' She looked pensive. 'I must talk with Dr Verney. He will want to know of the diseases I found there and the remedies I used with his help. I shall tell him how you brought the box safely to me and how it made so many cures possible.' Rollo frowned and looked resentful as if she forgot his part in this. She held his hand. 'My dear love. If you had brought me nothing, I would have loved you, but that box wrought its magic in a way that I can never forget. No other man could have done so much.'

He laughed as if to dismiss the idea but looked pleased and when the ship gained the mouth of the Thames he was in a good mood. In spite of their underlying sadness, they revelled in familiar sights and heard English voices as they anchored ready for the tide to take them further up the estuary. 'Did you know that the Dutch came and captured the *Royal Charles*, the King's flagship, right from the Medway under the eyes of the forts?' asked Rollo with pride as if he had a part in it.

Anna regarded him in dismay. 'The *Royal Charles* was an English flagship, Rollo!' She tried to smile. 'There are times when you are more Dutch than British. It was the Dutch who made that sad conquest.'

He reddened. 'I heard so much in Amsterdam that I almost believed I had a part in their victories. As an Englishman, they never let me forget their battles and the victories won against us.'

The Tower showed grey against the dawn as the ship sighed on bent oars and little sail on the tide. Anna shuddered, sensing the misery oozing from the stone walls and recalling that Sarah's lover had died there. The tragedy of many princes and nobles and the envy of the great seemed to give the greyness a dimension of pain and she was glad to see it disappear as the ship was edged into the dock at Bartolph's Wharf near the Custom House.

'We shall dine at the Old Swan while word is sent to my house for men and conveyances,' said Rollo, firmly. 'It shall be so,' he insisted when

Anna protested that she should send word to the Verneys that she had arrived and could be taken by hackney while her baggage was loaded and brought to the house. They looked at each other helplessly as they sat over a good shoulder of mutton and strong ale. The inn was well-filled and several men came over to speak to Rollo. Anna felt that a gap was forming between them as if the tide took them by separate channels, but when his carriage arrived, Rollo pressed her hand and whispered that he would be with her soon. 'Have no fear, my love. All will be well.'

He looked up as the carriage came to the door and saw that Willem sat on the box with the coachman. Rollo sprang up beside him and embraced the grinning man, speaking quickly in Dutch and then laughing as if he was delighted to see him again. Anna waited, half smiling and understanding nothing, until the two men seemed to remember her. Rollo jumped down followed by Willem who regarded Anna with cautious approval. 'The lady in the picture!' he said, and beamed. 'You are welcome, *Mevrou.*' Anna laughed. It was strange being welcomed to her own country by a foreigner. 'But you are almost Dutch,' he said, 'And so are doubly welcome.'

'I have forgotten any Dutch I once knew,' said Anna, ruefully. 'It is a lack that I regret and I hope to learn again soon.'

'You wish to travel again, and to our country? Rollo is now familiar with Holland and the other low countries and will be able to guide you.'

'That would be kind,' she murmured and

avoided looking at Rollo.

'I promised not to let you linger by the ship,' said Willem with an apologetic air. 'You are awaited with much eagerness and I have been ordered to bring you home.'

'I shall take Mistress Anna home first,' said Rollo.

'There is no need,' she said, and was pale and tense. 'I see the Verney coach coming and I think we must part ... until later.'

'Until later,' he echoed and had no chance even to hold her by the hand again before Sam drew up the coach with a flourish of his whip and grinned from ear to ear with delight.

'Miss Anna! My Lady is waiting for you and the family are all there. Miss Kate came from the country when Christopher brought horses to market and stayed to greet you knowing you would come in the next few weeks.'

'Kate?' Warmth flooded back and Anna felt excited. She sat in the coach and recalled that the cushions had been recovered since she left. The smell of new cloth and beeswax and the sights of the widened streets made her forget that she was sad and she was conscious of her welcome even before she reached the house.

'They stayed to get ready and sent me in a fine old flurry, I can tell you, as soon as they heard that you had come ashore,' shouted Sam from the box. 'Deb has arranged your own room and your clothes are aired and pressed, and have been this three weeks.'

'And my husband? How is he?' she asked, with a mouth that could hardly form the words.

'The colonel is staying with his cousin and has not had the news of your return. We sent gallopers to find him and he will be here shortly, never fear, Miss Anna.'

Anna gave a deep sigh and thanked God for being good, but Sam frowned. 'It's not the homecoming you thought, is it, Miss Anna? It isn't the same without the colonel and you will want to care for him as you did before when he was sorely ill.' He laughed. 'He's a lot better but not right and he has a nice surprise for you. I shouldn't say but there's a house in Chelsea awaiting a mistress,' he added, with a broad wink. 'As pretty a place as I ever saw and Debbie would give her eyes to serve in it, but Lady Marian wouldn't let her go, and nor would I.'

He prattled on, happily content to let her sit back and pretend to listen, then blew on a horn when they reached the house and helped Anna down from the coach. 'My dear!' Anna was enveloped in a warm embrace as Lady Marian hurried out on to the porch and almost dragged her inside the house. 'Don't weep, my dear! You are home now and soon will be reunited with your dear husband.' But the two women clung together, with tears coursing down their cheeks and when Kate saw them, she laughed and asked if they had attended a funeral, but her own eyes were wet as she held Anna close and said how much she had been missed.

'Daniel has seen the best of physicians and is much better, but they say that he may be retired on half-pay soon,' said Lady Marian. She smiled. 'With you beside him, my dear, that is no trial as

393

Edward is pleased with your investments and you are a very wealthy woman. I am sorry for one of his brother officers who has no wife with means and only an aged father with a small estate in Wales to which he must go, if he wants it or not, as the only way open to him.'

'The army is his life,' said Anna. 'What will he do, Lady Marian?' She sipped the tea set before her more to gain time to think than because she craved a drink. It was as if they discussed a stranger. 'He does not farm or rear stock and apart from his scientific studies, he has no diversions. The theatre is no amusement to him and he thinks and lives the army.'

'I shall ask Rollo to use his influence and Vincent will help, too,' said Lady Marian. 'Edward says that there is a position in the arsenal that he could fill and be useful.' She sighed. 'I wish he was here to greet you, but London bored him and he went riding with his cousin and to take the country air.'

'I need time to sort out my clothes,' said Anna, and tried to forget the arms that had held her for so many nights and in the soft light filtered through a veil during the hot afternoons, in another world fast slipping away. Her bedroom was as she remembered, with the huge tester bed and truckle beneath it. She changed her clothes and relapsed into doing her hair carefully and with ornaments, and Debbie brought cream for her hands, clucking over their condition and sighing over the darkened skin where the sun had not been kept away.

'I have invited Rollo and his wife to supper,'

Lady Marian announced later. 'He pleaded that he had to make ready to meet the Duke again tomorrow, but I insisted and Helena was eager to meet you.' Lady Marian unfolded a sheet and threw it down when she saw a rust mark on the cloth. 'That will have to go back and be done again,' she said. 'Helena is a pretty little thing. I think she may run to fat later but as yet, she is trim and has fine hair and skin. She learns fast and can now speak quite well in English and has a better idea of our ways now that she has taken the reins in her own household. I think she likes London and may well divide her time between here and The Netherlands in future, especially as Rollo says he may have to go away again.'

Anna made polite remarks and as the day progressed and she was busy, she had no time to dread the next meeting with Rollo and now, his wife, and when Debbie called her to say that the guests had arrived and would she take sack with Mr Verney, Anna was composed and dressed elegantly as if she had never left England.

She forgot to put down the book she was carrying and had it in her hand when she entered the drawing room. The past hour had fled as she studied the latest papers on the lectures from the Royal Society and knew that Daniel had left them for her. At first, she had smiled, ruefully. Other men give me rubies and flattery, Rollo gave me my heart's desire and my plants, but my husband gives me heavy reading, knowing that I welcome it, she thought.

She put the book down on a small table and went to meet Helena. She sensed that the girl was uneasy and yet had a kind of defiant courage. She knows about us, Anna decided and glanced quickly at Rollo's stony face. Helena smiled and held out her hand, greeting Anna in careful English and looking pretty in an unsophisticated way. The two women exchanged small talk and then Kate rescued Anna with the plea that she had seen her only briefly in the last two years, and Helena walked across to her husband and smiled at him in a proprietorial way.

Lady Marian talked fast and too brightly, suspecting that something was happening under her nose of which she had no inkling, and Rollo kept his distance from the woman whom he loved above everything.

'Mother confided in me that it is thought that Sarah had another lover, a French count who was here for only a few days,' whispered Kate. 'I have seen the miniature of the child and it is very like a foreign face.'

'I don't believe it,' said Anna, with some heat. 'Sarah was a wilful child just as Alice was but she was never immoral. When a girl of that age loves, she gives her whole heart and does not dally with others.' She looked across at the pendant that Lady Marian wore and which she had studied earlier. 'I impressed on Lady Marian that a foreign woman who saw only a small picture and not the baby could not know the father. I see that she is wearing it tonight and she promised to keep this vicious rumour from Alice. It would break her heart, for she above all people knows the truth about her dear friend.'

Marian persuaded Helena and Kate to play at

cards with Edward and Willem, and the rest of the company talked and strolled through the hall and the new orangery. 'I must speak to you,' whispered Rollo and led Anna through the ferns and the damp plants to a dimly lit corner. 'I am summoned to Holland!' he said.

'By Helena?' Anna was pale. 'I see how she looks at you and I know that she will never give you up easily.'

'If that were all, I would take you now and carry you off before all the assembled company and not look back even if the King took away all my English possessions,' he said in a harsh whisper.

'What has happened?'

'The rumours are true. The King has signed a treaty with France to exclude the Dutch from the triple alliance of Holland, England and Sweden and to attack the Dutch shipping again. The Treaty of Dover is a fact now and not rumour. The King will find some excuse to quarrel with the Dutch again now that France has added weight to his cause and strength and we shall be at war within the next few weeks or months.'

'And so you are torn, Rollo, as I am torn, by duty and by love.'

'Torn and commanded, Anna. I am to go to the Dutch Court as a diplomat, with free right of passage if war is declared. It was hinted that I can be of use to the King and as I have a Dutch wife, I may be *persona grata* in both camps.'

'When do you leave?' Her face was calm as if fate had done its worst and she was ready for death. 'Do you think we shall ever meet again, my love?'

'In a few months: in a year, when this has settled and I can plan for the future,' he said, eagerly. 'Or come now while they sit at cards, and take the next packet to Ireland or Belgium.'

She touched his hand. 'No, we cannot avoid our duty. You because you have too much at stake and could never live in obscurity again, and me because I am a creature of duty and depend on it as a baby depends on its nurse. I am happier serving and I cannot leave Daniel now that he is beaten. He will be here tomorrow or the day after and like all men will need his pride nourished so that he is not a failure in his own heart.'

'I shall come back for you, Anna, if it takes ten years. I cannot live unless I have that hope.' He kissed her hand.

'Yes, come back when you can,' she said, as if consoling a child. 'And God speed you, my love.'

'You are saying goodbye?' Helena stood by the door. 'It is sad to go, but we must go home now. Yes, Rollo?' She smiled. 'Men make war but women make homes, and we shall have many babies now, I think. I have learned much about the English and now I am Lady Fitzmedwin, I am like you, Anna, Dutch and English and will please my husband.' She put a hand on Rollo's arm and Anna watched them leave, then picked up her book and went to her empty, lonely bed.

The publishers hope that this book has given you enjoyable reading. Large Print Books are especially designed to be as easy to see and hold as possible. If you wish a complete list of our books please ask at your local library or write directly to:

Magna Large Print Books
Magna House, Long Preston,
Skipton, North Yorkshire.
BD23 4ND

This Large Print Book for the partially sighted, who cannot read normal print, is published under the auspices of

THE ULVERSCROFT FOUNDATION